Saving Us

THE BILLIONAIRE BROTHERS OF NY DUOLOGY

A BRU SPINOFF: BOOK ONE

KRISTA SWANSON

MODAMA PUBLISHING

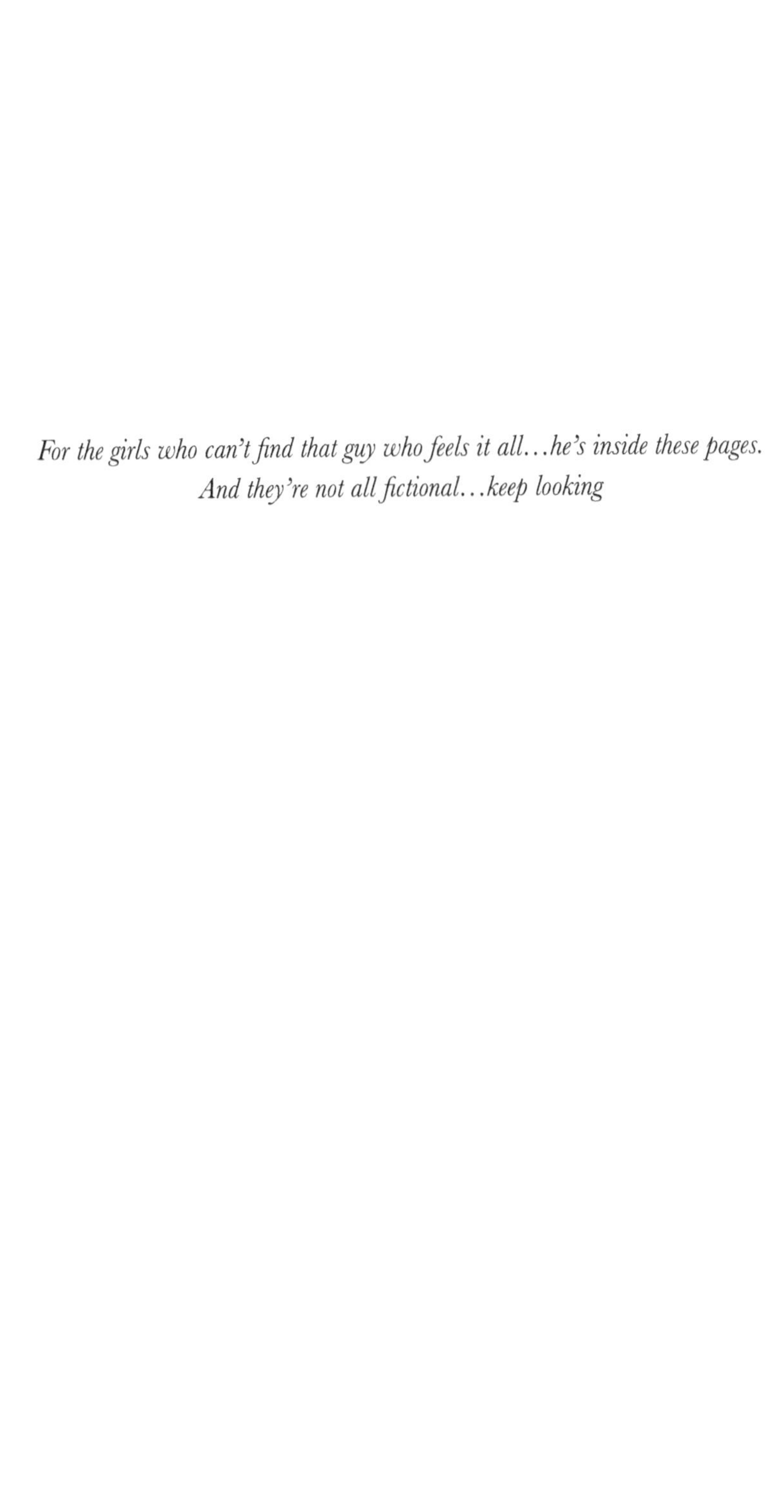

*For the girls who can't find that guy who feels it all…he's inside these pages.
And they're not all fictional…keep looking*

CHAPTER 1

Gage

"Hey, asshole," Chase said from over my shoulder, and it made me jump in my chair. He got a look at my phone before I had a chance to close the screen. "Who's the hot chick? That's some rack she's got."

Looking at her green eyes on a phone didn't do them justice. As brilliant as they appeared through a screen, they were breathtaking in person. More than breathtaking—they were captivating. And that was what she did to me. She captivated me. But we weren't meant to be.

How the fuck did my brother get into my office, literally behind me while I was sitting at my desk, without me noticing?

This was my problem lately. I was consumed by thoughts of her and oblivious to everything else around me.

Becca.

That was who she was.

But I needed to forget about her.

"No one, just a hook-up from my time down at BRU."

BRU: Blue Ridge University. It was where I'd gotten my under-graduate degree instead of going to NYU like my parents wanted.

Like Chase.

And BRU was where I returned, or rather escaped, for a few months last fall to start my graduate degree. When the shit hit the fan last year during my contentious divorce, I took it upon myself to take a leave from work to further my education.

"A hook-up? You're telling me you only tapped that once while you were down there? What a waste."

I swiveled in my chair to respond, no, *to retaliate*, but he'd already moved away from me to the well-stocked bar in the back of my office. I left him to his own devices and returned to my thoughts. Staring out the window onto Nassau Street in lower Manhattan, I hoped the views would distract me. But nothing seemed to work lately.

She consumed my thoughts. All. The. Time.

Some people never fall in love. They never get to experience that feeling when the most beautiful creature they've ever seen walks into the room, and their heart melts. Or that reaction when they gently run a finger along an arm in passing and it stops your breath.

And I believe most have not experienced it twice.

But I did.

I'd also had my heart broken.

Twice.

The first time I was blindsided. She tore it out, stomped on it, and took a piece with her. And to make it worse, it happened quickly and while we were young. Shit, I was still young. After that, I guarded my heart.

But I made a mistake and let my guard down.

I didn't think I'd allowed my heart to open. But apparently, I didn't have as much control over it as I thought I did.

It was supposed to be sex—just sex. And it started off that way. She was a siren in bed, and out, for that matter.

Full of life, mouthy, seductive.

She was exactly what I needed at that moment in my life to make me forget.

She brought me back to life after…Rebecca.

But I let it go too far, and we both got hurt.

It wasn't my intention. We talked about it and outlined what we wanted from the start. We went into it with boundaries. But my fucking heart got in the way.

Not my dick, my heart. Figured.

If I were more like my brother, none of that ever would have happened. The heartless son of a bitch never fell in love. At least I didn't think he did. Lately, I was left wondering if his latest breakup hit him harder than I'd realized. But we didn't really talk about shit like that.

I needed to delete the pictures I still had of her, and us, on my phone. Too much of my time had been spent scrolling through them, staring at her sparkling emerald eyes as they looked at me through the lens. It was as if those eyes were still staking a claim on my heart every time I looked at them, breaking it in two over and over again.

This particular picture was taken by the pond on the campus of BRU, right as she was heading off to class. Her smile was wide as she turned away from me and the breeze caught her hair a bit, those red highlights in her dark strands shining in the sun. It was the same day we came up with our "agreement": supposedly keeping it simple, only hooking up, no strings.

It was also the first day I touched her. The first day I heard her moan. The feel of her skin against my fingertips made my dick hard, that was all it took. My thoughts traveled to that day often, remembering how her tits felt in my hands, the weight of them. How she spread her legs and let me know exactly what she wanted me to do to her. Just thinking about running my fingers along her pussy and pushing them inside of her was making my dick twitch in my pants now.

Chase's footsteps approached, and I quickly adjusted myself and closed the screen of my phone. Turning toward my brother, I saw the glass of amber liquid in his hand. He motioned to it as he took a seat in the chair in front of my desk.

"Want one?"

"No," I answered, my disbelief evident in my voice. But I was sure my tone was lost on him. He didn't mind a few drinks daily. I'd been trying to stay away from drinking during the day while at work. Having a bar in our offices was a tradition set by our old-school father, and our clients appreciated the drink when they came in for meetings. But performing at a high level at work and day drinking didn't really mix.

At least for me.

"So, did she get the job done?" he asked, his drink motioning toward my phone, which was now on my desk.

Staring blankly at him, I wondered for a moment if he had read my mind and was truly asking me if she was able to get me off. Was he that much of an ass? Or was it just me? Back when we were growing up, he and I actually got along. We used to hang out together.

We had some of the same friends in high school and, believe it or not, used to confide in each other.

I wasn't sure when that all changed for him, and us.

"Gage, c'mon," he scoffed as he leaned back in his chair, swirling the contents, making the large, singular ice cube clink against the sides of the expensive crystal. He took a generous sip of his bourbon before speaking again. "Did she make everything go away? Did she help ya, man?"

It was my turn to lean back in my chair. My hands went behind my head, fingers interlocking, as I looked up at the ceiling, doing whatever I could to avoid answering his question. It seemed to be a sincere question. Swiveling the wheels away from him, I turned to look out the wide, expansive, floor-to-ceiling windows that took up one wall of my office.

It was a bright, sunny, cool spring day in New York City. It had been a few months since I'd returned from Virginia, putting off my decision to pursue my advanced degree for the time being. The cars and people on the street below looked tiny from forty floors up, but they were bustling about, all going about their day, oblivious to the pain some people around them might be dealing with.

My eyes remained fixed out the window. I couldn't bring myself to look at him. He could always tell when I was lying. We may not hang out as much as we used to, but that didn't change the fact that we were still brothers.

And I had to keep reminding myself: I was done with relationships. No more. Nada. Stick to anything but long term. I was never a one-night stand kind of guy, always leaning toward relationships for some reason. But if that was what it came to, then that was what it would have to be.

"Yeah, she got the job done." I propped my feet up on the tiny table behind my desk, securing my position turned away from my brother. "She, um…" I blew out an unsteady breath as I sat forward in my chair. "She definitely helped me forget about Rebecca."

CHAPTER 2

Harper

"Shut up!" My hand slammed down on my phone as "Walking on Sunshine" by Katrina and the Waves blared from it. My original thought of it being a perfect song to wake up to was going to have to be reconsidered. And how was it possible that my alarm was already going off? It had to be a mistake. It felt as though I only slept a couple hours. When I got home from the club, I couldn't even bring myself to wash my face I was so tired. And the evidence of that was now all over my pillowcase.

Waiting tables at one of the most exclusive clubs in New York City had its perks. The biggest one was, of course, the tips from the rich men who were the main clientele. It also allowed me to work my day job since the club was evening hours only.

My day job.

That was what I really loved to do.

I worked at Fiona's Flower Shop. And I was her lead floral designer. We weren't your everyday, run-of-the-mill floral shop. We had high-end corporate accounts as well as taking care of numerous weddings weekly. My team took care of the corporate accounts primarily, making floral arrangements for their entryways and offices on a regular basis.

My end game was to own my own shop, hence the day job and the night job. Either way, it was probably necessary living in NYC. I wasn't interested in doing corporate, though I didn't mind that part of my job. But I liked the interactive parts of the business: meeting the customers, seeing their smiles when the bouquet landed in their arms.

Katrina and the Waves was blaring from my phone again.

Shit! And now I was going to be late to that day job if I didn't get my ass out of bed.

And I couldn't be late. Fiona was giving me my big chance today.

My first-time meeting with a client face-to-face, alone, to further the account. This was the break I'd been waiting for, the opportunity I needed to move on one day and do this myself. I was going in early to meet with them before store hours so that we wouldn't be interrupted. I felt that was a good move on my part.

Scrambling out from under the big down comforter, I ran to the bathroom to take a shower. My literal shoebox of a studio apartment was all I could afford, but thankfully I had my own bathroom. There were so many apartments here that didn't if you could believe that. If I had to stroll down a hallway in my current state to pee or shower, it would be good for no one.

There was no time to wash my hair, so up in a bun it went as I jumped under the spray. It wasn't as hot as I would've liked, it never really got to the ideal temperature if you asked me. The best type of shower was when your body was beet red when you were done, and the room was so foggy you couldn't see a foot in front of you. But in this building, we settled for lukewarm at best.

Working at the club had its downsides as well. Me scrambling to get to my day job because I was exhausted from my late hours was the main one. I rarely got home and into bed on my club nights until around three a.m. Granted, I only worked at the club Wednesdays through Saturdays, so it wasn't every day I dealt with this. But the days I did were tough since I needed to be at the shop by ten.

Drying my body as I dashed around my apartment, I hoped to find some clean clothes in the mess scattered across the floor. One aspect of my life that fell to the wayside because of my hectic schedule was cleaning and laundry, but something had to. And those were things that didn't pay the bills.

My love of flowers and plants had been a lifelong passion, and I'd turned it into a new hobby of starting plantings in unique items. Currently, I had a fern growing from a boot, an aloe plant thriving in a conch shell, and some begonias just beginning in an old teapot.

Once they were sufficiently cared for, I found a pair of jeans that were clean and a white t-shirt that would do. Swiping on some mascara and some lip balm, I grabbed my backpack and headed for the door. But I stopped myself and went back for my jacket since it was still cool on April mornings in New York.

Today would have to be one of those days I bought breakfast on the run. I didn't enjoy having to do it; the cost made little sense to me. I could make perfectly good coffee, even better coffee, at home for a fraction of the cost. And the food was mainly processed. I'd been trying to eat healthier when time allowed. Who knew this adulting thing was so time-consuming?

"Hey, Harper, haven't seen you in a while," Rex said as I walked into the local bodega. It was on my way to the shop and the perfect spot to grab a quick meal. Plus, Rex was a great guy. Albeit a huge flirt. But he was harmless considering he was married with four kids and did most of his flirting with his wife standing right next to him.

"Hi, Rex." Racing around, I looked for my usual, a yogurt

parfait, grabbed it and hurried to the counter. I was so happy to see my tea waiting for me. As I was tapping my card on the reader, I looked into the kitchen. "Where's Maria?"

Rex shook his head, and a deep rumble came from his chest. "Ahh, two of the kids are home sick from school. She's with them." He pointed above us with his finger, motioning to the apartment they lived in over their store.

"Hope they're better soon. I'm sooo late, gotta run!"

He waved as I took off out the door, not watching where I was going.

That was when I plowed into…something.

It obviously had to be a person. It was the only logical possibility this close to the door as I exited. There were no phone poles close to Rex's entrance. But it was sooo hard. Like, rock hard.

And then hands grabbed my arms to steady me.

But not before my hot, steaming tea hit the ground and my yogurt parfait hit me…splattering all over the sidewalk, my pants, and sneakers. My eyes went wide at the mess and a small whine escaped my lips. Hearing the sound, the arms holding me pulled me in closer, as if to protect me from whatever harm this could do to me.

I found my head flush against a soft wool jacket and was suddenly overcome with the scent of leather, mixed with spice and maybe a note of cedar or pine. My dismay at my current situation was temporarily halted by the divine smells invading my nose. It was almost putting me into a trance-like state as I leaned into the hard body holding me close and continued to, literally, sniff his coat.

But then, as if realizing the error of his ways, he pushed me away, his eyes glaring down at me.

"Jesus Christ, watch where you're going!"

His voice whipped me out of my stupor, and I ripped myself from the stranger's hold.

"I'm so sorry, I was in a hurry to get to work as I ran out the door and I didn't see you both." My words were weak, but I was surprised by the collision and his harsh words.

When I looked up, I was staring at two of the most gorgeous men I'd ever seen. And working at the club, I'd seen my share.

They had to be related. Other than a variation in coloring, they looked similar. The one standing closer to the curb had lighter brown hair and almost hazel eyes. And although they were looking between me and the yogurt splattered on his expensive-looking loafers, they held a hint of playfulness in them.

The other, the one that had obviously just been holding me, was darker. Darker hair, a bit of scruff on his face, and darker eyes —more my type. But his eyes held something beyond darkness in them. And those dark eyes glared at me and the mess on his pants. His grip may have been soft on my arms, but his look held the anger he truly felt.

"Gage, cool it," the lighter one warned his evil twin. He had a look of apology all over his face as his eyebrows lifted and he shrugged his shoulders. "I'm sorry, we ran into you as well. We could've watched where we were going. And now …" He gestured to my breakfast that was currently forming a river running into the gutter of the already garbage filled street.

As he talked, the other one only continued to glare. And move further from me as he inspected the mess I'd made.

"It's fine," I said, gesturing to my now soupy mess on the concrete. My stomach was rumbling underneath my sweater as we stood there, indicating that it was indeed not fine. I used the napkins still in my hands to address the mess on my pants, but it didn't do much in the way of cleaning them. I would have to deal with it once I got to work. "And I really am sorry, but I need to get going. I have an appointment at the shop, and I need to open up today. My boss'll kill me if I'm not there to meet my clients."

Moving away from them both, the friendlier one stepped in front of me, blocking my departure. His hands were up in front of him, making sure he kept himself a decent distance from me. I wasn't sure if it was for my sake or his.

"Let me replace your breakfast." His hand reached to his back pocket, I assumed to get his wallet.

"No, really. That's very nice of you, but I've gotta go. Fiona will kill me. We have very important clients coming today and she gave me this meeting." I looked at my phone and realized it was almost nine; I wasn't going to make it. "Fuck, I'm gonna be late," I muttered.

"Fiona?" the other one asked. "Is that the owner of the flower shop?" he said to the man who had to be his brother.

They shared a look before both sets of eyes landed back on me.

"Sorry again," I said, looking mainly at the curmudgeon's pants. "I, um, can get those cleaned for you if you want."

"No, you can't," he said, very matter-of-factly.

My head snapped to his at the words, but he was done with me. They both were. But as they walked into the market, the nicer of the two pushed his brother and said something to him as he did. But I couldn't hear him.

My pace needed to be quick. Those two took up precious minutes that I needed to make it to the shop. By the time I unlocked the door, it was already a little past nine, but lucky for me, no one was waiting to be let in. I raced to turn on the lights, adjust the thermostat, and put on the instrumental music that I loved to have on while I oversaw the shop.

Looking around, I realized everything was where it needed to be. I had left it in pristine condition when I closed the day before, thank goodness. That gave me a few extra minutes to try to clean myself up before my meeting. Running to the restroom, I grabbed a hand towel and ran it under the tap. I figured most of the mess on my pants would be covered by my apron, so I focused on my sneakers, and thankfully it came off the leather easily.

Feeling more at ease, I grabbed my apron, and worked my way through the store to the office in back, pulling the account binder from the desk. Opening the calendar, I double-checked who I was meeting with. I always liked to know the name of the person I'd be talking to.

Maryellen McEntyre

I remembered her. Beautiful girl. Hard to pinpoint if she was around my age or older, though. She seemed much more sophisticated than me, probably a result of working in the environment she did.

At that moment, the bell rang over the front door, alerting me my meeting was about to start. Grabbing the binders and paperwork necessary for the next thirty minutes, I bounded through the opening separating our office from the showroom, my arms full of portfolios with photos of the arrangements I'd been working on for weeks leading up to this meeting.

"Welcome, Maryellen," I said, as I bounced into the showroom, the contents in my arms hitting the massive wooden workspace.

Fiona took my advice regarding this amazing table. We had two active workspaces, one in the back, but one out in the open for the customers to see the magic taking place. It was a massive square table, a beautiful piece of mahogany wood measuring a spacious six feet by six feet. It was surrounded by numerous stools to enable the customers to sit and watch their bouquets and arrangements being made, enjoying the simplicity of individual flowers being turned into enchanting designs.

"Maryellen couldn't make it this month," a deep voice responded.

My hands froze while opening the catalog of photos.

The voice.

I knew that voice.

And I was afraid to look up.

In the next moment, in my peripheral vision, a yogurt parfait and tea were set on the table in front of me.

And a small gasp escaped from my barely open mouth as my head moved ever so slowly to see who had placed it there. Though I had no doubt who it had to be.

There was only one person it could have been.

Well, one person and his grumpy companion.

A mixture of confusion and exhilaration consumed me. I lifted my eyes, and they grew wide as I stared at the pair in front of me. Each man stood at least a foot above my five feet four inches as they held their own coffees in their hands. But the looks on their faces were distinctly different.

Mr. Grumpy was still, well, grumpy. His harsh look as he stared back at me forced the breath I was holding to escape from my mouth, making a quiet swoosh sound as it exited. His face held a myriad of emotions as I scanned it quickly. I sensed a note of triumph as he gave his sidekick a glance, as if to drive home the notion he was right about me being the one who would come strolling through the door. Then it morphed into a softer look that started on my face and swept down to my toes, which I wasn't expecting.

He did it swiftly.

Almost so quickly, I questioned if it happened at all.

But my body warmed at the thought of him looking at me that way.

And all of this happened in about three seconds.

Then he seemed done with me.

His, I assumed, brother was more jovial as he shot me a thousand-watt grin. And he knew he was hot. He was the guy I would've hung out with in college, a typical frat guy. He seemed easy-going and smiled. A lot.

"Here ya go," he said, pointing to what had been placed on the table in front of me. "Figured it was the least we could do."

"Thank you. You didn't have to do that, really," I said, a bit embarrassed.

"No worries," Frat Boy said. "And the market guy knew your order, so it should be right."

And then he flashed that white drop-your-panties smile again. But as I glanced at the other, his look was different.

His look wasn't superficial like Frat Boy. His was more serious as his eyes bored into mine.

Then I pulled myself together.

My professional self got us back on track.

"Well, you both must be from Parker Financial Associates. I'm, uh, very glad to meet you." My hand went out to Mr. Grumpy first, hoping to warm him up a bit. His grip was tight, his hand warm, but his demeanor remained cold.

As I turned toward the other, I watched a calculated veil shield his face. He went from sweet frat boy outside the coffee shop to the all-business-billionaire executive in the blink of an eye.

"I'm Chase, this is my brother, Gage," he offered, his tone adding to the professionalism he was forcing into the situation as he shook my hand. "And, yes, Parker Financial is our company. Although it is technically still our father's company, we're running it."

But then he took a step back.

It was obvious he was not the real one in charge.

And I wouldn't be dealing with Frat Boy, but with Brother Curmudgeon.

Maryellen was the one from the company I normally met with.

She was the sweetest, and I was missing her a ton at the moment. Why had she sent them instead? This seemed out of the ordinary, and I was confused.

I needed to get a handle on this meeting though, and quickly. They were one of our most important clients and Fiona was trusting me to take over this account. Turning back to the table, I opened the catalogs and portfolios to the many arrangements that they've used from us in the past.

"Well, gentlemen, welcome to our shop." I gestured around the space, my arms spanning wide, as my eyes connected with Mr. Grumpy, who I knew now was Gage.

And my confidence drained, immediately.

He looked…bored.

But of course they'd be bored. Why in the hell would the-next-in line owners of a multi-billion-dollar company be the ones standing in a floral shop picking out designs for the summer arrangements?

But then I looked at Frat Boy. His eyes were trained on me as I spoke, his dedicated attention easing my nerves a bit.

"In front of you are photos of all the arrangements used in your building in the past for the upcoming season." My voice was strained from the pressure to get it right. I was trying hard not to blow this account simply because I couldn't keep it together in front of these two. "I also have some updated ideas for the season over here."

As I reached for the other binder, I was stopped dead in my tracks.

"Well, if the arrangements you make are half as pretty as you, then we'll be fine," Frat Boy, otherwise known as Chase, threw into the conversation.

Looking up at him, the smug grin plastered across his face was that of a guy who always "got the girl." For him, this was no longer a business meeting, but a pickup opportunity. And although I felt he was my only ally at the moment, I wasn't interested in what he had in mind.

Glancing at Mr. Grumpy, I could tell he wasn't either.

"Chase." The terse way he said his brother's name was full of warning. "Ignore him," he directed at me.

My head snapped back. It was almost an order.

But Chase didn't take the directive too kindly. He shot up on his stool, the metal falling to the floor, and stormed out of the shop.

Stunned by what had just happened, my heart sank as I watched my only ally desert me. And I was left with the man who looked like he wanted my puppy to die.

"I'm serious. He's not involved with the bottom line in the company as much as I am. He has no idea how much money we give you guys," Gage said. "He also has no idea how important first impressions are when people enter our building. And once we started using your arrangements, we had data proving those statistics improved."

But now, as he spoke, I found myself wanting to listen to his words.

Don't get me wrong, he was still a curmudgeon.

But he was a sultry curmudgeon. When he put that many words together, and I had the opportunity to hear his voice for a prolonged period, they sounded like melted caramel sliding from a spoon. Silky but thick as it warmed you from the inside out.

Okay, maybe it was because I hadn't eaten breakfast that I found his voice so delicious. But his voice didn't change the fact that half of my account had stomped out of our meeting.

"Well, I appreciate that, and I'll be sure to share that information with Fiona. She'll be happy to hear it." My voice trembled slightly, and I didn't know what to do with my hands, opting to rearrange the piles of papers and photos in front of us into different stacks. Sweat formed on the back of my neck and my temples.

I screwed up.

As I began to gather my materials for the meeting, his hand landed on my arm. "What are you doing?"

I looked up, not sure what to expect. Looking at the now empty doorway that was Chase's escape route, I turned my attention back to Gage, his expression softer.

"This meeting isn't over. Oh, and by the way, if you're going to make it in this business, you should make sure to introduce yourself to your clients when you meet them." He actually chuckled under his breath as he took a seat on one of the stools and opened one of the binders.

Fuck.

Holy Shit.

Did I never give them my name? Oh my God. I couldn't believe how badly I screwed this up.

"I really would like to start this whole day over again," I mumbled, mainly under my breath, but I knew he heard me. I moved to stand next to him, and we were eye to eye only because he was sitting down. It reminded me of crashing into him not fifteen minutes ago, and how my face was flush against his chest. His hard, solid chest.

He was tall. Like seriously tall. My eyes, when he stood, were looking straight at his pecs.

But now, as he sat and spun on his stool to face me, we were looking right at each other.

I extended my hand.

"Hello, Mr. Parker, my name is Harper Wilson. It's very nice to meet you."

He took my hand. And he didn't just shake it.

He held it.

And looked…*into* me…with those caramel eyes.

"Harper," he said.

But as he said my name, a feeling hit my spine from top to bottom. It was the way he said it.

"That name suits you."

And then he let go of my hand. But he didn't take his eyes off mine as he swiveled back toward the table.

"Let's get to work, Harper. Maryellen tells me you're the best at what you do, so show me what you've got."

And that's what I did.

CHAPTER 3

Gage

Why does he have to act like such a child all the time? My only wish is that my father was still around more to keep him in control. I mean, technically I'm now his boss, but he doesn't see it that way, not yet anyway. He's not professional enough when it counts, he drinks too much here at the office and at night when we go out with clients. I'm surprised he didn't do more damage when I was away in Virginia last fall. When will he learn that he needs to step up and take a bigger role in this company, more than him being the playboy of floor thirty-five?"

When I stopped my rant and turned away from the window toward my desk, Maryellen was sitting stoically in her chair across from me. Her blonde hair was pulled tight on top of her head and her razor-sharp blue eyes narrowed in on mine as she held her iPad in her hands, waiting for our actual meeting to begin. She seemed to work hard to make her appearance not the focus while maintaining a high level of professionalism. But there was no denying she was a beautiful woman. I had no idea how old she was, my guess ranging anywhere from late twenties to mid-thirties. She was crafty at thwarting the attention of the many male clients that came through my office.

"Sir," she started.

"Maryellen." The sternness in my voice was met with a chide smile on her chiseled face. She knew I didn't like when she did that.

"Gage," she started again. "You know as well as I do that he's struggling since he and Amy ended. He hasn't been the same since. It's almost as if he's on a destructive path intentionally to hurt himself sometimes."

Both of us Parker boys have had bad breakups in the past couple years. And I guess he wasn't handling it as well as I thought he was.

"I wasn't aware he was still struggling. I guess since I haven't been around."

"Exactly, and now you do, so I think you should cut him some slack," she reprimanded.

I felt some remorse about my words with her response, but not enough to be sorry. "I can hardly cut him slack when he's acting like a dick in front of clients or customers. He was a total asshole to Harper from the floral shop yesterday. He actually tried to pick her up."

She balked a bit at that news, the frown visible on her face. But it disappeared quickly. She had such a soft spot for him.

"But the floral invoice came through this morning, so I guess it's safe to say you rectified whatever Chase almost screwed up."

I slumped into my chair, tired of my own complaining.

"Yeah, I stuck around and made sure it got done."

But sticking around caused another issue.

Sticking around and finishing the meeting forced me to spend more time with Harper. Which I found hard to do. Because she was gorgeous and smelled amazing, things I shouldn't have been noticing during a business meeting.

The exact things I sent Chase away for.

Maryellen started tapping away on her tablet, leaving me to the notes in front of me for a few minutes. Thursdays were spent wrapping up, preparing for the following week. I never liked to leave that for Fridays; employees weren't as sharp on Fridays. The current invoices were on a shared document for Maryellen and me to go over as well as my social calendar with the company for the coming week.

"She's really good at what she does," Maryellen said.

I looked up, acting confused, because I really didn't want to continue talking about Harper. At all.

"The flowers," she said.

"Fiona?" I asked. "Her shop is nice, yeah."

"No, not Fiona. Harper," Maryellen responded, kind of emphatically. "She's the magic behind all of what gets made in that place."

"Oh, yeah, she seems great. And her arrangements are amazing. We see how everyone loves them here." Yeah, not only are her arrangements amazing, but so many other parts of her as well.

Christ. What the fuck was wrong with me? To be thinking about a girl I'd just met, let alone a vendor of ours, was the last thing I needed.

Maryellen continued to stare as I worked on our schedule. She was acting weird, but I chalked it up to me being my typical annoying self that tended to get on her nerves. Then I noticed a new addition to the calendar.

"What's this event you have on the schedule for next Saturday?" It was common for Chase and me to entertain clients who were in town. New York is an exciting place to visit for our European clients and they usually expected to be wined and dined. "I don't remember there being a night out next weekend?"

Maryellen didn't answer me right away as she continued tapping on her tablet. Finally, her eyes connected with mine.

"That one just came across my desk late yesterday. He's the son of Ronald Weaver, the owner of Gold and Sons, the company you just acquired last week. He's meeting with you because he's moving to New York since it was decided he will run that sector of the company."

I nodded along at the information she provided and noticed that Chase was on the calendar to join us as well. That usually meant it would be a very late, drunken night.

But I figured I was due for one of those.

"What club do you have us booked at? I've never been to that one."

The Velvet Rope.

"Oh, it's been around. I hear it's a very good one, you just need to get out more." She gave me a glance from under her long eyelashes after that comment. "I booked you a room in the VIP lounge. You'll have a private server and bartender, as usual. It's all set up, no worries."

There was never anything to worry about when it came to Maryellen and her ability to handle my business life, or my personal life, for that matter. Somehow, she always got it done.

"What's this I'm hearing about a night out next week?" Chase said cheerfully as he bounded into my office. His feet seemed to be bouncing in delight as his strides took him to my couch. "It's about time we get a night out, bro." His arms fell against the back of the sofa as his feet crossed at the ankles midair before landing on the table in front of him.

A silent look of tolerance was shared between Maryellen and me as she stood from her seat. She understood that we would have to finish our meeting later and excused herself without a word. But I did catch Chase watching her as she left.

"Don't you ever work?" I chided as my eyes returned to my computer.

"Dude, we are among the lucky ones, where going out on a Saturday night, to an exclusive club, *is* work."

He wasn't wrong there. And I was due. I just didn't think I was ready. But for the sake of the new co-worker, I'd put the happy face on and entertain away.

"Well, that's still over a week away. We have a company to run until then if you haven't noticed. And," I paused as I glanced at my watch, "we have a staff meeting to get to. We should head downstairs now."

Every Thursday we held a breakfast meeting for the entire staff at 10:00 a.m.

That was almost one hundred employees that we fed every Thursday morning.

My father wasn't too thrilled with the idea when I came up with it last year, but participation during the meetings increased tenfold since. In addition, since starting the Thursday brunch, productivity had improved as well as employee approval ratings. It couldn't all be coincidental.

Our father was playing around with the idea of selling the company. We were brought up being told this company would be our bread and butter, that it would be ours. Yet, he was thinking of taking it away from us. I wasn't sure if I wanted that to happen or not. In the meantime, I'd make sure the company remained productive.

And I would do it in his name. They thought the brunch idea was his.

I had a reputation to uphold: curmudgeon.

Chase was the fun playboy brother that everyone could joke around with in the office. I, on the other hand, ran the business.

Therefore, I had the stress of making sure the company made money at the end of the day. Not always an easy task.

Hence, curmudgeon.

But I felt as though Maryellen knew the real me, which most here didn't see.

At that exact moment, the knock came on my door.

Her head popped in as I was standing from my chair.

"I know, Maryellen, we're heading to the meeting now, thanks."

"You should have included mimosas in the Thursday brunch menu," Chase commented to the back of my head as we walked down the hall to the elevators.

It didn't warrant a response.

AFTER THE MEETING, Chase and Jared walked with me back to my office. Jared was a lawyer in our company. We not only worked together in my company but had been best friends since college. We were roommates and in the same frat down at BRU. He wasn't happy, though, when Rebecca and I used his services to finalize our divorce. He felt that "put him in the middle," considering he was friends with us both. But we made our divorce easy enough for one person to handle. She took nothing, I wanted nothing. We just went our separate ways, so it worked. The three of us were something of a trio back at school, and he was as upset as I was when things didn't work out between Rebecca and me.

He and I were like brothers, maybe more like brothers than me and Chase.

"Hey," Chase said as we got close to my door. "Ya got a minute?"

"I'll wait in here," Jared said, heading into my office.

Turning toward my brother, he looked uncomfortable.

"So, hey, I'm sorry about what happened yesterday," Chase said.

"Yeah, I meant to talk to you about that. It wasn't very professional what you said to Harper."

He leaned against the wall and let out a sigh as his hand scrubbed at his face. "I know, man. I'm sorry." Unbuttoning the jacket of his suit, he turned toward me. "You know I'm not really cut out for this corporate shit, especially the meetings. I'm better on my own, sitting at my desk with my computer. Or the going out part, I'm good with the socializing stuff."

He was right. And I should respect that. Knowing one's strengths and boundaries was important, and I should limit his responsibilities to what he felt comfortable with. I'd work harder on that for him.

"So, anyway, I was thinking I might reach out to her, see if she wants to go out," he said.

And my stomach dropped.

Yet I had no idea why this should even bother me. I made the decision I was done with women. Well, done with relationships. So, if he wanted to reach out to her, he should.

But my gut was telling me no.

That I shouldn't let him.

So, the jealous asshole in me answered him, not the brother.

"Not sure we should mix business with pleasure."

He appeared a bit stunned by my response as he stood in the hall, across from me, silent. I walked to the door of my office to meet up with Jared.

Turning to him, I asked, "Anything else, Chase?"

"Nope." Spinning on his heels, I watched him walk to the elevator and hit the down button.

CHAPTER 4

Gage

I decided to pay the floral shop a visit the following week to settle our first installment in person. There was no reason the check needed to be put in the mail when the shop wasn't far from my brownstone. Besides, I should probably meet the infamous Fiona anyway. Considering how much our company paid hers each year, I should put a face to the name.

Their listed hours online indicated they were open until seven tonight. I left the office a little early so I could swing by the shop before they closed on my way home.

As I pushed the door open, the bell announced my arrival, just like last time. The music inside was inviting: some coffeehouse instrumental type stuff similar to what I'd listen to while working at home. No one was in the front room, so I looked around while I waited.

"Can I help you?" a familiar voice said.

Turning toward her, she was a vision as she stood behind the large table. She had a bunch of flowers in her hands, as if she were in the middle of a project I interrupted. Her hair was in a one of those messy knots on top of her head again and a flush developed when she saw it was me.

"Hi," I said.

I knew our first meeting didn't go as she'd planned. Between our run-in beforehand, Chase's comment and sudden exit, and me being my usual grumpy self, she probably wasn't all that happy to see me.

But I have not been able to stop thinking about her.

And considering I didn't want to *be* with anyone, that was a problem. So, coming to see her, and figuring out why, was in order.

"Mr. Parker," she said. "Nice to see you again."

"Gage, please."

Her blush deepened. Interesting.

"What can I do for you, Gage?" She put the flowers on the butcher-block table and walked toward me while untying her apron. As she pulled it up and over her head, her hands snapped the apron into a ball and onto the table all in one graceful motion. I found myself staring at her every move.

And then I realized she was watching me watch her.

And I liked that.

But then another, younger girl, came out from the back room.

"Harper, what do you think should be added to the arrangements for the King account? They don't look complete yet," the girl said as she opened a cooler looking inside.

"Excuse me." Harper motioned to me with her hand as she helped her coworker with the flowers in the case.

As I watched them, I questioned what I was really doing.

What were my motives for being here? I suddenly felt as though my visit was simply to piss off my brother.

And maybe cockblock him.

The envelope burned a hole in my pocket the longer it stayed there. Taking it out, I was tempted to place it on the table and leave.

"Sorry about that, she needed to finish up that account before leaving," Harper said, looking at her watch.

And that was a perfect segue.

"You're closing. I'm only here to pay our invoice." Handing her the envelope, her eyes dropped to it as it landed in her hand.

"Oh," she said slowly. Disappointment dripped from her words, which was surprising considering our last encounter. But she seemed to push it away, literally shaking her head. "Of course."

But as she looked up, I was rendered speechless by her crystal blue eyes. I don't think I really noticed them last time. They were striking. The color of the Caribbean Sea.

"I have some of the new arrangement ideas from our meeting prepped in my portfolio. Since you're here, we could go over them."

Her words were lost on me as I watched her move around the room, appearing to tidy up and prepare to close the shop. Her occasional glances told me she was still waiting on my answer.

Why was I so enthralled by this woman?

And as she waited for my answer, my dick wanted me to say yes.

But my brain and heart both begged me to say no.

She walked to the front door, locking it and turned the sign to say "Closed."

A distant voice from the back of the store yelled, "Bye Harper, I'm heading out!"

"Bye Callie!" Harper yelled back.

And then we seemed to be alone.

And she was standing in front of me, hands on hips, an expectant look on her face.

"I have a few minutes," I told her.

A curt nod was all she gave me as she walked into the back room, essentially leaving me alone. "Have a seat, I'll be right back," she called from the back.

Christ, what was I doing?

Walking out the front door was what I should be doing, that would be my smartest move. But apparently, I was going to listen to my dick, since I pulled out a stool and took a seat.

Talking myself into this being a business meeting as I sat waiting for her to return was the only thing keeping my ass on the cold metal stool. Finally, she came walking through the doorway carrying a large binder in her hands.

"Here we go," she said as she plunked it down next to me. "It's perfect timing you're here. I'm not too far into the designs, so you can tell me if you like them."

I wasn't sure if this was the normal process Harper and Maryellen went through, we never discussed this in our Thursday meetings. All I ever did was sign off on the invoices to be paid. When Maryellen suggested that I come this month to see where the money goes, I agreed it was a good idea.

Now I wasn't so sure. For a variety of reasons.

One being the dirty-blonde sitting next to me who smelled amazing. I mean, yeah, we were surrounded by flowers. But there was something about how she smelled that was different, yet floral at the same time.

And it was driving me fucking insane the closer she got to me with every page she turned.

"And see this one? This is for the main lobby…"

I couldn't pay attention to what she was saying, not one word. Her gaze hopped back and forth between me and the pictures, and the little wisps of hair would float around her face. It would make her scent waft through the air even more, and it was intoxicating.

She was bent over the wooden table, engrossed in what she was telling me, yet all I could do was look at her neck. With her upswept hair, it left the smooth skin leading to her also exposed collarbone free to view.

I suddenly wanted to touch her.

I wanted to do more than touch her.

My hands had a mind of their own and continuously wanted to reach out and run my thumb along the vein in her neck, to feel her warmth.

Instead, I busied them with my pen as it clicked and clicked and clicked. Even I was annoyed with me.

"Can you see the pictures from where you are, Mr. Parker?" she asked.

We both knew I couldn't. And I was sure she was confused by my sudden disinterest in the meeting. But I couldn't think straight.

She wasn't even my typical type. She was pretty, don't get me wrong. Even more than pretty, beautiful.

But she seemed…nice.

And I wasn't normally attracted to nice girls. I liked them a bit feisty, ones that gave me a run for my money.

"It's Gage," I reminded her, rather curtly.

"Oh, right, sorry."

She spun on her heels as she apologized, her body now aligned with mine, literally standing between my bent knees as my feet were perched on the stool. She didn't expect to end up so close to me, I could tell by her reaction.

Which was a sharp intake of breath as her eyes landed on mine.

But she remained frozen where she was, standing between my legs.

Neither of us quite knew what to do with our hands, though mine were aching to reach around and pull her even closer. Hers, I noticed, she kept rubbing along her jeans.

"No need for apologies, Harper." I made sure to look at her, really look at her when I spoke.

The animated swallow in her throat as she held my gaze spoke volumes.

She was attracted to me.

Seeing that made me want to grab her, strip her of her clothes, push her onto the table, and hold her down by the throat while I pushed her legs apart with my other hand. Turn this innocent dove in front of me into something a little darker.

And thinking about that made my pants get tighter.

Instead, I stood, forcing her to back away. As she did, her eyes widened as she looked up at me.

"I need to go." My words were firm as I moved toward the door. "I'm sure whatever you come up with will be fine." Reaching the door, I turned the lock and pulled it open, harder than I intended to. The bell above rang loud in the silent room.

Walking out the door, leaving it open as I went, I knew I'd made the right decision.

And hearing her close and lock it behind me confirmed she agreed.

CHAPTER 5

Harper

My hand shook as it lingered on the lock. Resting my head against the window shade of the door, I allowed my heart rate to slow. Him walking out that door was the right decision. For both of us. He's a client. Nothing good would have come of it if anything had happened.

And I was delusional to think anything was about to happen.

He truly was just done with me and looking at the pictures.

What CEO of a huge financial company has any interest in the floral arrangements that will be in the foyer of his building? Or the girl responsible for making them?

As I returned to cleaning up the remnants of stems and petals left behind from today's jobs that were strewn across the table, and about to get the broom, there was a knock at the door.

Sometimes we had some latecomer customers trying to get bouquets to bring home, but it was not happening tonight.

"We're closed," I said through the locked door. Turning the exterior lights off, I hoped the message was made even more clear to my late-night intruder.

But the knock sounded again. And it was more forceful.

Lifting the shade, I recognized my visitor. Contemplating whether I should unlock the door, I finally turned the bolt and pulled it open.

Standing in the doorway, leaning against the frame, was six feet four inches of a dark, sexy, and stormy grump whose expression displayed as much confusion about what he was doing as mine.

Without words, he stalked into the shop and closed the door behind him, locking it. Turning back to face me, our eyes connected, and I was frozen in place. Two steps, and his body was almost touching mine. His finger gently lifted my chin, forcing me to look up at him.

"Leaving was the right thing to do," he said.

My breathing was choppy as he continued holding my face, not letting me look away.

"But I couldn't stop thinking about you once I did."

Then his eyes closed, and a huff of what sounded like frustration escaped from his lips, and I couldn't help thinking he regretted his decision to come back. But his thumb came up to rub along my cheek, a very sweet move from a guy I wouldn't consider sweet.

And my choppy breathing altogether stopped.

"It's like you put a spell on me or something, or maybe it's this place." He looked around the shop, then back down at me. "Your scent intoxicates me. It pulled me back and made me want more."

And then his eyes shifted a tiny bit, as if he couldn't believe he'd just said those words. He almost looked disappointed, maybe second-guessing himself. His hand fisted, seemingly in frustration, against my cheek as he backed away.

And I surprised myself at being let down by his slow retreat, my body leaning toward his ever so slightly as he moved. But he didn't go far as he leaned against the refrigerator case closest to him and put his hands in his pockets.

As he stood there, looking all sexy and shit, my mind raced. My thoughts bounced back and forth between disbelief that he was here, showing interest in me, to thoroughly enjoying his attention.

And crazy enough, I think I wanted more of his attention.

The butterflies in my stomach were evidence of that.

It had been way too long since I'd gotten any male attention that didn't come in the form of my ass being grabbed.

And though I didn't want to admit it, he was hot.

Like, seriously fucking hot. And his broodiness added to it.

He cleared his throat as he lifted his eyes, finding mine, and it seemed as though he was about to say something as his mouth opened. But he clamped it shut, as if suddenly changing his mind.

So many possibilities went through my mind of what he might have said:

Want to get a drink?

Can we see each other again?

I hope it's not too forward that I came back…

But instead, we both stood motionless, staring at one another. And as we looked at each other, one would think it would've been awkward, but it wasn't. Instead, the longer we stood there, those crazy feelings in the pit of my stomach started to settle, to calm down. And that caught me off guard.

I didn't know him, yet all I wanted to do was force my feet to move in his direction.

Watching, I could tell his indecision about his next move was weighing on him as the seconds ticked by. He broke our gaze as his eyes bounced around the shop, not settling on any one place for long. But then his eyes settled back on mine, and he smiled. As I smiled back, one hand came from his pocket and went through his hair, mussing it up a bit. It made him seem more real somehow, as though he wasn't so perfect.

Maybe he was nervous after all.

"Fuck it," he said, almost to himself, as he advanced toward me. His hands went to my waist, and he started walking us back a couple steps until my thighs hit the table. His hands framed my face as he leaned forward, our mouths coming dangerously close. "I'm going to kiss you."

And I nodded as a soft moan escaped my throat.

Because I wanted this kiss. More than I realized.

His full lips came to mine, soft at first. Then harder, as his lips opened, his tongue begged entrance into me. His fingers threaded in the loose hair around my neck, pulling more from my bun as he gripped me. Our tongues danced together, soft and gentle.

He was a contradiction. Everything I knew of him so far was rigid, hard.

But his kiss was…tender.

And it made my insides melt.

My hands went to his face, almost on instinct, and were rewarded by the feel of that scruff along his jawline. My nails gently dragged through the roughness, enjoying the feel against the pads of my fingers.

Getting kissed by Gage Parker was not on my list of things to do today.

But I wasn't the least bit sorry it was happening.

He parted from me slowly, peppering me with tiny pecks around my lips. Eventually, he withdrew completely, looking down at me once again.

"I needed confirmation that you tasted as sweet as you smell," he said. His hand cradled my cheek after he whispered those words.

This moment was surreal.

He wasn't real.

"And you do," he continued.

Stepping back, he left me against the table, weak in the knees. I mean, he wasn't a complete stranger, but he was damn close.

Yet, that kiss.

It was swoon worthy.

Backpedaling toward the door, he said, "But I should go, for real this time. Don't forget to lock up again."

And then he opened the door, closing it this time, and left.

GOING OUT ON A TUESDAY, especially for drinks, was not the norm for me. But after what happened at the shop, I texted Victoria and begged her to meet me for one. I had to talk this out. There was no way I'd be able to go to sleep tonight without getting someone else's perspective.

Walking into the bar, I looked around and found her sitting at a booth, the wild blonde curls giving her away. Plopping across from her before she saw me made her jump in her seat.

"Fuck, Harper, a little warning!"

"Love you, too, bestie," I said, blowing her a kiss across the table. Vic and I have worked together at the club for a few years now and became fast best friends. Living in a city like New York, both of us being outsiders, gave us a lot in common right off the bat. We didn't have a ton of time for each other, with my second job and her still going to school part-time. But whatever time we did have, we made good use of together.

"What's up?" she asked. "Your text was very cryptic."

She'd ordered some wings and had two beers on the table for us already, which was one of the things I loved best about her. She knew me so well. Chugging almost half the beer before I even thought of starting the story, she stared me down from across the table.

"Well?" she asked. "I don't have all night, I've still got home-work to do, Harp."

"Ok," I said, ready to start. "You're not going to believe this." Leaning in over the table conspiratorially to start my story, her eyes got wide. "Do you remember the two brothers I told you about from the other day?"

Nodding, she said, "Yeah, Frat Boy and Curmudgeon. But if I remember, you said they were both hot."

They were both hot. But now I kinda thought one was hotter than the other.

"Yeah, they are. So, I was closing tonight, and Curmudgeon showed up." Chuckling at his nickname, I grabbed a wing and started nibbling on it. "He said he wanted to pay their invoice." My skepticism wasn't lost on Vic.

"In person? Isn't that a bit '90s?" She laughed out loud. "Does he realize how transparent that is?"

Just thinking about Gage made me blush a bit. Tonight was so unexpected.

Victoria stared at me as I continued to eat my buffalo wing.

"Harper," she said. "What did you do?"

Reaching for another wing, I did my best to avoid her question for the moment.

"Harper!"

But it was why I asked her here.

"Well, we may have kissed."

The gulp of beer that was about to go down her throat instead sprayed out of her mouth, across the table, and all over my food and face. Literally, I was soaked. Grabbing my napkin, I wiped my cheeks.

"Seriously?" I asked as she laughed out loud, and I pushed my plate aside.

"Curmudgeon!" she howled.

I was sure my face fell, and she saw it. Her laughter subsided, and she watched me carefully as I took a swill of beer.

"You like him," she said.

"Maybe, but can I like someone I don't even know?" I responded. And it was true. I knew nothing other than he was the heir of a billion-dollar company, a client of ours, and a grump. "But I liked what he did."

That piqued her interest. She sat back against the booth, beer in hand, and waited for me to continue.

"Well, first I started showing him some work pictures, and he was like making me call him Gage, not Mr. Parker, and then I stood up from the table, and I was, I don't know how, but freakin' right between his spread legs on the stool." I was rambling, I knew that. But I needed to get it all out before I lost my nerve. "And the tension, Christ, when he looked at me. But then, bam, he got up and left. Like, just got up, said 'I have to go' and left."

Her bulging eyes told me she was with me on the story.

"There's no kiss in that story, Harp," she said.

Rolling my eyes, I threw a paper napkin at her chest.

"I know Vic, but this is where the story is like one of those books we read all the time," I said. "He came back. He literally knocked on the locked door of the shop and came back. When I opened it, he came strolling in and went right for my face, like literally stroked my cheek. Then he looked confused for a minute, but then he walked me back against the table and kissed me."

Victoria's slow smile spread across her face. "That doesn't seem very curmudgeony."

We laughed together.

"Did he talk? Did he say anything or just kiss you?" she asked.

"He may have, but nothing I can remember." Those details were left out intentionally. Because the words he'd said to me were definitely not the words of a grump. And I also wanted to keep them to myself, keep them special. At least for now.

As I reflected on the events of my night, I found myself absently drawing pictures in the dew on my glass.

"Well," Vic said, drawing me back from my thoughts. "That sounds super sexy and romantic. And I'm happy for you, babe. You guys gonna see each other again?"

And that was where my magical encounter seemed to take a cliff dive.

The slow shake of my head coupled with my eyes not meeting hers I knew was telling Victoria more about this experience than I really wanted her to know.

It was forcing me to admit to myself more than I wanted to.

"Well, we, uh, didn't exchange numbers," I told her.

"Hey," she said, the pity already in her voice. "Harp, don't worry. In this day and age, that's not a problem. We can figure something out."

But she could tell by the look on my face that there was more to my concern. Much more. Victoria slumped back against our booth with a frustrated huff.

"Harper, you have to stop thinking every guy you meet is going to be like Asshole. He was a special breed, not everyone will be like him. You need to put yourself out there."

The asshole she was referring to was my ex from right after college. Well, we met when I moved to the city and were together for a couple years. He was on the fast track to become partner at a law firm. But once he landed that job, image was all he cared about. It completely changed him. Or maybe I just never saw who he really was. But once I did, he was ugly. Every aspect of him was ugly. He had no regard for my goals in life at all, only his.

"Chicks before dicks, right?" I said, and we clinked our beers to that.

Vic wasn't looking for a boyfriend while she was still in school and working all the time. Hookups only were her thing.

And she wanted that to be mine as well.

But as hard as I tried, I wasn't built that way.

"Right," she said.

But somehow, one specific dick was stuck on my brain.

CHAPTER 6
Gage

Our weekly meeting would be starting momentarily, but I needed to finish one more spreadsheet before Maryellen came in. The company was doing better than expected this quarter, but still not where we were this time last year. And although it was simply a sign of the economy, my father would see it as a failure of mine, I was sure.

Just as I hit save and send, the knock came on my door.

"C'mon in, Maryellen," I called out.

She came walking in with her tablet, always ready to go. Sitting in her accustomed chair in front of my desk, she crossed her legs and put her phone on my desk.

"We don't have too much today, si—Gage." The smile made it to her eyes this time as they lifted to look my way at her blunder. She was starting to get it. It was hard being under the formal rule of my father for so many years before he left. I was working hard to make things different here at Parker Financial and bring it into the twenty-first century. My hope was that it would pay off.

"Sounds good, what's up first?"

She started off with some basics from human resources and

some forms I needed to sign about benefits and insurance. Then we moved on to the topics I would need to address at the faculty breakfast meeting coming up. We finished up, and she was standing to leave.

"Oh, there is one more thing," she said, sitting back down. "A call came through late yesterday. Harper Wilson put a request in for you to go to the shop. She said she needs your approval on the summer lineup."

Trying to disguise my stunned face was challenging, but Maryellen seemed to not notice.

"Is this how *you* handled the flower account?" I asked her.

She seemed surprised by my question, flustered even. "Well, yes, sometimes I'd need to approve the designs, I guess, if they were completely new and never used before."

Flowers. We were investing this much time into flowers. Don't get me wrong, I clearly understood the aesthetic value they added to our space. But something wasn't adding up.

"Fine, let her know I can stop by tomorrow afternoon on my way home."

And it sure as hell wasn't adding up that this had now become a responsibility of mine.

Maryellen nodded with a slight smile and let herself out of my office.

And I spun in my chair to look out my window.

To think.

And fuck, the only place my mind went was to Harper's round ass as she bent over that table. And how her tits filled out her t-shirt as it stretched across her chest. And the fact that not only was I paying her another visit, but looking forward to it was a big red flag. I'd had enough red flag relationships lately to last a lifetime. I was supposed to be staying away, fooling around only.

So maybe that's what this would be, could be.

Maybe Harper Wilson would be a hookup.

MY NERVES WERE SHOT as I approached the door of the shop. Maybe my assumptions about this meeting were wrong. There could be a need for approvals I was unaware of. I was new to this side of our business, what did I know? My thoughts about Harper wanting me to come by morphed from wanting to see me to it most likely being business, all in the last three steps before the door. And I was not accustomed to feeling insecure.

Pushing the door open, the bell announced my arrival. But once inside, the shop was already dimmed as if they were closed. Looking at my watch, I knew they were open for a few more minutes but thought I could have gotten the hours wrong since it was Friday.

"Hello?" I called out.

"I'll be right there."

Just hearing her voice did things to me.

Then she came strolling through the door, nothing in her hands. Just her. This time, her hair was long, hanging in waves past her shoulders. She was in jeans again, but a tight pink V-neck sweater hugged the curves of her breasts.

"Hi," she said. Her voice was quiet, almost shy, as she stopped feet away from me. Leaning against that massive wooden table, her hands wrapped around herself, almost protectively.

But all it really did was push her full breasts out more, her cleavage displayed by the neckline.

"Hello," I said.

I allowed the awkward silence to linger just a bit.

"Maryellen said you called, needed me to come by."

She was nervous. Her hand went to her hair as her fingers ran through the long strands. There was a slight tremble to her hand as it came back down and settled against her torso again.

"Um, yeah, well, about that," she started. "There aren't really any papers to sign…I just…" She turned bright red.

"It's just that, when you left the other day, I didn't get your number. The only number I have is Maryellen's."

"So, you thought calling a fake business meeting to get me here was the way to go?"

I thought it was smart if not a creative way to get me here. But risky.

As I closed the gap between us, Harper's eyes widened with each step I took. Completely thrown off by my question, she had no idea how to read me as I approached her.

My own intentions were clear to me when I was coming here. Then a haze fell over my mind, clouding my judgment. But that cloud seemed to be lifting with her words.

Seems she had the same idea.

I mimicked her stance, leaning my hip against the table, my arms crossing my chest. My movements caught her eye, and she glanced up from under her lashes.

But then I saw her steel her emotions and throw her shoulders back in defiance.

"I'm sorry I lied to you," she said, keeping her gaze locked on mine. "I, um, didn't know what else to do. After you left, and after that kiss, I…"

"I wouldn't have come to this *meeting* if I didn't want to see you." *And maybe get more than another kiss.*

That made her smile. She was still nervous, but a bit less knowing I wanted to be here. She went to some lengths to get me here, and it felt pretty good being pursued. Even though I was fairly used to recognition from women, I usually took the aggressive role.

But this felt good.

"I guess I dropped the ball on that the other day," I said. "But I do have your shop number."

And then she looked a bit put off, almost nervous.

"So, should I have waited for you to call?" she asked.

Stepping closer to her, the urge to scoop her up and make her understand that wasn't what I meant was strong. I was usually a lot smoother than this.

Why did she take me off my game? This was going to be a hookup, nothing else. But she already had me feeling things inside.

"No," I said. "Not at all. I'm glad you called our *meeting*."

Her breaths became choppy with my words, and her eyes rolled back a bit before her lids slowly covered her deep blue irises. Maybe she was still nervous, or possibly my words calmed her. Regardless, she looked damn sexy. And I felt, like the other day, as though I couldn't keep my hands from touching her.

Gently wrapping my fingers behind her neck, I pulled her closer to me.

Taking her face in my hands with my other hand, I guided our faces close, our lips gently touching. She gripped my shirt in her fingers, pulling me closer yet. She opened her mouth to me, our tongues tangling together, my hands moving behind her head and into her hair.

She wanted this as much as I did, it seemed.

And I wasn't sure how far this was really going to go, or how far she was willing to let it go.

But I knew how far I wanted it to go. I came here on a mission.

So, I took a chance.

My hand trailed from her hair to her neck again, that warm spot I'd been daydreaming about. But I didn't stop there. Instead, my hand continued down her chest, a finger daring to touch the top of her breast peeking out of her sweater. Her skin pebbled from my touch, and she pushed her body against mine.

"Is this okay, Harper?"

She mumbled an incoherent agreement into my mouth, not wanting to pull away.

Cupping her breast, the weight of it heavy in my hand, I pushed it against the other. My thumb felt for her nipple through her sweater, her bra, and it responded immediately.

Suddenly, she pushed me away, and I wanted to whine like a bratty kid. Staring down at her pouty lips, all I wanted was my mouth on them again.

"I think…" she started.

But I put my finger on her mouth to quiet her. We didn't need words. I moved in to replace my finger with my lips, but she pulled out of my hold.

"Gage, should I maybe go lock the front door? It's not locked yet."

My hands found her ass, and I pulled her against me, eliminating the space between us. Grabbing hold of her as I stood from the stool, I lifted her up and onto the table next to us, her laugh lighting up the room.

"Oh my God!" Her wide eyes looked at me as a smile spread across her face.

Then I was standing between her spread legs. And it felt good. She wrapped them around me and pulled me against her, locking her feet behind my thighs. I was tempted to take her right then and there, screw anyone walking in on us.

But the sensible side of me won over.

"I'll go lock the door, don't move. And you're sure that'll be okay?" I walked toward the front of the store but kept my eyes on her. "What about Fiona?" I asked.

"Everyone already went home for the day, I'm closing."

Her sly smile made my feet move faster. Not only did I lock it, and double-check, but I pulled the window shade down as well. By the time I turned back around, Harper was undoing her jeans.

"Stop," I instructed her.

Confusion set in all over her face as I stalked back to her. She sat motionless on the table, her legs hanging off the side. Her innocence was screaming for me to be careful with her.

I didn't know what it was about her that brought out the animal in me. Her bright blue irises peeked out from under her long, dark lashes and I swear I saw the hint of moisture in her eyes. I didn't want to scare her, I wasn't a monster, but the domination I felt was definitely a turn on. My hands landed on her thighs, above her knees, rubbing gently, making their way to the top. My fingers curved in, thumbs pushing between her thighs, and I could feel the heat emanating from the spot, even through the thick fabric.

Her eyes closed slowly as my hand rubbed over her pussy.

She was turned on, too.

"You like this?"

She immediately got flustered by the verbal interruption, her once-closed eyes popping open.

"I do," she replied.

She stared at me while her hands plopped behind her on the table to support her weight as she leaned back.

But all that did was push her tits closer and higher out of her low-cut sweater. I couldn't wait to feel them in my hands, not through the sweater or bra.

"So, we're doing this, here, and you're good with it?" I asked.

I don't know why I needed confirmation, but I did.

And she gave it to me by sitting up and taking off her sweater.

And she unveiled a completely see-through white lace bra.

Fuck.

I could see the outline of her nipples clearly through the thin material, and it begged for my mouth to suck on them. But I withheld.

Instead, I reached out and rubbed my fingers across them through the lace. She closed her eyes and rolled her head back, relishing my touch.

Then I grabbed one between my fingers and rolled it, feeling it grow and get hard.

"Oh my God," she moaned. Her body relaxed under my touch, and using my other hand behind her head, I gently lowered her to the table, all while still working her nipple between my other fingers.

Once she was flat, I noticed she'd been hiding a fit body under her clothes, the tight lines of her abdomen showing muscles that had been worked. But there was still a curvy softness to her, a femininity that trumped her solid body. My fingers found her nipple again, and bumps arose on her flesh, begging my other hand to caress her skin. Her legs instinctively spread wider, allowing me to push myself against her, the pressure intensifying.

I couldn't hold back any longer. My mouth landed on her breast, sucking the taut skin deep between my lips as my hands pushed her breasts together. Her back arched, pushing them against my face. Taking advantage of her moves, my hand went behind her, and holding her up, I maneuvered the clasp of her bra, pushing it from her shoulders.

Harper helped pull it away from her arms and settled back against the wooden slab. Then she reached up and pulled at my tie, my buttons, then my jacket.

"I think it's time we got some of your clothes off," she said.

Stepping back to help, I took my jacket off and laid it over a stool. Taking my time, I unknotted my tie and loosened my shirt. Harper sat up and keenly watched every move I made.

Leaning back on her elbows again, smiling up at me, she

looked so fucking adorable. But not so cute that I didn't want to take her pants off. Moving closer to the table, I slid the zipper down on her partially opened jeans and noticed she had a white lace thong on. There was something about the matching set under her clothes that turned me on.

"See something you like?" she asked.

"Something like that," I responded. My hands reached behind her, anxious to finish the job of getting her naked.

But then, standing there, almost naked, in front of me, she was suddenly shy. Her eyes avoided mine, scanning the room and looking anywhere but at me. She fidgeted with her hands, covering herself for a few seconds here or there. They needed something to do.

"Take my belt off."

It worked. She settled and her hands came to my waist, fiddling with the buckle and sliding it from my pants.

"Should I keep going?" she asked. She looked at up me as she asked her question, her blue eyes wide and bright, the color of today's sky.

"If you want."

And she did. She moved to the button and the zipper, a slight push allowing them to fall to my ankles. I kicked my shoes off, and the pants followed.

We both stood there, facing each other in our underwear. I was thankful she left the thong on. I needed to see how her ass looked in it. And I would have some fun taking it off myself. Reaching out, I picked her up and placed her back on the table. Keeping my hands on her ass once putting her down, I enjoyed the feel of her flesh on my fingers as I massaged her cheeks. Her legs fell open, allowing me to step close, our centers aligned, almost touching.

But I didn't give in to that, yet.

Her hands went behind me and wrapped around my waist as she attempted to tug me against her, to rub against me.

"Uh-uh, not yet. Patience."

The tiny moan of disapproval quickly turned into a sly smile when my hands came around to the front of her and my fingers rubbed along the outline of her panties. She suddenly seemed to be on board with making this last.

Although my dick was rock solid already, and I knew if she stroked it once or twice, I would probably shoot my load right then. It had been too long.

"It looks like you're ready to go now, though," she said as she stared at my cock.

"Don't you worry about me," I said as I spread her knees wider.

A squeal sprang from her lips as my hands dropped to the thin strip of cloth covering her pussy.

"Fuck," I said. As I ran a finger from top to bottom, her panties were already wet. "It seems as though I'm not the only one ready."

My thumb found her clit through the lace and pressed down on the now hard flesh. Harper's legs instinctively tried to close in on my hand, but I held her legs open, and her body writhed on the table beneath me.

"Oh, fuck," she moaned as her hands reached for her breasts. Her back arched as she gripped them, pushing them together, pulling on her own nipples with an intensity I wasn't expecting.

My thumb started swirling around the tight nub, pushing into the lace. My other hand skimmed the seam of her panties, lifting the fabric just enough for the tip of a finger to dip inside. She gasped at my touch as I found her entrance and immediately plunged my finger deep inside her while my thumb continued its assault on her clit.

Her eyes popped open, finding mine and begging for more. She needed more as her hand came over mine and pushed it deeper into her pussy.

"Does this feel good, Harper? You like this?" Before she could answer, a second and third finger made their way inside her tight opening, pumping into her.

"Fuck, yes, please, don't stop!"

Her hands thrashed, pulling at her tits and slamming against the table. Her legs pushed against my arms, but I held them down, my elbows against her knees.

Then I had an idea.

My hand stilled and she whined. Pulling my hand from her pussy, I laid them on top of her thighs.

"Do you trust me?"

She looked at me with wary eyes, and I knew it was an unfair question. My smile warmed as she continued to think about my question.

"*Will* you trust me?"

"Well, I must trust you on some level already to be letting you do this to me, right?" she said. "Why?"

"I want to blindfold you, Harper. I want to cover your eyes so you have no idea what I'm going to do to your pussy. What do you say?" I didn't wait for her answer as I reached for my tie that had been tossed to the floor. Coming back up with it in my hand, I showed it to her.

There was a moment of hesitation.

Then she smiled up at me, a nod following.

"Say it, Harper. Use your words and tell me what I can do to you."

She blinked several times, looking a bit stunned at my demand. But she regained her confidence quickly.

"Blindfold me, Gage."

I'd never done this before. But something about our spur-of-the-moment hook up had me pushing my own boundaries.

Smoothing out the silk with my fingers, I lowered it over her eyes.

"Lift your head a bit." I wrapped it around and tied it on the side of her head. "Are you comfortable?"

"I am," she said.

But her words were breathy, and the rise and fall of her chest indicated some stress. My lips grazed her forehead and trailed tender kisses toward her ear.

"Relax," I whispered. Kissing her lobe caused a shiver to run through her body, but her breathing started to even out and she settled. "That's it," I murmured in her ear. The back of my fingers rubbed across her cheek, over her lips.

Her lips were plump and cherry red without any makeup on. My thumb glided over the smooth skin, pulling down on the bottom lip slightly. Leaning down, I planted a gentle kiss on her mouth. That seemed to calm her even more.

Standing, I reached across Harper's body, grabbing hold of the first "toy" I planned on using.

A pink, long-stemmed rose.

Dragging the bloom across the tip of her nipple, I watched closely for her reaction.

Her body froze as her mind processed what was touching her. But there was no denying that her body liked it as her nipple hardened to a peak. Moving to the other breast, I swirled the flower across her skin, the velvety petals leaving a path of goosebumps.

"You're being such a good girl, Harper, and I can tell you're enjoying this."

I moved the flower to her upper lip, rubbing it under her nose, allowing her to smell and identify what I was using. She smiled as I pulled it away. Dragging it in a line between her breasts and down her belly, stopping at the line of her panties.

Pulling them down a bit revealed a little patch of light brown hair manicured so perfectly atop her pubic bone.

"Turn over for me, Harper. I need to see that ass of yours in this thong," I ordered.

She turned over, her feet coming to the ground as she bent over the table. Her ass was an offering to me. The full, round cheeks fit perfectly in my palms as I gripped them, pulling them apart to see that strip of cloth down the middle. Pulling the thong from her, the temptation was strong to reach out and play with her tight, puckered hole.

Instead, the rose made a pass along her tight back opening, her body stiffening at the touch. A moan left her lips at the same time, so I made another pass, and she pushed her ass closer to me, almost in invitation.

But I still decided to wait.

"Take your thong off for me, Harper, and then get back on the table."

Harper willingly obliged, and when she laid back down, she spread her legs even more.

And what a fine sight she gave me. Her cunt was the same color as the rose as I slid it from top to bottom. My free hand rubbed the inside of her thigh as the flower continued teasing her.

Her body jerked with the sensation as my other hand moved closer to her core, desperate to feel her again. I placed the flower on her belly and moved both my hands to the insides of her thighs, moving upwards as my fingers reached the lips of her pussy.

A tiny gasp escaped from her, and her hands came around to mine, prodding me to continue.

And I liked that.

But I still needed more.

"Can I taste you, Harper?" I asked.

As I looked up her body, I saw an enthusiastic nod, the silky ends of the tie flailing about.

Spreading her open, I pulled her clit out and lowered my mouth. My tongue made slow, languid circles to the taut tip as her body tensed.

Moans followed, so I knew she was enjoying it.

But my patience had waned; I couldn't wait any longer. My finger found her entrance as my lips sucked her clit into my mouth.

"Oh, Gage!" Harper screamed as her legs crashed against the sides of my head.

Her muscles tightened around my finger as I fought to put another in. Instead, my tongue bathed her slit from bottom to top, and I returned to the bottom to force it inside her, needing to taste her again. My thumb pulled at her clit as she writhed under me—

"Stop!" she yelled. She sat up and ripped the tie from her eyes, nervously looking to the back of the store. "Shit, did you hear that?"

I froze and listened.

And then I heard what sounded like a key jiggling in a door.

"Who is that, Harper?" I asked as I found my pants on the floor and handed hers to her.

"It must be Fiona. Fuck, fuck, fuck…"

She was frantically looking for her underwear on the floor, almost in tears.

"She gave me this opportunity, this account with your company, and I'm fucking you on the table!"

She was full-blown crying now.

"Harper." I grabbed her by the arms and forced her to look at me. "You need to calm down and get dressed right now. We'll talk about everything later, you can do this."

I handed her thong to her, and she quickly got dressed. My

clothes were on seconds after hers and then we heard the voice from the back.

"Harper, are you here, honey?"

She was panic-stricken, with an expression like she was about to vomit. I nodded, trying to instill some confidence in her. She wiped away a few stray tears and nodded back.

"Yes, Fiona, I'm in front," she said. Her voice cracked slightly, but she did good.

"Okay, I'll be right there, I have some stuff to get from the truck."

Harper grabbed her apron from a hook, tying it around her back.

"Okay, I've got this, I can do this," she said to herself as she sat on a stool at the table. "Can you sit with me? Will you stay?"

I would have preferred to make my exit, sticking around could easily give the impression I'm looking for something more. But this was not a situation anyone should have to deal with alone, especially since it was created by us doing this together.

"Of course I'll stay."

I heard the back door open again and knew her boss would be joining us. That was the second I noticed her white lace bra under the stool I was about to sit on. Grabbing it from the ground, I stuffed it into my jacket pocket, next to my tie, just as a tall, dark-haired woman of about sixty years came through the doorway.

"Well, I didn't know Harper had a meeting tonight," she said, walking up and reaching for my hand.

I stood to take it, shaking it vigorously. "Yes, hi Fiona. I'm Gage Parker. It's nice to meet you. We're just about done here. She did a wonderful job setting us up with our summer lineup. I look forward to seeing the new designs in person."

"Oh, Mr. Parker," she said with enthusiasm. "So nice to put a face to the name. I met your dad years ago."

Fiona's proud smile went in Harper's direction. She obviously cared deeply for her and entrusted her with her company, which said a lot.

"She's amazing, isn't she?"

"Oh my God, please stop, Fiona," Harper said, looking embarrassed. She stood and started cleaning the table, shifting the lone pink rose to the side. "I'm going to finish up with Mr. Parker and then enter the order into the system. Can you open the front door, I had it locked."

Harper snuck a smile my way as Fiona went to the front door.

"Don't mind me, you two. Act like I'm not here. I wasn't supposed to come in, but I had some flowers I needed to drop off. I'll only be here a few minutes and then I'll be out of your hair," Fiona said as she walked past us toward the back.

Harper slouched against the table, looking exhausted.

"I'm sorry," she whispered. "This was a disaster." Her hands covered her face and were trembling.

"Hey," I wanted to go to her, it was my instinct. To take her hands in mine and make everything okay. But I saw the red flag warning pop up in my head, telling me I was doing what I always did: moving too fast. I stayed where I was, trying to console her with my words. "This was not a disaster. Maybe it was just the universe's way of telling us to slow things down."

"Yeah." She nodded, but her voice sounded…disappointed.

She picked up the pink rose again, wistfully holding it against her chest as she started gathering her portfolios and papers.

"I had fun, Harper. Maybe we can try this again sometime."

She didn't stop organizing her things as I spoke; she felt dismissed.

But that was what I wanted, wasn't it?

CHAPTER 7
Harper

Saturdays. Most people loved them. I, on the other hand, have come to tolerate them. Working both jobs made for a long day. I enjoyed my time at the shop, but Saturdays were busy. But that did help the hours fly by. Most of those hours were spent creating, which was my favorite thing to do.

Though I was distracted by the memory of what Gage and I did on this table.

"What are you smiling at?" Fiona asked as she came out from the back with another order. "That looks like the face of someone who's gotten laid."

"Fiona!"

Fiona was like having a second mother. I think she felt she needed to take over the role since my mom was so far away. But she got it confused at times. Although Fiona was about thirty years older than me, she still acted like she was my peer. Talking to her about things like sex happened more often with her than they did with my best friend. So, the mom role she tried to take on was more in her head.

"What? It's the same face I make whenever Jim and I get

around to doing it. That's why you don't see that face on me that often." She walked around the showroom, gathering the blooms that would be needed for the next order. After placing them on the table near me, she hesitated before heading to the back room. "Anyone I know?"

"Stop it!" I screamed. But I knew it was no use with her, and I obviously couldn't tell her the truth. "And, no, no one you know."

And most likely it wouldn't happen again, for all I knew. Things ended…weird last night. I mean, we got interrupted and that didn't help. But then he just kind of left. Just like the first time.

Christ, I was almost shitting my pants when he walked in. I couldn't believe I went through with that call to Maryellen. Setting myself up for a one-night stand was so out of character, but I needed to push out of my comfort zone. I'd had enough confidence calls at night with Vic to last a lifetime, encouraging me to just start having sex with whomever I was attracted to. Besides, Gage Parker did not come across as a relationship type of guy.

How we left it didn't make me feel as though he and I would be seeing each other anytime soon. And that was exactly how one-night stands worked. It's also probably why I never really liked to experience them.

Fiona finally gave up her inquisition and went back to her books and bills in the back room. Looking at the clock, I was happy to see only a few minutes left for me here.

"Bye, Fiona, I'll see you Monday," I yelled to the back before heading out.

Racing home, I felt ready to crash for the night, my feet yelling and begging to be propped on the couch. Unfortunately, there wasn't much time before they had to be stuffed into stilettos. Only a mere few hours after the shop closed, I had to be ready to go at the next job.

The stilettos got paired with an outfit unsuitable for the streets of NYC; at least not if I didn't want unwanted attention. However, once inside the walls of the club, the short skirt and cropped tank (let's face it, I was basically wearing a studded, lacy bra) were what paid the rent.

And stuffed my savings account for my future.

A means to an end.

But hopefully, I wouldn't need to do it much longer. That savings account was growing nicely. Another year or two and I was sure I'd be able to get the loan I needed to start my own shop.

The pink rose in the bud vase caught my eye as I made my way to my closet; it had opened all the way. I'd have to remember to hang it upside down tomorrow to start drying it. It was probably wrong of me to save the damn thing considering how abruptly he left, for the second time. But there was something about him…

As I stuffed my sky-high pumps into my backpack, the toaster and phone pinged at the same time. But I didn't even have time to check my phone as I added a smear of cream cheese to my bagel and headed out the door.

My short walk to the club had me there in minutes, and I pushed through the back door. It was like entering my second home—a place that felt familiar, even if I didn't feel like being there.

"Hey, beautiful," a voice sounded from behind me.

Spinning toward the sound, Pete almost ran into me with his hands full of bottles. "Shit, I'm sorry," I said, attempting to steady his hold on the booze in his arms. "Had no idea you were that close to me."

"Any guy would be a fool to not come up close on that ass, Harper."

Pete was a notorious flirt, and he and I flirted back and forth all the time. His boyfriend, Neal, worked here as well, and we were all good friends. They were adorable together.

"I'm wearing the baggiest sweats I own, Pete. How can you even see my ass?"

"I know full well what it will look like in five minutes in that spandex. It's engrained in my memory, baby girl. Trust me, any guy would be lucky to have that ass in his hands."

Pete was not only one of the good ones, but he was hot. Like really freaking hot. He had that sexy black hair that flopped over the top onto buzzed sides. And it framed a face with chiseled cheekbones, dark blue eyes, and full lips. Plus, he was no stranger to the gym, making sure to showcase his muscles with sleeveless vests as his uniform of choice. He played the game right to get the tips he needed. The female customers had no idea he was gay, but somehow all his male customers did. It was amazing to watch.

Absolute perfection.

"Stop!" I said, my hands pushing against his muscular chest. "I need to go get dressed, speaking of spandex. And check the schedule. I have no idea where I am tonight."

"I do, baby girl. You're with me, right where you should be," Pete said as he continued down the dark hall and up the stairs to the lounge rooms. "We have VIP rooms together tonight. Also, the way it should be."

Oh my God, that made me so happy. Lounge nights were so much easier than being on the floor. We were responsible for two VIP rooms that were connected to each other. And even though that made for a lot of work, it was still easier than being on the floor. Typically, they were small groups of friends or business associates that made for a more enjoyable night, plus a guaranteed huge tip.

And Pete and I did well together.

I hustled to the locker room since I still needed to get into my uniform and touch up my makeup. As I approached the door, the level of noise coming from the other side made it sound like a high school gym locker.

"Can I borrow your boob tape? I ran out."

"Anyone have a tampon?"

"Can someone work for me tomorrow night? I have a date!"

The questions and statements were all blurring together as I rushed into the room, finding my locker, and quickly spinning the numbers on my lock.

"Hey, Harper, you made it. I was thinking you weren't coming in tonight. You didn't answer my text."

I turned to the sweet voice next to me and smiled at Victoria, whom I didn't know was also on tonight.

"I'm sorry, I was running late getting here and didn't have time to even see who texted me." I slumped on the bench that ran along the lockers.

"You look exhausted, girl. Did you work all day again at the shop?" she asked.

"Yep, from ten to six."

She shook her head, the compassion evident. "But you have your dream, and you'll be out of this place before you know it. I have faith in you."

Stuffing my bag into the locker, I moved on to pulling the tight shorts on and stuffing my boobs into the lacy top.

"We both will be out of here, Vic, because you'll be done with school, and I'll be ready to open my shop."

She leaned in for a hug before moving back toward the makeup tables.

Then I stared at my true nemesis.

Those five-inch stilettos.

I hated them.

Like, really hated them.

The day I walked out of this club, I would never wear another pair of high-heeled shoes.

Ever.

With a grimace, I slid one foot into a shoe at a time. The pinching feeling immediately hitting my toes as the back dug into my heel. I gave up on bandages, they never stayed on. Standing still, eyes closed for a moment, I took a few deep breaths to allow my feet to adjust.

They always did.

They had to.

"Don't forget your choker," Victoria said to me, as I was about to walk away.

Shit, I did almost forget.

A black velvet choker, with hot pink script letters across our neck.

The Velvet Rope.

CHAPTER 8

Gage

Saturdays were my sacred day. It was the one day of the week I intentionally did not work. The door to my home office remained closed, and I even steered clear of checking my work email. Of course, there was the occasional emergency that required attention. But other than that, it was the one day I kept all for me. My reason was solid: everyone hated Sundays, anyway. That dreaded feeling of having to head back to work the next day was already hanging over your head. Why not get a head start on it all then.

So, Sunday mornings, I would have my coffee at my desk at home. I loved my home office. The natural light it captured was amazing, especially in the mornings. I would pull back the curtains and let it stream in as I propped my feet on the two-hundred-year-old mahogany desk. The townhouse I had temporarily while down at BRU last year was not exactly my style. The firm sent a designer down to decorate for me, but it never quite felt like home.

My place in New York, however, was exactly to my taste. It was not what most people my age or of my financial standing normally called home. My brother had his penthouse apartment on the

Upper East Side. But me, I loved my brownstone in the West Village. I had a rooftop terrace, a yard, everything to make it a real home.

It was the home that my ex and I made together.

My marriage to Rebecca was supposed to be forever. We met during college at BRU and fell in love. We were *that* couple in college that everyone was jealous of and thought would be together forever. We were together for three years before graduating and moving up to New York. My father loved her as much as I did and wanted her with the company. She and I thought it would be great to work together.

And it was…until it wasn't.

We spent *too* much time together. We never had a break from one another. And with a brand-new marriage, that was probably not the best formula.

My father's solution was to send her to London on assignment.

And the absence did make her heart grow fonder, only it was for someone else.

She met someone, asked for a divorce, and the rest is history.

I never really had time to fall out of love with her, nosediving from love to hate.

But I didn't fall out of love with my brownstone. Making a few changes was all I needed to do to remove *her* from the place. It was definitely my safe space, and I loved my weekends here.

But there were certain Saturdays, like this one, I had to work.

Although, if you asked Chase, heading out to a club on a Saturday night was the furthest thing from work. But Chase and I had different definitions of what work was. He wouldn't be too concerned about the whereabouts of our client, soon to be co-worker, once we arrived at The Velvet Rope.

But until tonight, the day was mine.

First on the agenda, I was heading out for a run. Grabbing my sneakers, I plopped on the sofa to tie them up as my phone vibrated with an incoming text.

> Chase - Hey man just a heads up I'm bringing
> Amanda tonight Maryellen set it up

THAT WAS INTERESTING. Why would Maryellen have done that and not arranged someone for me? I quickly checked the calendar to see if I'd missed a note about the night, someone that I was supposed to pick up for the event. But there was nothing noted.

But that left me to deal with the new business associate, which surely was Maryellen's plan.

> Me - Sure, it'll be good to see her

AMANDA IS one of Chase's on-again, off-again girls that he couldn't ever figure things out with. When they were together, they were great together. He seemed happy, as if he would want to have a relationship with her. But the moment she was gone, he reveled in the peace of being alone. Since Amy, I really think he'd just gotten used to the bachelor life.

God knew I had as well.

Right?

CHAPTER 9

Harper

"So, we have some hotshots here tonight on one side, apparently. Some millionaire brothers from a financial company downtown, wining and dining their clients. I don't think they've ever been here before," Pete explained while he stocked the bar. I was getting the tables cleaned and prepped for the group. We only had about ten minutes before their scheduled time for the room began, but they never arrived that early on a Saturday night. Most business types were out to dinner first and would get to us by 9:30 or 10.

"What company are they from?" I asked as I was lighting the candles in the dimly lit space.

The VIP rooms were on the upper level of the club, with a perfect view of the dance floor and DJ below. There were eight private lounge rooms on this level, four on each side of the wide opening to below, all visible to each other. Seemed a bit haughty if you asked me, as if they wanted to parade amongst themselves who could afford the life. But I understood the aesthetic of it. They were all open to the middle of the club overlooking the dance floor, with their own staircase directly to the action. There were two bars on each side of the upper floor, so

Pete and I had two rooms to work. The lounges were separated by a ceiling high wall of opaque glass, but were open to each other at the bar. It allowed me to bounce between the lounges easily.

Pete pulled out the portfolio and looked at the calendar.

"PFA."

That didn't ring any bells.

"And the other room?" I asked as I came behind the bar, searching for the champagne flutes. We always had champagne on a silver tray for the guests upon their arrival. I realized Pete wasn't answering my question.

"Pete?"

"You don't wanna know," he eventually whined.

I stopped pulling out the flutes and stared at him.

"Nooo," I complained as my elbow flopped on the bar in front of him, my chin landing in my hand. "Again?"

"Yep," he sang in response.

Ugh.

Another bachelor party. But then I had an idea.

"Who's working the other bar next door?" I asked.

"I think it's Garrett," he answered as he finished cleaning his last glass.

"Does he owe you any favors?"

His sly smile said it all. "No, but he thinks you're the hottest thing in this place. I bet if you asked him, he would change rooms with you."

I wasn't so sure; bachelor parties were the bane of everyone's weekend here. Even a bachelorette party was better. For some reason, the guys got really carried away at these things. And most times it wasn't the actual bachelor but his married friends who hadn't been out enough that caused the problems.

I bounded out the back of the room and down the hall to the

other set of lounges. It was worth a shot, and I wasn't below begging him. Peeking inside the dark room, I didn't see anyone at first. The candles were lit, the flutes full of bubbly, so maybe their guests were about to arrive.

"What's up, Harper?" a voice said from behind.

"Shit," I said, my hand flying to my chest. "Becky, you scared me. How the hell are you able to walk so quietly in your…" I peered down at her feet and noticed her wiggling toes.

"Fuck that, I can't put those things on until the guests are walking up the stairs. What's up?" she said as she walked around me, her arms full of cloth napkins and small plates.

"Is Garrett on with you tonight?"

Becky kept walking away from me, obviously still needing to prep her room. She flitted around, setting the napkins and plates where she wanted them before heading to the bar and reaching for her bag. I felt her pain as she stuffed her feet into her shoes.

"Nope, he called in tonight. Lisa's on in here with me, she ran to the cellar to get more tequila. Can I help with anything?"

Damn. There went my idea. Eh, I liked Becky too much to give her the bachelor party anyway, probably was for the best.

"No, had a question for him, I'll catch him next time he's in, thanks. Have a good night."

She barely smiled, but I got it. It was crunch time. Checking my watch, I realized how late it had gotten and that I was wasting valuable time over here rather than in my own lounges getting them ready. Running back down the hall, the best I could in the death-inducing spiked heels, I rounded the corner, barely staying upright.

And ran right into a hard, rock solid chest.

That smelled divine.

And familiar. Very familiar.

Firm hands grabbed me by the upper arms to ensure I would stay upright as my eyes lifted to confirm my assumptions.

It couldn't be.

How was this happening?

"Harper?"

The voice was deeper than I remembered, but full of surprise. He himself not expecting to see me here. The deep notes of his voice seemed to reverberate in parts of my body a voice shouldn't hit. His hands were still holding my arms as I stood motionless, almost in a stupor, as my eyes slowly moved up to his face.

"Hi," he said, his voice warmer yet, if that was even possible.

How can one little word sound dangerous while turning you on?

I was totally flustered. This was not what I was expecting for my night. I wasn't embarrassed about my job here, everyone in my life knew about it. But for some reason, I didn't want *him* to know about it. Backing away, almost shrugging out of his hold, I knew I probably came across as cold and somewhat apathetic.

PFA.

Shit, I should've realized. I should've known it was them: *Parker Financial Associates.* We had our official meeting last week, their acronym was in my own calendar. My disbelief had to be what he saw on my face as I stared at him. But I had to resume my professionalism regardless of us knowing each other outside of the club.

Regardless of him having his mouth between my legs just last night.

On my worktable, at the shop.

Probably the best almost-sex I'd ever had.

I couldn't breathe. But that would be expected. He was a beautiful specimen of a human being; any breathing female would be attracted to him. That's all it was. I was attracted to him; there were no feelings involved.

At. All.

None.

My thoughts of him on and off since last night, on the table, were normal. That was a unique experience. Anyone would think about it.

Constantly.

Straightening my back and pushing my shoulders up, I tore my eyes from his, as I took careful, measured steps to the table on the side of the room. Once the tray was firmly in my grip, I spun on my heels, plastered my fake club smile on my face and got to work. I approached Gage and his group that had gathered, with my offering of champagne filled flutes.

"Welcome to The Velvet Rope."

CHAPTER 10

Gage

"Isn't that the chick from the flower shop?" Chase whispered in my ear as I walked over to the bar. I was trying to ignore the feelings I was experiencing from seeing her again. Here. Only twenty-four hours after having my fingers inside her, my mouth on her. And those feelings surprised me. Though I guess they shouldn't have. I knew she was a pretty girl—okay, more than pretty. Her day job attire was not something that truly accentuated her assets, however. But, fuck, if she didn't come alive in the tiny outfit they had her wearing in this place.

And I wasn't necessarily pleased about it.

Case in point, Chase already noticed her.

"She has a name, ya know," I responded, and my back was all he was getting. I was still pissed at him for how he treated her at the shop last week. Plus, how does he forget the name of someone he wanted to ask out? I know he apologized to me, but she was owed one as well. At twenty-four years old, I wouldn't think I'd still have to parent his behavior.

"Well, I wouldn't need to know her name if she was under me or on top of me, I'd have her screaming *my* name the whole night."

Motherfucker. How was I going to let him get away with talking about her like that? His assumption would automatically be that *I* wanted something with her if I came back at him.

And I didn't. Right?

However, my hands rolled into fists as the bartender came to take my order.

"What can I get you?" he asked.

"Bourbon on the rocks, please." My words were curt, but he had no idea why.

"Sure," he said, "and just so you know, Harper can take your order if you'd rather not make your way to the bar, sir."

My breath hitched at the mention of her name, more so because I was hoping my brother was no longer standing behind me. When he moved on to make my drink, I slowly turned to my left to find Chase watching me closely. The look on his face immediately made my hands curl at my sides again.

"Harper," he said, almost to himself. And the curl of his lip as he smirked told me all I wanted to know about his newfound intentions about her. "That's right. She's fucking hot. I know you said no business with pleasure, but shit, she might be worth crossing that line for." His elbow nudged me as he went in for another sip of his drink. "I probably owe her an apology, though, huh? Maybe I should go give that to her now."

The bartender placed my drink on the bar in front of me. I took my time picking it up, swirling it in the glass. Smiling down at the liquid, I was happy to see this place used highball ice as it clanged against the crystal. Eventually, I turned toward my brother and locked eyes on him. My composure needed to be in place for the rest of this conversation.

"Maybe leave well enough alone, Chase. I restored our relationship with her and their company, one that you threatened to destroy with your immature outburst."

He chuckled at my reprimand and proceeded to down the bourbon in his glass, slamming it on the bar once done. But I was trying to do whatever I could to keep him away from her. And to not give away that I'd had my fingers in her and my mouth on her a mere twenty-four hours before this.

"Well, isn't that what big brothers are for, bro?"

The level of cockiness in his voice was troubling. He was drunker than he should be for just arriving.

"Where's Amanda?" I asked. Scanning the room, I found her sitting at one of the tables talking with our man of the night, Nate Weaver, and his wife Cami. They brought some friends with them, as did we. It was more fun that way in these lounge rooms. "Go take care of your girl, Chase. She came with you tonight."

He pushed off the bar, stumbled a bit, and started walking away. "Yeah, whatever *bro.*"

Hopeful he could keep our new staff member entertained for a bit, I remained at the bar with my drink.

Right then, I heard loud shouts from around the corner. There was another lounge slightly visible from where I stood at the bar, and I was able to notice a large group of raucous guys next door, their party just getting started.

And Harper was right in the middle of them.

With a tray in her arms, high above her head, full of bottles and glasses, she was bouncing from guy to guy as they appeared to be…grabbing at her ass?

"She's okay."

The voice echoed in my ear between the pulsing and pounding of my heartbeat I also heard in there. My head snapped in the direction of the voice, realizing it was the bartender.

"She is," he said with confidence as he wiped down an already clean and dry bar between us. "We do this every weekend, and she's a champ. They won't even know they're getting turned down as they are, because, you know, we work for tips."

He reached his hand out and I stared at it, momentarily numbed by the information he had just provided. But I quickly recovered and offered my hand in return.

"I'm Pete. You seem to know Harper, so I thought I'd introduce myself. Any friend of hers is a friend of mine, she's one of the good ones." His smile was completely genuine.

Yeah, I knew Harper. And this guy had me wondering how well he knew her, too. But that really shouldn't matter to me. She shouldn't matter to me.

None of this should be bothering me, yet it was.

I've sworn off relationships, women in general. And I'd sure as hell learned my lesson on dating people from work.

Yet, here I was, seeing her again, and the damn giddy feeling it gave me inside was pissing me off.

What the fuck was going on with me?

"Nice to meet you, Pete. And, um, well, Harper and I know each other through our, uh, day jobs, I guess you would say."

He nodded, obviously understanding what I meant. My eyes traveled back to the other room, noticing that Harper was no longer amidst the men but along the side of the room, clearing some tables of empties. Regardless of how adept she was at handling herself in such situations, it didn't make it any easier to see her having to deal with it. It was like she was in a room full of Chases.

And I didn't like how it was making me feel.

I drained the drink in my hand, and as I placed the glass down, a new one landed in front of me. Pete's slight smile and nod as he backed away from the bar let me know I'd probably be regretting this come morning. But as I brought the fresh drink to my lips, I didn't care too much about tomorrow morning. I needed to get through the night.

"I see you've made friends with Pete."

Her voice.

My dick was throbbing just at the thought of looking at her, knowing what I *would* see.

Those perfect tits pushed together by that ridiculously low-cut thing barely decent enough to be called a top. And it was basically see-through, most of it black lace other than the front covering up the important parts. The parts I was longing to have my mouth on again.

And then there were the shorts.

Though more of her ass was showing out of them than not. Her perfectly tight, round ass that I envisioned pushed up against a wall with me in front of her.

And of course, I liked seeing it.

But so did every other fucking guy in here.

She most definitely did not resemble someone wholesome anymore, and it was messing with me.

Taking a deep breath, I turned toward her and smiled. "I did, he's the one to have as a friend in a place like this, right?" I tilted my glass her way before taking a sip.

"Absolutely. And let me know if I can get you or your guests anything else. Any food, for example. Would you like to see a menu?" she offered, as she reached across the bar.

Rather, over the bar.

With her ass up in the air and her heels lifting from the ground.

My gut reaction—well, I had two of them, really.

One: I wanted to pull her off the bar, cover her with my jacket, and never let another man look at her the way I knew they all were at that exact moment.

I wanted to protect her.

Hide her away forever.

Make her mine and never let anyone touch her ever again.

What the fuck was wrong with me? That was the exact opposite of what I knew was right.

And two: I wanted to slam my body up against her ass as she reached across the wooden slab. I would tell her to hold on to the other side as I spread her legs open with my knee. Then I would slide that small slip of fabric between her legs to the side, knowing full well there was nothing underneath, and expose her. She would shake with excitement, and she would be wet, really wet. My finger would start by teasing her soft skin, but then it would slip right in, and that innocent voice, she'd moan. Loud. I would rub my dick, still in my pants, against her pussy, and she would want to pull away from the bar. But I'd force her to stay exactly where she was. And then…

"Gage?"

Fuck.

"Did you hear me? Here are some menus, do you want me to ask your guests, or would you like to take care of that?"

Why was she acting as if yesterday didn't happen? As if I didn't have my fingers inside her pussy just last night?

"I'll take care of it." My words were gruff, probably more than they needed to be, as I took the menus from her hand and stalked to the other side of the room. I knew what we did was a mistake, and this was the proof I needed. She wanted it to be a one-time thing, and frankly, I should, too. I had to stop my habit of turning everything into a relationship.

I wasn't doing relationships. Right?

The group was already lively, and I guess I had Chase to thank for that. At least he was good for something. I threw the menus on the table toward him and he understood the assignment. Moving to the club side of the room, I took a seat on one of the stools along the half wall looking over the dance floor. The club was packed with people grinding up against one another, making it hard to tell who was with whom. I was sure those things changed by the end of the night, anyway.

"Looks fun down there." A voice next to me caught my attention.

Looking to my left, I found a pretty blonde standing against the velvet rope railing. She was looking off into the distance, admiring the party atmosphere down below, giving me the opportunity to admire her.

The music was loud up here, but somehow their sound engineers configured the speakers below in a way that still allowed us to be able to hold a conversation. Even still, I think I only grunted as my reply.

"Not a fan of dancing?" she asked, turning her body toward me, in an attempt, I knew, to get my attention.

And it worked, she was worth looking at. Her deep-dipping black minidress, covered in some kind of sparkles, left little to the imagination. And if she bent over, we would all know whether or not she had panties on.

"I'm Chelsea, by the way." And she used her voice well. It was seductive and sweet at the same time.

"Nice to meet you, Chelsea, and no, dancing is not my thing," I answered, returning my eyes to the movements below. "But be my guest," I said as I gestured to the staircase leading to the dance floor. "I want everyone here to have a good time."

She took the rejection in stride as she strutted down the stairs, knowing full well I was still watching her. She wasn't done with me, she and I both knew that as she glanced my way one more time.

"She's one of Amanda's friends, she's a nice girl," Chase said next to me. The change in his demeanor threw me for a moment, him sounding like he cared. "I told Amanda to bring her along tonight, thought she might have a chance with you, ya know, with you being celibate for months now and all."

And he ruined it by continuing to talk.

I got close to having sex very recently…but he didn't know that.

"Dude, it's written all over you. You looked ready to fuck Harper right there on the bar before."

My head snapped toward his.

"Hey, I get it. You've had a dry spell."

He might be my brother, but I didn't need to sit here and allow him to counsel me on my sex life, or lack of it.

And it was a choice to not have sex.

It got in the way down at BRU, and I needed a complete break for a while. Heading down there to get my mind off Rebecca, my now ex-wife, only to meet Becca, was not the intended course of therapy. Escaping one heartbreak to head into the hands of another forced taller walls of avoidance to build around me.

It was obvious sex got me into emotional trouble. I wasn't good at separating the two very well. My hand and porn were taking care of the job just fine up until now.

I don't know why I thought I could do one-night stands.

"Gage, listen, I know you better than you think I do." Chase's voice held a hint of sympathy. "And I know you won't touch Harper for the exact reason you gave me."

And I nearly choked on the air I breathed. I quickly took a long chug of my drink to hide my response.

"No one wants a repeat of what you've already gone through with Rebecca, man."

His elbow went into my side and almost sent me off my feet due to my stunned state from his words. I righted myself as we both leaned against the velvet railing that mimicked a rope and observed the anarchy on the dance floor below.

My eyes found Chelsea as Chase and I continued to survey our surroundings. Both our heads turned slightly toward the other, a knowing look between us. There were plenty of guys giving her the attention she wanted, she deserved.

"Chelsea is hot," I told him.

"There ya go!" he yelled while hitting me in the arm. "Right? She's fucking hot as hell. If I wasn't going home with Amanda tonight, I'd be trying to tap that."

I shook my head, already knowing the answer to the question I was going to ask him.

"Do you have to have a girl every Saturday night?"

I chuckled as he stood from the rail and we both started moving toward the crowd that was surrounding and almost attacking the food that had come from the kitchen. Chase stopped me, though, his hand on my arm, and turned me to face him.

"The bigger question is, why don't you? You're a young guy, have money, and not to be weird, but we know you're good looking." He primped himself, grabbing his lapels before continuing. "Of course, not as good looking as me, but you should get your fair share. Why are you not enjoying yourself with the ladies? That's the real question."

Everyone thought they knew what went down between Rebecca and me, and for the most part, they did. But our marriage was, essentially, a sham. And it happened out in the open for the entire company to see.

And that really sucked.

But what no one knew was how my heart got broken a second time. And I didn't plan on telling anyone about that. And here I was, brooding over a girl I hooked up with once simply because other guys were checking out her ass.

"Someone has to focus on the company, little brother," I offered as my reason. And it wasn't a complete falsehood. He and I both knew he wasn't ready to be in the role he was. That was apparent during the time I spent at BRU last semester.

"Yeah, well," he started before stuffing a huge piece of shrimp cocktail into his mouth. Through the food, he attempted to complete his thought. "Good seggs doesn't haf to take that long."

His garbled words gained him some laughter from our audience that had crowded around us and the food.

"Is that so?" Nate, our future co-worker, questioned with a hearty laugh afterward.

His wife chimed in. "Oh, Nate, what are you laughing at? I thought that was your motto?"

"Oooh!"

"Ouch!" The crowd was full of sympathy for our man of the night.

"Touché, my darling." Nate reached out with his arm, pulling his wife close, and they shared an intimate moment that ended with a kiss.

It was refreshing to see a couple that was apparently…healthy.

"They're cute," a small voice said next to me.

Chelsea had returned. And this time, I made sure to really look at her.

Her long straight blond hair was in a tight ponytail high on her head, the hair still flowing a bit past her shoulders. I could see tiny droplets of perspiration dotting her hairline, I assumed from her dancing ventures down below. She wore a lot more makeup than I usually liked to see on girls, especially since she didn't seem to need it; she looked like a natural beauty. And the dress she was wearing, it was still as short as I remembered from a bit ago.

And her legs were something to see.

Long. Lean. Smooth. Tan.

They looked as if they literally had oil on them. Was that something girls did?

"They are," I replied. "I'm not sure how long they've been married, but I know they have three kids, so they're doing something right."

She quietly agreed as she took a sip of her drink. Her eyes remained locked on mine over the rim of her glass. Her intentions were obvious.

This time, I made sure to keep eye contact with her.

I'd made up my mind.

She would be my distraction. A means to an end to rid my mind of Harper Wilson.

Another Saturday night alone was not in order for me tonight.

"Please tell me it's almost closing time," I complained to Pete as I handed him some empty glasses. "And I need two whiskeys, neat, a chardonnay, two bottles of Lite, and one Manhattan."

As much as I didn't want to see Gage all over that leggy blonde, I still would have preferred to be in their room. The bachelor party in the other lounge had begun to get out of hand with some of the guys even encouraging their conquests of the night to dance on the tabletop. And the girls were more than willing to oblige if it kept them in the lounge room, they weren't fools.

Pete rushed around behind the bar, filling my order as I looked between both rooms. Gage's group was…civilized. They were talking, laughing, drinking, but with both their feet on the ground and all their clothes on. I didn't need to look to the other side to know that several guests were in different stages of undress, some on tables, some on chairs, some on top of other people on tables or chairs.

It hasn't been easy distracting myself from Gage's interest in that tall beauty. Or in the way our interaction went the complete opposite of how I wished it had. Knowing he was here on business, I worked hard to keep our conversation professional, but that seemed to backfire.

"It's like a fucking frat party over there," Pete said.

"No, this is worse. Most of these guys have wedding rings on. This is way worse." But we've all seen our share of forbidden secrets while working at this place that must stay locked up in our individual vaults. I could literally write one of those spicy romance novels Vic and I always read.

Pete slid the tray full of drinks to the edge of the bar top, and I secured it under my hand before lifting it high above my head.

"And no, sweetheart, we still have another hour to go," Pete told me, the disdain plain in his voice.

My head snapped his way, and my disappointment had to be all over my face.

"It's okay, you've got this. And I'm right here if you need me," he offered. "Go make us that amazing tip you always do and before you know it, you'll have those feet wrapped cozy in your socks and your body cuddled up in your bed."

He had me dreaming of my night ahead as I strode into the land of the misbehaved, and I wasn't paying attention as well as I should've been. I didn't quite walk into him; it was more like he jumped down from the table next to me, landing at my feet.

My grip on the tray wasn't the issue.

It was the fact that I had to move the tray to my side, out of his way, to avoid him knocking it out of my hands. That allowed our bodies to…collide. We were chest to chest.

"Whoa, sorry, beautiful. I didn't mean to startle you," he said, reaching out to steady both of us as my feet stumbled a bit.

But his hands didn't grip me in what would be considered a usual or appropriate place. No, I felt his arms go around my waist and hips. Then his hands landed firmly on my ass, gripping it with his fingers, literally digging them into me right at the hem of my shorts.

But I kept my cool, looking up into his eyes. He wasn't a bad-looking guy if you could see past his sweaty, drunken state. His shirt was undone by about three buttons, and his tie was barely hanging around his neck. But his smile was genuine as he tried to stay upright, his body leaning into mine. And at least he wasn't one of the married ones, or well, he didn't have a ring on. I got the feeling that if he remembered this in the morning, he would actually regret it. Didn't excuse where his hands were, but so many of these guys did stupid shit when they were this drunk.

"I'm fine," I said as sweetly, but neutrally, as possible. My eyes then gestured to the large tray of drinks above our heads. "One of these yours, by chance? I do need to keep working, ya know. Your buddies need their drinks still."

He pulled away, but only by inches, refusing to let go of the hold he had on me.

"Let me put this down, okay?"

Twisting my body toward the table next to us, I was able to place the tray on the surface, the drinks safe. But somehow his hold remained on me, only now it moved to my hips, dangerously inching lower. I wasn't happy with that.

"You are so hot." His words were slurred as he spoke up against my ear. Then I felt the entire length of his body up against the back of me and my original opinion of him changed. I needed to put an end to this.

Grabbing one of the beers from the tray, I spun around again, realizing I was more comfortable when we were face to face. This happened at times here, and I always got myself out of it. Sometimes it took a bit more work than others.

"Thanks, but let's cool you off with one of these, okay?"

Grabbing one of his hands away from me, I forced the beer bottle into his grip. He looked down at it as if confused by how it got there but proceeded to put it back on the tray. I took advantage of that and pulled away, creating about a foot of space between us. I smiled wide as I went to pick up the tray, but his hand forcefully pushed the tray back to the table. Some of the drinks rattled, and I needed to steady the bottles.

"Oh shit, I'm sorry about that," he said. And he sounded truly apologetic.

I turned to him, his hands now up in a defensive move.

"But what's wrong, can't we hang for a bit?" he asked.

Keeping my smile in place, I gave him my routine response.

"I've gotta keep working. I'm on duty here, taking care of both rooms. Matter of fact, I'm getting behind. There's definitely some food I was supposed to bring out to this room by now. I should probably go check on that."

The mention of food usually gets most guys' heads thinking in a different direction, allowing me to break away.

But not this guy. Even though he wasn't the most obnoxious I'd run into, he was very persistent.

"Take a look around, no one here is missing any food you might need to get. Everyone is either too wasted or busy with someone," he said as he scanned the room. "Let's just go hang out by the rail and talk for a bit."

"I really can't, I…"

He attempted to pull me toward the rail, but I resisted, pushing him off me as nonchalantly as I could.

And then I heard that deep, familiar voice again.

"I think you must not understand the message she's sending you."

The harshness of his clipped words and how he said them

should have made me jump, but it didn't. Instead, a calm settled through me, and I didn't need to turn to see who it was.

His voice was already recognizable to me.

But my aggressor jumped, and the anger poured out of him with Gage's words.

"Who the fuck are you?" He stepped back as he postured himself, pushing his chest out as he stood up tall.

It was then that I was able to completely back away and observe the scene since the drunk guy was now distracted. And his loud words attracted the attention of some of his friends, but Gage didn't seem to care as he stood toe to toe, towering over him, staring him down.

Gage looked lethal.

"It doesn't matter who I am."

His words were measured, calm, and murderous.

"She was clearly trying to get back to work, and more importantly, trying to get your hands off her. She was just too nice to tell you to fuck off."

But now his words made me nervous. This was my job, my wages, and he was putting them both in jeopardy. My eyes scanned the room for Pete, hoping he was witnessing this and would help me take control of the situation, help me put an end to it before Dean, the manager, showed up.

"I'm fine, Gage, really." My hand landed on his taut forearm in an attempt to pull him away from my offender, and thankfully that got his attention. His eyes landed on mine, but the rage in them took me off guard. They softened slightly before he turned back toward the drunken asshole.

"Well, let's just make sure you're fine," Gage said as he started moving forward, making the other guy take steps back.

But then the other guy stopped.

And they were chest to chest.

"Dude, I'm not afraid of you." Though, as the guy said it, his voice cracked, and he couldn't quite keep his eyes on Gage completely.

And none of his friends moved close to him in a show of support.

He was completely alone.

"I think you should be," Gage said. "You owe her an apology," Gage's hands fisted at his sides as he restrained his anger.

The guy laughed out loud. "For what? She rubbed her body up against me, she was coming on to me first, dude."

My body stiffened in anger at his lies, and I wanted to intervene. But I knew I couldn't, he was a customer.

But Gage wasn't done.

"I watched the entire scenario asshole, that is not how it happened. Care to try again?"

The guy stared up at Gage, caught in his lie, getting more agitated. He was bouncing back and forth on his feet, his eyes now shifting from Gage to the ground. Suddenly, his hands came up, pushing Gage at the chest. "Fuck you, asshole! You don't know what you're talking about!"

Gage looked down at the guy, I think somewhat startled that he even touched him.

"That was a mistake." Gage's voice was calculated.

His one hand went around the guy's neck, gripping it tight. And then he was almost holding him by the throat, the guy's legs flailing, as they both scrambled across the floor. Chairs scraped along the tiles and got pushed aside by their advancing bodies, as Gage threw his opponent onto an empty table that skidded to a stop against a wall.

My heart was pounding as I looked around the room, noticing

the horrified faces of all the guests. Even some people from Gage's room had joined to watch the show he was putting on, including his brother, Chase.

Chase had a proud grin on his face.

I, on the other hand, was mortified.

But it was anger that bubbled to the top.

I was no damsel in distress who needed saving. Even though this guy was a tougher character to get rid of than most, I would've been fine, even if Gage hadn't stepped in.

"What's going on?"

Pete's worried words echoed my concern for the growing spectacle that Gage was creating as he continued his assault on the guy, pinning him to the table while muttering words in his face.

"We have to stop him, Pete, before Dean gets word of this." As I moved toward the two men in an attempt to pull them apart, I felt an arm grab me by the middle.

"Uh-uh, if he thought this guy was trouble, you're not going anywhere near this. Stay away, princess. I'll take care of this."

Pete hustled to the chaotic scene and reached for Gage by the shoulder to pull him off the guy. He finally got them separated, and we were able to see the blood coming from the guy's mouth as he lay splayed across the table. Gage, fully enraged, pulled back and spun around with a formed fist, ready to fight, but stopped when he saw it was Pete.

"Dude, we can't have you doing this here," Pete said, trying to calm him down. "C'mon back to your room, man. He's not worth it. He won't be bothering Harper anymore."

Gage's eyes surveyed the room, taking stock of the amount of people watching what went down. He looked at the guy on the table, now moving away, over to his friends, away from us.

And then his eyes found me.

But I thought I'd see something very different in them. He had just gotten done fighting someone for me, in my defense.

But what I saw in his eyes was anger.

The pit in my stomach clenched tight as I fought back tears. And I hated that he solicited this response in me.

This was why I'd sworn off men in my life. My visceral response was always too raw, too naïve. I put too much stock in trusting them and their intentions.

And it always fucked me over.

And right on cue…

"Gage, are you okay?"

The gorgeous, leggy blonde had come to take care of him, rubbing his face as she wrapped her body around his in every way she could.

"I'm fine," he said.

But his eyes remained on me. He allowed her to take his hand, but he walked toward me with her by his side and I felt trapped. I didn't want to talk to him, not after the searing look he'd just given me.

And how it crushed me.

"Harper," he said, his voice low and gravelly. "I'm sorry if that caused you any trouble, but I couldn't stand by and watch that."

We both looked into the other room, noticing the guests were packing up and starting to head out. Apparently, the fight put a damper on the mood. I didn't care, I was happy to see them go. But I was nervous that the main client wasn't going to be happy with his night being cut short, and our tip would be affected.

"At least they're leaving," Gage said.

"Yes, that's good," the blonde said. "What happened, Gage?"

"Chelsea, can you go get our coats? I think it's time for us to leave as well."

"Of course, baby," she cooed.

And I almost vomited in my mouth.

My dagger eyes shot to his, but he refused to look at me. The anger that rolled off me had my muscles tensing as my fists coiled at my sides.

Thankfully, Pete came to my rescue. His arms came around my shoulders and he pulled me in for a hug, a kiss to the top of my head. He knew me well enough to know that I wasn't happy with how my current conversation was going.

"Hey, guys, it's almost closing time, so with everything that's happened, maybe we should call it a night with everyone, what do you think?" Pete said.

Gage shoved his hands into his pants pockets before letting out a sigh. "Listen, I'll talk to your manager if necessary to explain the situation and let him know that there was nothing either of you did wrong. That this was all on me." There was a bit of shame in his words but not enough to satisfy me.

Pete shook his head before responding. "No worries, man. I don't think it'll come to that."

Gage nodded before walking off.

Turning toward Pete, my eyes watered, the anger now converting into frustration.

"What the fuck?" I yelled.

Pete squeezed me harder, though it didn't make me feel any better about what Gage had done to us, to me, tonight.

And that was it.

The rooms cleared out, and Pete and I were left alone.

Left to clean up the physical mess left behind. And I was left hoping I wasn't going to pay deeply for the emotional mess he left, as well.

"HOLY SHIT!" Pete screamed. He was running back into the lounge room as I was sweeping the floors and finishing the mopping. He ran right to me, lifted me up and spun me around in circles until I was dizzy.

"Oh my God, Pete. Stop, I'm going to throw up! What's up?"

He finally put me down, and at least I had my sneakers on so my feet were steady.

"You're never going to believe this, Harper," Pete said. He was so excited, his smile made me laugh.

"What, Pete? Jeez, what are you so happy about?"

"Oh, sweetheart, come on over here," he said as he strutted to the bar. "You'll need to sit down for this." He pulled out a stool, and I sat as he went to the other side so he could face me.

He tossed a thick white envelope onto the bar between us.

Thick white envelopes usually only meant one thing.

And I never had thick white envelopes handed to me. Ever.

"Pete, where did you get that?" I reached out, afraid that it wasn't real.

But then Pete pulled out another of equal size from his back pocket. "This one's mine."

"Pete, what's going on?"

He pushed the envelope toward me, but I was still hesitant to pick it up. Good things like this didn't happen to me. I've had to work hard for everything I've ever gotten in my life.

My dad was my favorite person when I was a little girl. We had a special relationship. I was your typical "daddy's little girl." And I think because he and I had such a strong bond, my mom and I weren't very close when I was young. We lived a comfortable life in New Jersey, and they were both hard workers. My dad worked in an insurance office, a typical nine-to-five, and my mom was a hairdresser. That most likely played a role as well, since she worked so many nights and weekends, those were the hours I had with my dad alone.

But then my dad got sick. And I was young. He died when I was thirteen. Needless to say, I was crushed, destroyed. But so was my mom. I was too young to really understand how much in love they really were, consumed by my own life. But seeing how lost she was without him, it was obvious. Through our loss of him, we became closer. It wasn't a very typical mother-daughter relationship, but we created one.

But we found out, even though my father worked for an insurance firm, he didn't have his own life insurance policy. My parents were not prepared for him to leave us so early. Life became harder. My mom needed to take on another job, and when I was old enough, I had to work to help pay the bills as well.

She has since moved to Florida, enjoying the sun in her retirement. I see her when I can, which isn't often because it takes money to get there that I can't spare. But we talk a couple times a week. And in recent years, I can say our relationship has gotten even stronger, even if it was only from our chats over the phone.

But things were never just handed to me. I've had to work for everything I've gotten.

So, staring at this envelope, this fat envelope, made me nervous.

Because good things didn't happen to me.

"Pete, where did this come from?"

"Well," he said, "turns out your buddy tonight must have thought that the bachelor party would stiff us. To be honest, I thought they were going to as well, but they didn't." He pulled out another envelope, one that more commonly resembled our tips after a lounge night. "Seems the bachelor felt really bad. I guess that asshole was his soon-to-be brother-in-law, and he made sure to leave us a tip, a pretty decent one."

I looked inside and found a thousand dollars, five hundred for each of us. A very generous tip, all things considered. Closing the envelope, I rubbed my finger along the edges, my nerves ratcheting up. Pete pushed the other envelope across the bar top.

"There's a note inside."

"Just tell me who it's from, Pete, and how much it is." Although, it was pretty obvious who it had to be.

"Sweetheart, your boyfriend from tonight, well, in addition to keeping you safe, took care of us. He left five thousand dollars, for *each* of us."

What?

"Read the note, sweetie. Although, I'm sure yours says something a bit different than mine does." He leaned over and kissed the top of my head. "Don't take long, I'm walking you home and I'm leaving in ten minutes. So, get your sweet ass downstairs soon."

He left me with my envelope and my note.

Harper,

I hope this finds you well. My apologies if what happened tonight caused you any issues with your boss. That wasn't my intention. But I won't apologize for what I did. I couldn't stand by and watch him do that to you. It pained me to see you in that situation and I'd do anything to know you'd never be in one like it again.

The included money is to cover my tip and what I'm assuming will be lost wages for the other room. I'm thinking they won't be leaving you the tip you deserve. I hope this more than covers both.

Gage

Well, I knew I should be thrilled. And I was.

Five thousand dollars.

It would have taken another two to three months to make that much in tips, and Gage gave it to me in one night.

But why did I still feel like crying?

CHAPTER 12

Gage

The sun was streaming through the window, warming my face. I should have remembered to pull the curtains closed before climbing into bed last night.

Climbing into bed.

I suddenly remembered why I didn't think about the curtains. My eyes popped open, but I made sure to keep my body frozen and I listened, really listened, for any other sounds in the room. Sure enough, I heard the soft breathing of someone still in bed with me.

Turning to my left, I saw the naked body of Chelsea.

She was still here.

Why the fuck did I let her stay the night? Having a one-night stand was one thing but letting her sleep over was too much. I shouldn't have given in to her almost begging and going on about not wanting to take an Uber at three in the morning.

But I continually surprised myself by proving I indeed was not a monster and agreed with her. I was fully aware no female should be sent into a stranger's car, alone, in the middle of the night. But I also knew I didn't want her here when I woke up.

Yet, here we were. It was always awkward figuring out the

easiest way to send them off. And it being a Sunday would make it even harder. Thankfully, I did have some work to do, so there was that.

Jumping out of bed without a glance in her direction, I locked myself in the bathroom and started running the shower.

This really sucked because I loved my Sunday mornings, especially when the weather was as nice as today. My coffee tasted better in the yard or up on the roof, not sure why, but it did. Staring at my reflection, it made me wonder why I allowed myself to get into this mess.

And then I heard the timid knock.

"Gage?"

My head slumped between my shoulders in defeat as my hands rested against the vanity. Moving to the door, I unlocked and opened it, but held it against my body, a shield that would hopefully protect me.

"Hey, I just wanted to say goodbye before I left." She was fully dressed, purse in hand. And her weak smile told me she read the room and knew where I stood.

Yet why did that make me feel like an asshole?

"Oh, one sec, let me shut off the water, I'll walk you down."

As we exited my room, the small talk started.

"You have a lovely home, it's just you in this big place?"

"Uh, yep, just me." Insinuating that I could possibly be cheating on someone wasn't going to get her a second invitation, not that it was going to happen anyway. We made it to the bottom of the staircase which led into the foyer, and I turned toward her before opening the door. "It was nice meeting you, Chelsea."

She tried to hide the disappointment, but it slipped through. "Yeah, it was a great night." Her heels clicked on the tiles as she started making her exit, but then she stopped and turned around.

"Ya know, both Amanda and Chase warned me that you'd be closed off, told me you've had a rough year."

I did not like where this was going.

"I'm not looking for anything serious, so if you want to get together sometime, give me a call. We could just, I don't know, hang out."

My head fell softly against the door as I continued to hold it in my hands. She was pretty. And nice. I should want to see her again.

But I didn't.

"Yeah," I told her. "I'll call you sometime."

But she knew. Her small wave as she walked out to her waiting car was a goodbye. And I was okay with that.

Closing the door with a click, I locked it up and headed for the kitchen. My shower would have to wait until after coffee.

As I waited for the cup to fill, I took out my phone and shot Jared a text.

Me - Hey man wanna hang today tell Delia it's my turn with you

HE LIVED WITH HIS GIRLFRIEND, so finding time with him wasn't always simple. But Delia was a cool girl and gave us our guy time when we needed it. I finished making my coffee and walked toward the back slider, making my way into my sanctuary of a yard. It wasn't the biggest, but it was exactly what I needed to feel like I was escaping from the city. It had a small patch of grass, a tree, and when the weather warmed up, it would be filled with pot after pot of vegetables and flowers. Just as I was sitting on the small couch on the paver patio, my phone buzzed in my pocket.

· · ·

PERFECT. I had just enough time to get my work done. Then the rest of the day we'd be hanging out like old times.

"THIS IS AWESOME, Gage. When did you put it in?" Jared asked.

He was referring to the outdoor tv on my patio. Thankfully, it was warm enough for us to watch the game outside.

"Last summer, right before I left for BRU. But I didn't have much time to use it before leaving, and I can't be out here in the winter. I was torn between putting it out here or on the rooftop deck to use with the hot tub."

Jared and I had gotten settled on the patio couch with our beers, plus a pizza and some wings I had delivered.

"I think you made the right call, makes more sense out here. You'll use it more being able to just come right out back instead of having to walk all the way upstairs for it."

I nodded in agreement. It was the reasoning I had for why it should be out here as well, even when Rebecca wanted it on the rooftop. I was glad I went with my gut.

"How have things been for ya lately, man?" he asked. "I know she's been across the pond since the divorce finalized, so that has to help a little." He threw his feet up on one of the soft ottomans as he took a chug of his beer. "We haven't seen much of each other outside the office since you've returned."

My mouth was full of a couple bites of pizza, and I took my time chewing and swallowing since I wasn't looking forward to talking about my ex-wife. But to be completely honest, it was probably why I invited him today.

"Yeah, well, I think it's good she transferred permanently. It made the most sense." Leaning forward, elbows perched on my knees, I put my beer on the table. Jared would not have a clue what I meant by that. Rubbing my hands across my face, I prepared myself for the telling of the story. "I mean, you heard the rumors, you filed all the papers, so you knew she was cheating, right?"

He nodded. He remained relaxed against the back of the couch, but he could tell I was stressed and remained quiet.

"Well, yeah, she cheated. But all that time she spent in London, she, uh…" I almost couldn't bring myself to say it aloud. "She was basically living with another guy over there."

Jared bolted upright.

"Holy shit." Jared's words were a hushed whisper as he sat in disbelief.

The three of us were friends since college down at Blue Ridge University. Jared and I were freshman roommates and eventually frat brothers. Jared met Rebecca in their pre-law classes and introduced us.

And she and I were inseparable from that day onward.

Really, the three of us were.

But Rebecca and I just had a lot of sex.

All the time.

Our college years together as a couple were among my favorite years of my life. They were idyllic.

It was part of why I thought heading back there for graduate school might help me. It was always a place that I associated with good thoughts and memories.

"Yeah, and the worst of it is that she started seeing him about a month after she got to London. So, yeah, most of my marriage was a sham."

Rebecca and I got married six months out of college. We figured why wait; we felt we were meant for one another. We were going to be working together in my father's company, so we went against both our families' guidance and married at twenty-two years old.

When my father sent her to London on assignment, he thought he was doing us a favor. He felt that a bit of time apart since we lived and worked together would be good for our relationship.

But then she started requesting to be there more and more, longer and longer.

"*The job is more complicated than we expected.*"

An impromptu visit brought it all to light.

"Fuck, Gage, I'm sorry, man. That really sucks," Jared said. "That pisses me off that she did that to you."

I laughed. "Yeah, you and me both."

We fell back against the couch and watched the game in companionable silence for a bit, Jared still processing my news.

It wasn't easy for guys to sit around and shoot the shit about their love lives.

So, I decided I wasn't going to anymore.

"Want another beer?" I asked as I walked in toward the kitchen.

He got up and followed me. "I'm assuming you heading back down to BRU had something to do with wanting to, what, get away or something? We never really talked about that. You kind of just up and left. I came into the office one day and Chase told me you were taking the year off to go back to school."

We popped the tops off our bottles and leaned against the kitchen island. I figured he was going to bring this up, and the guilt I felt over it overwhelmed me. But I was spiraling down a dark hole back then and needed to do something.

"Yeah, sorry about that, man. I didn't mean to just leave. And I'm sorry there wasn't really any communication while I was down there." Leaning against the marble, I stared at the floor in front of me, too ashamed to look at my best friend.

"Hey, no worries, I get it. Once I put two and two together, knowing what was going on with you and Rebecca, I figured it was a soul-searching kind of thing."

Looking up, I found his eyes on me, studying me.

"What? What's that look for?" I asked him.

He started laughing quietly.

"You went back to BRU." He shook his head at me and took a long chug of his beer. "Don't you realize that it's every guy's dream to be able to go back to college? To actually go back and live there? Shit, you relived the best thing we had going, Gage!" He rushed around the island toward me. "C'mon, tell me about it. You had to go to parties, I'm sure, right? And did you, ya know, hook up with anyone?" He punched me in the arm with a wide smile on his face.

My plan to not talk about the rest of it wasn't panning out.

"Well, it was kinda cool being back down there, but you can never *go back*. Ya know what I mean?" My tone was more serious than he anticipated. He was hoping for recounts of frat girls and tailgates.

And I guess I could just give him what he wanted.

But there was too much of me that stayed behind at BRU to be excited about telling him my tales.

"Where did you live? Were you in the same complex we lived in?" Jared asked.

We both laughed, thinking back to our senior year. We lived together with two other frat brothers. And, well, we had fun.

"No," I told him. "And thank God, that was a shit hole. I was in the place over off Prices Road, those townhouses. They're pretty nice for college kids."

Heading back out to the yard, Jared followed, but kept up with the questions.

"So, are the girls still as hot down there?"

Jared made a name for himself at BRU. He and Delia didn't meet until he moved up here to New York. His bachelor years spent at college were…notorious. If anyone could be accused of being a manwhore, it would have been him. But the girls loved him, undeterred by the sheer volume of other girls he'd hooked up with.

"I guess."

"Whoa," he almost yelled. "What do you mean, 'you guess'?"

Suddenly, the paper on my beer bottle became the focus of my attention. I almost had it off all in one piece, which was a huge accomplishment, and I hoped Jared would let me be and work on my current project.

"Dude, what happened down there?" he asked.

My head snapped up and I looked at him, trying to hide my surprise at his revelation. But I failed. He saw it.

"That's why you came back to work early, I'm assuming."

Throwing my head back in defeat, I knew I was destined to tell him everything.

"Dude, are we really doing this?" I asked, looking up at the ceiling for an answer. I walked back out to the patio, sitting on the couch again.

Jared sat back against the couch as well. "That's on you, man."

But we both knew I needed to get it out.

"Yeah, I needed to leave there. I, uh, met someone there. But it was the wrong time for her and me. She was on a break from her boyfriend." I stopped to regroup, pulling out her picture on my phone. Handing it to Jared, he let out a whistle.

"Damn, she's fuckin' hot."

I closed my phone before I saw her face staring back at me again. Too many nights had been spent looking into those green eyes.

"Yeah, she is. And we said it would just be sex, but…"

Jared barked a laugh out loud.

"What?" I asked, a bit annoyed with him finding humor in this.

He didn't answer me right away but started shaking his head as if in disbelief. "Dude, you should know as well as I do, you're not built that way. You don't do 'just sex.' It's never been your thing. Even that girl before Rebecca, what was her name?"

"Sara."

"Yes! Sara. And you were convinced freshman year, the first girl you hooked up with, was 'the one.' I'm sorry, man, but you should've known better."

Thinking back, I didn't remember it quite like that, but Jared did have a better memory than I did.

"Well, I'll have you know I had 'just sex' last night. Didn't even take the girl's number."

Slamming my bottle on the table in a show of triumph, I looked to Jared for his reaction. It wasn't what I expected. Instead of a conspiratorial shit grin, his eyes were turned down and his mouth a grim straight line.

"You're not getting what I mean, Gage." He placed his bottle on the table next to mine and appeared to be thinking very seriously about his next words. "Listen, don't take this the wrong way, any of it. First, you're a good-looking guy. I'd go so far to say, a hell of a lot better looking than me. Women are always checking you out." He paused, rubbing his hands on his knees a bit.

Yeah, he seemed to be nervous.

"All things considered, you should have notches in every bedpost and up and down your door frame, but that's not you, man. Never has been, and I don't think it ever will be."

Clearing his throat, I got the impression things were going to get even deeper.

"I'm no professional, but don't ya think it has something to do with, I don't know, your mom, maybe taking off on you guys so young? And her cheating on your dad. And don't get me wrong, I'm not saying the way you are is bad. I should have been more like you in college."

Our collective laugh and his self-deprecation lightened the mood. But he wasn't finished.

"How did last night make you feel?"

Fuck.

He was going for the jugular. And he knew what he was doing. Instead of answering him, I jumped from my seat.

"I need another beer, you?" I asked. My pace to the kitchen was quick, but he caught up to me.

"Hey, how 'bout we head out to a bar or something? Let's get out of here, change of scenery," he offered. "Delia is out to dinner with friends, I actually have all night."

It would be good to go out, just hang out at a bar. Hadn't done that in ages with all the time I'd been devoting to work. And maybe in a public place he'd lay off the inquisition.

Though, to be honest, I knew it was why I asked him here.

As I started cleaning up the pizza box and bottles from the kitchen counter, I stopped and looked his way. "You'll get a kick out of this," I said. "The girl I met at BRU? The one I was hoping would take my mind off, well, everything. Her name was Becca."

Jared froze mid-step and his head snapped in my direction. "You're fucking kidding."

Shaking my head, we both shared a laugh.

"You were fucking a Becca to forget about Rebecca?" he asked, the humor not lost in his words.

"Yeah, she never quite understood why I called her *Becca, not Rebecca.* Thank fuck her name was just Becca."

"Only your luck, dude, seriously. Only you," he laughed.

He went back to cleaning up the food so we could head out. But I was stuck on the question he had asked me but I refused to answer. Keeping my back to him, too afraid to make eye contact, I finally decided to answer it.

"Last night made me feel like shit."

Yeah, we were freshman roommates. And yeah, we joined the same frat. We were forced into so many social situations during college that it was inevitable we'd be friends. But there were many other reasons he remained my best friend now, years since college.

And this was an example of one of them.

"Yep, and that's why we're getting out of here. Let's go get drunk."

CHAPTER 13

Harper

"Oh my God, I'm so drunk!" Victoria and I were at brunch at one of my favorite spots in the West Village, Bobo. We were two hours in on bottomless mimosas and feeling no pain at all. These Sunday afternoons always did us good after a long Saturday night. And we were celebrating a rare occasion: we both had the same night off. That never happened.

"I'm pretty wasted myself," Victoria said as she drained the flute in her hand. "But we deserve this. It's not often that it's us drinking the drinks."

It was almost four in the afternoon. We always got a late start on Sundays and thankfully these brunches ran almost all day here in the city.

"I still can't believe the night you had last night." Vic filled up our glasses with the last of our current pitcher. "Should we get another?"

"I don't think so, my stomach is about to revolt from the juice."

I wasn't sure I could even finish the glass she poured. But I chose to put it to my lips to avoid talking about last night. Vic had been trying to get the details out of me all day, but I'd been resisting.

But she's been relentless.

"Pete told me the guy that left the huge tip is into you, Harp, so what's going on? The entire locker room was talking about how he fought someone 'in your honor.'"

She literally finger-quoted her words.

"It's no big deal." But I knew I was going to have to tell her it was Gage. She would figure it out eventually.

She only knew about the kiss, not anything else we did the second visit he paid me.

Our server saved my ass and showed up at the table.

"Can I get you ladies anything else?" she asked.

"Just the bill, thanks," I told her.

Reaching for my bag, I pulled my card out and put it on the table.

"My treat," I said.

Victoria sat back in her chair, ready to protest, her hands coming up from her lap to grab her bag.

"Nope, I mean it. Let me put that monster tip I made to good use."

She shook her head, and I knew what she was going to say before she said it.

Victoria and I both had plans for our futures. It was the only reason we worked at The Velvet Rope. The money we made there was helping us achieve our dreams. She knew about my plan to open up my own shop. But Victoria, who was still going to school part-time at NYU, was majoring in marketing. Her dream was to, one day, work for one of the big social media giants. She needed the money because she was paying her way through school, and that wasn't cheap.

Shaking my finger at her, I took the bill and walked it up to the podium, making sure she couldn't help pay. When I returned to the table, she had some bills scattered about.

"I'm leaving the tip."

I didn't argue.

"Careful when you get up, I was a bit unsteady on my feet." I started giggling as I watched her stand from her chair, balancing on two wobbly, drunk feet.

"We're not done yet, Harp," she said. Grabbing me by the arm, she pulled me along and we walked out the door onto 10th Street. "Let's go to a sports bar. Aren't the Yankees playing a double-header today? We can catch the second game, if not the end of the first."

As we were walking, arm in arm, I got the sudden urge to tell my bestie my dirty little secret.

Damn champagne.

"So, remember romance novel kiss guy from last week? The one from the shop?"

I felt her nod against my head since she was leaning her entire body into mine. It seemed like we were trying to hold one another up as we walked.

"Well, there's more to our story, something else happened between us, and, well, he's the guy that got into the fight and left the big tip last night."

Victoria stopped dead in her tracks and grabbed me by my upper arms. Her deadly stare spoke volumes. I could see the headline now: *Girl murders best friend for withholding sexy details for days.*

"What the fuck, Harper?" she screamed. "You're just telling me this now? Why didn't you say something last night? And it's what… Sunday! When did this *something else* happen?"

Shrugging out of her hold, I hooked our arms together and continued our stroll.

"Well, he came back to the shop on Friday. But don't hate me.

You know I've been working a ton, and you had school. We didn't even talk until we saw each other at the club. And there was no time to tell you then."

She remained quiet for a few moments, our steps falling in line. But then she turned her face my way with imploring eyes.

"I'm waiting…you don't think you get to stop there, do you?"

"Um, well, we kinda hooked up in the shop."

Even though I couldn't see her face, I knew she was smiling. The fact that she wasn't yelling or screaming something at me told me she had a big, fat grin on her face. I risked a look up at her and sure enough, teeth and all.

"Now it all makes sense," she said. "Everyone in the locker room was talking about how fucking hot he was, so you scored, sister." She barely took a breath between questions and comments. "Oh, and don't think you're done yet, Harp. I need dirty details, like the nitty gritty."

She stopped us from walking and started making her way to the curb, pulling me down and across the street. Noticing a small playground ahead, I knew we were stopping.

She wanted the whole story.

"Sit." She pointed at the bench with a stern finger but a warm smile. "Now, talk."

I knew to listen when she got bossy, so I sat on the bench we found.

"Well, I told you about the kiss already," I said. "And how he left."

She nodded but waited for me to go on.

"Yeah," I said. "Um, but then I called his office." Knowing my cheeks were red, my hands covered my face as it dropped to my lap. "Oh my God, saying it out loud makes it sound so desperate."

"No, it doesn't, you took charge," Vic said. "What happened? Christ, this is better than my books."

"Well, I arranged for a meeting and he came back to the shop."

Slapping her leg, she hooted so loud the people around us stopped and stared. But then she got serious.

"Oh my God, Harp, that's freakin' amazing! You arranged it like we talked about? I didn't think you'd go through with it!" she screamed.

I did. I arranged our hook up. The nightly convos with Vic convincing me to do it finally worked. It was subconscious on some level, but not entirely since I wore my best bra and panty set that day.

"Look at that smile on your face, you're acting like you'd like to see him again."

I nodded and hoped I could leave the story there.

"No, no, no you don't. You don't get to skip over the best part. Tell me about the chemistry and what happened next, that's the best part, Harp. Sex is sex, it's all that other stuff that makes me swoon." As she spoke, her hands were wrapped together over her heart.

"Jesus, Vic, it happened so quick. I don't know, he walked toward me, leaned against the table, looked down at me."

Clamping my mouth shut, I suddenly got embarrassed. These things never happen to me. It has never happened before that I've randomly hooked up with a guy out of nowhere. I think that was why it bothered me so much at the club when he was acting as if we barely knew each other.

"Um, then, he, uh, put his hand on my cheek."

My cheeks were red from telling the story, and I really wanted to stop.

"That's actually so sweet, Harper." She reached out and took my hand in hers. "And then what happened?"

There were so many moments from our time that I wanted to keep to myself. Some good, and some not so good. I didn't want to tell her that he left without asking for my number. Or that he apparently went home with someone else from the club last night. Pushing those facts from my brain, I focused on the romantic details. And even though I was convinced we'd never see each other again, it was still special to me. Though I wasn't ready to share it all with her.

"Well, he's very talented with his fingers, let's put it that way," I told her.

She liked that little tidbit. But I knew the inquisition was far from over.

"Well, how big is he?"

And there we go, that was the Vic I knew and loved.

"Well, the closest I got to his, you know…"

"Dick," she provided.

"Yes, his dick, was seeing it in his boxer briefs. From that sight, it looked scary big, to be honest."

Her eyes went wide, the question about to pop out of her mouth.

"Nope, we didn't have sex. Believe it or not, Fiona interrupted us."

The bellow that emitted from her mouth made the pigeons near us take flight. Moms with their children at the playground looked our way to make sure we were both okay.

"You have got to be kidding me. Fiona barged in on the two of you? What did she see? His face between your thighs? His hands down your pants? How far did it go before she cockblocked you?"

"Christ, Vic, quiet down."

Victoria was trying to talk softly, but the alcohol we consumed had her voice octaves louder than it should've been. She looked around, giggling while doing so. Leaning in, trying to find my ear, her loud talk-whisper almost hurt.

"I'm sorry," she said, then pulled away, giggling some more. "But inquiring minds have to know. Spill."

Victoria knew that I hadn't been with anyone in quite a while. My last relationship was with a guy named Chris, who came into the shop a lot. He eventually asked me out, and we were together for a couple months.

That was almost six months ago.

And casual hook ups were not my thing.

Not until the other day. With Gage.

She knew as well as I did that this was a big deal for me. But she was also drunk, and so was I.

I put my hands up around my mouth, ready to tell the biggest secret of my life to my twenty-six-year-old best friend in the middle of a NYC playground. "Well, he may have been going down on me when we heard the key in the back door."

"Yes!" she screamed. "On the fucking flower table?"

Grabbing her arm, I hauled her off the bench and pulled her along the sidewalk, far away from little ears.

"Yes," I told her, and she squealed with delight as we started walking.

Except, our steps weren't very steady, and she almost veered off the sidewalk right into an oncoming car.

"Vic!" I yelled and pulled her back.

We both started laughing hysterically, so much so I needed to cross my legs.

"Fuck, I should have peed before we left," I said. "I don't know if I'll make it to the bar. Where are we going, anyway?"

She pulled me along, the pace quickening, as we darted between people giving us dirty looks.

"Let's go to Sullivan's, they have a ton of screens, so we shouldn't have trouble seeing the game there. And maybe you'll decide to tell me some more of your dirty secrets."

⁂

THE BAR WAS CROWDED. I don't know why that surprised me. First, it was Sullivan's, a popular bar even when there wasn't a big game to watch. Second, it was one of the first warm days in New York, and Sullivan's also had a great patio with a second outdoor bar. People were hanging out the front open windows while sitting at their pub tables with more people crowded around the L-shaped bar along the side. And the patio was the most crowded of all, with people clamoring for a chance to snag a bistro set or a spot on one of the couches.

We had walked our way through the entire space, deciding where to set up shop. Both of us decided inside would be our best chance at seeing the game. There weren't as many TVs out back. Making our way back to the inside bar, Vic started pushing through the crowd to get the attention of the bartender.

"Hey, it's Theo working, he'll take care of us."

Theo had done some bartending at our club on occasion when we were short-staffed. I let Victoria work on getting our drinks while I searched out the possibility of two seats. But the prospects were grim. Thank God I had comfortable shoes on, at least.

"Here."

Vic handed me a cold bottle, tapping it, before we both went for the first sip.

"That tastes amazing. Ice cold beer after that walk, mmm, nothing better," she said, taking another long chug. "No seats?"

Shaking my head, I continued looking around, taking in my surroundings. It had been a while since I'd been in a bar as a patron. It felt good to be here and not have to be the one serving the drinks. I wasn't going to stress about finding a seat, but instead enjoy my time with my bestie.

"Looks like we'll have to watch the game from here," I told

Victoria. We were standing behind the seated patrons at the bar, so we had a decent view of the wide-screen televisions.

"It also looks like we have some admirers," she cooed in my ear. "Two o'clock, sitting at the bar, which is perfect. Maybe they'll give us their seats."

My eyes scanned the other end of the bar for who could possibly be the guys she spoke of.

And then our eyes connected.

The hints of caramel in his brown eyes stood out, even from across the room.

My body broke out into a sweat while at the same time a shiver went down my spine.

"Shit, Harp, you've got some game lately. Look at you making eyes with the hottie over there."

Victoria had to nudge me to break the trance-like contest between us.

"That's him," I said. But it was so quiet I wasn't sure she heard me.

"What?" she asked.

Looking his way again, he still stared at me but was talking to his blonde-haired buddy at the same time. A slight smile touched his lips, I believe due to something his friend said, but he never took his eyes off of me.

"That's Gage, the guy from the shop."

CHAPTER 14

Gage

As Harper and her friend approached us, a panic settled into my bones. Jared didn't know anything about her. I wasn't planning on telling him any of what happened this past week. The way I acted at the club both surprised and concerned me.

I didn't know her.

Well, I'd kissed her. And touched her. Gone down on her and almost made her come.

But I didn't *know* her.

And this was why I was no good at the "just sex" thing, no matter how hard I tried.

"Hey, Jared, so listen. Those two girls are going to come up to us because I know one of them, just a warning."

He pulled his eyes from the game to follow where I was looking. "Which one do you know? And how well?" His elbow hurt my ribs.

Then I noticed that Harper was physically being dragged by her friend to our corner of the bar. She looked mortified as they approached. But her friend was all smiles and full of laughter while pulling her along.

"Well, look what we have here," her friend said as they got to our corner. "Harper tells me you are the one and only Gage."

She stuck her hand out to me, and I took it. And by the redness in both their eyes, and the tiny slur to her friend's speech, I made the determination she'd consumed quite a bit of alcohol. The girl with Harper was taller, with blonde curls and deep brown eyes. But in addition to her good looks, I could tell it was her personality that got her what she wanted, whenever she wanted it.

"And don't worry, she gave me the abridged version of what you two did. I don't know *all* the details."

Harper pulled her friend's hand from mine and pushed her out of the way.

"Vic, what the hell?" She tried to be quiet, but she wasn't.

So, Harper was drunk as well. She turned toward me, and a pink blush crawled across her cheekbones.

She was fucking adorable.

"Hey, so this is my best friend, Victoria. Vic, yes, this is Gage."

That blush was now spreading from her cheeks to her chest. Her chest that was on full display in her floral sundress. The dress was covered in these big pink flowers, which made sense to me knowing her, and you'd think it was innocent enough. But her tits were basically hanging out of it, and it barely covered her ass.

"Who's your cute friend over there?" Victoria asked.

"Harper, Victoria, this is my friend Jared."

Jared came around from his stool to meet the girls, shaking each of their hands. He might have a serious live-in girlfriend, but he still knew how to make a first impression.

"Nice to meet you, ladies. Would you both like to sit down?"

They both mumbled a "thank you" as we gave them our seats. I pulled out my chair for Harper, and her body grazed against mine as she sat. Her hair was cascading down her back in soft curls, blonde highlights on the tips. Something I hadn't noticed before now. The temptation to reach out and run my fingers through her hair, to knot it in my hand and pull her against my chest, was strong. I wanted another look at that long, slender neck.

"Right, Gage?" Jared asked.

"Huh?"

He knew he caught me completely checked out. His eyes motioned to the two beautiful girls with us, now waiting for my response to a question I hadn't heard.

"I said, Sullivan's is such a great bar. We come here quite a bit, you and I."

Harper fidgeted in her chair, adjusting how she was sitting so she could see both Jared and me as we talked. As she spun around, her shoulder rubbed against my hand holding the back of her wooden stool.

Her skin was like velvet, and instinctively, my finger rubbed against her. She momentarily froze but then leaned into my touch.

"Yeah, we do come here often, though not much lately. I was away most of last fall and this is our first time out since I got back."

Wow, having just realized that it made me think more and more that I was becoming a workaholic. But Jared was no different. We saw each other at the office several times a week, but it was all work there.

"Well, Harper and I come here a lot, too. I'm surprised we haven't run into you guys before. I definitely would remember seeing either one of you."

Victoria turned herself so her body was almost completely touching Jared, and we had no room to move away with the crowd surrounding us. She didn't know she wasn't getting anywhere with Jared, but this would be fun to watch.

"Can I get you guys anything?"

Finally, the bartender came to take our order. It had been over thirty minutes since we got our last beers.

"Yeah, we'll—"

But I was interrupted by the curly blonde.

"Theo, keep 'em coming man, hook us up," she said, flashing him a thousand-watt smile with her bright red lips.

Oh, she was a firecracker. If she had long dark hair, with some red highlights, emerald green eyes, and was a shit ton prettier, she just might remind me of someone back at BRU.

But then I looked at Harper, sitting quietly in her chair, looking around the bar. Her thick hair wasn't adorned with anything, nor was her face, yet she was stunning. Much prettier than her friend. She seemed to have a natural glow about her that didn't require much enhancement, very different from how she needed to dress at the club.

"So, you guys know the bartender? That makes going out to the bar a whole different experience," I said.

Victoria smiled in my direction. "It doesn't hurt, that's for sure. We know him from the club."

"Oh, you guys work together? Jared," I motioned to them with my fingers, getting his attention. "They both work at The Velvet Rope. Have you been there? It's a cool place. It's where we just had Nate's event this weekend."

"I have not," he said, as an intrigued look came over his face. He smiled at the girls, his award-winning smile. "But I think I need to get there."

I swear, him and Victoria would be perfect for each other. But I liked Delia.

"Yes, we work together, besties at work. We have fun," Victoria said.

Four beers were slammed on the bar behind them, and they turned, waving to their friend. Grabbing the bottles, they each handed us one, and we prepared to make a cheer.

And of course, it was Victoria who chose to speak.

"To wooden bar tops," and she slapped the wood next to her. "May we all have sex on them one day!"

She and Jared clinked their bottles. But what they missed was the look of horror on Harper's face.

I, on the other hand, did not.

"Jesus Christ, Vic, are you fucking serious!" Harper cried out as she slammed her beer down, She almost fell from her chair as she launched herself from her seat, landing in my arms, and stormed away, toward the back of the bar.

In tears.

A hush came over the three of us, though Jared was left utterly confused.

And I just lost some respect for her best friend.

Victoria was standing on the rungs of her stool, searching for where Harper ran off to.

"Shit," she murmured. Then she looked at me, the apology clear in her teary eyes. "I'm sorry, I shouldn't have said that. I think I should go find her."

As she started getting up from her seat, I stopped her.

"Are you good with me going?" I asked.

All she did was nod. Checking with Jared, our unspoken communication was clear. He would stay with Victoria while I did what I needed to do.

Heading toward the back, I had no idea if she went to the restroom or the patio. Looking out the back door first, a quick scan didn't turn up anyone in a pink flowery sundress. Moving down the dark hallway, I noticed a line for the ladies' room, and saw a hint of pink a few girls up. Moving past the girls in line, I reached out and pulled on Harper's finger, gently, to let her know I was there.

Her head snapped my way as a lone tear fell from her eye. She wiped it quickly, hiding her face behind a curtain of hair as she looked at the ground.

"Hey," I said, moving close to speak as privately as we could. "Can we go talk somewhere?"

She glanced up, as her arms wrapped around her waist, making her look completely vulnerable and closed off at the same time.

"Well, I actually really have to go to the bathroom, bad," she said. A soft laugh followed.

But then the girl behind us barged in on our conversation.

"Hey, is this guy bothering you, hon?"

Both Harper and I turned to her.

"No, I'm fine, but thank you," Harper said.

I smiled at them both. It was refreshing to see girls standing up for each other.

"Okay, will you meet me on the patio when you're done?" I asked.

She nodded, and I left it at that.

It was only about ten minutes before I saw her walk through the door and start looking around the large space. I made sure to not miss her so she wouldn't get nervous. Walking right up to her and taking her by the hand, I led her to the back of the patio where there was some room.

"Are you cold?" I asked. But I was already taking off my sweatshirt and offering it to her. There wasn't much sun where we were and no patio heaters in this area. She took it from my hand and pulled it over her head.

It was almost as long as her dress.

"That wasn't cool what she did, I'm sorry that happened." I lifted her chin to make sure she heard my words. "Don't be embarrassed about telling her about us," I said. I couldn't help a smile from forming when I said that. "It kind of makes me feel good knowing you did."

That got her to smile as well.

And fuck if that didn't make my heart swell.

And as crazy as it sounded, I felt as though from that moment on I wanted to make her smile at least once a day.

"Thank you for saying that, I just don't know why she did that. We had a lot to drink at brunch, I'm going to blame it on the alcohol. She isn't normally mean."

Harper looked away as soon as she stopped talking. She's had trouble keeping eye contact with me since getting here.

"Listen, Gage, about the other day at the shop. I don't…do that. I don't usually hook up with people I don't know."

She still wasn't looking at me. So, I reached for her chin again. Her wide, blue eyes stared up at mine, and I wanted to toss all this talking bullshit out the window and kiss her right then and there.

But that wasn't what she needed.

"And I know I was the one that got you to come to the shop, and that looks bad, like it's what I wanted. But it was more that I just wanted to see you again."

I waited to make sure she had said all she wanted to say.

"And I'm pretty sure that's one of the things I'll like most about you once I get to know you," I said.

Now it was my turn to pull my eyes from her because this was not in my plan for the day. I wasn't expecting to ever see her again. Yet here I was pledging to get to know her.

And I was suddenly okay with that.

"Our start has been anything but conventional. The club incident alone needs its own conversation. But I'd like to think that the universe keeps putting us in one another's path for a reason," I said.

She let out a bit of a sigh, which wasn't quite the response I was hoping for.

"You don't agree?" I asked her.

"I think I do, but I have a few questions."

And she went back into her defensive mode, her arms around her middle and refusing to look at me.

I could add obstinate or headstrong to the list of characteristics my head was keeping on her.

Then I noticed a big chair open up near a space heater. Grabbing her hand, she let out a small yelp, unsure of what I was doing as I pulled her toward the seat. The race was on to get to it before anyone else, and we won.

"C'mon, let's sit down and talk, it'll be more comfortable."

"But it's only one chair," she said.

Sitting down, I pulled her down with me. The chair was wide enough that both our bottoms had cushion, and I simply pulled her legs across my lap so we could talk.

"Are you okay with this?" I asked, as my arm went around her back to support her.

"Well, it is more comfortable. I stand so much at both my jobs, sitting is a luxury."

We settled in to the chair and savored the heater's warmth for a moment.

"Do you want a drink?" I asked.

"I'm good."

"Okay, you have questions," I said. "What are they, Harper?"

She was wringing her hands together, showing me she was nervous, but so was I. I'd promised myself I was steering clear of this. Of any girls that were potential for a relationship.

And Harper was one hundred percent a relationship girl.

"Well, the night at the club, I was getting mixed messages. Like, a lot of them. You were acting like you'd never really seen me before, even though the day before your hand was knuckle-deep inside me."

Well, shit. She wasn't mincing words.

"And then you fight some asshole, which, by the way," she said, raising her voice and staring straight into my eyes, "I'd have been fine even without your help; I handle that shit all the time." She settled back against my arm before continuing. "That spells out: 'I care for her,' or something along those lines. But then you leave with that blonde tramp, and fuck if that didn't mess with my head right after you did the most chivalrous thing anyone's ever done for me."

I felt like an asshole. A complete and total asshole. When she said it like that, there was no reason she should ever talk to me again.

And she had yet to ask a question, but she obviously needed to get this out, so I let her keep going.

"And then let's get to the tip and the note," she said.

"Wait, you're mad at me for the tip I left you?" I asked, genuinely surprised.

Harper put her face in her hands and took a moment to collect herself. My hand went behind her neck and turned her toward me, our faces almost touching.

"Hey, relax," I whispered against her cheek.

She let her forehead drop to mine.

"I sound like such a brat right now," she said. Her words tickled my cheek, her lips were so close to me. "And no, I'm not mad at you for the tip you left me. Well, yeah, I guess I am. It was unnecessary, Gage. Way too much. I actually want to give it back to you."

She pulled her head from mine, but I didn't let her go far as my hand came around and held her cheek. She tilted into my hand.

"That will be a discussion for another time. I'm still curious what your question is?"

She chuckled at that and pulled away.

"You're distracting me, that's part of it," she said, then laughed. "My question is, what does all this mean? We fooled around, but were you going to ever call me after that? You have yet to even ask me for my number. You fight someone in my honor but go home with another woman. Where does this leave us?"

All very valid questions, and ones I wasn't sure I had the answers to. But she deserved something from me after my actions over the past few days.

"Well, for starters, that girl meant and means nothing to me. I'm sorry last night even happened." And I was. "And I know I've done nothing but think about you since I was 'knuckle-deep' in you, so if that means anything."

That got her laughing, and I laughed along with her. She turned her body more toward me on my lap, opening up more. Getting comfortable.

"That actually means a lot," she said.

"Listen Harper, I'm going to be completely honest. I was not looking for a relationship. I just got out of a couple things that were very complicated, and they kind of fucked me up."

Her look remained serious, but her eyes softened at my words.

"A relationship was the last thing I was looking for, but you keep showing up. And I can't stop thinking about you. But I don't know where that leaves us." My damn heart was surpassing my brain and going in for the kill. "But if you'll have patience with me, I'd like to figure this out with you."

Her eyes searched mine, for what I wasn't sure. Maybe to detect if I was being honest with her or not. But then she leaned back against my arm, seeming to be satisfied with what she saw.

"I think we can do that." Her small smile grew wide.

"Yeah?" I questioned.

"Yeah," she replied.

Her hands gripped my face, and she moved in closer. Her lips rubbed gently against mine before she talked in a hushed whisper. "I'd like to see where this goes."

And then she kissed me.

My arm went around her waist, pulling her in while the other went in her hair, keeping her in place. I didn't want her backing away from me anytime soon. This needed to last.

"Harp?"

Our lips came unlocked immediately to find Victoria and Jared standing over us. Victoria's eyes were red, possibly from her drinking or maybe she'd been crying.

Jared, on the other hand, had a smirk on his face, one of complete disbelief in all the stories I'd been feeding him today.

And we'd been interrupted, again.

"Hey, Vic," Harper said as she got off my lap.

"Honey, I'm sorry, like really sorry."

Her words were apologetic, and her voice was full of remorse. I felt bad for her. Then she looked at me.

"Gage, I'm, uh, sorry. I don't even know you. I hope we can try this again when I'm not a drunken lunatic."

I nodded as I noticed her tears flowing again. Harper pulled her into a hug, and they shared a few quiet words. Jared came to me, and the smirk hadn't left his face.

"Favor, pal," I said, standing.

"Yep, I've got ya covered. I already know where she lives. She'll get home safe."

After shaking hands, Jared escorted Victoria away as she waved to us both.

Harper turned toward me once we were alone again. Well, as alone as we could get in a bar full of people. She gestured to the chair, and we returned to our seats, her on my lap. I liked the look of her in my sweatshirt. The idea of her in any of my clothes was a welcome thought.

But then the doubts filtered in, even while still looking at her bright smile and big blue eyes.

Should I be doing this right now?

So soon after the divorce…and Becca.

Thinking about Becca as I looked at Harper, I realized something. Becca was never mine, she was never meant to be mine, and I knew that going in. It was my own fault for allowing my emotions to cloud my judgment. But Jared was right about me when he said I was no good at casual. And this beautiful creature sitting on my lap didn't deserve any games from me. I couldn't play with her heart. This had to go slow so that I could make sure I knew if I was ready.

Ready for anything at all.

"What do you say I walk you home?" I asked her. "Well, I guess I need to know if you're walking distance from here first."

"I'm about six blocks, just north of Washington Square," she offered with a smile. "And I'd like that."

Standing, she offered her hand to pull me up. I took it and pulled her into an embrace as I stood, her looking up at me as our bodies came together.

"I'm only walking you home. I'm not coming inside. We need to start fresh and do this right, don't you think? And give me your phone, so I can put my number in it."

Her smile grew wide again, and I noticed a small dimple on her left cheek I'd not seen before.

Fucking adorable.

"I think that's sounds perfect, Mr. Parker."

CHAPTER 15

Harper

Dreams. They can tell you a lot about yourself. For example, I have a repeated dream of falling down the stairs. It's a terrible feeling, but I learned it doesn't mean I'm clumsy and need to always live in a first-floor apartment. Rather, it usually means you're missing control over something in your life or maybe it's going in the wrong direction, both very logical possibilities with me. And the fact that it's a recurring dream, analysts say that I'm really avoiding the problem that falling dream is telling me.

However, the past couple nights, I wasn't falling in my dreams. Well, not falling down any stairs.

I was having sex. A lot of sex. With Gage.

It doesn't take an expert to analyze what those mean.

And when the dreams woke me, I'd grab my phone and reread some of the texts he'd sent me.

Gage - Hey we talked about dinner, does Tuesday work

- I'm glad fate stepped in and put us on the same path three times last week

- Btw did you know you have the cutest dimple on your left cheek

- I'm looking out my office window and the sky is reminding me of your eyes

- When do you think I can be knuckle deep in you again

- OK, ignore that last text, we're going slow, right?

- But it will happen again

AND I MIGHT HAVE DONE some other things when the dreams woke me as well…but he'd never know about those.

The sun wasn't even up yet, but I was wide awake. I was pretty sure it was because Tuesday finally arrived. When Gage walked me home, we talked about going out on some dates and getting to know one another, taking it a bit slower. And I really appreciated that, considering most guys, well, would rather just get right back to business.

But here I was, only a little over a week since last seeing him, and my mind was consumed with sexual thoughts and passionate dreams. It didn't help that I didn't work at the club Sunday nights, and the shop was closed on Mondays. And Victoria was in class all day yesterday. Having nothing to distract me from my own thoughts these past couple days other than a spicy book or a show filled with sex wasn't working.

There were three hours to go before I needed to be at the shop. That was too much time to sit around my tiny apartment. Going for a walk in the park would be just the thing to start the day right.

Once I was dressed for the crisp morning air, I made sure I had my safety whistle and pepper spray. My mother hated that I was living in NYC alone and sent me self-defense gadgets all the time. These early morning walks were times I made sure to take some along.

And I could catch up with my mom. She was always up early, and it was a perfect time to check in.

She picked up on the second ring.

"Hey honey. Out for a morning walk?"

"I am, and it's finally starting to warm up a bit up here. I bet you're already out on your lanai having your second cup of coffee, aren't you?"

Her chuckle into the phone made me smile, but the slurp of her coffee made me laugh.

"You know me so well. Are there other people around you? You're not completely alone, are you?"

Washington Square Park was beautiful. Though nowhere near the size of Central Park, its size was decent. It had plenty of green space to give you the feel of nature when you needed it. But the main attraction was the arch and fountain in its center. During the day, all year long, the number of people in the fountain area was immense. This early, it was locals only, but it still attracted enough people to make one feel safe.

"There are plenty of others out walking and running right now, no worries."

Her hum of approval was all I was going to get.

"Weather good, Mom? Have you been getting to the beach?"

One thing I was super jealous about her living in Florida was the year-round beach weather. Growing up in New Jersey, we spent our summers and vacations on the Jersey Shore. But it was such a limited season. May through September were the only months bearable to sit on the beach. Maybe October. But the water didn't get truly warm enough to enjoy going in until well into July. But some of my best memories from childhood are of us renting a beach house on Long Beach Island in NJ.

But we stopped doing that once my dad died.

We couldn't spare the money for vacations. But any chance I got to take a day trip down there, I went. And I still loved it.

"It's already starting to get really hot here. I've only got about another month before I'll start my hibernation."

As much as my mom loved living in Florida, she didn't truly love the heat and humidity. And not having enough money to have a house up north as well, she wasn't a typical snowbird and lived in Florida full-time. So, during the hottest months, she rarely did much outside.

"Well, it's that or come back and deal with subzero temps and snowy winters. I don't know what to say, Mom."

"Yeah, no, I'm good with my hot, gross, sticky summers down here. So how's my favorite daughter?"

Our little running joke considering I'm an only child.

"I'm gooood," I responded. And with that, she knew I'd called with a hot topic.

"So, is this work related, or does he have a name?"

I laughed out loud. "He has a name." And then I didn't know what I wanted to say next. My mom and I were close, but we didn't really talk about my sex life. Yet this directly involved that. What was I really going to ask her?

"His name is Gage, Gage Parker. We don't know each other that well yet, but things moved kinda quick the first time we met. And, well, now he wants to slow things down." After pausing for a second, I realized she wanted me to keep going. "And that's not necessarily the problem, although it might have made me second-guess if he was truly attracted to me."

I hadn't realized that was a concern of mine until I spoke those words aloud. Insecurity wasn't something I was plagued with normally, but it hit every now and then. But why would a guy, who had gotten as far as Gage did with me, not want to keep it going?

"I'm wondering how you knew. When you first met Dad, when did you know he was the one you wanted to spend your life with?"

Wanting to focus on our conversation, I plopped on a nearby bench. It took a minute for my mom to start talking.

"Let's unpack this, Harper. First, the whole sex thing. You haven't been with someone in quite a while, so I get that you would want to, you know, keep it going."

Jesus Christ.

"Mom, this is not supposed to be about my sex life. And how do you know when I do and don't have sex?"

There was a slight chuckle through the phone line. "Oh, honey. Moms know. Besides, you don't keep secrets well and I'd know if you were hanging out with anyone, and you haven't in almost seven months. You keep yourself too busy working both those jobs."

This would be a topic for another day, but I'd learned to keep my mouth shut about certain things.

"Now, regarding your father and me. I don't know if love at first sight is really a thing, but I knew early on that we would be together, that we'd get married. It's just something I felt in my gut, my heart. When I was around him, I felt whole. And when we were apart, it was as if some part of me stayed with him, and I never felt whole unless we were together."

My tears fell silently.

There was no way I was going to turn this into me crying about my dad, or us losing him. But my heart broke for my mom realizing that she felt…part of a person without my dad with her.

"That's a beautiful way to describe your love, Mom."

And then I heard her blowing her nose.

My dad's been gone for thirteen years, but she hasn't stopped loving or missing him. That's true love.

"So, if you're asking me this, Gage must be pretty special," she said. I could hear the smile in her words.

Sitting back against the bench, I noticed the sun starting to come up over the tall buildings surrounding the park. Looked like it was going to be a perfect day, again. Gage told me he was picking me up at 6:30. I had to push for that extra half hour considering the shop only closes at six. There was no way I could be picked up from work to go out, not on our first official date.

"I don't know, I think he could be, Mom. We've had somewhat of a rocky start, but he's got promise. I'll, uh, keep you posted." Realizing it was getting late, I stood and started heading back home. "Enjoy the beach today, Mom. Find a shell or piece of sea glass for me."

"Love hearing your voice, babe. Love you."

And she hung up.

THANKFULLY, the day was flying by at the shop since we were swamped with walk-in orders as well as a corporate order that was due tomorrow. Fiona was busy handling the walk-ins while I worked in the back.

Fiona questioned why my hair was in loose curls when I came in this morning. Didn't take her long to figure out I had a date tonight. Since I was going to be so short on time, I needed to do my hair in the morning, before work, for this evening. The amount of hairspray I put in it gave me a headache, and I still wasn't convinced it would hold. When I asked Gage, in our numerous text conversations since leaving the bar on Sunday, why we had to leave so early, he was elusive. And the "picking me up" part was interesting as well. Maybe we were taking a car service? He was wealthy, so maybe that was how they did things. Unlike us common folk who walk or use the subway.

As quick as the day was going, it still wasn't quitting time. Three more hours to go yet. I couldn't remember the last time I was this excited to see a guy again. But these floral arrangements needed to be finished by day's end, so I needed to hustle.

"Harper?" Fiona yelled. "Can you come up front? You have a visitor."

Unsure if it was a customer or not, I removed my dirty apron and walked through the doorway.

Standing next to Fiona was the most handsome, sexy guy in a business suit I'd ever seen. His five o'clock shadow was always perfect. He must trim it that way. Always just the right amount to not look like a full beard but grown in enough to look groomed. And his suits looked like they had to be custom, fitting his thighs and arms just tight enough to see he was muscular, but not so tight that he couldn't move.

I swear he was a full foot taller than me, and standing next to Fiona, I could get a sense of how tall he really was. He towered over her, and I was even shorter.

And I was going on a date with him that night.

His warm brown eyes sparkled as he smiled when I walked in.

And I made sure to smile back.

"I'll, uh, give you two a minute. I think he's here to pay an invoice," Fiona said. But her sideways look as she walked past me told me she could see something between us beyond customer and client.

"Hey," I said.

"Hey, yourself."

His voice. I didn't think I'd ever get tired of that smooth, deep timbre that almost made my insides vibrate every time I heard him talk.

"What are you doing here?" But as soon as I said it, I wanted to take it back. "I mean, I'm glad you're here, I just wasn't expecting to see you until tonight."

He stalked over to me, his slow measured steps echoing against the tile floor. I'd never felt more like prey in all my life.

And it excited me.

"When the invoice came across my desk this morning, I figured, why not bring it to you in person. What a perfect excuse to see you," he said as his hand moved a stray curl behind my ear.

And my body tingled. Everywhere.

"I like the curls," he said.

I felt the blush start on my face and cover me all the way to my chest. A simple compliment from him had me speechless and thinking about the other things his hand had already done to me.

"Thanks, and it's nice having an impromptu visit from you."

He undid the button on his suit jacket and put that hand in his pants pocket.

Why is that such a sexy move from a guy in a suit? And why do I think he put his hand in his pocket to stop himself from touching me again?

"Yeah, I've been having trouble concentrating in the office today. I've been, uh, looking forward to tonight."

A boyish grin spread across his face as he looked at me through half-hooded eyes. I didn't trust myself with the way my mind had been betraying me all day with thoughts of him, but the physical pull he had on me currently was strong. My hands went up to his chest, gripping his lapels, hoping that would stop me from doing what I really wanted.

"Yeah, me too," I said. I looked to the back room, and he understood completely.

"I won't keep you. Here," he said. In his hand was an envelope, with I was sure his company's payment due for the floral order. "I'd like to see that dimple before I go." He leaned in, his lips close, the words tickling my ear. "I mean, this place does bring back memories of other parts of you that I'd, of course, like to see, but the dimple will do for now."

His words warmed my entire body. My smile must have given him what he wanted since he smiled in return. Then, leaning in, he placed a tender kiss on my cheek, on my dimple.

"I'll see you in a little while."

Watching him go was a fun activity, his swagger accentuating his features in that suit. But the moment that door closed, she emerged.

"Well, well, well, looks like someone has a suitor." She stood, an accusatory look on her face. "When were you going to tell me?"

She was showing her age.

"Fiona, who calls it a suitor these days? And it's nothing, we are going on a date, that's all."

She went back to making an arrangement that was due to be ready in the next few minutes. Standing by her side, I admired her work. She did beautiful work, still. Regardless of her being in the business for over thirty years, she kept herself current and on trend. For example, we had more wildflowers in stock than we did roses.

I was going to miss her when I got my own shop.

She was still quiet, but I assumed she was concentrating.

"Just be careful, Harper."

Her words caught me off guard. Stopping mid-step, I spun toward the table, leaning on it. Yeah, the exact spot.

"What do you mean?"

"Well," she started. But then she hesitated, seeming to really think about her words. She put the stem in her hand on the table and gave me her full attention. "I don't know him, but I know his type. He's a big executive downtown. His lifestyle is so different from what we can even begin to comprehend. So, just go in with your eyes wide open, that's all." She went back to her flowers, and I slowly stepped away from the table.

"But you both look gorgeous together, thought I should tell you that."

CHAPTER 16

Gage

"M r. Parker, I need a minute. I know it's late," Maryellen said. "This just came across my desk, and I thought I should alert you of it immediately since it's actually only a few weeks away. I don't understand how these groups can't give better notice for things like this. I already checked your sched-ule, and we would have to move a few things around for you to make this, but I'm sure you'd want to."

Looking at the invitation in my hand, my stomach fell slightly.

"I guess this is for the endowment we give them each year?" I asked.

She nodded while tapping on her tablet.

"I was thinking, sir—"

"Maryellen, please."

"Gage, I was thinking this might be a good trip to send your brother on."

My head snapped up to hers at that idea.

"He needs a bit more responsibility placed on him, and this might be just the thing. I thought you might not want to head back down to Virginia so soon after coming home." She continued tapping on her tablet. "He doesn't have nearly as much to move around on the calendar, so it would be easier. And BRU only needs a rep from Parker Financial, they don't need their alum."

Plopping in my chair, I was once again silently thanking my father for hiring Maryellen. It was one of the best decisions he made before making his quiet exit from the company. Although not official, he hasn't been in the office in over four months. He's basically retired.

"Did you know that I'm a graduate of Blue Ridge University?" Maryellen asked.

My eyes couldn't have grown wider after that statement. There are so many things that remained a mystery when it came to Maryellen McEntyre. But this was not one I expected.

"I did not know that, Maryellen. I'm assuming we weren't there at the same time?"

That comment got a rare smile out of her, and her face lit up. And suddenly I realized how wrong I'd been. We weren't that far apart in age, after all.

"We, sir, were actually there together for one year, but that's it. My senior year was your freshman year. I don't think we would have crossed paths."

Twenty-nine years old.

"I think your dad hired me, specifically, because of my schooling. He talked about you all the time and how proud he was of you not falling into the cookie cutter trap that happens up this way." She laughed, thinking about the memory. "He loved that I went to BRU as well."

"How did I not know this?" I asked, completely dumbfounded.

"I don't know, si—Gage. We don't really sit around talking much about our personal lives. But I thought I'd let you know that little tidbit."

She stood from her chair, about to leave my office.

"Hold on," I said. "I have an idea."

LIVING IN THE CITY, I didn't have the opportunity nor the need to take my car out that often. But having her was one of the reasons Rebecca and I chose to buy the brownstone we did. It has a garage. Paying to store a car is ridiculously expensive and a huge pain in the ass. I loved the convenience of taking her out for a ride whenever the mood hit. And yeah, the car is a 'she,' as all cars should be since they can be so temperamental.

Unfortunately, it wasn't the best night to have the top down. The temperature had dropped a bit, and we had a decent ride. Once I pulled up to her apartment building, I shot Harper a text.

Me - I'm here and don't forget a sweater or jacket

Harper - KK I'll be right down

DOUBLE PARKING WAS a risky business on her street, it was narrow and hard for other cars to get by. Thankfully she was coming out the door before I caused any issues.

"Well, I don't know much about cars," she said, plopping onto the passenger seat, "but I know enough to realize that this one is special."

She looked around the interior, admiring it, and that made me happy. But all I wanted to do was admire her. The curls she had in her hair still looked amazing, maybe even better since I'd seen her earlier. And the dress she was wearing accentuated every curve of her body.

"So, what do you think of Shelby?" I asked.

She looked completely confused as I started driving. But looking out the windshield, she put it together and laughed. "Shelby? You call your car Shelby?"

"Well, she *is* a Shelby, so it only makes sense that's her name."

Laughing out loud, she rolled down the window and put her hand outside. "I like it. I like that she has a name. She's a Mustang, I know that at least."

But I couldn't concentrate on what she was saying, even if she was talking about my prized possession.

She had her head against the headrest and was staring out the window as her hand played with the wind. The sun kept hitting us in between the buildings as I drove and would bounce off her face, illuminating her skin. Every time I saw her, I found something else that intensified her beauty.

Then she realized we were heading to the Holland Tunnel, and she sat up as she took notice.

"Are we heading to New Jersey?" she asked, excitement in her voice. Looking over, she spun her body in her seat to face me completely.

I nodded and couldn't help smiling at her.

"Did you know I'm from New Jersey?" she asked.

So fucking adorable.

"I did *not* know you're from New Jersey." That was information I would tuck away for later. "I hope this is a restaurant you'll like."

We were doing okay on traffic through the tunnel. Our reservation was at seven thirty, and even though the drive was only a little over five miles, it could easily take us an hour at this time.

"Well, where is it? But to be honest, it won't matter where we're going."

She turned away, looking out the window since we exited the tunnel and were now in her home state. There was something about this whole night now that made coming here a bit more special.

"As long as I'm with you, I don't care where we eat."

When she said that, I was tempted to pull the car over and drag her onto my lap. Instead, I reached across the console and gripped her leg just above her knee, right below the hem of her dress. She kept her eyes looking out the window but put her hand over mine. And squeezed it.

"We're almost there."

THANKFULLY THE WEATHER HELD OUT, and we were able to eat at the table I reserved on the patio. Batello's is one of my favorite restaurants in Jersey City because of its view of downtown NYC over the river. But I have to say, the view I had across the table stole all my attention during our meal. And the best part was her complete ignorance of how beautiful she was and that everyone in the place stopped and stared when she walked in.

Her dress was simple but pretty. It was pale pink and hugged every curve. Yet I noticed she paired it with flat shoes. I was missing those stilettos she wore at the club. But it didn't dissuade my mind from having thoughts of taking her into the back somewhere. Maybe find a wooden table…

"That was delicious," Harper said. "And this place really is a beautiful spot. I've never spent time in Jersey City. When I was growing up, it wasn't so up and coming as it is now."

She held her wineglass close to her mouth as she looked over the rail we sat up against. The sun had already set behind us and the city lights illuminated the horizon. It framed her perfectly, and

I was tempted to snap her picture, to always remember this moment.

"What a view," she said, looking across the river.

It was a spectacle. Living here, I didn't appreciate the beauty of the city enough, instead noting its daily shortcomings. It was nice to be reminded of its beauty now and again.

"How is it that you're single, Harper? You're stunning, funny, fun to be with, smart. All the things that anyone would want. Why are you not with anyone?"

I loved how the blush on her cheeks spread to her chest whenever she was embarrassed. It made me want to reach across the table and touch her, to see if her skin was as warm as I expected it to be. Shaking her head slightly at the compliments, she took a moment to respond.

"Well, I was, for a bit. Last year I had a guy I spent some time with, but it wasn't anything serious. And he wasn't really on board with my plans for staying here in New York, so it would've never worked." She appeared distracted as she looked out at the river, a boat catching our attention as it raced by. "There was someone serious right after college, but, well, it didn't work out." The amount of wine she drank after that declaration told me not to push on the topic.

"What about you?" she asked. "All the same positive traits could be said about you, but we must add successful to the list. So why is there no soon-to-be Mrs. Parker on your arm?"

It was my turn to take a gulp of wine.

"Well, there was a Mrs. Parker. And now there isn't."

She was surprised, but she recovered well.

"I'm sorry."

"It's fine. I'm better off, believe me." My sarcastic chuckle didn't go unnoticed.

"So, it was divorce," she said rather than asked. "That couldn't have been easy to deal with this early in life. I mean, I think we're close in age, so that kinda sucks, I'm sorry."

The regret at bringing up the topic must have been all over my face. But Harper had no idea how new this situation really was for me, so this was my fault, not hers.

"How old are you, Gage?"

Her warm smile was welcome as she easily changed the subject.

"What do you think?" I asked her.

She contemplated that for a moment, staring me up and down as she did. The wag of her eyebrows lightened the mood as she blatantly checked me out. We both let out a laugh.

"Well, you're pretty advanced in your career, but I do know it's a family business," she started with. "I think you're the older brother between you and Chase, so that's another clue." She took a long sip of her wine, finishing it off. She held her glass out for me to refill for her, which I willingly did. "He seems pretty young, if you ask me. So based on my limited information, I have you at twenty-eight."

Staring at her, I was mentally attempting to deduce her age, knowing full well that was the next question. And that's always a tougher question with women.

"You're not far off, but I'm not quite there yet," I told her. "Twenty-six in a few months."

That seemed to surprise her.

"I won't put you through the torture of guessing mine," she said. "I'm twenty-seven." Her eyes narrowed as she watched me carefully. "Does that bother you?"

"Do you take me for being shallow? You're a year older than me, Harper. There's no issue with that for me. Is there for you?"

"Nope," she said matter-of-factly as she put her glass on the table. And it appeared the topic was closed. "Do you have any other siblings?"

"No, just me and my brother. What about you?"

I knew we were at the "getting to know you" stage, but talking about family was one thing I really didn't want to do. Nothing good would come out of Harper learning too much about my family.

"Just me, myself, and I. Well, and my mom, but she lives in Florida now, so it really is just me I guess."

A veil of sadness floated over her as she stared out at the river again. It appeared she also didn't want to talk about her family. I wasn't sure if changing the subject again was in order or letting her work through her thoughts in her own time.

Instead of either, I reached across the table and took her hand. Her fingers gripped me back before her gaze met mine. An appreciative smile let me know she needed those few quiet moments.

Her hand pulled from mine as her hand went toward the vase in the center of our table, her finger grazing the flower.

How ironic it was a single pink rose.

"Pink is my favorite color," she offered as her finger gently rubbed along the petals. Her thoughts seemed distant as she said it. "It has been since I was a little girl. My dad would always bring me a dozen pink roses for my birthday and Valentine's Day every year. He bought red for my mom, but pink for me. He said they meant different things for different people."

I nodded as she paused in her story. Her eyes scanned the river, contemplative. But then her gaze locked with mine, ready to talk again.

"I don't know if him bringing me those flowers all those years played a role in me loving them as much as I do. I'm sure it did. But it definitely played a role in pink being my favorite color."

Her small smile held some pain in it. But I felt as though her sharing that with me was a big step for her.

For us.

"You look beautiful in pink, so it's a great favorite color," I told her.

And the slight pink blush that fell upon her cheeks was close to the color of her dress.

"Hey, can we take a selfie?" she asked as her chair scraped against the pavers, ready to change the subject again.

She was up and finding the perfect backdrop before I could make it to her side of the table. Grabbing a hold of her around the waist, we put our heads together with the lights of downtown behind us. She snapped a ton of pics as we laughed.

"May I, sir?"

The waiter came to see if we'd like him to take a picture for us.

"That would be great, thank you," I said.

Harper handed over her phone, and we struck a more formal pose, her hand around my middle as I held her close. Then I felt her tug on my tie.

"Ya know," she whispered, quiet enough so our photographer wouldn't hear, "I can't look at a man's tie the same way anymore."

"That's enough, thank you," I firmly told the waiter and held out my hand for her phone. Once I had it safely in my pocket and knew we were alone, I spun on her and pulled her against me, my mouth against her ear.

"I take it that means you liked what I did to you on the table?"

Her simple statement had me wanting to beg her to let me take her right here, in the restaurant. Somewhere. Anywhere.

But slow...I said we would go slow.

She nodded.

Still pressed against her and holding her head close, my fingers dug through her hair. I know she felt my cock as it hardened against her belly.

"You can't say things like that to me when I'm trying to be a gentleman, Harper. Slow, remember?"

Lifting her face up to mine, she made sure our eyes connected. "Gage, I appreciate your intentions, but when we've already done what we've done, why wait? We're both adults."

My mouth crashed against hers as the last word left her lips. I gently cradled her face, but it was an oxymoron to what my mouth was doing to hers. The lashing of our tongues was like a dance between our lips.

I pulled away, breathing heavy against the side of her mouth. "I think I should get the check."

"I think that's a good idea." And then she placed a tender kiss on my cheek before her words echoed in my ear. "Hurry up."

DAMN IT. Why did I choose a restaurant so far outside the city? And why was there traffic heading back at nine thirty at night on a Tuesday? All these thoughts were running through my head as Harper tried to keep the conversation light. And why did I insist on driving? I should have used the car service.

"So, Maryellen is your secretary, I'm assuming. She's the nicest in the world. When you and Chase walked in that day, I have to say, after our little run-in that morning, I was slightly upset it wasn't her I was meeting with."

Finally! We were out of the tunnel, and the traffic was moving better now. My phone indicated we'd be at my place in ten minutes.

"Uhm, yeah, I know. When Chase and I heard you say something about Fiona when we first met you, we knew going in we were gonna see you. Well, obviously, we brought you your breakfast."

Looking her way, I needed to just blurt my question out.

"The drive home kinda killed the mood, are you still up for

hanging out? I know it's already late and we both have work, but if you'd like to come…"

"Yes," she said firmly. "I'd like to still hang out."

Got her answer just in time to make the turn to my place.

"We'll go to my place if that's okay, since I have my car. Too much of a hassle to find parking and I have a garage."

Her neck looked like it could have broken it snapped so quickly in my direction.

"You have a garage? Like, your own on your property for your car?"

The disbelief in her voice was comical.

But many didn't come from the world we lived in. I've tried to stay humble and not flaunt what my father has built for us, but sometimes things slip out. Like this. And I really hated how it sounded.

"Um, yeah."

Her hand went immediately to my thigh and squeezed. "You should never be embarrassed about your successes in life, Gage, and I'm sorry if I made you feel uncomfortable. I can't wait to see your place."

Fucking hell, where has this girl been?

"Well, most of the success is due to my father, he only recently left the company in our hands. He was working full-time up until a few months ago."

Hitting the button on my visor as I turned the corner down the alley, I saw the door rising. It was tight back here, and I was always nervous pulling this car in and out, but it was still better than having an attendant doing it anywhere else.

"That's awesome that you've been able to work with your dad. I mean, I'm assuming you worked with him for a while leading up to him retiring."

Talking about my father would do the complete opposite of the mood I wanted to be in when we walked inside.

"I wouldn't call it retirement for him, but we can talk about him another time," I said as I put the car in park and turned it off.

By then, she was looking around the garage in awe. She opened her door, though, and quickly realized how tight the space was.

"Yeah, it's tight, but I don't complain because it's amazing I found a brownstone that I not only fell in love with but also had this."

Once out, she met me at the front of the car and grabbed my hand.

"C'mon, I can't wait to see your place!"

The two of us walking into this house together as I held the door for her, and her smiling up at me walking through it, felt... real. I hadn't brought anyone back here, truly willingly, since my divorce. No one that I had intentions of wanting to spend time with.

And it scared the shit out of me.

CHAPTER 17

Harper

Knowing Gage would not want me to gush too much about his place, I tried to keep my reactions to a minimum. But holy fuck! His place belonged in one of those coffee table books about the best apartments in the city, from the chef's kitchen to the patio and yard, a full gym, all the way up to the hot tub on the rooftop terrace. And let's not forget to mention the attention to detail when it came to the decorating was impeccable. I was definitely biting my tongue during most of the tour.

We finished back on the main floor, and he pulled a bottle of wine from his bar fridge.

"Want a glass or is it too late?" he asked.

Already resigned to the fact that I was going to be tired at work tomorrow, another glass would help bring our mood back to what it was at the restaurant.

"I'll definitely have a glass," I said. "But I need the restroom first."

He pointed to the door off the kitchen. Once inside, I tore open my bag and took out the small number of tools I had with me to work with. First, I spritzed a few sprays of my scent on my neck and wrists. Next, I checked my makeup. It wasn't too bad, and all I brought with me was my lip gloss, anyway. Finally, I ran my fingers through my hair, attempting to rid it of the knots eating outside inevitably created. It didn't have the effect I wanted, rather, my hair became a bit wilder looking. Smoothing it with my hands wasn't doing much good either.

It would have to do.

Opening the door, I walked right into a wall of muscle. As his arms encircled me, he pulled me against his body, my own arms trapped against his chest.

"We have to stop meeting like this," I said. Breathing him in, the scent of cedar, spice, and leather overwhelmed my senses.

"No," he said. "I think meeting like this is exactly the way things should be for us."

His words made my knees weak.

He handed me my glass of wine as I noticed his tie and jacket were no longer on. I wondered if one of them might show itself again tonight.

I didn't just wonder, I hoped.

"Harper, I don't want to play games right now. No beating around the bush. We're doing this," he said. "I've got the fire going, so if you're good with not fucking me in a bed, I'd like to stay down here."

How does one respond to that?

All my body allowed me to do was nod. His straightforwardness was a turn-on. I loved him taking charge.

"Is your phone on silent? I don't want any interruptions this time," he said, looking back at me.

"It is."

He led me into the living room by the hand, and I saw the fire roaring inside its hearth. The lights were dimmed, and he even lit some candles. I took a generous gulp of my wine and put it on the table in front of the couch. He sat on the wide cushioned sofa, and as I was about to join him, he put up his hand.

"Stay standing." His eyes roamed me from top to bottom. "I want you to take your dress off for me."

My body was not something I could afford to be shy about, not with the outfit I wore at the club. If this was something he wanted and enjoyed, I was more than willing to oblige.

And again, I liked handing over the control. Something I never knew about myself.

"You'll need to unzip it for me," I said. Gage gave a drowsy blink and rose from the couch, approaching me with a predatory gaze. My breath caught as he stood over me, then put a rough hand on my shoulder to turn me around. He swept my long hair over one shoulder, a puff of breath from his nose meeting my neck. Every sense was heightened, his finger trailing behind the slow pull of metal down my back. He already had me flustered, and I had to clear my throat to speak. "You don't have to undo it all the way, just start it for me."

Wordlessly, his footsteps retreated from me. I peeked over my shoulder to find him sitting back on the couch, watching me. Reaching around, I found the zipper and slowly pulled it the rest of the way down. The top of the dress fell from my shoulders as I held it up over the front of me.

Slipping one arm out of the dress, I kept the rest of it in place.

"You're good at this," he said.

I snuck another look at him over my shoulder.

Both his arms were stretched out along the back of the couch, his glass of wine in one hand. He was slouching a bit against the cushion, his long legs almost reaching the backs of my knees. His shirt sleeves were rolled up against his forearms, the veins prominent along his skin.

And again, his clothes looked custom as they clung to every line of every muscle. His thighs seemed ready to burst through the expensive wool while his biceps stretched the cotton to its limits.

He brought his glass to his lips, draining it while we maintained eye contact. Reaching behind, he placed the glass on a sofa table and resumed being my audience.

But not before he rearranged the large bulge growing between his legs.

"Why did you stop?" he asked. But the smirk he wore told me he knew exactly why.

"Well, you're a bit distracting," I told him.

"Please, keep going, beautiful."

I felt as though I was way out of my league. He was a different kind of lover. The tie was my first clue, but there was something in the way he looked at me that made me feel nervous.

Yet intoxicated at the same time.

My hands went to the other sleeve of my dress, working my arm out. Holding it over my breasts, I spun to face Gage. His hooded eyes took me in as his one hand rubbed along his hard cock through his pants. He flicked the button of his trousers open, and I found it hard to swallow as I watched him. My hands were eager to pull his zipper down for him, but I had a strong urge to not disappoint him. Remaining where I was, I continued watching as he undid his own zipper and opened the top of his pants.

Underneath were dark boxer briefs stretched to unimaginable lengths, the outline of his thick cock prominently in view.

Stepping forward, I found myself standing between his separated knees. He rubbed his legs against mine just as my fingers let go of the silky material.

It lay in a puddle between our feet.

Neither of our eyes followed it. Instead, they remained on one another.

But then he glanced lower, taking in my sheer black lace bra and thong and gave me a Cheshire cat smile. My nipples hardened under his stare.

"Black lace. Very nice choice, Harper."

The only parts moving on him when he spoke were his eyes as they roved over me, and his hand rubbing himself through the cotton.

"Should I keep going?" I asked.

He contemplated as he looked me up and down. "No, keep them both on for now. Come straddle me."

Thank God. I couldn't wait to feel him up against me. Spreading my knees apart and placing them on the couch, my ass slid onto his thighs. I was about to push myself farther up, eliminating the space between his cock and my pussy.

But he stopped me.

"Not yet. Stay there for now."

The whine I emitted told him how I felt about that.

And the temptation to reach down and rub myself was so strong, I don't know how I resisted. The hope of him touching me soon was the only thing keeping me going. I felt as though I would combust.

Finally, his hands moved from the back of the couch. They came to my waist and gripped me, his thumbs skimming the top of my panties along my hips.

"You are so fucking amazing to look at, Harper. Do you know that?"

I may not be shy, but I did not do well with the compliments. Because I had not been told that.

Ever.

And it was overwhelming, but I refused to succumb to the emotions. I was going to enjoy every moment of this.

"Answer me, Harper," he said, as his fingers slid under the strings of my thong. "Tell me you know you're beautiful."

My skin burst alive, his touch scorching a path across my hip bones. But his head tilted, and he stopped the advance of his fingers, looking at me for my response.

"What I know is you make me feel beautiful, Gage."

Reaching for his face with my hands, I ran my fingers through his thin beard. I'd never dated a guy with facial hair before. And now I didn't think I would ever not.

He was so fucking sexy.

His hands were still firmly on my middle, though his thumbs made their way down to the edge of my underwear. Shivers went through my entire body with the anticipation of his hand moving over the material covering me and finally touching me.

"This black lace looks amazing against your skin," he said.

Suddenly he grabbed the top of my panties in one hand, pulling them up, against me, into me. The thin material between my legs went taut against my pussy. At the same time, the thumb of his other hand went to my clit, now fully enlarged and pushing against the lace of my panties.

My moan was loud.

"Fuuuck, Harper," he growled. "You like that, huh?"

All I could do was nod as I held onto his forearms and my head rolled back. He brought me to the border between pleasure and pain. But the scale tipped to pleasure as his thumb rubbed and flicked my sensitive, hard skin that was tight against the lace. He pulled the material up against me; so tight the string of my thong pushed along my ass, creating more intensity.

"Answer me, Harper. Do you like this? Will this make you come?"

"Yes," I moaned. "I love it, Gage. Make me come."

His thumb applied more pressure, the circles getting smaller and smaller as he focused on the sensitive tip of my clit. My fingers dug into his arms as I held onto him, my legs aching to close.

Instead, I pushed my ass against his thighs, trying to drive my body closer to his rock-hard dick. But his hand kept me firmly in place as the orgasm started taking hold of me.

Then I felt him pull the material to the side, just enough for my clit to be exposed. The cool air mixed with the warmth of his touch on my skin was an intoxicating combination. He pulled the edge of my panties against my pussy lips, again that combination of pleasure and pain.

Then he was doing something to me I'd never felt before.

I felt my clit between two of his fingers.

"Oh, my God, Gage, what are you…doing? Fuck!"

My body instinctively rocked back and forth, riding the waves as they started to hit me. My orgasm started off intense without being able to close my legs.

"I'm pinching your clit, Harper," Gage said. "Come for me, baby. Let me watch you come for me."

And that did it.

His words, his hands, all of it combined, sent me over the top. Writhing like an animal as his hand continued its assault on my body. When I couldn't take anymore, my hand covered his and stilled him. Looking down, his smile made me grin right back at him.

But then I collapsed into his arms, and he wrapped me in an embrace.

"I don't think I'll ever get tired of watching that," he whispered.

I giggled as I sat up. "Well, that's good for me, I guess. That was amazing." Pushing back on his legs, I undid the top button on his shirt and continued down the line. "You have too many clothes on."

He sat forward, allowing me to slide his shirt down his arms.

Lifting the white cotton undershirt at the hem, I pulled it over his head.

It was nice to see the chest I'd only been able to dream about. He was all muscle, but not to the point of being bulky. There was the tiniest bit of chest hair, enough to run my fingers through, but not so much it got in the way of tasting him. My hands slid down from his pecs to his torso, the many ab muscles tight due to how he was sitting.

And then there was that perfect V line leading into his boxers, his "sex lines." They were so pronounced it was obvious he worked hard to get them. Running my fingers along them, I was glad to see his skin pebble from my touch.

He was perfect.

"I'm gonna take your pants off now," I told him as I undid his belt and zipper.

"Well, you're not naked yet. I think that needs to happen first."

Standing up and reaching around, I undid my bra, letting it fall from my arms straight to the floor. I caught him staring at me, at my breasts.

"Perfection," he said. "Touch them for me, Harper. Push them together."

Something else he was helping me discover about myself: I apparently liked being told what to do sexually. When he ordered me to do things, the rush of adrenaline it produced in me was surprising.

His eyes were glued to my one hand as it rose from my side, touching my breast, pushing it against the other.

"Pinch your nipples for me, make them hard," he instructed.

I did as he said, and the warmth was already building between my legs again. One hand stayed high, but the other reached between my legs, searching for my clit.

He liked that. As I touched myself, his hand went to his cock, gripping it and rubbing it through the cotton. I watched it grow under his hand and I became hungry for it.

My hands went to the straps of my thong to pull it down, but he stopped me.

"Turn around."

Without question, I did exactly as he said and started pushing them down my thighs.

"Don't let them fall, bend over," he said.

When they got to my knees, I bent at the waist, pushing them further down my legs.

As soon as I did, his finger swiped from my asshole all the way to my clit. And before I could react, his tongue followed the same path.

Just once.

It was torture.

When I was convinced he wasn't going to touch me again, I spun around. And my eyes were drawn to his lap, though now not watching him touching himself.

This time, it was to see that the tip of his cock, at full size, was poking out the top of his boxer briefs.

My swallow may have been audible.

He wagged his finger, beckoning me to come closer. Kneeling on the floor in front of him, I grabbed the waistband of his pants and underwear together and pulled. He lifted his ass, allowing them to slide off easily.

And we were finally both naked.

My instinct was to jump up and sit on him; I wanted to feel his entire body up against mine. But he'd been so selfless up to this point, he deserved more from me.

Inching forward, I got my body up against his spread legs. Leaning over him, my mouth landed on his stomach, my tongue licking across every indent his muscles created. But in doing that, Gage's dick landed right between my breasts.

My hands fell to the sides of each breast, pushing them around his hard cock, as my tongue inched lower and lower.

"Shit," he murmured as I peered up to see him throw his head back against the couch. "Jesus Christ, Harper, that feels amazing."

At that, I sat up, forcing him to sit with me, keeping a firm hold on his cock between my tits. My fingers came together, interlacing around him and me, feeling the bulging veins of him beneath my palms. A rhythm began as my hands slid up and down.

His tip glistened in the light of the fire. I stopped stroking him and held him tight against my chest, bending my neck to reach him. My tongue darted out, licking across the thick head of his cock, taking the precum into my mouth.

"Yes," he moaned.

My lips stayed around him, sucking on the top, my tongue swirling around the tip. The muscles in his legs tensed under me as his hands went to my head.

"Harper," he moaned. "Listen to me, this…I won't last long. I'm fucking you tonight, I am not coming in your mouth. But I need this a little longer."

As soon as he said that, I released the hold my tits had on him and gripped his cock firmly in my hands. It took both hands to hold him entirely.

"I don't think I can take all of you, Gage, but I'll do my best."

"Baby, even if just the tip of me goes in that hot mouth of yours, it will make me almost shoot my load."

Putting his smooth shaft back against my mouth, it stretched wide and opened for him. As I slid my lips down his shaft, it hit the back of my throat only halfway in.

"Holy fuck, Harper!"

His thrusts were slight, because there just wasn't enough room. And as he pumped, the gagging sounds turned him on even more.

"Jesus Christ," he said, pulling himself out of me so quick he was already standing.

I was left sitting on the floor, him above me, drool coming from my lips.

"You're a fucking dream," he said as he reached for my hand, pulling me to stand with him.

His mouth covered mine as he licked my lips dry. He spun us around so that I was close to the couch, and he turned me away from him.

"Be a good girl and get those knees up on the couch and bend over," he said.

Ha, little did he know this was my favorite position.

"I think I can make it work," I said sarcastically. Kneeling on the cushion, I took hold of the back of the couch. In preparation.

"Get my fingers wet, baby," he said right before shoving two of them into my mouth.

Those fingers were then rubbing me at my opening, priming me, getting me ready. But I was already there.

"You're dripping, Harper."

His words were making me wetter.

Then I heard the rip of a foil package and him rolling it into place.

Grabbing me at the hips, he positioned the tip of his cock against me. Rubbing it up and down, he pushed the tip in the slightest bit. The anticipation of him entering me was exhilarating.

My fingers dug into the cushion as my pussy clamped around the intrusion.

"I'm going slow at first."

And he did. He slid himself deep inside me inch by inch until he was fully seated.

I took all of him.

But then he pulled out slightly and pushed himself back in. Still gentle.

But I needed more.

Pushing my ass against him and grinding, he got the message.

"I take it you're ready for me to fuck you, Harper."

"Please, Gage."

He pulled out of me again, more this time, almost all the way. His fingers dug into my hips, gripping my bones.

At the same time, he slammed into me while pulling me onto him. My involuntary moan echoed against the walls of his house. Without stopping, he reared back again, hammering into me over and over again.

The sweetest agony burned between my legs as I pushed against him with every thrust.

"Come up toward me," he grunted between thrusts.

He helped pull me upright, holding me against his torso, an arm around my middle. We balanced ourselves on the edge of the couch as his other hand pulled my head to the side, his mouth landing on my neck, sucking hard. His mouth remained there, while a hand traveled to my breast, squeezing it.

I was, once again, teetering on the edge of pain. A delicious pain that heightened my senses as he drove himself into me.

The need to touch myself, to rub my clit, overcame me. Reaching down, my fingers joined in on the pleasurable assault of my body.

"That is so fucking hot, Harper, Christ," Gage said as he watched me touch myself over my shoulder. His moans grew louder against my neck, more frequent. "Fuck!"

The force of his movements shifted as he pushed my chest onto the couch again. His grip tightened on my hips as he now raised my ass high, pulling and pushing my body every time his cock impaled me.

"Oh…My…God!" I cried out as the peak of my pleasure began rolling through me.

His movements were manic, those of a man starved for his own release.

One more solid thrust, and he stilled. Falling against my back, his body trembled as he came inside me.

Our quick breaths and the crackle of the fire were the only sounds to be heard. A wave of contentment rushed through my entire body as we lay there together. Eventually, he pulled himself out of me and moved to the side but didn't let me out of his hold. Tiny kisses tickled my shoulder blade, and his hand went to the curve of my ass.

We were quiet for a while, so long that I thought he may have fallen asleep. I felt close to sleep myself. Between the wine at dinner, the time, and the sex, I was exhausted. But he started moving next to me, got up, and headed to the bathroom.

When he returned, he snuggled in where he had been, but this time covered us with a blanket.

"I hope this isn't too forward, but I'd like you to stay tonight. I can have my car service bring you home in the morning." The gentle touches never stopped as he talked. "It's kind of late, and to be honest, after that, I don't want to let you go."

A smile formed on my lips of its own accord. I was glad we weren't facing one another. I probably looked like a giddy teenager.

Christ. What were we doing?

CHAPTER 18

Harper

The past two days, I felt as though I'd been floating with every step I took. Tuesday night and into the morning couldn't have gone any better with Gage. And him asking me to spend the night…plus add his sweet text messages since.

Gage - I haven't been able to stop thinking about you

Me - I know, last night was amazing

Gage - Thursday night can't come soon enough

> Gage - Morning beautiful

> Me - Good morning

> Gage - I have a meeting that won't be over until after 6 I'll come by as soon as it's over

> Me - Sounds good

I HADN'T STOPPED SMILING.

The alarm blaring its sunshine-y music in my ear couldn't even bring me down today. And that was saying a lot, considering I took a shift at the club last night, so I'd be working on about four hours of sleep.

The club was an exhausting job, but since it paid so well, I didn't have to work more than three nights a week to make good money there. And my seniority gave me the best nights, Thursday, Friday and Saturday. But Gage had a meeting Wednesday night this week and begged me to try to rearrange my schedule. Turns out, Victoria had exams on Thursday and needed to study Wednesday night, so us switching worked for her as well. So, my rare Thursday night off was going to be spent on a double date with his friends Jared and Delia, which I was excited about.

Inside scoop from friends was important.

Hopping out of bed, I walked into the kitchen and noticed the pink rose in its bud vase, officially on its way to being dead. But I wasn't throwing it out. No, that would be hung to dry.

It had to be preserved. Like the memory, it would always be in my mind.

Dumping the water into my kitchen sink, I carefully hung the stem from the pendant light by my window. Looking up, I noticed the time on the wall clock and realized I had to get going if I was stopping for food.

Finally making it out of my apartment, I raced to the bodega and pushed the door open, expecting to see both Rex and Maria.

But it was only Rex again.

"Hey, Rex, can I have my usual?"

He nodded while I went for my yogurt parfait. As I approached the counter, I knew something was off. His normal smile was missing, and he wasn't even looking at me. Torn between how to proceed, I chose to ask about Maria.

"So where is your better half, Rex?"

When he lifted his head, there were tears in his eyes.

"Oh my God, Rex, what's wrong?" My heart went to my throat as my pulse shot up.

"Oh, mija, she got some bad news," he said as he grabbed a napkin for his eyes and nose. "She's got some cancer." And then his chin fell to his chest. The cries were soft at first, but his shoulders started shaking as the sobs began.

"Rex, oh man," I said, moving around the counter to go to his side. "I'm so sorry, how are the kids doing?" I wrapped my arms around him, and his head fell to my shoulder. But then he sat back on his stool, a big sigh coming from him.

"We haven't told them yet, but they'll figure something out soon. She's so tired and not really eating. And…" He paused.

And I waited.

"We don't have insurance," he said. And his tears started falling again.

Of course they didn't, he owned this place and was self-employed. I was sure they barely made it by with the amount of business his store did. But I knew from when my dad was sick that there were programs out there for situations just like this.

"Rex, have you looked into any hospitals or doctors that might still treat Maria even though you're not insured?"

He shook his head. But he didn't need me giving him false hope, either. I decided I would do some research, look for myself and find out what I could for them.

"I'm so sorry, Rex, please let me know if I can do anything."

I slapped a twenty on the counter, grabbed my breakfast, and walked out the door.

I would look into this for them. Cancer was not always a death sentence and maybe I could make a difference.

For them, anyway.

Fiona was already at the shop when I got there. We had a big wedding to get ready for on Saturday and would be very busy these next two days.

Weddings were probably my favorite floral designs to create. Aside from the brides usually being very creative, I loved knowing where they were headed once we made them. And this one was a barn theme, my absolute favorite. All the bouquets and table pieces were wildflowers.

"Fiona, I'm here," I screamed to the back. "I'm going to set up in the front and get started on the tablescapes."

There were some noises from the back, but no response from her. I went to the refrigerators and started pulling the stems I needed to make the arrangements when I heard her struggling with something. Looking up, I saw her carrying a huge basket of what looked like some kind of fruit. I ran and grabbed it from her arms, placing it on the table.

"What on earth is this?" I asked her.

"You tell me, it came just a few minutes ago, for you." She handed me a card with my name on it. "Well, open it. I'm dying to know who it's from."

Of course, I most likely knew. And I wasn't sure I wanted her to know we had seen each other again. But it didn't seem I had a choice.

> *Harper,*
>
> *What to send the most beautiful girl who works in a flower shop? Can't send her real flowers, so I sent you 'fruit-flowers.' I hope you enjoy them. I'm sure they're not as pretty as what you create. And maybe save some of those strawberries, I can think of something fun we can do with those...*
>
> *Gage*

THE HEAT WENT from my cheeks to my chest. There was no way I was reading this out loud to her.

"I'm guessing you're still seeing our Mr. Parker?"

I was conflicted about answering her, but she would know if I was lying.

"Are you okay with it if I am?"

She stopped shuffling the papers she was organizing and stared at me.

"Why wouldn't I be?" she asked.

Plopping on a stool, I popped a piece of the pineapple from one of the flowers in front of me. It was perfectly soft and sweet. "Eat some. This will go bad before I can finish it all."

She sat next to me, and we continued snacking on the fruit flowers in an uncomfortable silence.

"He's a client, I didn't know if you'd be upset with me for

seeing him. I mean, it's so new, we've only seen each other…a few times."

"Sweetie," she said. "First of all, you're both adults. Regardless of what happens, I think he's mature enough to handle things here appropriately. Second, Christ, he's a sex god, you deserve this and I'm happy for you, Harper." Standing, she grabbed my cheeks in her hands, giving them a squeeze. "You two must make quite the couple when together."

I SPENT my lunch hour on the computer doing research about hospitals in New York City that treat cancer for people without insurance. It turned out that there were several options—New York Presbyterian even had a program. I printed out the contact information for Rex and Maria and made a mental note to drop it off on my way home.

And as expected, the day flew by with how busy we were. In addition to the wedding prep we had, there were ten walk-in orders as well as a corporate account to get started on. Fiona was going to have to think about hiring more help. We weren't going to be able to keep up with these orders if any more work came in with us and the couple of afternoon high school kids.

And I'd like to start training someone for her so when I leave, she's not left in a lurch.

"Fiona, I'm taking off. I have a date tonight!" I yelled to the back room. We were closed, but she would be there for hours.

"Have fun, girl! Make sure to have sex more than once each time you're with him, that's my tip. Because it won't happen when you get older." She started cackling to herself and then the music turned up louder.

Huh, more than once each time.

We would have to get on that.

Fiona liked for me to lock the front door on my way out since she was working in the back. Once I did, I grabbed my bag from the ground and spun on my heels to start my walk home. I needed to hurry to have enough time to freshen up.

"Hey, beautiful."

I knew that voice. It did things to my insides. Turned them to mush.

Looking around, I found it coming from a rolled-down window of a limousine. He was opening the door as I walked toward the car.

"What are you doing?"

"What do you mean? I'm picking up my girl for our date. Meeting got cancelled so I thought I'd swing by and get you home quicker so you could get changed. And we could use the car to go to the restaurant then, too."

I don't know about a car being quicker in the city, but he already had me in his arms, his caramel speckled brown eyes staring into mine. His perfectly manicured beard was begging for me to drag my nails through it. So, no complaints.

Plus, the driver of the limo was now holding the door for us.

"Thank you, Thomas," Gage said as he led me to the backseat.

Settling in and looking around, I realized this was my first time in a limo. From the sound of it, however, it was not Gage's.

"Thomas, this is Harper."

The driver smiled in his rearview mirror as I waved through the opening separating front to back.

"Is this *your* limo?" I whispered.

He grabbed my hand, rubbing small circles on the back of it with his thumb.

"Mmhmm," he said. "Thanks for agreeing to go out with Jared and his girlfriend tonight, he's been on my case to do it since meeting you at the bar. He said he wanted to be able to 'officially' get to know you since he was put on babysitting duties that night."

I felt shitty about that. It wasn't fair that he was left with that responsibility simply because Victoria and I were drunk. An apology was in order.

"Oh, Thomas! I'm sorry, can you stop here real quick? I need to drop something off." We were right in front of Rex's, stopped in traffic anyway. Hopping out of the car, I ran to the door, but it was locked. Very unusual for this time of night. I decided to slide the papers I printed for him under the door in case I didn't get in to see him in the morning. They were in a folder with a note on top.

When I got back in the car, Gage's look was full of questions.

"Rex, you remember him, our yogurt fiasco? Well, his wife is sick, and they don't have insurance. I researched some doctors and hospitals in the city they could contact."

Leaning into me, he placed a gentle kiss on my temple. His hand came to my face, cradling my cheek, our heads touching. My insides were melting with every touch of his.

"Of course you did. I knew you were special," he said.

My confusion must have shown as my head shook slightly at his comment.

"And you're even more special that you don't even realize why," he whispered against my lips. "Let's get to your place and both get changed. I want to get to dinner and show you off."

Most NYC apartments were tiny, mine was no exception. And I was not embarrassed by it one bit. I worked hard for every dollar I used to pay its rent.

But as Gage and I ran up the stairs together, I wondered if he'd ever been in one so small. After seeing his home, this could only be described as insignificant.

Opening the door, I did a quick scan and was happy the only

issue was I didn't make my bed. There were no dishes in the sink, no dirty clothes on the floor. Odd for me, but a lucky day.

But that was the thing.

I could see all of that from my front door.

"Welcome," I said. "This is literally the epitome of a humble abode."

He looked around the space, walking up the table of pictures, looking at them all. Then he found the corner filled with my plants and flowers.

"Those are interesting," he said.

"Those are my plant babies."

"Plant babies?" he asked as he looked at each one. "Why are they planted in all these different containers?"

Walking over, I looked at each one with admiration. I couldn't wait to go thrifting for my next container.

"Well, I like to rehome discarded things and use them as planters. I like to think I have a vision for it. Take this teapot, for example. The hole on the side is the perfect spot for a new stem for a flower to grow through."

"They're cool," he replied.

He continued his cordial survey of my studio, but I decided to cut him some slack. He didn't have to truly appreciate my love of quirky plantings just because I did.

"I'm assuming you're changing too?" I pointed to the bag he brought upstairs with us.

"It's a bar-type place, no need for the suit."

"Okay, well, you can use the bathroom if you want," I told him.

He threw his bag on my couch and stalked toward me as he removed his jacket. "Are you telling me you've become shy now, after what we've already done?" His chuckle was downright seductive. "Harper, there's no way I was waiting in the car while I knew you were up here, taking off your clothes without me. That's why I'm here, to witness the beauty of Harper Wilson again."

He reached out to the hem of my sweatshirt, pulling it up and over my head. Problem was, I wasn't expecting him to see me like this, under my clothes. My hands went to cover myself up.

"What are you doing?" he asked, pulling my hands from my chest.

"I wasn't really prepared for this. I'm in a sports bra, Gage, not very sexy."

Taking me by the hands and spreading out my arms, he stepped back and looked me up and down.

"Harper, anything you wear you're sexy in," he said, moving closer. His finger went to the curve of my breast at the top of the cotton material. "This right here, how your breast is peeking out the top, that's fucking sexy. And your neck," he said with a growl. His mouth was on me in his next breath, sucking and licking behind my ear.

Within seconds, we both had the rest of our clothes off, shirts and pants flying across the room. As he stalked toward me, I watched him roll the condom over the top of his rock-hard dick.

As I watched him, I realized how much I loved that we were just doing this. Out of nowhere. With his driver waiting for us downstairs.

His hands went under my ass, and he lifted me against him as I wrapped my legs around his waist. Finding the closest wall, he slammed me up against it as his mouth devoured mine. His one hand slid between my legs, finding my entrance, pushing inside.

"I love how wet you get for me," he said, moaning into my mouth.

"Only for you, Gage."

"Fuck, Harper," he said as he reached below and gripped his

rock-hard cock. Using the wall and one arm to support me, he guided himself into me, slowly.

The stretch was painfully perfect.

Neither of us cared what I was wearing.

No one paid any attention to the unmade bed.

Nothing was said about the fact that my living room and bedroom were in the same space.

None of that mattered.

Only we mattered.

Walking into the bar, I was happy to see it was as casual as Gage said it would be. Comfortable now in my jeans, I relaxed into his hold as he guided me through the place. Eventually, I saw the guy I knew to be Jared and a beautiful blonde sitting with him. He stood up when we got to the table.

"Gage, Harper, you guys finally made it," he scoffed.

Gage and I shared a silly, conspiratorial grin, his hand on my ass giving it a firm squeeze. Was the look on my face a dead give-away that I had just orgasmed all over his dick? I hoped not.

Jared came around the table, engulfing me in a hug.

"Harper," he said as he pulled back. "This is my better half, Delia."

His gaze fell upon the tall beauty who was coming out of Gage's hug. She turned to me with open arms and pulled me in, holding on with a ferocity that surprised me.

"I've heard a lot about you already," she said, almost in a whisper as we pulled apart. "Come, sit next to me, we have to be able to talk without shouting across the table."

The dinner conversation was light and simple. We drank and ate and drank some more. I learned that Jared and Delia met once he moved to New York, that she was also a lawyer, and that they'd lived together for almost a year now.

Learning that the guys met in college was a treat, because Jared was more than willing to share lots of stories about Gage from their days at Blue Ridge University together. Frat parties, old girlfriends, spring breaks gone awry. The stories were endless.

"Where did you go to school, Harper?" Delia asked.

"I went to a small state school in New Jersey, got my business degree there."

I didn't want to get the same questions I always got: Why do you work in a flower shop? Why do you serve in a club? You have a college degree, when are you going to use it? So, my standard reply, a rehearsed speech by this point, started coming out.

"My dream is to own and open my own flower shop one day," I said. "I worked at one during high school, and college, part-time for money. And I got hooked. I learned a lot from the floral designer I worked with in high school. And now with Fiona, well, I couldn't have a better teacher. But I wanted the business degree, so I'd know what I'm doing when I finally have the money to do that."

"That's awesome, Harper," Delia said. "I want to come by the shop you're working at now and see some of what you do."

Delia and I fell into a conversation about a few things privately while Gage and Jared talked about sports or something. But I caught Gage looking at me while they were talking, a pensive look on his face.

Eventually, it was late enough to call it a night. Standing up from the table, we said our goodbyes.

As Jared came to give me a hug, I offered my apology.

"Hey, Delia is great. And I wanted to apologize for leaving you with Victoria last week. I don't usually drink that much, neither does she."

"Listen, I see something in you, in you and Gage. If me taking her home gave you guys a chance to do whatever the hell you did, all good. My pleasure, Harper."

Nodding and smiling, I made my way to Gage. Jared and Delia started walking after we said our final goodbyes on the street, and then, like magic, Thomas and the limo showed up.

"It's not a night we can usually spend together, but do you want to come over? You can spend the whole day at my place tomorrow if you want. Maybe use the hot tub, and I can come home for lunch."

I loved that he knew my schedules, for both my jobs. Sometimes I couldn't even keep track, but he knew my days on and off by heart already.

A quick thought of us moving too fast flickered in my brain, but I forced it away. I was the one that moved us along. We were adults. Not even that young anymore. I was allowed to do what I wanted to do.

"I'd like that."

We climbed in the car, and he pulled my legs onto his lap, taking my shoes off.

The foot rubs started early with him. As soon as he learned how much my feet hurt from being on my feet all day and night, he spoiled me.

"Ahh," I said, leaning into the corner of the long bench seat. My eyes closed and I felt as though I could fall asleep. "I like your friends, Gage. They seem like good people."

He clucked in approval. "They are. Jared and I are like brothers. And Delia is great. She's perfect for him. I think they'll make it."

It was nice to see a healthy couple in the flesh. They did seem to be the type that could last. "I got Delia's number, too. She seems really cool. If we can find some time, her and I might get together."

He sat quiet against the seat as he continued to rub my feet.

"So, I didn't know you wanted to open your own shop," he said. "That's ambitious. I can, uh, help you with your business model if you need it."

My eyes opened, but I didn't move because I didn't want to run the risk of his hands stopping the divine work they were doing.

"I'd love some advice from you. Anything to help me get there. It seems like it's never going to happen." The lament in my voice was a bit dramatic, but by twenty-seven years old, I thought I'd already be doing what I had planned for myself.

I'd be a fool to turn down help from a billionaire business mogul.

CHAPTER 19

Gage

We'd fallen into a routine, Harper and me. We spent Sundays together, since she was off from both her jobs on Mondays. She took her time getting up and out, and I have to say, I loved seeing her in my bed as I left for work. Monday nights were usually good for us both, so we either went out or brought food in. She was off from the shop on Fridays, too, so I did my best to meet her for lunch.

It was nice. And some might think we were moving quickly, but I felt that our pace was just right—for us.

But then we decided we should spend more time as a couple with our friends instead of holed up alone in my brownstone.

Our plans today included a day with Jared and Delia at Coney Island, specifically to do go-karts. It was something Jared and I had been wanting to do, and the girls were on board. I wasn't sure if they agreed just to make us happy, but it did exactly that.

Jared and I were definitely like little kids when it came to our downtime activities. We both enjoyed golf, softball, going to the gym, basically anything physical.

But to top it off, we were competitive as shit.

Today could get messy. Harper hadn't seen this side of me yet, and I hoped after she witnessed how he and I got when we competed, she didn't want to just walk right away.

"Are we seriously taking the subway?" Harper asked. The incredulity in her voice startled me.

"Yes," I answered with a finality in my voice. "Why?"

Her voice went higher when she answered, giving a look of innocence. "Nothing."

Her *nothing* definitely did not mean nothing.

So, I continued to stare at her as we stood across from each other, my kitchen island between us. I'd been packing a backpack with some snacks and water bottles for the day, thinking we might want to sit on the beach if the weather held up. When she continued to say nothing, I stopped packing the bag until my stare got her attention.

"Well," she started. But the pause was followed by her shrugging her shoulders. "I don't know, all we've done so far is use your limo and Thomas. I just didn't think it was 'your thing.'"

And she used the air quotes.

"My *thing*?" I questioned. But I realized she was right. One hundred percent correct. Not sure if it was an unconscious thing, like I was low-key trying to impress her. Or maybe I'd just been overly busy since meeting her and recently getting back in the groove at work. But thus far, we'd only used Thomas to get around the city. "Well, I do get around like other people a lot of the time. It just hasn't happened much since we've met."

I thought my answer would satisfy her, but instead, she still looked thoughtful. I didn't want this to turn into something it didn't need to be, so I let it go.

"I'm looking forward to our day together, what about you?" I asked as I closed my bag. We were meeting Jared and Delia down the street at the subway station in fifteen minutes, so we needed to start heading out. I reached for Harper, my arm going around her waist as I pulled her against me. Her arms wrapped around my middle and her head fell against my chest.

"I am," she said, looking up at me. "I really like Jared and Delia. And believe it or not, even though I've lived in New York for five years, I still haven't been to Coney Island."

"Seriously?" I asked. "Well, then let's get going. It's iconic, and even though we're really going for the karts, I think I'll have to get you on the Cyclone. You do like roller coasters, don't you? I'm not sure this will work if you don't."

Her laugh filled the room, and I caught a glimpse of her dimple at the same time. I wasn't prepared for the warm feeling that consumed me hearing and seeing both.

"Lucky for me, and us, I love roller coasters," she said as she turned out of my hold. "C'mon, we're gonna be late."

Jared and Delia were at the corner as we arrived, and we all walked down the stairs to the subway station. I loved seeing how Harper and Delia ran to each other on the street and walked arm in arm toward our train.

"So, things seem to be going pretty well between the two of you for someone who said he swore off relationships," Jared chided. We hung back as the girls walked ahead.

"Yeah, well, we both know me, don't we?" I answered.

As hard as I may try, I wasn't built for casual or even short term. I was a perfect case study for some psychology student somewhere. But the best part was, I think I found my match in that department with Harper.

"I really like her, we've been having a good time," I told him. But I was playing it down. I more than *liked* her. At least, it was headed in that direction. And for some reason, I wasn't scared. With my recent past, I probably should've been, but everything seemed right with her.

"Well, then I'm happy for you, man. You deserve it after what Rebecca put you through. Just don't get totally swept away, I guess," he said, a bit of a warning in his voice.

The girls were up ahead, already through the turnstile, as he and I joined them waiting for the Q to arrive. The hour-long train ride to Brooklyn wasn't much longer than taking a car, so it made sense.

Delia and Harper were giggling and whispering to one another, about what, I had no idea. But it was cute to watch. I was happy to see them connecting, getting along. Harper said often that she doesn't fit into my world. But seeing her here, with me and my friends today, I knew there was no other place she belonged.

I knew I would heed the warning Jared gave. I was working so hard to stay vigilant about my feelings, not letting myself get too carried away. But all I saw as I looked at Harper was someone I could spend the rest of my life with. And maybe the timing wasn't the best. If I were being truly cautious, I'd take more time to heal from the divorce. But I wasn't about to let her walk away from me, either. The past weeks we'd been spent together had been amazing.

More than amazing.

"Gage, c'mon!" she yelled as she ran to me and grabbed my hand. "The train is coming."

Her smile was wide and her eyes bright as she looked up at me. I was oblivious to the smell of piss that surrounded us and the garbage down here in the underground station. She made all of that disappear.

She seemed to make so many of the unpleasant things in my life take a backseat.

And I wanted to see where it went.

CHAPTER 20

Harper

"Oh, think again! I'm not going to let you catch me!" I screamed over my shoulder to Gage. His go-kart was about to bump into mine as my pedal was pushed to the floor in a fruitless attempt to speed away from him. His laughter rang out above the roar of the engines as he pulled around the side of me, racing by. "You bastard!" I yelled at him as he sped past.

"Just keep up, babe, you and I are still beating the two slow pokes behind us," he yelled back.

We'd been competing as teams, and this was the tiebreaker. Gage and Jared weren't lying when they said they were competitive. But I fell into the trap of it with them as the day went on.

Delia and Jared were dealt two dud cars on this last run, and I was okay with that as Gage and I rounded the last turn of the course. We raced past the line as our time ran out, and our friends hadn't even made it to the last curve. Their frustration was clear on their faces as they pulled their karts into the line to park.

"You've got to be fucking kidding me," Jared complained. "This doesn't count, man. We had the worst cars out there."

"Hey, ya get what ya get, man," Gage countered.

Delia was chuckling as she stood from her car, her and I walking away from what we knew would now become a heated discussion between the best friends.

They were literally talking like little kids.

But I loved it. I loved seeing how they got along and the love they had for each other. It showed me a side of Gage I was unfamiliar with, and I liked what I was seeing. He was laid back today. Away from work, he was able to kick back and have fun.

"He really likes you," Delia said, interrupting my thoughts as we made our way to the exit. "I've been around for a while. Long enough to see him with others, and he's different with you."

Her words struck me, but I wasn't exactly sure how to respond to them, so I remained quiet as she and I walked through the gate.

"I mean in a good way," she continued, in tune with my silence. "Such a good way."

She took my arm in hers as we walked toward the towering roller coasters on the boardwalk. The sun was low in the sky, soon to set, as we made our way to the pier. Delia's small laugh as she continued talking made me look her way.

"Gage is not your typical guy when it comes to girls," she said.

"Oh really, in what way?" She had piqued my interest.

But just then, the guys came swooping in behind us. I'd have to wait to find out what she meant.

"Let's go, you two!" Gage hollered. "We need to get in line for the Cyclone again before it gets any longer." He grabbed my hand, pulling me along, Jared doing the same with Delia. The four of us ran to the queue for the ride like teenagers, laughing and out of breath. Once we came to a stop, Gage pulled me into his arms as he leaned against the metal railing.

"Having fun?" he whispered against my ear.

Nodding, I pulled away to answer him. "I'm having the best time. Today has been amazing."

His finger came to the side of my face, the tip touching the center of my cheek. "It must be a good day if it brought out your dimple," he said. "I love seeing it. It makes me happy when you're happy."

And that was just another example of what he'd been doing lately to make me think this could be…real.

Not just real, but long-term and real.

The guy who came across as Mr. Grumpy in the beginning was nothing but Mr. Softy in the end.

The entire day had been perfect. From him planning it, to us spending time on the beach, go-karts, and now the rides. We ate every imaginable bad food they offered, my favorite being cotton candy. The remnants of it were still stuck to the beds of my fingernails.

But day turned into night, and everything was shutting down. It was time for us to catch a train back home. The train was already coming as we got to the station, so we were booking it.

"Shit, are we gonna make it?" Delia squealed as we struggled to swipe our cards at the turnstile.

The four of us made it through and onto the train just in the nick of time. But as the doors were about to close, my eye caught sight of something under a bench. I made a move to exit the train but thought better of it.

"What is it, Harper?" Gage asked as we found some seats.

"Oh, nothing,"

But he kept looking at me.

"I, um saw something I would have liked to grab for a planter, that's all. It looked like something I've been looking for."

He sat back against the window, peering back toward the station we just left.

"What was it?" he asked.

Shaking my head, I really didn't want to tell him. But his persistent eyes told me he wasn't going to let it go. "It looked like one of those old metal lunch boxes, ya know, from when we were kids."

"Oh yeah," he said. "I never had one, but I remember some kids did."

We both fell silent after that, his arm coming around my shoulder. I knew I was tired from our day, and I was fully prepared to fall asleep against him for the hour ride.

Which I did. And it was a blissful sleep.

WAKING up in my own bed without Gage felt weird the next morning. But I had to be in the shop, and he had an early meeting, so we'd decided it was best. But it was odd to miss him already.

Running for the door, because of course I was running late, I almost tripped on a box in the hall. Looking down, I was surprised to see a bunch of beautiful, puffy pink peonies sticking out of the small brown box. Bringing it inside, I realized there was something else in the box with the flowers. Lifting it out, I was stunned.

It was a rusted, dented Marvel lunch box.

I was pretty sure it was the exact one from the Coney Island station I saw last night.

How the heck?

But I didn't have time to process any of it. I made sure the flowers had enough water and got myself to the shop.

As the bell alerted Fiona I'd arrived, she came from the back room.

"Morning." But the word was exaggerated, dragged out, as if she had something on her mind.

Something to say.

"Morning?" I responded, the question clear in my voice.

And we both stood, standing across from one another, as if in a standoff. One waiting on the other.

I gave in.

"Okay, what's going on?" I asked.

Her conspiratorial grin was aggravating as she started walking away from me.

"Uh-uh, not so fast. You don't get to act like this and just ignore me," I told her.

"Well," she started. She'd stopped her retreat and turned to face me, her silly grin still plastered on her face. "I had a visitor not too long ago, thought you might have some news for me, that's all."

Holy shit.

He came here for the flowers?

"A visitor?" I tried to play dumb, but the grin that formed on my face, I just couldn't hide it.

"Yep, a visitor. For pink peonies. And he texted me to come in early, can you believe that?"

But she wasn't mad. Not in the least. On the contrary, her smile rivaled mine.

My steps felt as if I were floating as I started making my way to the wooden table, not sure how I was going to work. My mind couldn't focus.

"Oh, and Harper," Fiona said as she was heading to the back room. "I think you can close your eyes with this one now. He seems like a keeper."

CHAPTER 21

Gage

"Hey, dick, what's up?" Chase asked as he came barging into my office. His typical behavior. His intrusion startled me from my thoughts. And I realized we hadn't touched base since he and Maryellen made the trip to BRU for the endowment dinner a couple weeks ago.

That was Maryellen's little idea. She tagged along to keep an eye on him and help with his responsibilities there. We decided it would make more sense for her to go rather than his assistant since she was familiar with the campus.

"Hey, how did it go in Virginia? Was the board satisfied with our contribution this year?"

He went to the bar and poured himself a drink before sitting in the chair by my desk. There was something that seemed…different about him. He looked more relaxed, a little happier.

But his day drinking was getting to me. The thought of having to talk to him about it ran through my mind.

"Yeah, they were all good." He sat back, looking at his phone, appearing to stall. "More than good, they were thrilled with our contribution and quite pleased with my speech as well."

Looking up, I gave him a quick smile.

"Good to hear. I've got a meeting to prep for. Was there anything else you needed?"

Draining his drink, he placed the glass on my desk. As he leaned forward, a seriousness veiled his face.

"Um, so yeah, that's a pretty nice campus. You have a nice school you went to. Can't believe I never visited you while you were down there."

What was he getting at?

"And?"

He stood, looking like he was going to leave, but turned toward me instead.

"So, they had some speakers at the dinner. Some big wigs with the school, but some student leaders as well. One was this chick who was president of some business fraternity."

Shit.

"She was expecting you at the dinner, not me," Chase said. "It was that girl on your phone, man."

Leaning back in my chair, I digested that bit of information. And I waited to see how it made me feel. Chase was staring, likely waiting for the same thing.

I hadn't thought about "you know who" in weeks as well. Considering Chase had been in Virginia, in her world, and not a single thought of her passed through my mind stunned me. Coupled with how well Harper and I had been doing, it was a win-win.

Surprisingly, I felt nothing.

Maybe a bit of flattery that she was seeking me out. But my heart didn't hurt.

"How is she? Did she seem happy?" I asked.

Chase sat down again, almost in relief, relaxing against the chair.

"I don't know, man, we didn't exchange numbers or anything. She seemed fine, I guess. I mean, she had a guy waiting for her after her speech."

Ty. She was still with Ty. That was good. I wanted her to be happy.

Getting up from my desk, I grabbed Chase's glass and walked to the bar. But instead of reaching for the bottle of Blanton's I kept out, I opened the cabinet and pulled out the bottle I'd only tasted once before. Even though he'd already had a drink, this moment was worth celebrating.

"Pappy?" Chase declared. "You're pulling out the Pappy?" He came up next to me at the bar, his hands rubbing together in excitement. "And why are you having a drink?"

Dumping the contents of his glass in the sink, I made two drinks, one less generous for him.

"Always neat," I told him as I handed him his.

We walked to my sitting area and sat across from each other, our drinks patiently waiting in our hands.

"So, brother, what's the occasion?" he asked.

Now that I'd poured the bourbon, I realized I was going to have to tell him. But I was proud of him as well, so I'd start with that.

"A couple things. I'm happy how things went for you on the trip. It sounds like you handled things with the board down there well."

Holding my glass out, the crystal of our glasses clinked, and I took a sip. The burn as it went down opened the taste buds for me, letting in the caramel and clove flavors. Among the best I'd tasted.

"Chase, make sure you do not chug this, please."

He took a sip, and his reaction told me he understood why. His eyes lit up as he swirled it in his glass, watching the brown liquid spin around.

"This is fucking fantastic," he said.

My brother was growing up.

"Yeah, anyway, I'm happy about the trip. I want to start giving you more responsibility, hopefully more in line with what you're comfortable doing. Do you think you're ready?"

He sat back against the couch, mulling over my question. That was not the reaction I was expecting. Eventually, he turned to me.

"Yeah," he said.

"Also, I had something else I wanted to tell you, and I guess kind of celebrate. I'm seeing Harper."

With this news, his face lit up. He held his glass out to me.

"Cheers, dude!" he said.

As our glasses hit again, he jumped up, unable to contain his excitement.

"You're not mad at me?" I asked. "I went against everything I told you not to do."

The smug smile that unfolded on his face spoke volumes. "You really think I didn't know what you were up to? The fact that it wasn't just a hookup for you is what makes me happy, man. I knew it! I called it that night at the club, didn't I?"

It was a nice moment for us. We didn't have too many of these anymore.

Our father tried to keep us happy, us boys. But he was always too invested in this company. Once Mom left, and it was just the guys, our father really didn't know how to parent alone.

Not that our mother was parent of the year. Far from it. But she was slightly better at it than he was.

But then she did what she did.

She walked out. On all of us.

For another man.

And another family.

And left us behind.

But that was almost fifteen years ago. And Dad was gone most of the time now, too. Plus, I didn't think Chase had finished growing up. I was left with a brother as a business partner who wasn't quite equipped to help run a billion-dollar company.

"Yes, you did, brother. And I'm pretty happy. I mean, it's only been like six weeks, but it's been good. So, when you come back from BRU with news of Becca and I'm okay with it, it's reason for a drink."

A contemplative look settled over him as we sat in silence, sipping our bourbon.

"Becca," he said. "Yeah, didn't know that was her name before meeting her. Got a thing for that name I guess, huh?" he said, then chuckled. "She's pretty young, yeah?" I wasn't sure if that was judgment in his tone.

"Yeah, the name thing threw me in the beginning. And she wasn't a mistake," I told him, assuming that was what he thought. I would never call Becca a mistake; we were never meant to be. But she showed me I could let my walls down, the ones I built up after Rebecca.

And that was it.

That was what Becca did for me. And that meant a lot. Because if I hadn't come to that realization, I don't think I would be opening myself up for what might happen with Harper and me.

"So, hey, Jared and I are going to the Velvet Rope tonight. Wanna come?"

Watching him throw back the rest of his drink in one gulp hurt my heart a little. But it lasting as long as it did was an improvement for him. He wasn't ready for the big boy stuff yet.

"You caught me on a Friday night with no plans, brother."

Standing from the couch, I joined him, now quite behind in preparing for my meeting.

"Heading there to keep watch on your girl?" he asked.

"What? Fuck no, I liked the place and wanna go back."

He started walking out, talking as he was.

"Sure, brother, sure. I'll see you there."

As JARED and I arrived at the club, I regretted not telling Harper I was coming. Just showing up at her place of work might not come across as endearing as I'd like it to. And what Chase said earlier had been stuck in my head ever since.

"Wow, this place is packed," Jared said as we walked around the corner from where Thomas dropped us off.

And it was. There was a line to get in. Walking to one of the bouncers, I asked a few questions, and he pointed around back. Handing him some money, I returned to Jared.

"C'mon," I said to him.

"Where we going?"

"Back entrance. Amazing what a couple hundred bucks'll do."

Jared started laughing out loud behind me.

"What?" I asked, continuing to walk behind the building.

"You're not too proud to buy yourself in, but you won't go in the front door?"

Jared knew me better than that. He knew even though I enjoyed the lifestyle the money provided for me, I didn't like to flaunt it. Walking into the club, ahead of all those people, was a dick move.

So, instead, we took the back door. No one needed to know. By the time we got to it, another bouncer was holding it open for us.

"Thanks, man," I said, handing him a hundred of his own.

It may have been a back entrance, but it took us right into the action. It was a side door off the main dance floor and no wonder they weren't letting anyone in at the moment. It was shoulder-to-shoulder in here.

"Let's see if there are any tables," I said. "If not, we'll head to the bar."

How the hell did Harper serve in this place? I could barely move between people, and I was holding nothing in my hands. But there were no servers anywhere near the dance floor, sticking to the perimeter near the tables.

I continued looking for a table, but there was nothing. So, I made a hard right and worked my way through the crowd toward the bar. Most people were waiting in line for a drink, not looking to sit. We found two seats at one end and grabbed them. It wasn't ideal because our backs would be to the club, making it harder to look for her.

"We don't get out enough, I guess. Either that or this was never really my scene," Jared said.

He and I were definitely more sports bar kind of guys. I didn't like the dance music they played here, nor did I dance. So, I concurred, this was not my scene.

But Harper was there.

And I was hoping she was on the floor tonight. It would really suck if she was in a lounge upstairs and I was stuck down here.

My phone pinged.

Chase - You inside? The line is around the corner

> Me - Go to the bouncer with the buzz cut, tell him you're with me and give him a C-note

"CHASE IS HERE, should be in soon," I told Jared.

Finally, a bartender came around.

"What can I get you?"

Jared ordered us two draft beers while I spun around, taking in our surroundings. And hopeful to catch a glimpse of some dirty-blonde hair or blue eyes. Scanning the entire room, I didn't see her anywhere. Discouraged, I turned around, grabbed my beer, and faced Jared.

"She might be upstairs tonight."

He stood in front of his chair, leaning against the bar top, looking around while drinking his beer. "Maybe she can help you," he said, pointing across the bar with his glass.

A big blonde bun was bouncing up and down, her hand waving erratically at the two of us.

"Did Harper say she goes to NYU?" Jared asked, shaking his head. "She doesn't seem the type."

But she did go to NYU, and she was headed our way, with a wide smile on her red lips.

"Oh my God! What are you guys doing here? Does Harper know you're here?" The strength with which she held onto my arm surprised me. Then she was twisting and turning, apparently looking for Harper. "I have to find her," she said, looking me straight in the eye. "I'll be right back, don't move."

She was like a tornado.

But at least she was finding Harper, so that meant Harper was on the floor and not upstairs.

"How was Victoria when you took her home that night?" I asked Jared.

"Actually, surprisingly nice, and easy to talk to. She seems to have two sides to her."

Suddenly, heavy hands landed on my shoulders, pushing down on me. Jared's face lit up into a shit-eating grin, so I knew who it was. Turning around, a familiar face wrapped his arm around my neck before I could get away.

"This place is crazy, brother," Chase said. "You must be dead set on checking up on your girl."

"Shut up, man," I said, shoving his arm off me.

That was not what I was doing.

Was it?

But Jared and Chase shared a look, and it pissed me off more. Ignoring them, I turned my attention back to the people around us, looking for either Harper or Victoria. But with so many people crowding the bar, I'd never see them approaching. Instead, I drowned my frustration in my beer, draining it and slamming the glass to the bar.

Chase and Jared rattled on next to me about work shit. But my eyes couldn't stop scanning the crowd, hungry to find her.

And then I did.

Her smile lit up the room from halfway across the dance floor. She worked her way to us. But literally was "working" her way to us. People were stopping her, and she was taking orders as she made her way to the bar.

On her final approach, she looked at nothing but me, our connection strong as she barreled through the last remaining people between us. Launching herself into my arms, I caught her around the middle, squeezing her.

She felt like home.

"Oh my God," she whispered into my ear. "What are you doing here?"

I put her to her feet, though the loss of her in my arms hurt a bit.

"Couldn't go another night without seeing you, beautiful."

Her smile did something to me, especially with those lips

painted hot pink. I leaned close to her cheek, talking quietly against her ear. "Your pink lips are fucking turning me on, Harper."

I loved when she had her hair up in one of those messy knot things on the top of her head, with pieces falling out everywhere. Paired with her makeup and uniform, she had that just-sexed look.

Her hand discreetly landed on my cock.

And my head rolled back in my attempt to not react.

"Hey guys," she said to Chase and Jared. "Come with me, I think I can get you set up with a table in my section." She grabbed my hand as we followed behind.

She was working a back corner of the room, off the side of the dance floor, and there were some booths and standing tables. She got to work clearing half empties from a tall table while we claimed it with Chase and Jared's drinks.

Her tray was full when she turned to us. "Can I get you guys anything? Food?"

They looked at me as if I were the warden.

"Get what you want, boys. I got what I came for," I told them. Turning to Harper, I gripped her empty hand, pulling her closer. "Can I steal you for a minute?"

Her big blue eyes stared up into mine.

"Give me a few minutes," she said.

Too distracted by her eyes, her ass, and what the rest of her was doing to me, I attempted to entertain myself by watching the dance floor. But it wasn't working. Harper took a food order from Chase, then left for the kitchen. All I could do was steal glances of her, especially as she walked away.

"You've got it bad, brother," Chase said.

Looking around for a drink, I realized I'd finished my beer when we were at the bar.

"But she's not a bad one to have it bad for. She's hot and she seems cool," he added as he leaned against the high top next to me. "I, uh, guess I still owe her an apology."

Harper returned with a tray full of drinks and food for us. She placed a highball glass full of bourbon I hadn't ordered in front of me. She put beers in front of the guys, plus a plate of nachos and some wings. The guys dug in to the food and drinks.

She scurried away, though, taking care of other customers. Bouncing from table to table, I was forced to watch guy after guy flirting with her. They would stand next to her, come up close, some would even put their arm around her. She was good at maneuvering out of their hold, but it was frustrating to watch.

But then one guy got really close. He followed her as she left his table, and I could tell it annoyed her. She turned to talk to him, seemed to point to his table, maybe telling him to go back and wait. It took everything in me to not go to her side and help her.

As she turned from him, though, he continued to walk next to her.

And then his hand went to her ass.

Harper froze.

And I stiffened.

But then I saw her hand go to the air, three fingers held high.

And within seconds, two bouncers were on the guy, and he was being tossed.

I turned to Chase and Jared to see if they caught the scene, but they were busy stuffing food in their mouths. Of course, I was uncomfortable with Harper having to deal with assholes like him, but I was happy they had a system in place to keep the girls safe.

Yet I still wasn't happy. And I never thought I was the jealous type. But her working in this setting had me turning into a green-eyed monster.

Then I felt that familiar tingle when a soft hand landed on my forearm.

"I have a couple minutes," she said. Grabbing my hand, she led us down a dark hallway that seemed to be designated for employees. "This is the access hall for the DJ, so no one should need to come down here."

The second I heard that, I spun her on those high heels, pushed her against the wall, lifted a leg and placed my hand under her ass, painfully close to her pussy.

"Christ, Harper, your pussy lips are almost coming out of these shorts."

Her laugh was warm against my cheek. "Well, I don't think I need to worry about anyone else lifting my leg sky-high like this, Gage."

My fingertips rubbed the silky skin slipping from the edge of her shorts, and the tiny moans escaping her mouth drove me crazy.

"I love when your hands are on me," she said.

My hand continued rubbing her from underneath while I ground my rock-hard dick against her, seeking her clit through the thin material. My mouth found that tender spot on her neck behind her ear that I knew drove her crazy, and I nipped at it with my teeth.

But then she tried getting her leg from my grasp, except my grip was fierce.

"We can't do this, not now, I won't want you to stop, and I have to get back."

And suddenly something snapped inside me.

"Harper," I said into her ear. "I don't want you to go back out there."

I knew I shouldn't be saying it. I knew it was wrong.

But I meant it.

"I know, baby, but I have to get back to work," she cooed.

She didn't understand what I was saying. My hands dropped from her as her leg fell to the floor, the tip of her shoe echoing against the tile. Stepping back from her so I could look at her face, I reiterated my feeling.

"Harper, I don't want you going back out there."

Her smile remained, but the confusion formed in her eyes. The confusion cleared as my words registered, then morphed into rage. Her shoulders came up as she stood tall, preparing for a fight.

"What are you talking about, Gage? I'm working. I have to get back to work," she said, very matter-of-fact.

"You don't need this job, Harper, and I don't want you working here anymore," I told her. "I don't need every guy in this place getting a hard dick when they look at you." I caged her in as my arms went around her head against the wall. "You're mine."

It came out like more of a growl than I intended.

Her fists balled at her sides as her anger flared. Then her hands came up to my chest, and with all her might she pushed me back, using the wall behind her as leverage. She actually moved me.

"Who the fuck do you think you are? You don't get to tell me what to do!" she screamed. "And I *do* need this job. You don't have the right to waltz into my life and tell me what I can and can't do, Gage!"

There were tears in her eyes threatening to spill over. But I didn't care. There was no way I could let her out on this floor another night with the likes of these guys, ready to pounce and put their hands on her. This obviously happened all the time, considering this was only the second time I'd been at this club, and it was the second time I wanted to kill someone.

"Harper, you don't need this money. I have money. I'll give you what you need for your shop. I don't want you here with these assholes touching you another minute. Stop putting yourself through this bullshit."

By now, her hands were on her hips, a snarky smile planted on her face.

"Putting myself through this?" Her hands flailed in the air around her. "I'm not putting myself through anything. It's called working. Holy shit, so you think you can just buy me? What the fuck, Gage? I'm not letting you just give me the money for my shop. Are you kidding me?"

She wiped at her eyes, her makeup smearing. Falling back against the wall, I shoved my hands in my pockets to prevent them from grabbing her. That would only make things worse.

She looked everywhere but at me.

But then her fierce blue eyes stared me down from a foot below me.

"I can't believe you're doing this to me at work. I didn't see you being the jealous type, Gage. You come across as a secure person." She paused, gathering herself and her words. "I'm heading back out there, and you won't stop me. And if you try to stop me from doing my job, I will raise my fingers for the bouncer on you." And I believed her.

CHAPTER 22

Harper

Making it into the shop Saturday morning was no easy feat. The rest of the evening at the club last night was…sad. That's probably the best word to describe it. Gage stayed for another hour after our fight in the hallway, but we didn't speak the rest of the night. It was best many things were left unsaid. I could sense his mood simply by looking at him. He went from still being mad that I stormed away, to looks of concern as he watched guys talking and flirting, to exasperation at the fact that I ignored him.

Asking Vic to take over their table was for the best. If I had to continue to be near him, I know I would have caved in to a conversation. And he didn't deserve one after what he pulled. He didn't get to tell me what to do. Once our shift was over, Vic wanted details about what happened, but I didn't have it in me to give them to her. I was mentally exhausted from getting through the night as it was.

And now having to put an entire day in at the shop when we weren't on speaking terms was going to be hard. But the pace here, coupled with how I could lose myself when working with the flowers, was my only consolation.

"What's with the long face, Harper?" Fiona asked.

As much as I loved working for and with Fiona, it was sometimes hard having two mother figures in my life. There were times, like now, that I just wanted a friend. And most friends would know that at that moment, I would talk only when I was ready to.

"Just tired. Long night at the club last night."

Thankfully, Fiona didn't push and moved along to the back room, leaving me to my designs and the front room. But the buzzing in my back pocket was a constant reminder of what my brain was trying to avoid.

His text messages started around midnight. I was still at work and didn't read them until I'd gotten to the locker room. About twenty of them had backed up by then. They continued on and off through the night. They ranged between apologies to him getting mad at me for not responding to his apologies.

Gage - Harper I'm sorry about tonight

- I know you're still working please call me when you get home

- I was a dick I'm sorry

- Call me

- Why won't you pick up your phone

- Answer your phone

- You're making me think something is wrong

Me - I'm home and fine

ONCE I LET him know I was safe, he stopped for the night, but the calls and texts resumed this morning. Finally, I ripped my phone out of my pocket and shut it down. There was no way I'd be able to concentrate with it vibrating every thirty seconds.

But as I walked to the refrigerator case, the door to the shop opened, and my heart sank. I couldn't bring myself to see if Gage was the one standing at the door. Slowly, I turned my head, and my eyes found a young woman looking at the premade arrangements.

Then I felt a gentle hand grip my shoulder.

"Head to the back, Harper, I'll take this one," Fiona said.

With tears in my eyes, I nodded as I rushed through the doorway and ran straight to the bathroom, locking myself inside. The cries instantly turned to sobs as my body curled in on itself and shook. Sitting on the closed toilet, I used some of the scratchy toilet tissue to blow my nose and wipe my eyes. Looking up, my reflection in the mirror stunned me. Red-rimmed eyes puffy from crying, mottled and blotchy cheeks from rubbing the tears away.

Pulling my phone from my pocket, I turned it on.

Fifty-two missed messages. Five missed calls. All from him.

I opened my phone and hit call.

"Mom?" My voice cracked the moment I said her name. I hadn't planned on calling, but I needed her; I needed to hear her voice.

"Baby, what's wrong?" she asked. "What did he do?"

We shared no words for a few minutes, her just listening to me cry as quietly as I could through the phone.

"Mom," I said again, not quite sure what I wanted to tell her yet.

"Harper, ya know, the beach has been calling your name down here. Why don't you hop on a plane, baby? Come see your mama. She could use a hug from you."

Holding the phone to my ear as the tears streamed down my

face, I nodded to myself in agreement. It would take so much arranging with both jobs. But I had time off. This was as good a reason to use it as any.

"Okay, Mom, yeah," I said, taking a deep breath. "I think that's a good idea."

The sigh that came through the line was one of relief. She didn't speak, but there was rustling in the background. I could only guess she was already hauling ass to start cleaning, making a perfect house more perfect.

"Okay honey, let me know what flight you can get on. What day do you think you'll try to head down?" she asked.

Thinking about it, I knew there was no other option.

"I'll be there today."

And I hung up.

THE HUMIDITY HITS like a wall the moment you step out of the airport. It's a phenomenon I won't ever get used to, no matter how many times I visit her in the warmer months. The air was so heavy with moisture that it's hard to breathe in, getting caught in your windpipe before it makes it to your lungs.

Looking around for my mom's blonde hair, I found her waving emphatically by her car. Dragging my bag behind me, I made my way over. The Fort Myers airport lacked the bustle and chaos of the NYC area airports. There weren't transit officers constantly blowing their whistles at the waiting cars here like up north.

But that was because there really weren't any cars waiting.

"Harper!" my mom screamed as she raced around her car to grab me into her arms. "Look at you, you look so beautiful."

She held me at arm's length after releasing me from her hug, studying me from top to bottom. Her hands went to my face, cradling my cheeks. "But you're sad, my angel."

Then she took my bag by the handle and rolled it behind her car. "C'mon, get in, let's get going. We've got lots to do."

Once I got out of the bathroom that morning at the shop, and Fiona got one look at me, she sat me down. I didn't tell her exactly what was going on but let her know I needed some time to visit my mom and get out of town. She gave me Tuesday and Wednesday off. My next call was to the club. It didn't go as smoothly with them calling out for that night, but I had the time off available, so I got it. I paid more for the flight than I wanted since it was the day of, but I would be with my mom from Saturday evening until Wednesday night.

"What do you have planned, Mom?" As I settled into the passenger seat, I fiddled with the vents, making sure the air blasted me in the face. And I was hoping she didn't plan a bunch of visits with friends or anything similar. She was known to crowd our social calendar when I visited.

"Well, we have to get to the beach, then there's this really cool beach bar that I've been meaning to try, but my friends are lame, so now I've got you to try it with. Then there's the pool in my complex, and then, well, back to the beach, I guess."

Her smile was infectious. She knew exactly what I was here for and what I needed. As she started the fifteen-minute drive to her condo, I realized I'd made the perfect decision abandoning my entire life up north for a quick escape to paradise.

And Fiona was the only one who knew where I was. Not even Vic got the call. I figured the fewer people who knew, the better.

"Thanks, Mom."

She smiled at me as she drove along, humming to the alt rock music she always had on in the background. She passed her love of that music onto me. Going to college in the early nineties, she had so many grunge and alternative bands that were just starting out to listen to that were still around.

The gate opened to her complex, and we drove around the winding road to her building. Pulling into her spot under the car canopy, I started to open my door, but she stopped me, her hand on my leg.

"Listen," she said. "I know you, and I'm not going to push. But you came all this way, so all I ask is that before you go home, you tell me what happened."

My head fell against the headrest as she spoke, and I worked hard not to let the moisture building up in my eyes spill over. As my head bobbed up and down, she smiled warmly and nodded back at me.

"Well, then let's go get ready for dinner," she said. "That beach bar has been calling my name for months."

My mom's place was on the mainland of Fort Myers, about a ten-minute drive to Fort Myers Beach. And this time of year, day parking was at a premium for going to the beach, so the next morning we decided to head out early. Besides, it got so hot in the afternoon, we'd want to head home by then, anyway.

We were sitting on the beach long before nine in the morning and were far from the first ones there. The sun was beastly hot already, apparently some freak heat wave for May. It forced us under the umbrella to be comfortable enough to read our books.

"I'm going in for a dip, want to come, Mom?"

"I'm good, sweetie. You go ahead," she said, not even looking up from her book.

The water of the Gulf of Mexico, especially when heading into the summer months, was more like a bath than anything else.

Being it was only May, it was still a bit refreshing when I first went in, but within minutes, it felt as warm as the air. And it probably was.

As I stood waist-deep in the calm water, my mind wandered to a certain person up north. Unlike the waters off the coast of New Jersey, there were no waves in the Gulf to distract me. The slow lapping water lulled me into a trance as my thoughts settled on him. I hated that I allowed him to hurt me, to interrupt my plan. He didn't seem the type to do anything like what he did.

But they never do.

"How was it?" my mom asked as I returned to our chairs.

"Like usual, I'll never get used to being able to walk right into the ocean. So unlike NJ water."

Plopping back into my chair, I looked at the horizon, thinking about who else I left back up north. I dug around in my bag for my phone, thinking I'd reach out to Vic and maybe clue her in to where I was. My home screen was filled with over two hundred missed texts and calls from him. And a few from Victoria.

I opened hers.

Vic - Where r u

- Ur bf is at the club rn looking for u I have no idea what to tell him didn't know u weren't working wtf is going on

- WTF he's going crazy girl he's like a lost puppy

"Everything okay, honey?" my mom asked.

Looking over at her, she was staring at me, book on her lap. I must have looked horrified reading about Gage being at the club last night.

"Not really."

She put her book down and sat quietly, waiting for me to be ready.

"So, it's about Gage," I started.

Looking her way, she nodded and pushed her sunglasses atop her head, her eyes sharp and focused.

"So, things were going great. He's this executive with a big company, a family company. That's how we met. We have their corporate account at Fiona's. I think I told you that." I paused as the memory of our meeting that ended on the table flooded my thoughts. My cheeks flushed, but thankfully it was camouflaged by the heat. "We've been spending a lot of time together. We even have this kind of routine already with our work schedules. It's been nice."

"Okay, but now you've hit a speed bump, I'm assuming. Tell me about it," she said.

"Well, it's more than a little bump, Mom. He wants me to quit my job at the club. He basically ordered me to. He came there the other night, and things seemed fine at first. But then all of a sudden, he was like, *I don't want you working here anymore.*" My voice elevated, almost yelling while we sat on the beach, my hands flailing. "I flipped out on him, told him off. *Absolutely not, you don't get to tell me what to do*, yadda yadda."

She studied me for a long moment before saying anything.

"That's not right he did that, of course, Harper. I mean, no one wants a controlling person in their life. Has he apologized? If he hasn't, then I'm with you, I think this probably needs to end."

I simply stared at her.

"What?" she asked. "Has he apologized?"

"Well, that's beside the point. He wants me to quit, and he said he would hand over the cash I need for the shop."

Her smile was small. But she smiled.

"Mom!" I yelled, completely frustrated with her. "He wanted me to just take *his* money for my shop. Can you believe him? Like, why would I take *his* money to start *my* business?"

She sat up more in her chair, looking a bit more interested in what I was saying.

"So let me get this straight. You want to start your own business and work two jobs to try to earn the money you need to do that. But he's telling you to quit one of those jobs and offering you the money you need to start that business. Do I have that right?"

Fucking Christ, she wasn't on my side.

I flung myself against the back of my chair.

"Mom, we've been together like six weeks. Are you really telling me I should be okay with taking tens of thousands of dollars from him to start my shop? Plus, I've skirted my responsibilities now with both my jobs because of him by coming down here. Because of a guy. Something I said I would *never* do again."

I was shocked at her insinuation. She couldn't possibly be telling me to give in and let him just…take care of me.

Jacob, and our years together, came screaming to the forefront of my memories. The way he wanted me to fit some kind of mold he created in his head to be his trophy girlfriend, and I knew eventually, wife. He was only concerned about appearances, as I eventually figured that out. But it took me years. All the money he spent on me, on us, was a ruse to get me to move with him wherever his life took him. He wanted me to be a stay-at-home wife, to create the perfect image for him and the firm. But that was not my plan for my life. And it took me longer than it should have to realize he didn't care one bit about my dreams and desires and what I wanted to do with my life.

I would not fall into the same trap again.

"Honey, I'm sorry, listen, let me clarify. You are a woman who wants to do things for herself—I get it. And I also think it's wrong of him to be making demands of you. I don't disagree with that. But if he wants to help you achieve your dream, especially if you see him as someone you could be with, maybe you should at least be open to that conversation. Possibly discuss him loaning you the money as an investor. And you would pay him back." She paused. "What I'm thinking you're not doing is talking about it. He isn't Jacob. Don't ruin every possible good thing in your future because you're afraid of what that one mistake did to you. Have you even told him why you don't want to take the money? Told him about Jacob? Has that conversation been had?"

She paused again, and I knew her tactics. She wanted me to give in to her reason, but I refused. I remained stoic, looking out at the water.

"And if he has apologized, or tried, you owe it to him to listen. If there is any chance this guy is the one..." She sat back in her chair and picked up her book again. I knew she felt triumphant with her words. "And I don't think you'd be here, with me, running away from him, if you weren't scared to death that he is the one."

The stubborn side of me would not give in to her. I sat there, watching the minuscule waves roll in, not speaking, for a good twenty minutes. But she wore me out.

"So that's it?" I whined. "That's all you've got for me. I flew all the way from New York for you to tell me I should listen to his apology?" My toes dug deep in the sand as I flung some in frustration.

"So, he *has* apologized?" she asked.

"Ughhh!" I screeched. "I guess so, he hasn't stopped texting or calling me since he left the club the other night. But he left and didn't look back." My arms were folded tightly against my chest as I stewed in my anger. "But I've only read a few of them."

She turned the page of her book, not very concerned with our conversation. And that seemed to anger me more.

"Maybe you should take the time to read some of them, sweetie. It might give you some insight into what was going on in *his* head, and it might be completely different from what you were thinking."

Uugghh!

CHAPTER 23

Gage

Where the fuck could she be? She wasn't at the club Saturday night. Victoria hadn't heard from her since they worked together Friday. She won't respond to any of my texts. She won't answer any of my calls. She doesn't seem to be at her apartment. I even asked Jared if Delia had heard from her, and nothing.

The past couple days have been a living hell.

Work yesterday was useless. I couldn't get anything accomplished because every thought was consumed by her. And by my asinine actions from the other night.

I didn't even understand where my jealousy came from. Although, having an ex-wife who cheated on you probably has some lasting effects. But it surprised me as much as it did Harper.

Sitting at my desk, staring out the window at the street below, I knew today would be another waste of time. But once the clock hit nine, I was making the call.

And it finally hit nine.

"Fiona's Flowers, may I help you?"

"Hi, may I speak with Harper, please?" With bated breath, I

waited for Fiona's answer. Intentionally, I did not tell her it was me, though I'm sure the caller ID alerted her.

The pause in her response wasn't very reassuring.

"She's, uh, off for a couple days. Can I take a message?"

I disconnected the call.

And grabbed my suit jacket.

Walking into the shop, the scent of flowers inundated me with memories of Harper. Her scent came rushing back as if she were going to be there, working at that wood table with her bright smile.

Instead, Fiona came walking through the back door, the bell announcing my arrival.

"Gage, what brings you in today?" she asked. She didn't seem all that surprised to see me as her eyes bored into mine, searching for something. It was as if she was looking for the answer in my face to her own questions, but I didn't have them for her.

But that told me she had some for me.

My hands shook with nerves as I stood, unmoving. Unsure of what my next move should be, I remained where I was, staring at the woman Harper respected as a mom.

"Fiona." My voice was feeble.

I wasn't myself. At all.

A broken version of me was standing in front of this person whom I now considered a friend. And my future was possibly in her hands.

"I need something from you, and you probably aren't prepared to give it to me," I said. Taking a few steps in her direction, I leaned against the edge of the table, using it to support me. I suddenly felt as though I was about to pass out. "I've, um, been trying to reach Harper since Saturday, and haven't been able to. We had a fight. She's not at her apartment. She's not here. I know we haven't known each other for long, and you owe me nothing, but if you could find it in your heart to give me some idea where I could find her, or at least make sure she's okay…"

The crack in my voice startled me. The last time I cried was the day my mother left when I was ten years old. And I hadn't cried since. Now I felt as though today would be the day. But I kept it in. The knot in my throat grew so large it felt like the air couldn't move past it. But I kept it in.

Bending over the table, despair ran its course through my body. My head hung between my shoulders as I realized how important Harper had become to me.

And she was gone.

"Gage." Fiona used a soft tone. "You poor thing."

Her hand went to my head, patting me, consoling me. I was too devastated to care about being embarrassed.

"She was just as shattered as you are," she said.

I looked up. The compassion her eyes held gave me hope.

"I see a lot of me and Jim in you two. And he screwed up a few times," she said, then laughed. "I would have wanted someone to push him in my direction if it was needed, or we wouldn't have the wonderful life we have."

But then she abruptly walked to her back room, leaving me alone. No words. And I was left wondering if I'd imagined what she'd just said.

But just as quickly, she came drifting back in with a piece of paper in her hands.

"Ran off to see her mom. She doesn't see her often, and this was a very sudden visit. I kind of knew something was up," she said. Handing me the paper, she closed it in my hand. "I hope I'm doing the right thing. Make sure you do the right thing."

Standing straighter and taking a full breath of air for the first time in what felt like days, I looked down at my newest ally.

"Thank you," I said as I bent down and hugged Fiona.

Walking out of the store, I pulled out my phone and made a call.

"Maryellen, get the jet ready."

I'D BEEN TO FLORIDA, but I'd never really *been* to Florida. A conference in Miami, a fishing trip in the Keys. But most of the time it was over the winter months, during the season when it felt great to escape the cold North to the warm South.

This heat and humidity sucked. And I jumped on the jet without a bag packed, still in my suit from the day. The car was taking me directly to Harper's mom's place. I'd worry about a change of clothes later.

But the first problem arose when we arrived at the gated entrance to the community where her mom lived.

I had no way of getting inside.

"Sir, what would you like me to do?" the driver asked.

I didn't have an answer for him. Being locked out of places wasn't something I was used to.

"Is there an office we can contact to let me in?" I asked.

"I don't believe so, sir. The only people that can open these gates are residents, it's a security measure."

There was an intercom with a button, so there was someone to talk to.

"I'll get out, thank you."

As soon as I got out, the sweat was dripping between my shoulder blades, hitting me at the waistband of my pants. The jacket came off, and the shirt was unbuttoned at the neck. As I rolled up my sleeves, I hit the button on the intercom. The static that sounded through the speaker was not the most encouraging sound.

I hit the button again.

And I was graced with the same static noise.

What if a resident needed help?

"May I help you?" a voice like tin said through the box.

"Yes!" I said a bit too triumphantly. "I'm here to visit someone. How do I go about that?"

"Well, they would have to buzz you in, sir? You should call them," the voice said.

Shit. I hadn't expected this literal barrier in my plan.

"But it's a surprise," I offered. "I've flown in to surprise my girl-friend for her birthday, and she's staying with her mom. Margaret Wilson, building four, number 4302."

There was a long pause with no words or static. I thought I'd been abandoned when suddenly, the static returned.

"Listen, I'm not supposed to do this. I'll buzz you in, but you have to come to the office. If you don't come here first, I will defi-nitely get fired."

The relief that washed over me was tangible. My back straightened and my shoulders raised just a bit as some confidence was added to my emptying tank.

"Thank you, which way to the office?"

She rattled off directions as the gate creaked open. I hoped I got the lefts and rights correct in my mind. Most people were driving through this maze, not walking. It took me ten minutes to get there, and by then the sweat was so profuse on my entire body that my shirt clung to my back. The front was completely unbut-toned, begging for any type of breeze to find my skin, but it wasn't happening. Finding the door to the office and knowing there would be air conditioning once stepping inside kept me going.

And what a glorious feeling it was. It's amazing how we take it for granted, and I don't think I will ever again. I welcomed the tiny bumps from the frigid temperatures that popped up all over my skin.

"You walked here? I thought you ditched me," a voice yelled from a nearby desk.

Turning to the voice, I found a thirty-something tired-looking girl, who I was sure didn't like her job but needed it. Her eyes inspected me from head to toe. Looking down, I realized my shirt was still wide open, my torso on full display. Pulling it closed, I moved toward her, my biggest smile of thanks on my face.

"Well, from the gate I did. I sent my car away when I couldn't get in, then realized that was a mistake five minutes later when I was sweating through my suit."

She, on the other hand, was wrapped in a sweater. They did like their air conditioning in this office.

"Yeah, this is a bit unusual for this early in the season. It's really hot out there the past couple days," she said. "Do you mind signing in and letting me see some ID?"

As I signed the clipboard, she scrutinized my license, for what I didn't know, then logged some information in a notebook.

"Thanks. We're really only supposed to let delivery people in here that don't have tags to open the gate. So let's keep this between us, if you don't mind," she said with a wink.

"Thanks again," I told her as I walked toward the exit. I wasn't looking forward to leaving the cool temps of the office, but I needed to get to Harper.

"Hope she has a happy birthday," she called from the desk behind me.

Once outside, the numbers on the buildings told me I'd have to make my way to the back of the complex to find Harper's mom's place. Thankfully, there was a tree-lined path that helped with the heat. As I walked, I realized I had no real plan in place for when I got there.

What was I going to say?

What if she refused to talk to me?

Once Fiona gave me the address of where Harper was, no thinking was involved. Jumping on the corporate jet to get down here as fast as I could was the only plan. My time on the flight was spent adjusting my meeting schedule over the next couple of days since I wouldn't be in New York. Maryellen got in touch with Chase and put him in charge of a few of them, so the hope was that he could handle it. He and Jared had been calling and texting since I landed, but I couldn't explain it to them. I didn't understand it myself.

I questioned if coming here was the right thing to do. Harper obviously went to extreme lengths to have me not find her. However, we're too far into this together for me to simply walk away.

I won't lose her over my stupidity. If she still doesn't want me after I apologize, well, I'll have to live with that.

Stopping, I looked at the building in front of me, building four.

Once I made it up to the third floor and was standing in front of the door to 4302, the panic set in. But I wasn't normally a nervous person.

I made people nervous.

My knuckles knocked on the door three hard times in succession, and then I waited.

And I waited.

Looking to my left and my right, as if someone might come out of another apartment. I realized no one was going to answer the door.

I was being hit with one obstacle after another.

Her mom's condo was near the elevator and stairwell. So, I

made myself comfortable on the steps, pulled out my phone, and tried to get some work done. Work was always something I looked forward to. It drove me when I woke each morning. But as I opened each email, my mind drifted from its contents to the way Harper walked away from me the other night at the club.

And the anger in her eyes.

Her anger for me.

She destroyed me. But I'd done it to myself.

Trying to work was useless. I moved on to social media, which I was rarely on. Maybe mindlessly scrolling through some TikToks would help pass the time.

But then the elevator dinged. Strolling out of it came two women.

One of them made my heart stop beating.

The other looked just like her, but with lighter hair and twenty-some years her senior.

Their arms were full of bags: grocery bags, beach bags, shopping bags. They were laughing and talking about their day. Moving from the stairwell, I took tentative steps in their direction for fear of scaring them. Her mom, Margaret, was the first one to see me.

She stopped talking. But it was obvious she knew who I was as her eyes lit up at the sight of me. Something of a smile started to form on her lips, but Harper was still going on about whatever they had been talking about.

"Harper," her mom said. "Let me take the bags."

"Why, Mom? I can help you. This is…"

She looked up at her mom and stopped talking, following her mom's gaze.

Spinning around, Harper saw me.

"Gage," she whispered.

Her eyes went wide as her body went limp. But she recovered, standing straighter, shaking her head from the cloud that had consumed it.

"Hi," I croaked out. I knew the moisture was building up in my eyes. Maybe it would be mistaken for the sweat dripping from my temples. But I didn't care anymore.

Finally, my manners kicked in and I raced to the aid of both women.

"Let me take these," I said as her mom unlocked the door.

Harper was stunned. She handed me the bags without complaint and followed me into the condo as if on autopilot. The kitchen was in plain view, and I placed all the groceries on the island. Mrs. Wilson had the other bags in her hands and was standing by my side as we both turned to face Harper. Her mom cleared her throat.

"Mrs. Wilson, I'm sorry to show up on your doorstep like this. I'm Gage Parker. It's nice to meet you." Extending my hand, she grabbed it firmly with both of hers.

"I know who you are, and it's so nice to meet you. And call me Maggie, please." Her look bounced between both Harper and me, settling on her daughter. "I'm, um, going to do a load of laundry with these beach towels, then head to my room. Give you two some privacy."

She scurried out of the main living space.

But Harper and I hadn't taken our eyes off each other.

She was still standing near the front door, her beach bag at her feet. I took a few tiny steps toward her to see how she would react.

"What are you doing here?"

Her voice was barely above a whisper, but the words cut through me like a knife.

"How did you find me?" she clarified.

My smile didn't get the reaction from her I'd wanted. Instead, her hands went to her head, fingers gripping her hair, as if it were about to explode.

"Hey, Harper, relax," I said, moving closer to her. "Finding you was no easy feat, I can tell you that."

And then she looked at me, really looked at me, for the first time.

"Why are you all wet? Why is your shirt soaking wet?" she asked. "And why are you in your suit?"

She was still struggling to put it all together.

"None of that matters right now. All that matters is that I found you and I hope you'll hear me out."

Her hand went to her mouth, covering it. Covering the gasp that tried to escape.

"Gage," she said.

And I did not like how she said my name.

There was a finality to it. A shudder ran through my entire body, head to toe, as my brain fought off the idea that she was about to reject me.

How could I have fucked this up? She was the best thing to ever happen to me. And I fucked it up.

Rebecca was my first love. But I think I always knew we never connected beyond the bedroom. We had fun in college and tried to make it into something it wasn't.

Becca tried to fix the cracks in my heart. But she didn't hand her heart over to me because it belonged to someone else. So, the cracks never healed.

But Harper.

The moment she ran into me, my heart was whole again.

But I fucked it up.

I lost her.

CHAPTER 24

Harper

My mind was racing as fast as my heart. And my brain was a big jumble of nothingness. Not a coherent thought to be had. I couldn't comprehend that he was standing in front of me. That he found me. That he came all the way to Florida…

For me.

"Gage."

His eyes, those brown eyes with caramel-colored specks, searched mine, looking for an answer I knew he needed. But I didn't have it yet.

And those warm eyes had tears in them. My heart was hurting. For him, for us.

My heart deceived me as it stole away some of my anger, dissolving it into thin air as he walked toward me.

"Gage, I…"

"Don't mind me," my mother said as she walked into the room, her hand blocking her face and eyes. She went straight for the kitchen, with a bag across her shoulder.

"Give me a minute," I told him, holding up a finger.

As I walked into the kitchen, she was packing up a few things from the grocery bags we had just brought in. Turning to me, she had a wide smile on her face. She pulled me aside.

"Hey, baby, you doing okay?" she asked and wrapped me in a hug.

"I don't know," I told her. "I'm shocked he's here, that's for sure."

She continued to hold me as we talked, and I liked the emotional support her hug was providing. The momentary break from being in the same room with him was allowing it to all sink in.

"The look on your face when you saw him told me a lot of things," she said against my hair. "Mainly, that you missed him."

I pulled away to look at her. "But I'm still mad at him, Mom."

"And you're allowed to be, but don't let it cloud your judgment. You need to make a decision. Are you willing to walk away from him without trying to fix this? Or is he worth the work a relationship takes?"

Her hands cradled my cheeks as I let her words sink in.

"And it doesn't hurt he's damn fine to look at," she said with a soft chuckle. "Don't forget what we talked about, about compromise in relationships. It's the cure for most ailments, trust me."

I nodded and she let go of my face. "I'm heading out." She reached down for her bag.

I started to protest but thought better of it. It was the right thing to do. Gage and I had a lot to talk about.

"I called a friend and I'm having a sleepover. You guys need some privacy. I'll see you tomorrow."

"Thanks, Mom."

Walking out to the sitting area, we found Gage standing in the middle of the room, looking completely lost. My mom walked up to him, reaching out for a hug. She whispered something in his ear, but I couldn't hear what she said. When she pulled away, they shared a look, even a smile.

"Get him a glass of water, Harper. He's gotta be dehydrated. And let him take a shower, he's sweating through his clothes," she ordered as she walked out the door.

Looking closer at him, I realized that was it. He wasn't wet—he was sweating.

"Oh my God, Gage, are you okay?"

I rushed to the kitchen and grabbed two bottles of water from the fridge. Turning to race back, I barreled into his chest, his bare chest, since he was standing right behind me. And his shirt was wide open. His scent was still there, despite the sweat.

Cedar, leather, spice.

He always smelled of this.

It was divine.

"Here," I said, pushing a bottle into his hand and trying to ignore that his close proximity made all the reasons I was mad at him dissipate.

He took the bottle and chugged it in one gulp. But all the while, his eyes were on me. When the bottle came away from his lips, I expected a smug smile to take shape.

But on the contrary, his look was wary. He looked…hesitant.

His downturned, bloodshot eyes looked tired. His entire body looked tired as he appeared to struggle to stay upright.

"Gage, drink the other bottle, please. You're scaring me."

Shaking his head was his only response.

"It's not water I need, Harper."

His voice cracked when he spoke, an echo of the strong Gage Parker he usually was. Looking at the ceiling, he struggled with what to say next. And I wanted to help him, somehow, but I didn't know what to say either.

But I saw him come together.

"Harper," he said, looking at me. "I was broken when we met, but you were fixing me. My heart was healing just by being with you. Seeing your bright smile and blue eyes reached some lost, broken part of me."

His eyes watered, a lone tear making a path down his cheek. My hand instinctively went to his face, but he stopped me.

"No," he almost begged. "Harper, I need to say this, to get it out."

The guilt tore through me. What a horrible person I was. Putting myself in his position, being completely ignored and abandoned after our first fight, made me see how immature I'd been.

I nodded. His one hand went to his head, his fingers nervously running through his hair. It stuck up a bit, still wet from his profuse sweating. I wanted to smooth it out for him.

I wanted to kiss him.

And this was exactly what my mother said would happen.

If he was the one.

"Harper, I am so sorry I said those things the other night. I had no right to make those demands. Jealousy, that's all it was. My jealousy of all the other guys that get to look at you while you're there."

Reaching out, I grabbed one of his hands, gripping it in mine, offering encouragement for him to say what he needed to say. Little did he know, I had already forgiven him.

He gripped my hand back.

"I'm in a place in my life where I expect people around me to do what I want them to do, need them to do." He stopped and looked at our entwined fingers, his thumb rubbing those tiny circles against my skin I loved. "But that's not fair to you. You're not one of my employees, that's not how relationships are supposed to be, not healthy ones anyway. But what I need you to understand is that me offering you that money wasn't even like that. It wasn't about you not working at the club. I seriously wanted to give it to you, just give it to you, because of who you are. You work so hard, and I want you to have your dream."

"But—" I started to say.

"Please let me finish." His hand came to my cheek, and I allowed him to cradle my face.

We were desperate for one another's touch.

"I've had some failed relationships, very recently, that hit me hard. I wasn't looking for what we'd started, but here we are. And when you took off, and I couldn't talk to you or find you…" He stopped talking, out of necessity. His sigh, his gasp for breath, described the emotion he was dealing with. "That's when I realized."

He hesitated.

"I realized that *you* are what I want. Fights and all. You're worth every fight we might have, but I know I'm *willing* to fight for us. I don't think I've ever felt that way before. And it will be on your terms. Don't take the money. I get how bold that was of me, I do. And I'm sorry. I would never want you to feel like I'm trying to buy your love. I want to earn it."

I nodded along with everything he said, but not until he saw the tears building up in my eyes did he stop.

That was when he realized that I was not only listening but hearing him. His hand relaxed against my face. I closed my eyes as his hand wrapped around my neck, into my hair, pulling me to his chest. His chin was atop my head as he continued.

"Harper, you just leaving, me not being able to find you or talk to you…it terrified me. Like I've never been scared before. I couldn't eat, I couldn't sleep, I couldn't work."

His arms tightened around me, as if he would never let go of me again. And that was when I heard the quiet sobs above me. His body shook in my arms.

"If we're doing this," he said, his words a whisper as his voice trembled, "if you'll forgive me, you have to promise me you'll never do that again. You can't run away."

The heaviness in my chest was enough to consume me; my heart fractured into pieces as he held me.

And then he broke.

I could barely hold him up as his body fell against mine.

My arms wrapped around his middle, struggling with his weight, as we stumbled a bit together. He steadied himself, reaching for the edge of the counter, but refused to let go.

"Gage," I said against his chest.

Taking him by the hand, I led him to the couch in the living room. My mind raced with all he had said. Of course, I knew he was trying to apologize to me the past few days, but I had no idea about the rest of it.

We got to the couch, him sitting against the corner, and I wasn't sure where to go. Did he want me close to him? In his arms? He still hadn't let go of my hand as I went to settle by his side. But he pulled me, full force, onto his lap, my legs going around his, as he got a hold of my waist, keeping me in place.

"I'm not letting you go," he said, looking up at me. "I need you close, Harper."

We'd been in this position before, several times. But as his fingers dug into my hips and his eyes pierced mine with his look, there was nothing sexual about this. There was a desperation to his touch.

He needed confirmation. About so many things.

His beard was thicker than normal, a sign of him not grooming for a day or two. I rubbed my fingers through the whiskers, the hair softer than when it was short.

I knew what he needed but had to make sure to get it right. He deserved that after these past few days.

"Gage." But my words got caught.

Then he pulled me close so quickly our chests collided, as my hands flew to his shoulders.

"Harper, all I want to know is if you forgive me," he said as his hands moved to my face, holding it with tender fingers. His lips trembled with emotion, on the border of breaking again, as he waited for me to answer him.

"Of course I do, but I owe you an apology, too."

His mouth crashed into mine with such ferocity it almost hurt. But then he started murmuring words against my lips, incoherent thoughts. Moving my mouth from his, he held us close, forcing our foreheads together.

And his silent sobs started again.

"I thought I'd lost you."

His stifled cry was painful to hear.

"Gage, calm down." Stroking his face, his breathing finally evened out. "I see now what I've done to you, and I'm so sorry. It was an immature response to our situation."

But then his tears started in earnest again. It seemed nothing I could do would remedy what he was feeling.

"I don't like that I felt so broken without you," he said. His head fell back against the cushion, avoiding looking at me. "And I don't know if we're moving too fast."

His words tore me up, but I knew to let him get it all out. He brought his eyes back to mine.

"It's not that I can't live without you, Harper. It's that I don't want to."

The tenderness that took over his face, his look, his eyes, moved me. Like magnets, our mouths were drawn to each other's, the kiss tender. His lips soft against mine, his gentle reminder that we were fixing us.

With his hands moving under my legs, he started repositioning me on his lap. "Let me hold you."

I fell into the corner of his shoulder as he held me like a child, cocooned by his arms across his legs. His hand that came around me rubbed my arm, and his breathing became rhythmic.

"Can I get you anything? You must be starving," I said, trying to sit up.

But he held me in place firmly.

"What about a shower? Will that make you feel better?" I asked.

I felt the shake of his head without looking up.

"Uh-uh. I've got everything I need right here." His words were quiet, even slow.

And he was asleep within minutes.

CHAPTER 25

Gage

Waking with a start, I was confused as to where I was. But then I felt the weight of her, asleep in my arms, and remembered. Looking down at her tiny frame on my lap, I knew we were starting something that we both needed to be very careful with. This whole debacle proved that. But I was scared, there was no denying that. Because I did not have a great track record.

And because of how I felt about her. It was happening hard and fast. But there was no denying it was happening.

It was dark outside, late into the night, I suspected. But the exhaustion of the past few days of lost sleep and our emotional reunion resulted in me crashing. And Harper didn't look ready to wake up yet, either.

But I felt disgusting. The sweat had dried on me in the form of salt crystals across my body hair. I needed a shower. Thankfully, she was light enough that I could lift her from me and lay her back on the couch. Once she was covered with a blanket, I went on the hunt for a bathroom.

Finding what appeared to be Harper's room, I turned on the

shower in the attached en suite. Stepping inside the roomy stall shower, I turned the water on full blast and waited for it to warm. Leaning forward against the wall, allowing the water to hit the back of my neck, I relished in the hot streams that fell across my skin, taking the grime of my day away with it.

Of course, I knew the potential outcomes of how today could have gone.

There was immense comfort knowing where we stood compared to how I felt even in the morning when I woke.

Suddenly, the glass door opened.

"Hey, you," I said, gaping at the sight in front of me.

She was stunning.

As she stepped in, I admired her now-tan skin glowing in the dim light as the water coated her. She wrapped her arms around my middle from behind, hugging me.

"Hey," she said. "I couldn't sleep without you."

Every little thing she said helped heal my heart a bit more.

"Let me wash you," she said, reaching for bodywash and a washcloth. After making the suds on the cloth, she rubbed it along my back and over my shoulders. The scent invaded my nose, floral with a hint of something woodsy.

It was all her. And it drove me crazy.

These past few days of missing her were a torment to my mind. Only once I saw her again did I realize how much I'd missed her body. Missed her touch.

"Gage," she said. The timbre of her voice shocked me, the sadness coming through in one word. Turning my head slightly to find her face, her downcast eyes confirmed my suspicion. "There's so much more that needs to be said, by me. I have to…"

Spinning to face her, my fingers went to her lips, silencing her pending apology. Shaking my head, I hoped my message came through in my look. But as she stood straighter, I knew it hadn't.

"I know you feel like you have to apologize, but I don't need that right now, baby. I've missed the feel of you. I thought I'd never have your skin against mine again."

Her hands came to my face, the apology in her trembling fingers as they gripped my cheeks. My hands covered hers as my mouth kissed her palm. She nodded up at me as she pulled her hands away.

"I promise we'll talk, Harper, we will."

"I know," she said with an acknowledging smile.

I turned toward the wall and reached for the hand still holding the washcloth, hoping she would resume washing me.

And she did. Her fingers trailing across my back. Her touch was what I needed, what I'd missed these past few days of thinking we might be over. As her hands and nails rubbed up and down, my body fought to respond to her touch.

The twitch of my dick went unnoticed at first. But as her hands lowered to my ass, I couldn't hide my desire for her any longer.

"Ahh, fuck, Harper," I moaned. My hands were against the tile wall in front of me as she dropped the washcloth to the shower floor. She gripped and rubbed me from behind, eventually working around to the side of my hips.

By now my cock was standing tall, desperate for her touch.

Her fingers glided along my sides, my hips, inching toward where I needed them to be. It took everything in me to not force her to grab my dick, cup my balls.

But delayed satisfaction had its benefits. I used it with her plenty of times. But experiencing it was torture, a sweet torture.

And she was playing my game. Her hands, instead of moving between my legs, spread to my thighs. Her nails dug in as she ran a path down each leg. My body trembled for her under the steamy spray.

But then the game switched. Or ended, I guess.

"I want you to fuck me, Gage," she said against my back, her mouth licking and kissing between her words. "Fuck me, make me come, please. We need this."

A primal growl came from deep inside me as I spun to face her. My hands lifted her by the backs of her thighs, pushing her against the wall, chest to chest. Her tits were pushed up against me and my mouth was drawn to the flesh, sucking it into my mouth. Her legs wrapped around my waist, my cock lining up with her pussy perfectly.

It would be so easy to plunge into her, right then.

And I almost didn't hold back.

But I did. Instead, I placed her feet back on the tiles, pushing her up against the wall. Her eyes peered up at me, droplets of water dripping from her lashes, as her damn tongue came out and licked her lips.

A seductress.

As she leaned against the wall, I dropped to my knees. Her hands went to the top of my head, nails digging into my scalp, fingers pulling at my hair, drawing me to her.

Spreading her pussy apart, I was desperate to get to her clit. Separating her legs further, she granted me access as my fingers pressed against the slick skin, opening her for me. The water trailed down her body, across her exposed flesh, making it glisten in the dim light.

"Oh my God, Gage, I love when you touch me," she moaned.

Looking up, I watched her head fall to the side as she arched her back, her breasts pushing forward. Reaching up, I took hold of a taut nipple, twisting it between my fingers. Her body froze. The pain seemed almost too much as her hand came to her breast, gripping the back of mine in protest.

"Relax," I murmured against the folds of her pussy. "Tell me if it's too much, but it'll feel good if you let it, baby." Waiting for a response and getting none, I prodded again. "Harper, tell me what you want, baby. Should I continue?"

"Yes," she whispered. "Keep going."

My fingers pulled and twisted, gently at first, but with increasing pressure. She began accepting the agony, allowing it to pass from pain to pleasure.

"Ahh," she mewled.

"That's it, beautiful. Surrender yourself to me."

As my hand continued the torment above, my mouth dove between her legs. Flicking her clit with my tongue, I savored her taste.

Like a sweet, delicate wine.

My lips circled around her, sucking her hard flesh into my mouth. The muscles of her thighs tightened against my head, clenching and squeezing, as I swirled my tongue around her clit.

"Christ, Gage, I can't…"

Lifting one of her legs over my shoulder, she opened even more to me. My free hand rubbed along her pussy, stopping at her entrance. Sliding a finger inside, her body trembled. Then her hands yanked at my hair with urgency.

"More Gage, that's not enough!"

My dick swelled with her command—and of course, I obliged.

Two, then three fingers pushed deep inside her as the walls of her pussy clamped onto me. As my hand pumped in and out in a torturous rhythm, my lips countered with a slow suck that pulled her deep within my mouth. All while I pinched and twisted each of her nipples.

It was the pleasure trifecta.

I knew when it started. The contraction of muscle inside her and out had my body in a stronghold.

And I knew not to stop. The sounds she was making, the moans and gasps, told me this orgasm was deep. Her bent knee over my shoulder pulled me closer, trying to keep me from moving.

Instead, using my other shoulder, I pulled her straight leg up and over.

She was balancing on my face, my hand, my shoulders.

And had no ability to stop me whatsoever.

I quickened my pace just enough to hear the change in her moan. That delicate balance between keeping her going and losing the orgasm.

I knew how to keep it going.

"Fuck!" she screamed. "Gage, please!"

She didn't know what she was begging for, but I did.

She wanted to come, but she didn't want it to end even more.

And I was here to deliver.

"Please what, baby?" I asked. "Should I stop?" I teased.

"Oh my God, Gage, please don't stop." She was begging, so close to the pinnacle.

The water streamed along my face as my mouth and hand continued to ravage her. Her legs tightened around my shoulders, my neck, as she rode the wave approaching. The high-pitched sounds coming from her sang a song of ecstasy and were music to my ears.

And I felt her reach the top as her body tensed against mine, holding onto my head for strength.

To endure.

With her body against the wall, my mouth against her pussy, and my hands gripping her ass, Harper reveled in the surge that consumed her.

She let herself go.

And I devoured everything she gave me.

I lapped it up as she screamed my name. Her body tensed as my fingers pulsed in and out, keeping the contractions going.

Then her muscles slumped, the exhaustion hitting her hard.

But I wasn't done yet.

Sliding her legs from my shoulders, I grabbed her ass, holding onto her and bringing us to standing. Her wide eyes watched me as I maneuvered us higher up on the wall.

Staring into those bright blue eyes, I got lost.

"You are so fucking beautiful, Harper, you know that?"

Her timid smile was fucking adorable.

"I love making you come. Your sounds, every move you make, all of it is sexy as hell."

She grabbed the back of my head and crushed her mouth to mine, our tongues doing a little dance together.

"I taste me on your mouth," she murmured against my lips.

The growl that came from deep within me startled us both.

"Saying things like that is going to get you fucked. Hard," I told her as I pulled her legs apart with my upper arms, opening her for me, as I lined her up against the tip of my dick. "Shit, let me get a condom."

Her arms flung around my neck, holding tight.

"No, don't," she said.

Looking at her with lifted brows, the question was all over my face.

"I'm on the pill and not planning on being with anyone else," she said. "Are you?"

"Never," I growled.

Lowering her pussy onto my stiff dick, I slid right into her. Taking it slow, I allowed her to accommodate me.

Her eyes flutter closed and her mouth fell open as her head tilted back. I pushed inside her all the way, making me harden even more. My mouth was drawn to her exposed neck. I began sucking on the wet flesh as the water covered us.

"Oh, Gage," she moaned. "You feel so good. So fucking good."

That was when I knew she was ready.

"Hang on, baby, we're going for a ride. This will not be gentle," I said in her ear. "Are you okay with that?"

Her response was to push her pussy down onto my dick. With force.

Rearing back, I slammed into her as her ass slid up the wall. With her on top of me, my entire length was inside her, reaching every part of her.

And she took it.

Her expectant eyes looked at mine, questioning why I stopped moving.

And that sent me on autopilot. The tension and emotion from the past few days were coiled up inside me and threatened to explode.

And they did.

In and out, pushing and pulling, slamming and stretching.

"Fuck…Harper…you're so fucking…tight!"

The spray from the shower trailed down our bodies, making her glisten. Her pebbled nipples bounced with each slam into her. Leaning down, I pulled one into my mouth, sucking hard. My teeth grazed the hard nub of flesh, biting at it.

That made her moans grow louder.

The tempo continued to increase, our bodies crashing against each other's.

"Fuck…I've missed you." My words tumbled from me as the clapping of our skin echoed against the tiled wall. "Look at me, Harper."

Her eyes found mine as I pumped in and out of her.

Those crystal blue eyes like the clearest ocean. And they held promise in them. An unsaid promise.

What I needed most.

"Look at me while I fuck you harder," I told her. "Watch the moment you take everything from me."

As I pummeled into her, my concern she wouldn't be able to do this disappeared.

Not only had she taken all of me, but she had stolen all of me.

"I'm going to come…Harper…watch me come inside you."

And she did. Her eyes on mine, my chest, our connected bodies, as I unleashed everything I had left in me.

I surrendered to her.

Body and soul.

CHAPTER 26

Harper

I always knew Gage and I were from different worlds. His was corporate, filled with suits and ties and business functions. Mine was vastly different, working in the shop and the club. But eventually, as a business owner, I thought our worlds would align more closely. That I could feel like more of an equal.

But when we boarded his company jet, I knew our two worlds were galaxies apart and might never cross.

The level of intimidation I felt was worrisome. And it wasn't just the jet. When we woke up the other morning to a knock at the door, the last thing I was expecting was a personal shopper to be dropping off clothes for Gage.

But Gage was the kind of person that had "people" to do things for him. A lot of people for a lot of things, apparently.

Yet, believe it or not, humble was a word I'd use to describe him. If I hadn't pulled this runaway stint, I'm thinking I might never have known about this jet. He wasn't flashy with his money or power, and he never made me feel like less.

And we didn't need another hurdle to clear when we had just

gotten through the first roadblock. I knew I was going to have to talk to him about how I was feeling.

We still had a lot to talk about, me apologizing for starters. And he didn't want to do it any time I brought it up. I think we left it for now. While on this flight back home.

A captive audience for one another.

"Let me take your bag," he offered as I looked around the spacious cabin.

There were a few traditional looking plane seats toward the front, I was assuming to use during takeoff and landing. But the rest of the space seemed to mimic that of a comfortable living room. There was a couch, table, and chairs along one side. They faced a wide-screen tv mounted on the wall that hung over a well-stocked bar.

Gage came up behind me, his hand on my lower back, guiding me to the seats up front.

"Let's take a seat. They want to take off in a few minutes."

I'd never even flown first class on a commercial flight, always economy for me. But as I sat on the buttery soft leather seat, sinking in to its comfort, I knew I was ruined.

How does one go back after this?

"Are you okay?" Gage asked as he buckled himself into the seat across from me.

His concerned eyes searched mine for any hint of a lingering problem. Or maybe it wasn't concern, but his own fear of what the next three hours might hold for us.

Our time in Florida together turned into what seemed like us living out the pages of a romance novel. We spent a full night and day after his arrival either in bed "making up" or out and about as if nothing had happened. But we both knew we needed to address a few things with each other…about each other.

"Yeah," I said. "This is just, uh, a lot to take in."

His soft smile reminded me that he was still Gage.

"Well, I remember when I saw this plane for the first time, it overwhelmed me, too. I was probably about ten years old when my dad took Chase and me on a business trip with him. We were both little shits the entire flight, I'm pretty sure the crew refused to work again if we came back."

We laughed together at his memory, but then I returned to being quiet. Leaning forward, he took my hand in his, rubbing the back of it the way he always did.

"Talk to me, Harper. We said that's what we need to do."

"We have three hours to talk, don't we?" I offered.

Just then, an attendant appeared.

"Mr. Parker, three minutes. Once we're up, I'll be by with drinks." She spoke directly to him but then turned my way. "Ms. Wilson, what can I get you?"

Another person waiting on him. And how did she know my name? I mean, I figured I needed to be logged in as a passenger, and there were only two of us.

Was I ready for this world?

"Um, I'll have a diet soda, please."

She smiled and moved back to where she came from, which was somewhere up front that hid her from us completely. My eyes fell back on Gage, who, it seemed, was amused by me.

"What?" I asked, my tone full of question and a splash of exasperation.

"Nothing, you're just fucking adorable," he said. "But, yeah, we have some time up here. And I agree we should talk. But I doubt that will take three hours." He sat back against his seat and his hand went to his face. As he rubbed his jaw, his sultry eyes devoured me from head to toe. "You didn't get the tour, but there's a bedroom onboard."

"Oh my God, I'm not having sex with her around to hear us!"

His look didn't waver, but I refused to give in to his seduction.

"Then stop looking so cute…and fuckable."

"Gage," I countered.

But then his demeanor did change.

"I'm sorry," he said, leaning forward as much as the buckle would allow. "But we do need to talk, and we should start with why you look so uncomfortable right now."

Having a man in my life who was in tune with my emotions as much as Gage could be my ruin. Most would think it helps create the perfect man. Yet, I'd spent the last few years building a wall to keep me from letting my emotions interfere with any guy I'd met.

But he was slowly chipping away at the wall.

And my tendency to run and avoid, I now knew, was only going to scare him away.

"Yes, we should talk." Trying to organize the jumble of thoughts in my head was taking me a minute. "Have you ever lived in a space where you can walk from one end to the other in three seconds flat?"

He sat against the back of his seat and his quizzical look told me he wasn't expecting that.

"I don't think you understand how it is for someone like me to be in a world like yours, Gage. When you gave me that five-thou-sand-dollar tip, do you even know how long it would have taken me to earn that on my own?"

The attention I was paying to my tone seemed to be working. He was still listening and didn't seem offended.

"My dad died when I was only thirteen. And he was the center of both my and my mom's world. Our lives crumbled. But smart with his money, he wasn't. We struggled. And that was even harder. So, I decided to never depend on a man. Especially for money."

Watching him closely for his reaction, I saw none. He was stoic. But listening, intently.

"Both my mom and I worked hard to get ourselves back on our feet, and we did it. Something I know I'm very proud of. Maybe too proud."

My hands were twisting in my lap as I avoided looking at him. I knew what I had with Gage was special. And I was concerned how our talk might affect it in the end. But I had to be more concerned with how not talking would ruin us.

The rumble of the engines under our feet told me the plane was ready to hit the runway. My gaze drifted out the window, the sun low in the sky. By the time we got to New York, it would be dark and late.

We did need to resolve this now.

Before going back to our reality.

The plane raced down the tarmac, its speed increasing. Chancing a look at Gage, his eyes were glued to mine. It made my heart race almost as fast as the plane. But I had to look away, break the stare, to continue telling my story.

"It's not just my dad," I continued as I stared at my hands in my lap. "There's an ex. And I didn't go in with eyes wide open. I fell for him, hard, but he wasn't in it for us. He was in it for appearances, for the idea of us. What *I* wanted wasn't important to him. And he never understood that regardless of all the talking I tried to do."

We were in the air, our altitude climbing as I watched the landscape of Florida disappear out the window. Gage shifted in his seat, drawing my attention to him.

"He was a bit controlling, and only wanted me to be an 'image' for him, nothing else. I couldn't have my own thoughts. He never asked about anything I wanted to do with my future. I finally realized because he didn't really want me to do anything for myself. It was all supposed to be for him."

Gage leaned forward a bit, his elbows resting on his knees, concentration evident across his face.

"It's hard to lose a parent, regardless of how it happens. I'm sorry to hear about your father. I didn't know," he said.

"I know, I really wasn't ready to tell you," I said. "As long ago as it was, it still hurts."

He reached out and took my hand.

"And your ex, well, Harper, we all have a past." He squeezed my hand. "It sounds like he was a tough one to deal with. But you're a strong woman, and what we learn from our pasts is what counts, and you're doing it all right in that department."

His tight-lipped smile conveyed his appreciation for my openness.

"And let's not talk about exes. I think I've got you topped in that department," he said, then chuckled. "You know I was married. Well, she cheated, which is whatever. That happens to lots of people."

The sadness of his words grabbed my attention.

But his demeanor told me there was more to their story, lots more.

"Rebecca and I met in college, and she wound up working in our company. May have been too much of a good thing, working and living together, who knows. But she was sent to London for work, and well, she met someone. Quickly."

The pause in his story lingered. I wasn't sure he was going to continue talking.

"How quickly?" I asked.

His eyes connected with mine at my question. "I don't think I'll ever know for sure, but I'm pretty sure she was living with the guy within her first month of being in London."

I didn't mean to audibly gasp, but it happened.

"Yeah, she turned out to be a real winner," he continued. "But better it happened as early on as it did, right?"

I wanted to hug him, but we were still buckled in from takeoff. Our hands were entwined as we bent as close to one another as we could.

And, apparently, he was on a roll with sharing.

"And then there's my father, who, unlike yours, was not the easiest to be around. He, uh …"

Gage released my hand, sat back against his seat, and stared out the window.

"He was tough. His expectations of me and Chase were high, probably bordering on the unattainable. But he was training us to ultimately take over his empire." A low chuckle was his attempt to lighten the mood. "Let's just say, he wasn't coming to any football or soccer games."

An announcement came over the speaker that we were free to move about the cabin. But this one was a little different, because it was addressed specifically to Mr. Parker. That doesn't happen in economy.

And as if summoned, the attendant brought our drinks to us.

"Thank you, Emily," Gage said as he took our drinks and placed them on our center consoles. Emily then promptly disappeared again.

Gage unbuckled, stood, and stretched. Reaching his hand to me, I took it, and we walked along the cabin.

"Let's get more comfortable over here," he said.

As we settled on the couch, he pulled me close and wrapped an arm around my shoulder. I pulled my legs up and cuddled into his side, appreciating the close contact. A kiss pressed on the top of my head.

"Some parents aren't meant to be parents. I'm glad you had

ones that were," he said, the sadness thick in his voice. "I thought my mom was. But when she left us, that changed my mind."

My head snapped toward his, though he kept his gaze trained out toward the middle of the cabin.

"I'm so sorry, Gage."

I watched him shake it off, though it was obvious it still affected him.

"It's been long enough now. I was ten when she left. I haven't seen her since. She, um…" He seemed so hesitant to continue. "She had another family by the time I was twelve, I think."

Holy shit.

Who in their right mind could do that to their own children? That meant Chase was only eight years old when she left. No matter how bad her marriage was, there was no reason good enough to leave her children behind.

Tears filled my eyes as a choked sob got stuck in my throat, letting on my emotional state. Gage pulled me to a sitting position, looking at me.

"Hey," he said, wiping under my eyes as the tears sprung free. "I'm okay. Us three guys did okay. We're doing more than okay, if you ask me."

His gentle laugh was his attempt at humor, trying to make light of his horrific story.

His sad, horrific story.

But he was right. He did seem to be doing alright.

"I'm sorry, Harper." He took my face in his hands. "I didn't mean to upset you."

Shaking my head, I needed to deter his attention from me.

"I'm fine, really," I told him. Taking a deep breath, I steeled myself to continue hearing what else he might have to say.

Looking at this beautiful man in front of me, I could only imagine how adorable he must have been as a child. How could a mother walk away from such a kind heart and warm eyes?

As I looked into those eyes, my heart broke for the boy he was, and the man he is. He was not healed from the harm she instilled in him. Probably never would be.

And I ran from him…abandoned him…just like she did.

"Oh my God, Gage," I said, with horror in my voice at the realization of my ways. I reached out for his face, holding it in my hands, gripping it tight. "I'm so sorry that I took off…"

Tears sprang from my eyes once again, fresh pain piercing my heart. He pulled me onto his lap, holding me close, our noses skimming. His fingers failed at their attempt to keep my cheeks dry.

"Gage," I started, knowing that so much more of an apology was due him. "I am so sorry. I should not have run from our fight, from us. It was a totally immature response, and I can only imagine what I put you through while I was gone." Rolling my hands together, the sweaty palms a dead giveaway of my nerves. "Jacob, my ex, was an ass, but as I'm telling you my story, it doesn't seem nearly as dreadful as what you've been through in your life, with your mom and your ex. It makes me feel as though I really overreacted here." A slow, rolling tear made its way down my cheek.

He shifted his position to align himself more with me. Our faces were directly across from one another, eyes connected.

"Harper," he said as he peppered my mouth with tender kisses, my tears making them salty. "You would never have known; this isn't a blame game. It's why we're talking, we have to get this out, let each other know."

Letting my head fall against his chest, we stayed like that.

Quiet, breathing, thinking. As he held me.

And he was right, this all needed to be said. Our pasts were what made us who we were, infiltrating every decision we make. But they shouldn't control us.

His fingers ran through my hair while his other hand rubbed my back. As we sat there, I felt myself calm down.

We'd done it. We talked about our pasts and our fight, and it seemed to bring us some closure on the past few days. The mood between us shifted. Things seemed…resolved.

"Your hair got so much lighter since you've been down there," he said as he played with a few pieces along my back. "It looks more like blonde now."

Sitting up, I slid the elastic from my wrist and pulled my hair to the top of my head into a messy bun. "I have what I call 'summer hair' and 'winter hair.' I'm light brown or dirty blonde until my hair sees the sun, then it bleaches out." I pulled at some pieces to make the bun just right but noticed Gage staring at me with an odd look. "What?"

He reached up and pulled on a loose strand of hair next to my ear before his finger ran a path from my neck to my now-heaving chest. Insane how a small touch or a simple look from him had me full of desire.

"You have no idea what you do to me, do you?" His question remained rhetorical.

But my own question was plain on my face.

"I love when you put your hair up, have you ever realized that?" he asked. "Your neck is so fucking sexy. It turns me on. And your little messy knot thing on your head…" He pointed to my bun. "It makes it look like you've just gotten fucked."

Both his thumbs rubbed across my shirt, my nipples reacting to his touch. But then his hands fell to his sides, and he looked at me, his eyes peering into mine.

"Harper, I will not fuck this up with you," he said as his hands gripped my hips. "What we have is too perfect. You're too perfect. I know I've said this already, but I will stay in my lane and let you live your life, as long as I can be by your side as you live it."

Looking at the ceiling, he paused. "I might still screw up every once in a while, but it won't be intentional, I promise." A small smile appeared. "Let's make a pact to talk, not run away, okay?"

Taking both his hands in mine and interlocking our fingers, I pulled his arms around me, forcing him to pull me in for a hug.

"I promise I will never run from us again, Gage."

My lips went to his, and it was a kiss with strong meaning. It held more than a promise—it held a vow we were making to one another.

"I'm not gonna lie," he whispered against my mouth. "I want you right now." His hands slid down my back to the top of my ass, dipping under the waistband of my jeans. "I want to take you into that bedroom back there and do things to you. But if all you want to do is lie here together, I'm good with that too."

His fingers grabbed a hold of the top of my thong and gave a little tug.

And hit me in all the right places. He knew exactly what he was doing.

"Well, I think I should at least get the full tour of this plane while I'm on it, don't you?" I asked, looking toward the door, which must be to the bedroom. "How much time until we land?"

He picked me up, and I wrapped my legs around his waist. This was his thing, holding me against him. He walked us to the room at the back of the plane and threw me on the bed.

"Enough time for me to make you come at least twice," he said as he locked the door, "before I fuck you."

CHAPTER 27

Gage

Being busy at work was usually my sanctuary. What I looked forward to. And it wasn't that I didn't still enjoy work, I did. But there were other things I enjoyed just as much, if not more, these past few weeks. And her name was Harper.

Since returning from Florida, things only seemed to be improving between us.

But work still needed to get done.

"Mr. Parker, the event this Friday is all set. For you both," Maryellen said. "The dresses are being delivered to Harper's apartment today for her to try on."

There was a formal dinner for a major client tomorrow night. It would be the first time I involved Harper in my work world. And I was kind of excited. I wanted to show her off to the entire world. Most of the shareholders from the company would be attending, as well as most of the corporate managers. Which meant Chase, Jared, and their significant others would be at our table, which would help put Harper at ease. Having Delia there would also help her to feel comfortable.

"Thanks, Maryellen, I appreciate you taking care of that for us.

She's nervous enough about tomorrow night. You taking care of the dress is amazing. And the fact that Delia will be there as well, she's looking forward to some familiar faces."

"Of course, sir," she said. "And, to clarify, we still have not heard from Rebecca. I wanted you to be aware."

I still hadn't told Harper that Rebecca could be at the event. My thinking was, why worry her if there wasn't a reason. But I was second-guessing my decision.

"I know." My frustration showed when it came to my ex-wife, but Maryellen's feelings about her were equally as negative.

"Does Harper know about her, Gage?" she asked.

"She does."

Her look of approval was short-lived.

She was tapping away on her tablet, as usual, while at our Thursday meetings. But her demeanor wasn't typical. She wasn't normally an emotional person, but she did smile on occasion. This morning, however, the scowl on her face was a bit concerning. And I don't think it was the mention of Rebecca that had done it.

"Everything okay today?" I asked her.

Suddenly, a mask came over her face, camouflaging the once noticeable emotion. My gaze remained on her as she struggled to maintain a neutral appearance. I may have noticed some wetness forming in her eyes, but I wasn't completely sure.

"There isn't much more we need to discuss, Maryellen. If you want to finish this later, we can."

I thought ending our meeting might give her the out she needed, but she remained sitting in the chair across from me, staring at her tablet, unmoving. Eventually, she looked up and her face had returned to what would be considered her normal composure. She gave me a small smile.

"I'm okay, si—Gage." Her smile widened at her almost slip. "I appreciate it, though. Just a little something I need to deal with on my own, that's all." She resumed looking at her notes. "The only task still worthy of discussing is next week's meeting with your father. It's scheduled for Wednesday. Does that still work? I know you have a long weekend planned."

Looking at my calendar, I realized how quickly it had come up. It was already the end of June, leading into July 4th weekend, and he'd been gone over six months already. This next meeting would most likely determine if he was leaving permanently. Retiring.

"Yeah, could you confirm with Chase, please?"

"I'll check with Simon."

That was a first. She would usually check with Chase directly, not bother going to his assistant. Simon and Maryellen didn't always see eye to eye. But maybe they were doing better with each other.

"Sounds good, Maryellen. Looks like we're all set."

She remained sitting in her seat, looking like she had something else to say. Leaning back against my chair, I waited.

"I'm glad it seems like you and Harper have worked out whatever was going on, Gage." She seemed hesitant to offer her opinion about my personal life, but I've tried to make her comfortable in this area.

"Thank you," I told her. "And I really am looking forward to showing her off tomorrow. I'm thankful she could get off work."

Fortunately, Harper was able to get off at the club.

The entire weekend.

Because the next morning she and I were taking off with Jared and Delia upstate to Delia's family cabin in the Catskills for the holiday.

It was setting up to be a great weekend.

"Oh, the club, that's right."

The club.

Did Maryellen know that Harper worked at The Velvet Rope?

How would she have known that? So many questions ran through my mind as Maryellen stood from her seat and made for a quick exit from my office.

"We do seem to be good, Gage. I'll reach out to Simon about the meeting with Chase and your father next week."

My impromptu visits to Harper at the shop had become somewhat of an inside joke between Fiona and me. She loved when I stopped by to surprise them both. Apparently, it was a reminder of how Jim, her husband, used to be with her in the heyday of their relationship: full of surprises.

"Mr. Parker," Fiona said as I opened the shop door, the bell announcing my arrival. "Fancy meeting you here."

Our greeting had now become a hug—I'd definitely won her over. And since Harper and I came out of the Florida thing okay, Fiona felt as though she played a role in helping us stay together.

"I'll go get her," Fiona said as she made her way to the back room.

"Thank you."

Harper walked into the front room, a smile lighting her face.

"What are you doing here?" she asked as she hustled into my open arms.

"Maybe I just wanted this hug?"

The feel of her was worth the time away from work these little trips cost me. And it seemed I was making more and more of these trips to see her.

But there was a purpose in today's visit. And I wasn't looking forward to bringing it up.

"Do you have a minute?" I asked her.

She heard the catch in my voice, and it showed as she pulled away, hands wringing together. Her nerves were on high alert.

"Sure," she said. "Fiona, I'm taking five." She walked toward the door and motioned for me to follow.

Privacy.

On a crowded New York street.

But I got it, it was better if strangers heard us rather than Fiona.

"Babe, relax," I said as I grabbed her hand, spinning her toward me.

"Hard to do with the way you asked to talk," she said.

Shit. This was already starting off bad.

"Harper, do you really think I'm here to talk about us? Like ending?" Her eyes went wide at my words, so I figured that was exactly what she thought. "Baby, that's not it at all."

I took her in my arms and leaned us against the building. "Listen, I do have something to tell you, and I'm not happy about it, but it has no bearing on us at all. We promised to talk, right? Talk, not run."

Looking her square in the eye, I waited until I knew she understood me. A few blinks later, her small nod was my green light. But she still looked nervous.

Or maybe it was me that was nervous.

"So, tomorrow night, at the event, there's a slight chance that Rebecca might be there," I said. "She's been a pain in the ass and hasn't responded so we have no way of knowing, and I thought about not even telling you. Because why even concern you about something that may not happen. But I didn't want you blindsided by it, or her, if she decides to show her face. Which she shouldn't do, because no one…"

She put her fingers against my lips.

Stopping my rambling.

Her smile made me calm down. Didn't realize how nervous I really was.

"Gage," she said. "Now it's your turn to relax. You have nothing to worry about. Thank you for telling me, but she works for your company. I'd expect you'd have to see her from time to time."

The steadiness of her words was a welcome surprise. And the breath I was holding came out as a loud sigh.

"Thank you," I said to her as I leaned my head against the window of the shop.

"What for?"

"I don't know," I said. "Being so mature about this, I guess. Not making a big deal, not being jealous."

She grabbed my face with both hands, pulling me in for a kiss.

"Let's not make problems where there aren't any, Gage," she said when her lips pulled back from mine. She went in for one more small peck. "I'm sure we'll have our share of issues to deal with. And we talk, not run, right?"

Hopefully, Rebecca wasn't going to be one of those problems.

CHASE AND JARED met me for lunch. I think they knew my nerves were shot about Rebecca and Harper possibly meeting at the event the next night. Harper amazed me with how well she handled hearing the news, but I was still nervous. So, when they both called in the morning suggesting we head to the bar for a beer and a burger during the Yankee game, I took them up on it.

Chase - Meet us at O'Hara's at 1:30

. . .

WALKING INTO THE BAR, I found them in a booth toward the back. Three burger platters and a pitcher of beer were already on the table.

"Hey, guys," I said.

Their mumbled hellos came through mouths full of food or beer as their eyes barely left the screen above our table. The game was in the second inning by the time I was able to make it out of the office. And the Yanks were already down by two.

"Looks like they're still missing Cole being on the IL," I said as I grabbed my seat.

My food was still warm, so they'd waited a bit to get the food. Jared poured me a beer, and our hungry silence resumed as we took monster bites of their famous burgers.

"Good choice for lunch, Chase," I told him. "We don't come here enough and it's so close to the office."

He nodded. "I agree, I think we should do this weekly."

"Well, maybe not weekly," I told him. "But we should do it more often."

"To getting out together more!" Chase hollered. And our three pint glasses clinked over the center of the table.

"To getting together more," Jared and I said in unison.

We settled into watching the game while finishing the fries on the table. The pitcher was long finished, and the game was already in the fourth inning before our waitress returned.

"Anything else, guys?" she asked.

We all looked around, unsure if we could spare more time together. By the looks on their faces, they were in no rush to get back to the office, and I didn't want to be the one to ruin our time together. My afternoon was free of meetings, just some paperwork on the books.

"Can we get another pitcher, please?" I asked her.

I caught the subtle smile on both their faces as I turned my attention back to the game.

"So, Amanda, huh?" I questioned Chase.

Jared perked up at my question as well. We both wanted to know more about what was going on with the two of them; it wasn't like Chase to see a girl on repeat.

"Don't read too much into it. I needed a date for this thing tomorrow and, well, she's the only one available."

That was total bullshit. Chase had his pick of girls at any given time. There was more to that story, but he clearly wasn't giving it to us. Our pitcher arrived and Chase filled our glasses.

"Well, I thought I'd let you know that I told both Maryellen and Simon today that they should come tomorrow night. I think it's about time we start including them in these events. They're just as important to our team as the investors, maybe more." Jared nodded in agreement with my news as I took a gulp of my beer. However, looking at Chase, I almost spit the contents out of my mouth.

He was as white as a ghost.

"Why would you do that?" he asked. It wasn't anger in his voice. He seemed more stunned at the news.

"*Why?*" I asked right back at him. "Are you going to tell me that Simon doesn't do more for you than anyone else in that entire building? I couldn't survive without Maryellen. If you don't feel the same about him, maybe it's time to start looking for a new assistant."

Simon had been in the company longer than Maryellen. I knew for a fact that he was the only reason Chase was able to maintain a professional appearance these past months. It was a false threat to get rid of him, one I would never allow to happen.

"He's fine," Chase said.

Something was definitely off with Chase.

"Well, Delia's looking forward to seeing Harper and Amanda, so I'm glad they'll both be there. We might get a chance to hang a bit with the guys tomorrow," Jared said.

Chase took advantage of the moment and went to the bathroom. I wasn't going to make anything of it. I wouldn't want him to do it to me.

"Yeah, I'm glad they'll have each other, too," I said to Jared. More glad than he would know, especially if my ex was making an appearance.

PULLING up to her apartment the next day in the limo, I texted Harper that we'd arrived. I'd decided that we would go alone. I wanted time with her before arriving, without the guys and their girlfriends. These functions typically required me to socialize with the shareholders to maintain a professional relationship with people I only saw a handful of times a year, so I could easily be busy most of the night.

Leaning against the railing, I waited for her and relished the warm June air. Being in the office all day, I hadn't realized how gorgeous the day was. Even my lunch was at my desk during a Zoom call overseas with London.

The inside door opened, and I caught a glimpse of her as she entered the foyer.

She chose the pink dress, her favorite color.

And just like I imagined it would, it looked amazing with her tan skin and accentuated her ass.

I knew before she even turned around that it dipped down low in the back. So low that I feared the top of her ass might peek out.

With how much skin these dresses showed, I was not entirely sure how girls wore undergarments.

"Hey, you," she said as she walked out onto the steps.

I held out the bunch of pink peonies I had been holding behind my back.

"For you, beautiful." I had them wrapped in a pink satin ribbon. Well, Fiona did it for me. It was helpful having her on speed dial for moments like this. Leaning down, I kissed her on her cheek. "Even though you work with them every day, you still deserve to be given flowers." She smelled better than the flowers.

She took them in her hands, her nose going straight to the blooms. Her eyes closed as she smelled them, then looked up at me through her long lashes.

"Thank you." She looked back at her door. "Should I run them upstairs?"

"No, I have a vase in the car for them. C'mon, let's get going. There's bound to be traffic."

As my hand went behind her to guide her to the stairs, it was just as I'd expected.

Completely bare back.

And sexy as hell.

Maryellen did an excellent job with the choices she'd provided. When she showed me the pictures of the dresses she had sent over, this was by far my favorite.

Thankfully, the crack of Harper's ass was not sticking out of the dress. But it was close. Her skin was glowing. And it took everything in me to not kiss every inch of her back as she descended the stairs ahead of me.

"Hi, Tommy!" she said cheerily as we got to the car.

"Ms. Wilson," he responded with a smile and a nod.

"Here, Gage, can you take the flowers and my bag, please?"

Harper lifted the bottom of her floor-length gown into her hands to get into the back of the car.

And holy fuck.

If that wasn't the hottest thing I'd seen…since the last time I saw her naked.

As she bent over, her ass was outlined so perfectly by the silky material. And as she lifted the dress in her arm, it showed off smooth legs that led to a pair of sky-high silvery heels, heels she hated wearing but did for me tonight.

Climbing in after her, we settled into the seat and Tommy closed the door. Leaning close to her ear, I whispered, "Are you wearing any underwear, Harper?"

Her scandalous smile gave me my answer.

"None of the dresses you had sent over lent themselves to underwear, Gage. I thought that was by design."

Looking at the front of her dress, the material draping low between her breasts, her cleavage on full display, I understood what she meant.

And then I knew I was going to have a hard dick all night.

My finger gravitated to the spot where her breasts were touching, pushed together in some magical way. As I skimmed the top of her breasts, I watched bumps appear on her skin. Her thighs clenched as my finger skipped over the material to her nipple that was hardening at my touch.

She was such a fucking turn-on.

Leaning low, I whispered, "How am I supposed to make it all night not touching you with you looking like this? Tell me that, Harper."

As my fingers pinched her nipple, a moan escaped her pink lips.

"Gage," she moaned.

But I had to stop. If I didn't, she would not look this beautiful by the time we reached the venue. Pulling my hands from her, I literally put them under my legs to keep myself from touching her.

"I don't want to ruin your perfect makeup and hair," I told her with a sly smile.

She leaned into me, fixing my bowtie, and placed a chaste kiss on my mouth.

"You look pretty good yourself, Mr. Parker."

Wiping her lipstick from my mouth, she sat back in her seat, grabbed my hand, and looked out the window. As she watched the scenery going by, I was content to stare at her profile. At peace with the fact that we were in a place, finally, that made us both happy.

I only hoped that there wasn't going to be a meeting between my past life and my current one. Although Harper assured me she would be fine if it happened, she didn't need to be subjected to Rebecca.

But I guess we would deal with it if we had to.

And maybe Rebecca would be an adult about us seeing each other.

She *was* the adulterer.

The unfaithful one.

CHAPTER 28

Harper

Gage looked amazing in his tux. His dark hair and caramel-brown eyes popped against the bright white shirt. And his clothes always seemed as though they were poured onto him, but in the most delicious way. His jacket hugged every line of muscle across his back, along his arms when he moved, yet he never looked constricted.

And I felt beautiful. When the dresses showed up at my apartment, I felt like a princess. Well, maybe at least a little like Pretty Woman in that scene when she goes shopping. And I'd go so far to say that we looked amazing together. Driving over in a limo made everything even more glamorous. It was setting up to be a night that should be special. We would be with his co-workers and his friends. And I knew several of his friends now and liked them. I was even looking forward to seeing some of them, especially Delia and Jared.

Gage brought me flowers. He even brought me my favorite flowers, pink peonies. My boyfriend was the most thoughtful person I've had in my life. He was complimentary to a fault. One devouring look from him, as his eyes raked over me from top to bottom, and my confidence went through the roof.

So why did I have a sense of doom hovering over me during the entire drive?

Was I nervous about possibly meeting his ex-wife? That was most likely it, but I didn't feel nervous when I thought about it.

My hands were shaking, so I kept them wrapped together in a ball in my lap. Could he feel my hand shaking when it was in his? As we pulled up to the hotel where the event was taking place, a heaviness settled in my chest.

Or maybe I was nervous about meeting his colleagues. These people were way out of my league. I was a florist by day and a waitress by night. Wearing a Dior gown and attending an event at the Plaza Hotel in New York City was not in my wheelhouse.

Gage exited the limo ahead of me, turned, and offered his hand to help me from the car. Always the perfect gentleman. As I stood from the door, he pulled me into his arms, a quick embrace, and brought his mouth to my ear.

"I can't wait to show you off to this entire room tonight. No one will look as beautiful as you," he whispered before placing a gentle kiss on my temple.

His words should make me feel weightless, as though I were floating from the compliment.

Instead, the dread remained. And was starting to make me feel sick.

Maybe I was truly nervous. He wanted to show me off. That had to be it. Different worlds. We've talked about it often, how I feel so disconnected from his environment. Once inside, I would get a glass of water and I'd feel better.

"Are you okay?" Gage asked as we walked inside, firmly holding my hand in his.

He squeezed it when he asked his question. Looking up, I nodded.

"I'm fine, I think I'm just nervous."

He looked down at his phone and smiled. "Delia is already here and waiting for you."

That offered a small amount of comfort.

My anxiety about the night dimmed even more as we approached the red-carpeted steps of the entrance to the iconic building.

It was stunning.

Each of the two doors was held open by a bellman as we moved through them, and I knew this was the closest to royalty I would ever feel. Stepping into the foyer of the classic space, we were surrounded by marble columns and flamboyant rugs and tapestries. The crystal chandelier above was a marvel.

But all it made me think about was *Home Alone 2*. And I let out a small giggle.

Thankfully, Gage was engrossed with finding our way, and my little outburst went unnoticed.

"Mr. Parker," a man dressed professionally holding a clipboard said as he came up next to us. "Nice to see you again, sir. And thank you for choosing The Plaza for your event." He fell in step with us as we moved along toward the elevators. "Your event is in the Rose Club, as was discussed. The guests that have arrived have been escorted to the room. Let me take you there, sir."

"Thank you, Martin," Gage said. "May I introduce my girl-friend, Harper Wilson?"

Swapping his clipboard around, he extended a hand. "Ms. Wilson, a pleasure."

Taking his hand in mine, I realized it was the first time I'd been introduced to a stranger as Gage's girlfriend.

And it felt nice.

It felt really nice.

"Martin, the room is set up with couches and chairs, as well as tables, correct? I wanted it to have intimate, comfortable areas for people to sit and socialize. Not just tables to sit around."

The gentleman referenced his papers and pulled one to the top of his pile.

"Here is the floor plan, sir. It is set up beautifully, if I may say so. The furnishings were brought in from a different room to better fit your requested contemporary theme. The gray, black, and pink color scheme looks impeccable."

They looked over the plan together as the elevator continued to rise. When it signaled our arrival to our floor, Gage made sure to take a hold of me once again.

"Ready?" he asked.

A simple nod was all I could muster up because my nervousness and the feeling of doom returned full force as we exited.

But the room was stunning. Martin and his team had done a fabulous job. We walked into a wood-paneled space that had a huge U-shaped bar with small chatting areas set up around it. Comfy gatherings of three and four chairs with a small table in the center were spread around the perimeter of the bar. Then, through a wide staircase to a lower level was the main sitting area. It was set up with small couches and chairs in the center, arranged in cozy groupings. Several guests were already sitting, eating from served hors d'oeuvres. Then there were several tall tables and regular tables set up around the room.

And the flowers.

They were stunning.

The arrangements were chock full of pink and white roses, peonies, fluffy hydrangeas, begonias, and even some hibiscus. The greenery mixed in was almost tropical in nature, with big green wavy leaves. Fiona would be in heaven.

But I had to wonder where he got them.

"Well done, Gage, this is amazing," I told him.

Leaning down, he whispered in my ear, "I'll tell Fiona you approve." His mischievous grin widened as I looked up at him.

"What?" I asked. "How?"

"That you will have to ask her. All I know is I commissioned the job with her but asked if she could keep it a secret from you, and she apparently did."

He was looking around the room in admiration as well. "And I can't take all the credit. Maryellen worked hard on this with Fiona. Many of the ideas were hers." Looking down at me, he smiled. "I do love that you chose the pink dress, you look amazing in it."

He plucked a pink rose from a nearby arrangement and placed it in my hand, a memory of what he'd done to me with one flooding my thoughts.

But then I looked around the room again.

"Did you choose this color scheme for *me*?"

"It is your favorite color," he said.

Staring around the room in stunned wonder, I acknowledged all the pink touches. From the pillows on the couches, the napkins on the tables, to the floral arrangements. So many shades of the color mixed in with grays and black. It was simple yet sophisticated.

Everything overwhelmed me.

"What if I hadn't chosen this dress?" I asked him, turning back his way.

"Well, you would have been just as stunning regardless of the color dress. But it worked out, and you will definitely be the most beautiful woman here tonight."

His hand went behind my neck, pulling me close as he bent down. Our mouths met and his pillowy soft lips lingered on mine as his fingers gripped the back of my neck.

"Hey you two, enough already!"

We startled at a booming voice right next to us and jumped away from each other. Jared and Delia were by our side, laughing as I blushed.

"Hi, guys!" Delia squealed. "Harper, you look amazing! Oh my god, your dress is to die for, turn around."

Delia grabbed my hand and spun me on my heels. She pulled on my long curls, admiring my hair as well. "And your curls look perfect."

She looked gorgeous as well. Her blonde hair pulled tight into a ponytail high on her head. Her classic hourglass body was covered in a skintight black dress and paired with red high heels and a red lip. Perfection.

"Christ, Delia, I wish I had your height and your body to pull off a dress like that. You look like a friggin model," I told her.

Jared leaned in and kissed my cheek next. "Hi, pretty girl, nice to see you again."

"Hi, Jared."

"Okay boys, I'm stealing her, you two can go do whatever business shit you have to do. I think I just saw Chase come in, so go grab him and do what you must. We'll be over here." Delia grabbed my hand and started leading me toward one of the sitting areas.

But Gage intervened.

"Harper," he said, taking a hold of my arm. Pulling me close to him, he whispered, "Will you be okay?"

We were in such a good place lately in our relationship. In the time since returning from Florida, we've made sure to talk openly about anything bothering us. Gage, especially, had gotten better at expressing when he felt insecure or hesitant.

"I'll be fine," I told him.

"She'll be fine," Delia said as she pulled me away from him, laughing as she did it.

The smile on his face as I strutted away told me he was enjoying the view. I made sure to accentuate my sway as I walked.

"Jesus, I told you he's got it bad for you, girl," Delia joked as she swiped two champagne flutes from a passing tray. Handing one to me, we walked toward a small sofa. "Let's go get comfortable. My feet are killing me already."

Before we sat, I stopped Delia, turning her toward me. "Do you remember when we were at Coney Island?"

She nodded, but looked confused.

"You were saying something similar that day, and that Gage was 'not typical when it came to girls.' Do you remember saying that?" I asked. "What did you mean by that?"

She turned me in the direction of the couch I knew she wanted to sit on and kept us walking.

"Well, Gage is a chronic relationship kinda guy. He can't help it. I know he wishes he wasn't, but he only wants to be in long-term relationships." She paused as if she didn't want to continue, but then turned to face me directly. "When he and Rebecca divorced, he kinda went off the deep end. He took off, left town, and I didn't really think he was gonna want to be in a relationship again for a while. But you came along." Her smile grew wide. "You, my dear, have changed his mind. I haven't ever seen him this happy."

I don't think that was what I was expecting to hear from her, but I wasn't unhappy with what she said.

We made our way to the couch, and once we sat, a few other women joined us. Some Delia knew, and some she didn't. We made the rounds, introducing ourselves and, had a nice little group conversation going within minutes. It started looking a bit like a high school dance: the guys taking care of business on one side of the room while the girls socialized on the other.

"Hi, Harper! Hi, Delia!" A voice rang out above the chatter around us.

We looked up to see Amanda approaching, which meant Chase had indeed shown up. I knew that would please Gage. He was never sure with his brother. And I was pleased to see another familiar face. We made room for her on our small couch, squeezing in together and giggling like schoolgirls.

"I'm so glad we're not hanging out with the guys. They're literally talking shop, like really boring shit, over there," Amanda said. "When we first got here, I didn't see you guys and thought I was stuck alone with them all night."

Amanda didn't seem to be Chase's type. But I wasn't sure anyone knew if Chase had a type.

"We don't want to be dragged into those conversations, do we?" Delia offered, trying to make Amanda feel welcomed.

A server had come by with some small bites on a tray, and we oohed and aahed over the variety of food offered. From shrimp cocktail to chicken satay, it all looked delicious. Just as I was about to stuff my face with a second piece of shrimp, Amanda grabbed my arm.

"Who is that girl next to Chase over there?"

Following her line of sight, I was pleasantly surprised to see Maryellen standing with him. And she looked absolutely stunning in a red slip dress that hugged her figure. Her blonde hair hung down her back, which I'd never seen before; she always had it pulled up while in the office or when meeting with me. She was with a man I didn't recognize while speaking with both Chase and Gage. They looked our way, her smiling in my direction.

"That's Maryellen, Gage's assistant," I told her. I was excited to see her. It had been weeks since we'd last talked. As I stood to walk toward her, Chase grabbed Maryellen by the hand and ushered her toward the bar in a hurried walk. The group they were with, including Gage, looked a bit confused as they watched them walk away.

As I sat back down, and tried to avoid looking at Amanda, I caught a glimpse of her looking at her phone, trying to act nonchalant.

But it was obvious she saw what I did.

A quick glance at Delia confirmed she did as well.

But then a pounding on a drum stole our attention across the room.

"The band is starting!" Delia screeched. "They're supposed to be amazing, let's go dance." She grabbed my hand, and we started toward the small space they left open as a dance floor.

Dashing away, we were intentionally trying to leave Amanda behind. Once we knew we were alone, Delia let loose.

"What the hell do you think that was about?"

"I don't know, do you think it really meant anything?" I asked.

But by the look on both their faces as Chase escorted Maryellen out of the room, it seemed pretty evident it did.

"Well, I'm not going to waste any more time thinking about it," Delia said. "Let's dance!"

She grabbed me by my hand and spun me around, both of us laughing out loud. A small group of others had joined us on the wood floor, and we were getting increasingly rowdier. The band was playing music from the late nineties, just my type, and I was losing myself in it. As I tossed my head from side to side, Delia whispered in my ear.

"You have an admirer."

Following her eyes, I found Gage watching me from a ledge overlooking the dance area. Smiling, I beckoned to him with my finger, swaying my hips to the music to entice him to join me. He shook his head, held up his beer, and continued to watch from where he stood. I knew he wouldn't join me. He didn't like to dance, but I thought I'd give it a shot.

But then I felt more hands on me. Turning around, it was Maryellen who joined us to dance.

"Hi!" I screamed to her over the music. Leaning in so she could hear me. "Oh my God, it's so good to see you. I didn't know you were going to be here and I feel like it's been ages since I've seen you now that Gage took over the flower account with us."

A sly smile took over her face as she shook her head a bit, almost in disbelief, and brought her mouth to my ear.

"I almost didn't come. But Gage made a big deal about me and Simon coming. He wants us to feel like we're a part of the team, and I appreciate that, so here I am."

She understood my confusion immediately.

"Simon is Chase's assistant. That's who I came with."

I gave her a nod. She was not *with* Simon. That made the interaction with Chase more interesting.

"Let's grab a drink," I said. I motioned to Delia that we were heading back, but she stayed on the dance floor.

"You look gorgeous, Maryellen." I gestured to her dress, then mine. "Thank you for the dresses you sent to me. They were such amazing choices, I had a hard time choosing."

We reached the conversation area and were lucky enough to find a seat. A server offered us champagne, and we both took a glass.

"Cheers," we said together, each taking a sip.

"You made a fine choice with the pink. Gage said that was the one you would go with," she said. Her look was conspiratorial as she continued to gaze at me. "I hope you two work out. He seems happier than he's ever been, ya know."

Laughing, I looked around, reminded of the décor, knowing

Maryellen probably arranged most of it. And then a thought struck me.

Could it be? Looking at Maryellen, the question was all over my face.

Maryellen McEntyre, mastermind matchmaker?

She looked me square in the eyes as she took a long sip of her champagne and smiled as the glass came down from her lips.

"Oh my God, you're behind this, aren't you?" I asked her.

At that moment, I saw Gage, still up on the same raised ledge, only now talking with a beautiful blonde. She stood closer to him than I would've liked, but I assumed she was a client, so I tried not to let it bother me. The music was loud—everyone had to lean in to talk.

Suddenly, Delia came running up on Maryellen and me.

"Harper!" she yelled. Her eyes bounced from mine to Maryellen, back to mine, then up to the ledge where Gage was still talking to the blonde. "Harper…" Her voice softened as she looked at Maryellen this time.

Delia came to sit with us while confusion set in.

"What?" I asked. "What's wrong?"

The two women sitting on either side of me shared a look.

"Nothing is wrong," Maryellen said, as she also looked up at Gage.

When I turned to look, my eyes connected with his. The solemn look on his face spoke volumes. He pointed to me, the blonde now looking our way.

And then I knew.

"It's okay," Maryellen said, taking my hand. "You're okay, Harper."

I sat as straight as I could while looking up at the man I knew I was falling in love with if I wasn't already there.

And I watched him have to talk to the woman who destroyed him.

"That's Rebecca, isn't it?" I asked.

"Yes," Maryellen said.

She looked nervous, as if she was telling me information she wasn't supposed to.

"And just so you know, he wasn't sure she was coming," Maryellen added.

"I know, he told me," I assured her.

She seemed to relax at that news as she nodded.

My mind wrestled with deciding if I should go to him or not. I didn't want to look like the jealous girlfriend, but I did want to support him. But as I watched their interaction, it was over before I could determine what to do. I excused myself from Delia and Maryellen.

Almost breaking out in a run to get to him before someone else did, we met at the bottom of a set of stairs. Grabbing him by the hand, I pulled him toward a darkened corner.

"Are you okay?" I asked him once we were tucked away from most of the guests.

His cocky smile wasn't what I was expecting to get in return to my question. As he leaned against the wall, bringing his bourbon to his lips, his smile grew even wider.

"Well?" The insistence in my voice only made him chuckle. But then his hand literally moved to his crotch, his head craning over mine to confirm we were alone.

"Your concern is making me hard, babe," he said.

Swatting his hand away from his pants, my grunt of disapproval was lost on him as he continued trying to make light of the situation.

"Baby, I appreciate your concern." His hand came to my face, cradling it the way he always did. "But I'm fine. I'm more concerned about you right now. It couldn't be easy seeing me with my ex-wife."

He felt my slight nod in his hand.

"Why on earth would you be concerned about me, Gage?"

His hand retreated completely, sliding into the pocket of his pants. He avoided making eye contact, looking at the crowd around us instead. It was as if a wall came between us, something that had never happened before.

And that dread I was feeling earlier came back with a vengeance.

A shiver went through my body as a cold sweat formed across my temples. That slightly sick feeling returned in the pit of my gut, making me want escape somewhere and be alone in my misery.

Was this what my mind knew was going to happen? She was going to come traipsing back into his life.

Did she still have a claim on his heart I was unaware of?

"Harper," he said, his voice firm. "Whatever you're thinking right now, knock it the fuck from your head." Both his hands gripped my upper arms as he pulled me close, our faces almost touching. "I see it all over your face. Do *not* let her do this to us. I will not let her come between us."

Staring up at him, I knew my eyes were watery. He was still holding my arms, so wiping the soon to spill over tears was impossible. I was not an overly emotional person. But the feeling that had been hanging over me since this morning decidedly messed with me.

"Gage," I started.

"No," he said, then let go of my arms. His one hand went straight under my chin, keeping my face lifted toward his. "Let me talk."

But he stalled, appearing to be at a loss for words.

"Listen, I had this vision of what I wanted tonight to be for us, and it didn't include my ex being here. The fact that she was unprofessional enough to not respond pisses me off. She's so much more calculated than I ever knew. She probably knows about us, had her plan to come and make a big entrance for all I know. But she means nothing, absolutely nothing to us. Don't give her another thought. She doesn't deserve it."

He was stroking my cheek, that strong thumb of his working its magic. His words were reasonable, but my anxiety was being persistent.

It was his fucking ex-wife.

When I looked up and saw the two of them standing next to one another, her smiling at him, they looked like they belonged together. She's from this world, it was obvious. She oozed glamour and professionalism.

And I wasn't expecting her to be so…hot.

"What did she say to you?"

Holding my breath as soon as I asked the question, I watched him closely as he paused before answering. I don't know why I asked because I wasn't sure I wanted to know. Morbid curiosity, I guess.

"Ha," he said, then kind of laughed to himself. "Well, she started off with an apology for just showing up." Leaning against the wall, his hands went in his pockets, and he looked uncomfortable. "But then she went right into the rest of her apologies about all the shit she did to me. And I didn't want to hear them."

He withdrew a hand, and it came up to play with a long curl hanging against my shoulder, wrapping it around his finger and pulling on it playfully. "I stopped her, told her not to waste her breath. Instead, I pointed you out and informed her that I was happy and not to waste another second thinking about us or what she did."

And then his hand came back to my face. My cheek nestled into his palm as his thumb stroked my cheek.

"I told her she did me the greatest favor. Otherwise, I never would have met you."

This man.

My God, he was going to be my undoing. The things he said to me made my heart break wide open and then become whole again with him inside it.

Last week he brought up the idea of us maybe moving in together. Not immediately, but for us to start thinking about it. The amount of time I already spent at his brownstone made it seem as if we were already there, but it's a major step to make it official.

And I think he knew I wasn't quite ready yet.

But moments like this got me closer.

"I guess I should thank her as well," I said.

We both laughed.

He grabbed my hand and led me back toward the party. The room was substantially more crowded with people than before we had retreated to our corner. Looking around, Gage understood who my eyes were seeking.

"I'm pretty sure she left already. But if not, I don't think you have anything to worry about when it comes to her. She won't bother you. She doesn't have many friends left in this office. I'm shocked she showed up at all." He swung around and pulled me against him, his arms around my waist. "You're hanging out with two of the girls who hate her the most around here."

My eyes wandered back to the couch to see Maryellen and Delia still chatting it up together. Their occasional glances in our direction made it obvious they were talking about us.

"Head back over to them. I have some business to go tend to. Have fun, but FYI, we aren't staying much longer," he said as his hands wandered to my ass. His lips were against my ear and his words a warm whisper. "As much as I love you in this dress, all I can do is envision you out of it."

His teeth nipped at my earlobe, causing my entire body to quiver in his hands.

"Yep, I want to make you shake just like that, but under me, Harper. And while I'm inside you."

Lesson learned: not wearing underwear when your boyfriend turns you on is problematic.

I was drenched between my legs. Literally drenched. With nothing to soak it up.

"Can we leave now?" I asked, smiling up at him.

He pulled at a long curl as he walked away, his wink as he went telling me he knew exactly what he'd done.

"Give me thirty minutes," he said, and disappeared into the crowd.

With my flushed face, I didn't want to go back to the girls. And I really did need a minute alone. Looking around the expansive space, I saw the sign for the ladies' room across the way and went in that direction.

You know you're in a special place when the counter of the restroom has a basket filled to the brim with any type of necessity you might need while out, including pairs of flip flops for your tired high-heeled feet. I contemplated grabbing them for a moment but resisted. Instead, I took a soft towel and blotted at my sweaty face, hoping to keep my makeup intact.

As the towel covered my face, the door to the restroom swung open. Quickly pulling it away, my anxiety returned tenfold.

Standing next to me, looking at her reflection in the mirror, was Rebecca.

And our eyes connected.

The lipstick she'd taken out of her bag remained motionless in her hands as we stared at each other in the mirror.

"You're Harper, right?" she finally said.

"I am."

In my mind were a million one-line zingers I should be throwing at her.

He's better off now, with me.

Thank you for not being able to keep your pants on.

Your loss is my gain.

What a fucking moron you must be for messing up a perfect life with him.

And if Victoria were here, she would have even better ones.

But as I looked closely at her, I could see that she was hurting. For some reason, I knew she wasn't going to sling any attitude in my direction, so I remained quiet. And waited.

"Gage looks happy," she said. And she smiled.

She was a very pretty woman. It made me a little insecure. Only a little, but it did.

"He deserves to be happy. He's a good guy that had a shitty thing done to him," she continued.

My gaze didn't waver. And eventually she couldn't maintain the cold stare I had for her as she chose to look down at the counter.

"He didn't deserve what you did to him. No one would deserve that," I told her.

The flinch was slight, and she tried to hide it, but I saw.

Her face lifted as well as her shoulders, an attempt to gain some confidence.

"You're right," she said, turning to face me. "I'm glad we ran into each other. Gage wouldn't have introduced us, I don't think."

I don't know why but hearing her say his name made my skin crawl. Even seeing her next to him and us standing this close didn't do to me what hearing her say his name did.

"But I can tell you're good for him. So, I'm happy to have the chance to tell you that."

Placing the towel on the counter, I picked up my bag. My

attempt at not being the jealous girlfriend was slowly fading. As I stood next to her, the green monster chipped away at my confidence and a strong desire to lash out at her overcame me. But the more I thought about the situation, the more annoyed I got.

She lived in London. You don't come to New York willy nilly without knowing. It takes a plan. At least booking a flight the day before kind of plan. She knew she was coming and chose not to tell Gage. Why, we won't know. But I didn't like that move on her part.

And I knew I should turn around and walk out.

But I couldn't. I didn't.

"Rebecca, I could sit here and bad mouth you because of what you did to him. But to be honest, you're not worth my time to do that. And yes, while I am good for him, your opinion has no bearing on our relationship one bit." Walking around her, I grabbed the door to exit. "Have a nice life, Rebecca."

CHAPTER 29

Gage

Harper seemed a bit off all night. From the moment I picked her up, until I helped her into the car to head home, there was something unsaid hanging in the air between us. Of course, her seeing me with my ex would create some tension, but she seemed off even before that. But once we got into the limo to head home, the tension seemed to heighten. Maybe it was because we were alone. Or maybe it was because I was able to focus solely on her.

I knew there was the chance of Rebecca showing up. The fact that she did meant we would probably have to talk about it, and I really didn't want to. Nothing related to that woman was worth wasting our breath on.

Harper held my hand in her lap, both her hands playing with my fingers, as the car weaved through traffic. It was too short a drive to be worth trying to talk about anything. Tommy would have us to my place within minutes.

But then suddenly, she spun in her seat and was facing me. Her eyes remained looking at our interlocked hands even as she started talking.

"When I woke up this morning, something just didn't feel right. I had no idea what it was, but it felt like a black cloud hung over me all day. Like this impending sense of doom that wouldn't go away, even with how excited I was about tonight." Her tiny smile helped me to realize that she was okay as she finally looked up at me. "I met Rebecca in the bathroom tonight a little while before we left."

Her words sliced me open.

Keeping them apart was the one job I gave myself once I knew Rebecca had arrived. I saw Harper go into the bathroom. That was when Rebecca came to say her goodbyes to some people nearby, probably leaving early because she realized she shouldn't have come in the first place.

But I got complacent.

She must have gone in the ladies' room on her way out.

"Harper, I'm so sorry. The last thing I wanted was for you to have to deal with her tonight."

Pulling her against my chest, I gripped the back of her head. But she pushed against me, struggling to sit up.

"Gage," she started. "I think it was good for me."

The irony of her smile wasn't lost on me. My look of confusion didn't surprise her.

"No, really. It gave me closure. I was able to get a few things off my chest, so it was good."

"What did she say to you, Harper?"

I didn't want my tone to deter her from telling me, but I was furious at this entire situation.

"Well, she told me I was good for you." Her smug laugh was adorable and actually calmed me down a bit. She resumed playing with my fingers as she continued. "And she said you look happy."

I fell against the seat of the car, letting that sink in. Never in a million years would I have predicted those words come from

Rebecca's mouth. Looking at Harper, she looked more relaxed already, just by telling me what my ex said to her.

"Anything else?" I asked.

"Well," she started. "I may have said something to the effect of *yes, I am good for him, but her opinion really doesn't matter so have a good life* and then I walked out of the bathroom, leaving her in there."

A triumphant smile spread across her face.

So fucking adorable.

And I was proud of her.

"C'mere," I said as I pulled her across my lap. Her cheek settled against my chest as I held her. "I'm sorry you had to deal with her at all, but it sounds like you handled it like a champ."

She nestled deeper into my hold, lifting her legs onto mine.

"Enough about her. I mean it, she doesn't deserve our time," she said, looking up at me, her hand rubbing the side of my face. "If I remember correctly, you made a promise about something you wanted to do to me once we left there."

That got my dick hard immediately. And it also reminded me that she was wearing nothing under this dress.

And her legs were bent conveniently on my lap.

"Do you really want me to start this now, in the car?" I asked.

Reaching up, she undid my tie and slid it from around my neck.

"This damn bowtie is too small for you to use on me like last time," she whined.

At that moment, the limo came to a stop.

"Well, lucky for you we're home, and I have an entire closet full of ties," I said as I pushed her off my lap and grabbed her roughly by the hips, pushing her out of the car. Tommy hadn't even gotten to our side of the limo, and we were out and across the sidewalk. "Thanks, man. See you after the holiday," I said behind me.

I heard his soft chuckle as he closed the car door. We scurried up the stairs as I struggled with my key. Harper was already undoing my belt. Pushing the door open, we fell into the foyer together, a puzzle of arms and legs entangled. My belt flew against the wall as the zipper went down on my pants. But then I pushed her back.

"Wait," I told her. "I've been dreaming of watching that dress fall from your body all night, Harper."

Taking her by the hand, we walked up the stairs to the bedroom. But then her hands were on me, pushing me up as she was attempting to run.

"Hey, I've been waiting long enough for you. Get a move on it," she ordered as she slapped my ass.

We took off together, laughing as we ran the rest of the way into the room. Her dress was wrapped around her arm to avoid tripping as we catapulted ourselves onto the bed, our guttural laughs echoing off the walls. Both of us rolled to our backs, but our eyes connected as our smiles remained wide.

Her smile lit up the darkened room. And as we lay there, our mood shifted from excited to serious, our eyes locked. We turned on our sides to face each other, almost nose to nose. Reaching out, I tucked a loose piece of hair behind her ear and took full advantage of my hand being that close to her face. Her skin was as soft as a rose petal as my finger drifted across her cheek. My thumb rested on her full lower lip, pulling down on it. The desire to bite it became too strong, and my mouth was on hers, kissing her, tasting her.

But I pulled back.

"Harper," I said.

Her closed eyes took their time opening at the sound of her name. Those long lashes framing her bright blue eyes. I'd asked her once what flower her eyes most resembled. Her answer was a forget-me-not.

How apropos.

"Would you like me to stand and take my dress off for you now?" she asked with a coy smile.

Ah, my little vixen.

"Not yet," I answered.

Her eyes widened at that answer.

"Don't worry, we'll get to that," I told her. "But," I started, then got a bit nervous. Because I wasn't sure this was the right time.

Was it too soon?

Looking at her, with those big blue eyes now staring at me, wondering what I was holding back on, gave me the courage I needed.

"Harper," I started again as my hand caressed her face. "I'm in love with you. When we're together, every breath of mine is measured by every move you make. When we're not together, I'm fighting the urge to find you, to be with you every minute of every day."

Seeing the wetness gather in her eyes melted my heart. Our lips came together for a soft, gentle kiss.

"I love you, Harper Wilson."

Watching her as she allowed my words to sink in, I grew nervous about how they made her feel.

"Don't feel like…"

But she stopped me by putting her fingers against my mouth.

Then by putting her mouth on mine.

Pulling away slightly, she whispered, "I love you, Gage. I've known I was in love with you for a while."

Taking her by the upper arms, I flipped her over and had her straddle me. Almost simultaneously, I lifted the dress up over her hips. When it got to her waist, she stopped me.

"Don't you…?" The question in her voice was enough.

"You can strip for me another time; I need to be inside you right now."

She lifted her arms and was free of the dress in seconds. Sitting naked on top of me was the most stunning creature ever made. Her perfectly round breasts begged to be held as my hands cupped them, squeezing them. Her head rolled back as my fingers pulled at her already taut nipples.

Pinching, rolling, and twisting. Eliciting that level of sweet pain she'd started asking for.

Her hands fumbled for my pants beneath her, struggling to get them off. I helped by lifting my ass from the bed, her rising in the air with me, and sliding them down my legs as far as I could without losing her from my lap. Sitting, I slid my jacket from my shoulders as her fingers nimbly opened each tiny button of my shirt in record time. She slid it from my arms, and I flung it to the floor.

Gripping her by the sides, I pulled her back and forth, her pussy rubbing along my already hard cock. Her wet pussy was like satin sliding along me, getting me ready for her.

"Be a good girl, Harper, and lift yourself up and put me inside you."

Her eyes went wide at the order, but she immediately lifted her ass and reached for my dick. Stroking it in her hand, she swiped it along her wet slit, settling it at her entrance. She slowly lowered herself onto me, my dick sliding into her inch by inch. Her thighs shook from holding herself up, but she didn't want to come down on me just yet, I could tell.

She was enjoying the slow torture as her pussy took its time taking me in. Her playing with me, like I do her.

But we had all night for torturous games with our bodies. I needed to feel myself inside her.

Now.

Grabbing her by the hips, I forced her all the way down onto me, a yelp escaping her lips.

"I'm sorry, but I need to feel you around me, Harper," I said as I pulled myself up and wrapped my arms around her. "Christ, you feel so good, so tight."

Sitting so our bodies were flush against each other, my hands splayed against her back. Her fingers gripped me by the hair as she stared into my eyes.

We stilled.

"I love you," I told her again. Forcing my lips onto hers helped stop the tremble that had started in them. My emotions were strong, this woman my undoing.

"I love you too, Gage," she whispered into my hair. She pulled me tighter against her, our bodies seeming to become one.

Any love I thought I felt in the past I now doubted. Those feelings were nothing compared to what Harper did to my heart.

I smiled up at her as the emotions filled my throat. "I've never been happier." I pushed my face against her breasts but kept talking. "You've brought light into my darkness and made me smile when all I did was scowl." I started laughing as my voice cracked, the emotions strong. "And now it seems you've made me into a Hallmark writer."

She gripped my face in her hands, staring into my eyes. "Hey, don't ever stop talking to me like that, Mr. Parker, do you hear me?" she warned with a laugh. She ground her pussy onto my dick for good measure. "If you know what's good for you, you'll keep the sappy stuff coming."

My hands went down, around the top of her ass, and started moving us in a slow back and forth motion.

"So, you like the sappy talk?" I asked, as we kept the movements going.

Her hands went to my shoulders, gripping for support, holding on, as our rhythm continued to progress.

"I do, especially when it includes you telling me you love me," she said.

She started lifting her pussy from me a bit, sliding it up only to come back down. As she continued, the pace quickened until she was bouncing on my cock.

Literally bouncing on me.

"You make it hard to sweet talk when you're doing this, Harper," I told her right before letting out a moan.

Her moans were coming between her grunts of exertion as she worked me.

"I have faith in you, Mr. Parker. You're ever the professional, you can work through…"

She paused in her thoughts as she let out a moan of ecstasy. But then gathered her composure as she slowed her tempo.

"You can work through any situation, I'm sure," she said.

She resumed the tempo from before, a daring smile across her face.

"I appreciate your vote of confidence, baby," I told her. Lying back, flat on the bed, allowing her to maintain her assault on my body, I appreciated the view her movements offered.

Her tits bounced up and down as she slapped her pussy against me. But I needed to focus on the sweet side.

"Your hair looks beautiful in the moonlight coming through the window," I told her, as I reached up and grabbed a breast. Two could play at this game.

Her head fell back. She loved when I played with her tits.

Snapping her head forward, she looked at me. She knew she lost some ground. She bent down, bringing our faces closer. Her fingers went straight to my scruff, something her and I both loved her doing.

"I love that you told me you loved me before we got into bed," she said.

I froze, my hand motionless on her breast.

And she sat up straight, looking a little nervous at my reaction.

Sitting up with her, I hugged her against me fiercely.

"You picked up on that," I said.

Her expression relaxed.

I pushed my dick into her slowly, not wanting our lovemaking to stop, but it needed to take a different direction.

The game was over.

"That was intentional," I told her, then kissed her. Hard.

My tongue found hers, and I devoured her. Our mouths still connected, I spoke against her lips. "I needed it to count, to not seem like it was only because of…"

She nodded against me, she understood.

We rocked together, in sync with one another, as if we were one.

Our rhythm became our love song.

Eyes connected the entire time.

Her arms around my neck, mine around her waist.

And we made love.

Literal love.

To each other.

WE LAY in bed for a long time after, simply holding each other. Then we would alternate between dozing and rubbing each other's backs. Everything with Harper was easy. Getting to know her was easy. Hanging out with her was easy. Her hanging with my friends was easy. Our schedule together was easy.

Loving her was easy.

And for the first time in my life, I didn't feel as though I was waiting for the other shoe to fall. It all felt right.

Glancing at the clock, it was already almost two in the morning.

And so much had changed in our lives in the past few hours.

She was on her belly, the sheet only covering her ass and legs. Her bare back looked like silk in the dim light. Her breast was peeking out next to the arm she had tucked under her head. She looked so damn sexy. But I curled my hands and resisted, though the temptation to touch her was strong.

"I feel you looking at me," she said, her face still squished into the pillow.

A boyish grin came over me, knowing she could sense me like that. We'd come far in the months we'd been together.

"Oh, do you? Well, could you feel my hands about to reach out and feel the side of your breast right here?" I said as I slid my finger along the smooth skin.

She giggled but didn't move.

My hand went to her cheek, stroking, encouraging her eyes to open. And they did.

"Are you ready for round two, Mr. Parker?" she asked as her sensuous eyes beckoned me.

Pulling her to face me, I shook my head. "No, that's not what I want. It's late, and we have to get up early tomorrow. I just didn't want to go to sleep for the night without telling you one more time that I love you."

Inching forward, her lips found mine.

"I love you, Gage Parker." Her white teeth seemed to glow in the dark room. "I really had no idea you were such a romantic, but I'm loving it."

Moving onto my back, I pulled her head into the crook of my shoulder, needing her to sleep against me. Her arm went across my chest as mine went around her shoulder.

"I wasn't. Not until you."

CHAPTER 30

Harper

Waking up in bed with Gage was definitely something I wanted to do more often. His warmth, his muscles, his scent. All of it. I wanted it all, all the time. But I wasn't about to tell him that. The fact that he told me he loved me was absolute perfection. I couldn't risk what we had by moving in together. I knew it was something he wanted as well, but I was scared it would be the ruin of us.

Because all good things I've ever had never lasted.

The men I've loved never stuck around.

And I didn't want to lose Gage Parker.

Beep…Beep…Beep

Gage's hand reached out for his phone on the nightstand. If the alarm was going off, that meant it was seven. But I'd been up for at least an hour, simply watching him sleep. The peace across his face as he slept gave me comfort, the opposite of that feeling of doom I had all day yesterday. I was thankful that day was over.

And contrary to what I feared, it turned out to be one of the best days of my life.

"Good morning, beautiful," Gage said as he turned over. "What are you doing up?"

He pulled me into an embrace, those sinewy muscles holding me tight. Sleeping naked would now be a requirement.

"I was enjoying the view." Balancing my chin on my hand against his chest, I peeked up at him. "Hey, didn't you mention something about a closet full of ties to me yesterday?"

His interest was piqued. But then he looked at the clock.

"How about I pack a bunch of my ties for our weekend?" he asked. "I will definitely make it up to you."

"Hmm, that sounds intriguing," I said. Then something hanging from his bedpost caught my eye. "Is that my bra?"

He turned his head slightly, then a broad smile covered his face. "Maybe."

Leaning forward, I plucked it from the wooden post.

"Is this the one I think it is?" My voice went up a few octaves, surprised by my discovery.

"It's exactly the one you're thinking of," he said. "When Fiona showed up, and we panicked, I found it on the floor. You had already run to the back room, so I stuffed it in my pocket."

I laughed out loud.

"It's mine now," he said, taking it from my grip. "Ya know, you told me that day at Sullivan's that you didn't expect us to do anything at the shop that night." His look was suddenly a bit accusatory, but with a side of humor as his smile grew. "But I'm not sure I believe you one bit, considering you had on a matching set under your clothes. And not just a matching set, but a pretty damn seductive one." He flicked my nose in jest, making sure I knew he was joking.

But I didn't realize he'd caught onto that. Shit.

"Well, it's now my memento from that day. We both have one."

He was referring to my dried rose. I guess he saw it in my kitchen.

"We do, don't we?"

He pushed out from under me, and I groaned in objection.

Hopping out of bed, he made his way to the bathroom, talking as he went. "Jared and Delia will be here at eight to pick us up, and I still have to pack."

The moment he left the bed, I missed him. But the view of his tight ass, with those little indents on the sides, as he walked away, almost made it worth it. Christ, his body was chiseled perfection. Lean, hard muscle.

"When do you have the time to go to the gym, Gage?"

He was already brushing his teeth but talked through the brush and paste.

"We have a gym at the office, so I usually get my workouts in during the day." He bent over the sink and rinsed, then leaned his head back out the door. "And on the weekends, I get in a run or two."

I felt so lacking in the exercise and healthful habits department. Looking down at my soft body, I wondered if he would prefer someone who was more like him.

"You're perfect." His words carried across the room.

Looking up, I knew he caught me looking at myself.

"Stand up."

His voice was firm, but I really didn't want to.

"Harper, stand up."

I did. He stalked toward me as if I were his prey. Once he was mere inches from me, his one finger trailed from my shoulder to my elbow.

"I've never felt softer skin. It's like velvet." Then both hands curved around my body to my ass. "And this right here, well, let's just say, I could get into a lot of fights if I let all the guys that stare at it get to me."

Scoffing, I pushed at his chest, but he held onto my ass, squeezing it, keeping us close.

"There is not a part of your body that isn't perfect." As he said that, his hands explored everywhere, from across my belly to my breasts, finishing at my face. "But it's not just physical." He put his finger on my temple. "Your intelligence, and drive, and the way you treat people, that makes up so much of what I love about you." And then his hand went over my heart. "That, combined with how you feel, and love. Your compassion is transforming me into the person I want to be." He gripped my face and came in for a kiss.

It was a simple kiss. And when he pulled away, he leaned down, our eyes level.

"You are perfect. Perfect for me. You have made me a better person. A person worth loving. So, don't ever question your worth. Ever again."

And all I could do was nod.

And smile.

"Okay, help me pack, because now we are getting picked up in forty minutes."

And I noticed him throw a few neckties in his bag before walking to his closet.

THE PASSING TREES were a tremendous distraction. Combine that with the music and the occasional conversation, and I was almost able to ignore the niggling feeling trying to worm its way back in. I was frustrated. As I leaned against the most beautiful man who declared his love for me just last night, why couldn't I just feel happy?

Maybe it was simply that I was afraid of love. And I was used to that.

Knowing my past, it would be expected for me to feel unsure about moving forward. And as close as Gage and I had become, it's been less than three months. When I talked to Vic about that, she said it was totally normal as we got older for things to move quicker.

Biological clock shit.

But this *feeling* felt…different.

I wasn't scared of commitment. As he held me in his arms, it was the one of the few things I looked forward to.

This was a legitimate sense of fear filling my entire core.

The entire time at the event, this fear invaded my every move. After my run-in with Rebecca, I'd thought that was it. And it lifted once I walked away from her, so I thought I was in the clear. But, when I woke this morning, it was back.

"You okay?" Gage asked me.

"Yep," I lied as we cuddled against one another in the back seat.

We had finally made it out of the city, over the G.W. bridge and were on the thruway. Jared was a good driver, which was not always a guarantee for a city dweller. But he wasn't born and bred here, I'd learned.

"So, where in Virginia are you from, Jared?" I asked.

He lowered the music so we could go back to talking.

"Falls Church, it's in NoVa," he said.

My confused look didn't escape anyone in the car. Delia chose to clear it up for me.

"He doesn't understand that people who aren't from Virginia don't understand the NoVa thing. It stands for Northern Virginia. It's basically the whole top part of the state that's outside of D.C."

"Ohhh, okay," I said, understanding.

Jared reached across the console and grabbed Delia's hand, holding it in his. From my seat, I was able to see her responses to his tiny gestures. We'd spent time together as couples, but I liked seeing them like this. It was obvious she was very much in love with him.

It was a seasoned relationship. They were in sync. They had a rhythm together. He moved, but she was ahead of his move waiting for him.

"And you guys didn't meet in college, right?" I asked Delia, forgetting their back story.

"Right, these two went to school together. I didn't meet them until they moved to the city. They're a package deal, though. They're a bit like chicks," she said, then laughed.

Gage pushed against her seat, and Jared poked her leg.

"What?" she yelled back at them. "Are either of you able to convince us otherwise? Is there anything you do socially without the other?"

Turning in her seat to be able to see them both at the same time, Delia's triumphant smirk spread slowly across her lips. "Yeah, I didn't think so."

My silent laugh wasn't so silent, and Gage pulled me into his side.

"Whatever," Jared conceded. "I'm man enough to handle being called a chick. What about you?"

Jared found Gage's eyes in the rear-view mirror, and they shared a conspiratorial look.

"Same," Gage replied.

Everyone fell back into a comfortable silence as the Range Rover hummed along the highway. I think I started falling asleep when I felt Gage reach into his bag at his feet. He pulled out his laptop.

"Sorry, babe, I have to return a few work emails."

While he got to work, I pulled out my phone and did a little research on the Catskills. I'd never been to the area and was looking forward to it.

"So, what're we doing this weekend, Delia?" I asked.

She spun around in her seat, the excitement all over her face.

"Fourth of July is so much fun at the lake!" she exclaimed. "I'm so glad you guys are coming. My parents' house is literally right on the lake, so we can go boating, fishing, or swimming whenever we want. But tonight, there's a big bonfire down by the main lake house. And tomorrow are the fireworks. Plus, we have s'mores to make, and there's this really amazing trail close by. I thought we'd go for a hike tomorrow morning."

Her smile was infectious. It all sounded idyllic.

Kind of made me think of my childhood summers on the Jersey Shore. I was thinking of asking Gage if he'd like to spend a weekend there this summer, take him to my old stomping grounds when I was a tween and on the prowl.

"It sounds amazing, thanks for inviting us," I said. "I'm a beach girl, but I love the lake. I just don't get to them often. This is perfect."

"Hey, babe," Jared said. "Can you help me with this?"

He seemed to be struggling to get his jacket off.

"I'm sweating my ass off, even with the air on. Can you pull this arm off for me?"

Delia pulled the jacket off his right arm.

"Shit," he complained. "I can't get my other arm out."

I heard him unclick his seatbelt and watched him pull the jacket off from behind his back.

But then everything happened in slow motion.

The pickup that was coming straight for us came out of nowhere.

Across the grass median.

At full speed.

In my periphery, I saw Gage looking down, still absorbed by his computer.

Delia was helping Jared with his jacket.

Jared was watching straight ahead and checking his rear-view mirror.

As he was trying to buckle up again, no one was looking at the median.

But there was no time even if he had.

Fractions of a second, I would find out.

"JARED!"

But I was too late.

His swerve did nothing to prevent the impact.

As it hit us, the front driver's corner of our SUV took the brunt of the collision.

The imagery created in the movies when a car flips: the slow motion as the crunching glass sprays across the interior of the vehicle, the passengers suspended in the air while upside down, as if time has stopped, the absence of sound, the deafening silence.

It's eerily accurate.

But then it all went black.

CHAPTER 31

Harper

"Harper." The voice saying my name sounded as if it was talking through mud or very deep water. I wanted to respond, but it was as if my mouth was frozen. My limbs felt heavy, too heavy to lift. But finally my eyes. My lids seemed to listen to my brain and move slightly. A sliver of light blinded me, though, forcing me to close them again.

"She's coming around," the voice said. It was a female voice, I could decipher that. "Harper, do you remember what happened?"

"Okay, good, she wasn't out that long," a second voice, definitely male, chimed in.

I felt a cuff tightening around my upper arm, and it was then I realized I was strapped tight, arms crossed, onto a gurney, in what had to be a moving ambulance. As the cuff started filling with air, tightening around my skin, it hurt.

But I didn't care.

I welcomed it because I did remember. And as the memories of what happened started coming back to me, I wanted them to go away.

Forcing my eyes open I tried to look around. But I couldn't, and

I realized I had one of those big neck braces on. My ankles and wrists lightly pushed against their restraints, testing how much room I had to move.

It was very little.

And all I could see was the ceiling as we bounced along the bumpy mountain road. The strong need to turn my head, to see who was here with me, took over, yet the collar around my neck wouldn't let me. I felt my heart rate rise, it beating against the strap holding me tight against the stiff board underneath me. Then I caught sight of the EMT sitting near me.

"Hi Harper, my name is Kate and I'm with Kingston Ambulance. This is my partner, Jack. Do you remember what happened?"

Tears welled in my eyes as I nodded yes to her question. It was all I could do, words wouldn't form. It was as if I spoke, it would make it real.

My body fidgeted beneath the straps again, sweat forming on my temples. I pushed my entire body against the bands and board, the panic setting in.

"Fuck!"

Kate turned my way, seeing me struggling. "Try to stay calm, Harper. Does something hurt?"

That was when I realized the intense pain in one particular spot. I nodded as my eyes instinctively looked toward my hand. "My," I said through gritted teeth, "wrist."

"Jack, can you cut her sleeve off."

Jack removed my one hand from the restraints, carefully cutting the material from my arm.

She came back around with a splint for my wrist and started wrapping it.

Jack sat on the bottom of the cot holding what looked like a tablet. "Does anything else hurt, Harper?"

"My head," I told him.

He made a note of that. "Are you nauseous or dizzy?"

I only shook my head.

"I know you'll be in a lot of pain tomorrow; it'll happen with a crash like that. But any other acute pain like your wrist? Any bones that we might need images of?"

A crash like that.

This was it.

This was my feeling of doom.

It wasn't Rebecca after all.

I knew something was going to happen—and it did.

Fuck, it did.

The anxiety started slowly. The panic started to bubble in my chest at a low simmer. But then it ratcheted up fast. My breathing became erratic while sweat formed on my brow.

"Kate, take her pulse," Jack said, an urgency in his voice. He came to sit closer to me on the cot, his hand now on my lower leg. "Harper, it's okay. You're okay."

Kate had her fingers on my other wrist and was looking at her watch.

"One forty" she said.

Watching them take care of me was helping a bit. It was distracting my brain from what it was trying to think about.

But I had to know.

"Where's Gage?" I screamed.

They shared a glance, and then Kate answered.

"Our main priority right now is you. Once we get to the hospital we'll see if there's someone there that can give you some answers."

And that was all I got.

X-rays. CAT scans. MRIs. Every type of test imaginable I'd been sent for. Then they had to cast my wrist. That was a whole other process. Being wheeled to another part of the hospital for them to set and cast me. Then back up to the ER.

A broken wrist. Two lacerations on my head that needed stitches, one on my arm. And a concussion. All things considered, I was in good shape, according to the doctors and nurses. Though I wasn't quite sure what that meant.

Compared to whom?

By the time they were done taking care of me, I was done with them.

"Will someone tell me where my boyfriend is, please?" I begged the nurse currently in my room.

"Did he come in with the same accident, honey?" she asked as she looked at my chart.

"Yes," I said, hopeful someone was finally going to help me.

"What's his name? I'll try and find something out for you."

"Gage Parker." The tears welled up in my eyes of their own volition. "Thank you."

As she was exiting the room and the door was open, I could hear a ruckus in the hall.

"…Wilson!"

It was Gage!

Getting out of the bed and making my way to the hall, I looked back and forth. Three doors down, he was standing in a gown, looking destroyed, bruised, and broken but more beautiful than I'd ever seen him.

"Gage."

His head turned toward me. And he took off for me, the best he could, crashing into me as he held me against him.

"Harper," he cried, his face buried in my hair. "Oh, fuck, baby, I thought I lost you."

His words were mixed with tears, his voice cracking.

Only when he pulled away did I realize he had been holding me with one arm, the other in a sling.

"Gage," I whispered, reaching out to his shoulder. "What happened to you?"

As I asked, he noticed the cast on my wrist, as well as the stitches across my forehead. His free hand reached out, gingerly touching the bandage on my forehead.

"Mr. Parker," a nurse said, sidling up next to us. "You can't be out of bed, sir. You have a pretty serious concussion. I need you to come back to your room."

He never took his eyes from mine but spoke to the nurse.

"I'm not leaving her side," he said with finality in his voice. "If either of us needs to stay overnight, please start the arrangements for a private room." He broke our stare, looking at the nurse, who looked confused by his orders. "Now."

She was stunned by his words, and a bit annoyed, but walked away.

"C'mere," he said, pulling me to him again. "Come to my room until we figure this out."

Climbing into bed with him was challenging, but it worked with my cast being on my left side and his sling on his right. Snuggling in, I finally felt as though I could take a full breath. My first one since waking up in the ambulance.

"I don't even know where to start, Gage," I said. And then the tears started falling. They quickly turned to sobs against his chest, my face twisting into his gown as I tried to cover them up.

"I ..." My words stammered from me as the shock from what we'd been through was setting in. "Do you have any information? Do you know anything? About Jared? Or Delia?" My voice escalated with each question, the panic starting once again.

When I was in the ambulance, they told me it was normal to deal with anxiety or panic attacks after a traumatic experience.

But this was happening several times an hour.

"Hey," he said, rubbing my back to soothe me. "Calm down, baby. It's okay, we've got each other now. We'll get through this."

But he didn't believe his own words.

Gage Parker seemed unsure.

He seemed full of fear.

THE ROOM they placed us in resembled a fancy hotel room. Who knew these even existed in a hospital? Along with it came a private nursing staff and chef's service dedicated to all the private rooms in this particular wing. Gage's concussion was quite a bit more serious than mine. Apparently, he hit his head hard against the side of the car. Hard enough to not only break the window but dent the frame. He'd been vomiting for a few hours before we were reunited earlier, but that thankfully had stopped.

The lacerations he suffered were stitched up on the side of his head as well. We would both have some scars to show for this: physically and emotionally.

We were able to request a bigger bed so that we could sleep together. As we watched TV, my phone lit up with a call.

It was my mom.

"Aren't you going to answer it?" Gage asked.

Shaking my head, I silenced my phone and put it away. He didn't ask any more questions. He understood.

It was only five o'clock in the evening.

Nine hours after Jared and Delia picked us up.

Seven hours since the accident.

One hour since we'd been moved to our private room.

And we still had no information about Jared or Delia.

"Can't we call their family or something?" I asked. "And you've tried both their phones?"

"Yes, Harper."

He was worried, but it came across as him being annoyed. I'd asked him the same questions quite a few times.

But I understood. These were his best friends, and we were in the same fucking building as them and couldn't find a damn thing out.

And then his phone buzzed. He had it on his chest for easy access, and when he lifted it up, the name DELIA showed across the screen.

"Hello?" he screamed into the phone while putting it on speaker.

But there was only silence on the other end.

"Delia!" he screamed, sitting up. The scowl from his pain didn't stop him from getting out of bed. The nervous pacing as the silence continued on the other end was maddening. "Is that you? Are you there?"

He was about ready to lose control. He looked at me, his red-rimmed eyes imploring for some type of answer. Anything.

"What do I do?" he cried.

Then we heard the small whimper through the line. Gage stared at the phone. He stared at it as if it would destroy him, like a bomb about to go off in his hand.

The whimpers from Delia turned into full-blown sobs.

"Gage!" The scream was so many things wrapped into one.

Fear, anger, agony.

Gage couldn't respond. He froze. Yet his knuckles turned white from the pressure of him squeezing the phone in his hand.

Taking it from him, I led him to the bed and sat him down.

"Delia?" I said softly into the phone as I walked toward the hall. Once outside the room, I tried to get through to her. "Where are you, honey? Tell me where you are?"

She couldn't calm down, hyperventilating while trying to talk.

"I'm…on floor…three…" she said. "Room…three…fourteen."

She was admitted, no longer in the ER.

"Okay, we'll be up to see you as soon as we can," I told her.

All I heard was some shuffling noise on the other end of the line and some light crying. Then there were some faint voices in the background, most likely those of a nurse.

And the line disconnected.

As I opened the door, I found Gage bent over the end of the bed, his feet propped on a bar, his elbow on his leg.

He stared across the room at nothing. A blank wall.

And was motionless as I approached him.

Sitting on the bed next to him, I was unsure of what he needed.

As I put my hand on his leg, he pushed it away. He not only pushed my hand away, but he also physically turned himself away from me.

"Gage." My voice was weak.

We were both breaking.

"Delia is on the third floor. We'll see her when you get out, okay?"

Gage was only supposed to be held for observation overnight. Once he got discharged in the morning, we'd see her then.

"No."

His strong word and voice surprised me. Our heads snapped toward each other.

"We're getting out of here now. Seeing her now."

Stomping to the armoire that held our clothes, he tore open the drawer and started throwing the blood-covered, ratty clothes from the accident out of the drawer to the floor.

"What the fuck are we going to wear!" he yelled. "I'm not putting this shit back on!"

Going to his side, I took the shorts gently from his iron grip and led him to the chair by the window.

"I'll find us both something," I told him.

He didn't look at me as he sat in the chair. His gaze went to the window, a scene of trees and a parking lot.

A nurse was able to locate some old clothes from a donation pile they kept. It wasn't much, but I put together some sweatpants and t-shirts. They were clean, that was all I could guarantee.

As I handed Gage the clothes, he stared at them in disgust. At first. But he adjusted his attitude quickly. I helped him with his pants, which went on easily. The t-shirt was going to be a challenge with his broken collarbone.

"You're going to have to take off the brace," I told him.

Once he did, we slid the gown off his good arm, then maneuvered it around the bad arm, keeping it close to his body. The grimace that formed across his face informed me of the pain he was in, but he made sure not to let on.

Then it appeared to be a puzzle ahead of me.

How to best put on a shirt when you can't lift an arm.

"Just put it over my head, Harper!" he yelled.

His impatience was understandable, but he wasn't thinking at the moment.

"That won't work," I told him. Taking the shirt sleeve and slipping it over the hand of his bad arm, I pulled it up and over his shoulder, then his head.

"Fuck," he whispered, the pain evident.

"I'm sorry."

He then pulled his good arm through the other armhole.

And we figured out how to get a shirt on him.

The next six weeks were going to be a challenge for us with his brace and my cast.

But we were alive…

He finally looked at me and gave me a small smile.

"Thanks," he said.

His smile made tears come to my eyes. But I didn't want him to see that. And I didn't want my tiny tears to turn into big tears, so I wiped them away as quickly as I could and got to work on getting myself dressed.

We gathered what few personal belongings we had with us, and happily turned our back on the room.

GAGE HELD MY HAND, which surprised me with how he was acting before we left the room. Not only was he holding my hand, but his grip was strong, painfully strong. There were no words. We left the room, passing the nurse's station without telling them we were leaving. After a short ride on the elevator, we stood outside room 314.

Neither of us wanted to go inside. I knew that. Going inside made it all…real.

But then we heard voices from within the room. Gage grabbed the knob and pulled.

The scene on the other side…was tragic.

Delia had a leg in traction but also in a cast. Her face was unrecognizable with a swollen, bruised eye and cuts and lacerations.

Four adults turned toward us as the door opened. One of the women walked toward Gage as we entered the room.

"Gage," the older woman said warmly as the tears streamed down her face. She had him in her arms, holding him tightly.

"Mrs. Foster," Gage said.

And then he broke.

He shook with sobs.

My man was reduced to a boy being held by the mom of his best friend who had died.

My only guess was she'd become a mom to him over the years.

They held each other for long minutes, both crying for the man they lost and for each other. When she pulled away from Gage, she held his face in her hands, looking him straight in his eyes.

"He loved you, sweet boy. More than you will ever know."

His nod was slight as he looked down upon her. But then his gaze shifted to an older gentleman, who I figured to be Jared's father. He stood by Delia's side, with whom I had to assume were her parents, and cried as he watched the two of them. Gage went to him, and they fell into each other's arms, their cries echoing in the room.

Looking at Delia, fresh tears fell for them as she took in the scene. She reached out to me, and I rushed to her bedside.

"Harper," she whispered.

Reaching down, I wrapped my arms around her and whispered my apologies into her neck.

"Delia, my God, I'm so sorry," I told her. "I…" But I couldn't bring myself to say what I wanted to. Not with Jared's parents in the room, it was too soon.

No talk about the accident.

Maybe ever.

This was hard. It was bringing back old feelings I hadn't felt for so many years. I didn't think Gage had lost anyone close to him before, but I was unaware if any of the others had experienced it.

"They were like brothers," Delia said, tearing me from my thoughts.

And she was right.

Jared wasn't just his best friend.

He was family in every sense of the word.

CHAPTER 32

Gage

Saying goodbye was never going to be easy. I knew that. But when it happened so suddenly. And so unfairly. And to someone that didn't deserve to leave in such a brutal way. That made it barely able to get through.

Harper wanted to be there for me. But I wasn't letting her. And I didn't know why.

And it started destroying her.

Jared's parents chose to have a memorial service a couple weeks after the accident. And those weeks leading up to it were a complete blur. When we got back to the city, Harper and I decided she would stay with me in the brownstone. After what we'd been through, neither of us wanted to be alone.

But even though we were together, we were still alone.

Even though I was going into the office, I was simply going through the motions. Thankfully, Chase had come through and was filling in the gaps I was leaving open. Jared's death had changed everyone in different ways. For Chase, he was stepping up and becoming the man I hoped he could be.

Harper couldn't work much with her injury. She couldn't serve at the club while wearing a cast, so that job was on hold. Floral arrangements were equally challenging, but she was able to still do some smaller jobs and help run the shop. Besides, being with Fiona during the day helped her stay sane. I knew the loss of Jared was hitting her hard simply because of her father. There was a dimness cast over her usual bright eyes.

And she was going through a lot of blame. We all were.

Harper felt if she warned Jared sooner, she could have prevented the accident.

Delia felt if she never let him take off his seat belt, he would still be here.

I felt if I had put work aside, for once, he could still be alive.

But I got myself to the office each day. What I got accomplished while there was a completely different story.

Sitting at my desk, staring down at the cars and people moving about, had become my most common pastime lately.

"Sir." The knock sounded as Maryellen opened the door simultaneously. "May I come in?"

Swiveling around in my chair, I tried to make it appear I was being productive by shuffling the papers on my desk and opening my laptop.

"Sure."

With unsure steps, she made her way to the chair in front of me, where she sat innumerable times before for our meetings. But as she sat in front of me this time, it was as if we didn't know what to say to each other.

"So, your father called again," she finally said, her words quiet.

Because she knew I didn't want to hear what she had to say.

Disgusted, I spun away from her and looked out the window, again, to ignore the news about my father. Why must he insist on us having this discussion? So close to Jared's passing? There was no way I'd be able to make sound decisions in my current state of mind.

But I was thinking he knew that.

I knew he was still considering selling the company. And if Chase and I held on, he couldn't.

"Anything new?" I asked.

Maryellen cleared her throat before speaking. "Well," she said.

I turned back around to face her in my chair since I didn't like the sound of that.

"He said if he didn't hear from you by the end of this week, he was coming next week, no matter what."

"Hmm," I said as I whirled my chair toward the window once again. The activity of life down below was the only thing that kept me sane lately. Life was still marching on with the rest of the world, even though my life had come to a screeching halt.

A pigeon landed on a nearby windowsill, his eyes locking with mine. A duel of wit and determination between us, who could withstand the staring match the longest. I had nowhere to go, nothing to do. It lasted for long moments.

I won. He flew off, obviously with something more important to do.

I was potentially losing my company, what I'd worked my whole life toward, and I didn't seem to care. I was more worried about beating a pigeon in a staring contest.

"I'll just wait for him to come next week," I told Maryellen.

Even without seeing her, I could feel her disappointment with my apathy toward…everything.

And that was it. I felt nothing.

Absolutely nothing.

HARPER WAS ALREADY HOME when I walked in from work, which was even early for her. I left the office hours before I should have, but it was another useless day for me there. Chase stopped by and tried to talk to me about some of the meetings he was running, but I couldn't do it. Too many of them would have involved Jared, and I just couldn't face those meetings without him.

Harper and I did a good job of dancing around one another these past couple weeks while home. The purpose of her coming to stay with me was for us to offer the physical support we needed with our injuries, but also comfort. But I wasn't letting her in, I knew that. She knew that.

I heard her moving around upstairs, so I grabbed a beer and went to the patio.

Something Jared and I did so often.

"Gage?"

She had walked into the kitchen looking for me.

"I'm out here," I said.

I didn't want to be so distant. We both went through a very difficult thing, the same thing, together. It was confusing me as to why I couldn't lean on her during all of this. Especially since she lost her father; having dealt with loss, she would most likely be able to help me deal with this easily.

"Hey," she said, sitting next to me. "So, I have an idea. I'm hoping you'll go along with it." Her weak smile made me sad. She was constantly nervous around me lately, never knowing what my reaction would be. "I packed some bags for us." She looked toward the kitchen, and I could see them. "And I spoke to Maryellen."

Normally, those two things, on a Thursday, would be red flags for me due to my work schedule. However, the only reason they were red flags at the moment was that I had no desire to go anywhere.

"Shit, Harper, you can't be carrying that stuff with your wrist," I told her. And I felt like a total ass that she did do it alone.

She took my hand in hers, our two good hands.

"Look at me," she said.

And I did, but then looked away. My walls were in no mood for being broken down.

"Please," she pleaded.

I found her blue eyes once again. They were sad. She wasn't crying, but the sorrow I saw in them went deep. And it was no longer for our lost friend.

It was for us.

"I'm taking you to my favorite place I used to go to when I was a kid. My favorite beach, Surfside, on Long Beach Island in New Jersey. I booked us a beautiful oceanfront room until Sunday. Three nights and days of calm and quiet beach time, together." She interlocked our fingers as her face transformed from its dismal state to one of hope.

And to be honest, it sounded nice. Maybe getting out of the city and away from everything that reminded me of him was what I needed. And it was what Harper and I needed as well. Some time to focus on us.

"It sounds perfect," I said. And I smiled.

And that made Harper cry.

HARPER HAD ARRANGED for Tommy to drive us down to LBI for the weekend as well, which I appreciated. Neither of us could drive due to our injuries nor were we in the mental state for it.

To be honest, I hadn't spoken to Harper about my fear of being in a car. Tommy was aware. He could sense it. But he was a good driver, the best I knew. Yet, it didn't calm my fears about the drivers around me.

And to think of all the times we'd driven in the limo without using our seatbelts.

"Hi, Tommy," Harper said cheerfully as she got into the car.

After I slid in, my eyes fell to Harper's waist.

"Put your belt on."

The words came out harsher than I intended as her head snapped in my direction.

She watched me snap my seatbelt in place and did the same. Her nod of acknowledgment was all I needed. She understood.

"I'm sorry," I said.

"Gage, you don't need to be sorry. You're absolutely right. We should have always been wearing them." She started looking around for something along the side of the car.

"What are you looking for?" I asked.

"Is there like an intercom or something to talk to Tommy? I want him to pull over so I can move closer to you," she said.

My heart felt like it wanted to break. But it was already too broken.

Instead, she was doing what she always intended to do: fix me.

I pressed the button. "Tommy, can you pull over?"

"Yes, sir."

The car stopped almost immediately. Harper unbuckled from her seat on the other bench and crawled to be next to me. I pulled the buckle across her body as she hugged me, our bodies melting into one.

Weeks had gone by, and I hadn't realized how much I'd been missing this: her touch.

Missing her.

With my good arm around her shoulder, I pulled her in close and kissed the top of her head. As she settled against me, I felt a sense of peace fall over us. It was as if we had shut out the world when we closed the door, and it was just us, only us. Even though the sensible part of my brain knew that wasn't the case, I would enjoy the two hours of peace I allowed myself.

"Sir." Tommy's voice echoed in the back of the limo.

Stirring against the seat, I peeled my eyes open to see Harper still asleep against me. Looking out the window told me we had arrived as we were driving down what appeared to be the main street in town. It was lined with small shops, eateries, and restaurants. Thrown in was a mix of small beach cottages and huge redone mansions. Turns out Long Beach Island truly was an island since I could tell the ocean was up to the right and a bay was to the left.

"Says the hotel is up another block, sir," Tommy said. "Maybe wake her."

He was right, she'd want to know we arrived.

"Harper," I whispered as I stroked her cheek. She stirred, and then those blue eyes popped open.

"Are we here?" she asked, sitting up in her seat.

Her eyes lit up as if she were a child.

"Oh, we already passed Ron Jon's. We'll have to go back later," she said. Then she looked back and forth between Tommy and me. "Did I tell you I booked a room for Tommy, too?"

I shouldn't have been shocked. That was the type of person Harper was.

Tommy had a huge smile on. "She did," he said. "And I appreciate it greatly. I actually have a cousin that doesn't live far. We're going to catch up this weekend."

Smiling back at Tommy, I realized I didn't know too much about him personally and I should change that.

We pulled into a circular driveway in front of the low-rise hotel.

It wasn't exactly what I expected, but looking around, there were no high-rise buildings.

"Okay, so listen. This is not the kind of place that has limos driving around. Once we valet this thing, I think we should plan on walking everywhere or using the bikes the hotel provides."

Harper was excited. Her energy was contagious.

"Sounds good," I told her.

The car was emptied of our bags, and we checked in at the front desk. Apparently, there is only one King Suite in this place. And due to its price, it was usually available.

As we stepped inside, I was pleasantly surprised. The line of sight throughout the entire space was the ocean. It was high enough over the dunes that we could see the break of the waves. The windows were of a quality that, when closed, we didn't hear a sound.

But when we stepped onto the balcony, the symphony of sounds that hit us was music to my ears. The crashing waves, the seagulls, the voices from the beach and pool below.

The sounds of summer and life happening around us.

Harper came up next to me, her arm going around my waist, and we stared out at the horizon. The sun was setting somewhere behind us and cast a magical glow on the water ahead.

"It's beautiful, isn't it?" she asked.

And even though it wasn't any different from most East Coast beaches, I felt the difference she alluded to. There was something about this place.

"It is."

"C'mon, let's unpack and get downstairs or to the beach. I don't want to spend all our time up here. We can do that later," she said with a wicked but hopeful smile.

We haven't had sex since the accident.

It wasn't a conscious decision.

But as I watched her flitting about the room, full of excitement and life, pulling her dresses and shoes from her bag, a sadness came over me. I wanted to be able to be as happy as she was. Why couldn't I? Why was I not able to move on and live my life with this beautiful woman? Leaning against the wall, I tried to hide it, tried so hard to not let it in, but it covered me from top to bottom.

And she saw it.

Walking over, she took my hand in hers and brought it to her mouth. Her lips were warm against the back of my hand.

"Gage, everyone's journey with grief is different."

The tears flowed freely after hearing her words, almost as if she gave me permission to feel.

Her hand came to my face, the way I usually held her, and my head fell against her palm.

"And whatever path yours is, I promise I'll be waiting for you at the end."

Her words broke me.

Falling to my knees, Harper came to the floor with me. Her arm came around me, trying to hold me up as I descended into my agony.

"Harper," I breathed out through my gasps and choked breaths. "I need you, baby, so much. I'm sorry. I'm just…I feel so broken. I'm so lost without him." With my one good arm, I gripped her with a force that probably hurt. "Save me, Harper, please. Save me."

I'd felt like I'd been drowning in muddy water, and I couldn't see the top, constantly struggling to figure out which way was up. But now I saw a hand reaching down, reaching for mine.

But as I looked at it, I realized it had been there all along. I only needed to clear away the murkiness to find it.

There we were, on our knees, on a tile floor, each with only one good arm.

Both sobbing.

Yet, I felt better in that moment than I had in weeks.

"I'm here, Gage. I've always been here."

Kissing the top of her head, down to her temple and around to her cheeks, I looked into those gorgeous blue eyes, mimicking the skies behind us.

"I know."

CHAPTER 33

Harper

The beaches of New Jersey always got a bad rap. New Jersey in general didn't get the love it deserved. But I would always be a fan of my home state. Not only were our beaches some of the most beautiful, but we had mountains and farmlands as well. And let's not forget our proximity to two of the biggest cities in our country, New York and Philly. And D.C. and Boston weren't that far.

We had everything going for us.

And now I was showing Gage our pristine Long Beach Island. However, my idea of using bikes for transportation was not well thought out considering our current disabilities. With my cast and his sling, walking was the only mode we had of getting around. Our first night we spent poolside and by the bar of the hotel. It was late when we got here, but not so late that we couldn't enjoy the amenities this place had to offer.

Gage wasn't in the room when I woke up, which I took as a good sign. There was a gym on-site, so I assumed he was using it. Or maybe out for a walk. He pushed himself to still use the gym even with his arm the way it was, and his doctor gave him the okay to do it if he was careful.

My plans for today were for us to go to the beach. As I was packing my bag with all the necessities, Gage walked in.

"Hi, babe," he said, more chipper than he's been.

Walking over to me, he handed me a takeout cup of tea and gave me a kiss.

"Let's take our drinks to the balcony," he said.

His breakthrough yesterday was heartbreaking, but important at the same time. Grief is a beast of horrific proportions. One day you might think you had it conquered, and the next it had you laid up in bed with a quart of ice cream.

Sitting on the cushioned chairs, we both looked out at the sun shining down on the Atlantic Ocean. It was another beautiful day. And it seemed as though it was going to be a hot one, too. Unfortunately, on this trip, we wouldn't be able to go swimming in the ocean, which was a favorite of mine.

"What are you thinking about?" Gage asked.

"Oh, just some of the times I spent down here as a kid. We used to rent a bunch of different houses. I can show them to you." Chancing a look at him, he appeared to be in a good mood still today. "We won't be able to go in the ocean on this trip, though, with our ..." Holding up my wrist and gesturing to his shoulder was all I needed to do.

We both hated talking about our injuries all the time.

"Next time," he said.

Next time.

"Want to go for a walk on the beach?" he asked.

"I would love that. We might as well pack ourselves up to sit there for a while. The hotel has chairs and umbrellas out there we can use. Let's get changed and head out," I said.

He stood from his chair before I did and leaned over me the

best he could. His mouth hovered over mine as I looked up into his eyes.

"I love you, Harper," he said. Then his lips covered mine. It was a gentle kiss. But it was perfect.

And it was the first time he'd said it in days.

"I love you, too."

THE WATER WAS STILL COLD—THAT happened in the Northeast. Many times, it wasn't warm enough to jump right in until the end of summer. But as we strolled along the edge, our feet got used to the temperature as the waves rolled along our toes. The shells tumbled against our ankles with each crash of the water, and I kept my eye out for any sea glass that might appear.

"So, I saw Tommy this morning," Gage said.

"Oh yeah? Did you guys meet for breakfast or something?"

Gage kept my hand in his but pulled me to stop walking, spinning me to face him.

"No, not quite. I, uh, needed a ride. He took me to a car dealership on the mainland," he said.

That was the furthest thing from what I was expecting to come from his mouth.

"Okay," I responded, a bit confused.

"I'm not going crazy, I promise," he said, then laughed. "I needed a car, because..." And he struggled with finishing his thought. "The Shelby is a great car, but she's not safe. Not safe enough. And even though we were in a Range Rover, they are very highly rated. If he only had kept his..."

Squeezing his hand, I hoped he understood he didn't need to finish his sentence.

"Well, um, they have a Land Rover dealer in town, and I

thought that getting a Range Rover would be a smart investment in us. Our future, and our safety."

If it weren't Gage Parker making a spur-of-the-moment purchase like that, I'd say he was crazy.

But he could afford it.

And this was part of his healing process.

"I think that's a smart idea," I told him.

He pulled me against him. It was one of my favorite places to be, against his bare chest. His scent surrounding me. With it mixing with the salty ocean air, I was in heaven.

"Yeah?" he asked. "You don't think it's impulsive?"

Shaking my head, I looked up at him. "No, not at all. Just not sure how we're getting it home."

His confident smile looked so much like his old self.

"One step ahead of you. Already arranged to pay Tommy's cousin to drive it back for us."

Smiling, I turned us around, pulling him along the surf. "Let's head back to our chairs. I'd like to read for a bit."

As we walked, he was looking at the monstrous houses lining the dunes. Needless to say, many of them had changed since I'd been here over fifteen years prior.

"Ever stay in one of these, right on the beach?" he asked.

"Oh, God no. We could never afford beachfront. Even back then, when they were still small cottages, we could only afford to stay like two blocks from the beach." Every year, we would rent a different house. My dad always thought we would find a better one that way. "There was one year we rented with my cousins' family, so we needed a bigger house. It was on the bay. That was fun. Being right on the water, jumping off the dock to go swimming. We fished, crabbed, we even took out this little boat that had oars."

Gage laughed at my last memory.

"You mean a canoe?"

"No!" I yelled at him. "I know the difference between a canoe and a boat. It was a small boat, like four of us could fit, but it didn't have a motor, a literal rowboat. We found it behind the house. I don't think we were supposed to use it, but my dad and uncle put it in the bay, and we all hoped it wouldn't sink."

So many memories of us being here flooded my mind. And in all of them, my mom, dad, and I were happy and smiling. In every single one of them. It was truly a magical place.

We reached the hotel, plodding up the beach toward our chairs.

"Want to grab a drink at the bar before you start reading?" Gage asked.

Letting him guide what we were doing seemed to be working. He was loosening up and acting so much more like himself.

"Sure."

As we sat, the bartender placed menus and coasters down. "What can I get you?"

"I'll have something fruity and frozen," I said. The club didn't sell frozen drinks, so I didn't get them often. Besides, they're a "vacation-y" drink.

He laughed then offered, "Well, there's a frozen margarita, piña colada or a watermelon daiquiri."

They all sounded amazing, but I stuck with my standby.

"Piña colada, please."

His smile moved onto Gage. "And you, sir?"

Gage inspected the menu, then looked at the bottles on the bar ahead of us. "What bourbon do you have?"

"Old Forrester, Woodford, and I have a special reserve of Maker's Mark," he answered.

"Maker's, neat please," Gage replied.

As I looked over the menu, I realized I wasn't hungry. Passing it on to Gage to see if he wanted anything, I spun in my seat to grab the view behind me. The bar itself was situated high enough on the property that the coastline was visible over the dunes. Sitting here, watching and listening to the waves crash with the soundtrack of the other island sounds mingling with it, made me long to spend more time here.

Our drinks were on the bar in front of us by the time I turned back around. As I picked mine up, I noticed Gage staring at me, smiling. Smiling back, I propped my elbow on the bar, my chin balanced in my palm.

"What are you smiling at, Mr. Parker?"

He took a sip of his drink before answering. "You," he said. "It's always you."

Movement behind the bar caught our attention, and we watched the bartender stand up on a stool to change the channel on the TV. Suddenly, the Phillies game got changed out for the Yankee game and several of the patrons cheered heartily.

And my heart sank.

Glancing to my right, nervous to know what I'd find, Gage was staring at his empty glass of bourbon. His hand wrapped around the tulip-shaped glass, knuckles white, as he gripped it so tight, I thought it might shatter. My hand went to his shoulder, but he shrugged it away. His eyes bounced around, looking everywhere but at the screen, or me.

"I can't do this right now," he grumbled, pushing away from the bar. As he did, his stool went flying to the ground behind him, attention being drawn to both of us. He stood stock still, hands fisted at his side, eyes fixated on the ground.

I struggled with deciding how to help him.

But then realized I couldn't. This was a battle he needed to fight.

His hand flew to his hair as he threw his head back in anger. Or frustration. Maybe both. Then he turned and walked away.

Grabbing the top of the fallen chair, I lifted it up as a server came to help me.

"Everything okay, hon?"

Scanning the bar area, no one else was still watching. The show was over. But the sweet girl next to me looked concerned.

"Yeah, he's just dealing with something," I told her.

Her slow nod as she stared me down told me she wasn't a believer. Especially once she saw my cast. Although she didn't deserve an explanation, I felt compelled to prove Gage was a good guy to this complete stranger.

"He lost his best friend recently," I said. Then, looking at the screen and gesturing to it with my shoulder, I added, "Watching them play was their thing."

This time, her slow nod was full of understanding as the sympathy rolled across her face. As she walked away, I was left standing alone, wondering what my next move should be.

Do I look for him?

Or leave him be?

He may have been fooled into thinking his grief had gone away. But it never goes away, especially not this early. It will subside with time. But then the pain gets packed into a remote section of our brains, and it pops out randomly, usually at the most inopportune moments.

For the rest of your life.

Strolling through the lobby toward the elevator, I decided to head up to our room. But as the doors slid open, soft caramel-brown eyes stared back at me.

"Hey," he said, the lilt to his voice full of apology. "You didn't deserve that." His hand reached out for mine, and I took it. He pulled me into the elevator just as the doors closed. "Let's go upstairs."

With his back against the wall and his legs spread wide, he

pulled me against him. As his arm wrapped around my waist, I dropped my bag to the floor. It had only been a few weeks, but it felt like months since we'd been in each other's arms, felt each other's skin.

His mouth covered mine with a lingering kiss. His hold on me was strong, fierce even, as his hand dug into my hips, my ass. I felt the desperation in every move he made.

But as we stepped off the elevator, I saw the glint in his eye.

It wasn't desperation.

It was one hundred percent desire.

As he opened our door, he peered back at me, his sly smile a dead giveaway.

"Sorry, but we won't be heading back to the beach today," he said. "You okay with that?"

Kicking the door closed with my foot, I lifted the thin material of my cover-up over my head and threw it to the floor. Standing in front of him in my bikini, I felt the bumps rise on my skin as his eyes devoured me from top to bottom.

The hungry look of a starving man.

As I lifted my hand to the string behind my neck, the veins bulged in his forearms from the fists he made to refrain from reaching out. I pulled the string, painfully slow, and watched his eyes waiting for the triangles of material to reveal his prize.

The bits of fabric fell against my belly, my breasts on display.

Gage licked his lips as he sauntered the two steps it took for him to scoop me up in his one good arm. His mouth latched onto my nipple as he walked us across the room and dropped me onto the bed.

"Look at you," he said, as he knelt over me, his legs on either side of mine. His elbows came down to the bed, his arm caging my head. "I've missed you, Harper Wilson. I've missed you, and us and…" His eyes gestured to my body in its entirety. "This," he said. "I've missed this body of yours, feeling it against mine."

And I couldn't say I didn't feel the same. My God, I missed him. And us.

His mouth found its way to that tender spot behind my ear that made my toes curl with every swipe of his tongue. How his lips on that part of me could make me heat with desire amazed me.

He knew exactly what he was doing.

It coaxed a moan from me so easily.

"I like the taste of the salty air on your skin," he whispered. "I think it might make other parts taste pretty good, too." Standing at the foot of the bed, he gripped the bottoms of my suit and pulled them to my feet, dropping them to the floor. Then, a hand reached behind me and with a pull, slipped open the knot holding up the top.

But then he walked away, to the dresser behind him. Rummaging in a drawer, he pulled something out that I couldn't see.

"You trust me, Harper?" he asked.

"Of course I do."

Walking around to the side of the bed, he propped the pillows in the center.

"Slide up here, baby," he said.

And that was when I saw the neckties on his nightstand. My pulse quickened as he picked one up and turned toward me with it twisting in his hands.

"I think I'm long overdue with this one, don't you?" he asked as he knelt alongside me. "I'm going to cover your eyes, Harper, then, as long as you're good with it, I'm going to tie your wrists to the bed."

His words made my body tingle. Tingle and warm in areas that I wanted him to do things to.

"Shit," I heard him mumble. "I actually can't tie these myself."

Realizing his struggle, I took the tie from him and covered my own eyes with it, tying it around my head.

And everything went black.

"If I loop these ahead of time, I'll be able to tie up your wrists," he said.

I loved that he wasn't getting frustrated.

He was gentle with my cast as he lifted it over my head.

"May I?" he asked.

Nodding, he carefully wrapped a tie around the plaster of the cast and chose to put that arm on the bed instead of high against the headboard. "This will be better," he said.

Realizing I wouldn't be able to touch or see him, I was torn about how that made me feel.

But the burning between my legs won out.

The silk slid around the other wrist, and he straddled me as he spread my arms wide, securing the tie to the wooden post behind me. Tugging on them, he determined they were tight. His fingers went to the insides of my one arm, trailing down, the sensation intense not knowing his next move. But then he stopped.

And swung a leg over me.

The bed lifted, and that was the only way I knew he got up. My remaining sense was heightened as I listened for every move he made. The Velcro on his suit ripping open was loud in the quiet room, and I knew he was now naked, somewhere, watching me.

"Are you comfortable, Harper?"

His words caused a sharp intake of breath, but I now knew he was at the foot of the bed.

"I am," I replied.

Suddenly, his hand was on my lower leg, lifting one at a time, shifting them, as he rubbed the muscles of my calves. His strong fingers dug deep into my muscles as I could feel him crawling up the bed, getting closer to me. Every inch he moved closer to me, his hand moved further up my thigh.

Finally, he was settled between me, on his knees, as far as he could go. His one hand gripped the outside of my hip as his body opened my legs wide for him.

"You are so fucking amazing to look at Harper," he said. "Every inch of you is beautiful."

As he said that, a hand slid around between my legs, hitting my core, his thumb rubbing along me from top to bottom. When his thumb slid down again, he dipped inside me.

"God, you're so wet already."

He took that slickness and rubbed it along my pussy, up to my clit. His finger lingered, rubbing slow circles on the hard bundle of nerves, my legs squirming from the intense sensations.

"Do I need to tie your ankles next time?" The sultry threat was followed by his elbows holding down my knees, forcing my legs to stay open for him. "That's it," he purred.

I could feel him working to change his position while keeping my knees pinned down.

"Do we think the salty air reached your pussy, Harper?"

Tiny puffs of air blew against me as he spoke. His mouth was so close to my opening, I wanted to lunge forward and force his mouth to taste me. My hands pulled on their restraints, the urge to grab his head and shove him between my legs strong.

But he had every part of my body restricted.

I couldn't move.

And I was never so turned on.

"Your pussy is glistening," he said.

And I knew it had it be, I could feel it.

"It's wet for you," I told him. "Only for you, Gage."

And he liked that.

His hum of approval was felt against my skin just as a finger plunged deep inside me. His mouth covered my clit, sucking it between his lips. As he pulled it in deep, my ass lifted off the bed, the intensity almost too much to handle. Using his good shoulder, however, he pushed me flat, forcing me to not move. His finger continued moving in and out of me steadily, the tension already starting to coil within.

Then he released my clit from his lips, allowing his tongue to take over. Circling and flicking it back and forth, my legs flailed under his hold. The clenching of every muscle in my body consumed my thoughts as the wave of orgasm started deep in my core.

The inability to touch myself in any way, the frustration it created, heightened the intense pleasure soaring through my body. My nipples ached to be touched, tortured, by his hands. They were hard, I knew that without seeing them. My hands pulled at their restraints as my need to pull on them increased.

And then he stopped moving. Stopped doing anything to me.

"You're getting close, aren't you, baby?" he hummed against me. His words made my legs tremble. "I like bringing you to the edge."

"Fuck, Gage," I begged. "Please don't stop."

He licked the inside of my thigh. But it wasn't enough, and I pushed my core toward his mouth.

"You want to come on my mouth, Harper? You want me to taste you?"

A simple moan from me was my only answer, and he drove multiple fingers deep inside my pussy.

My thoughts became incoherent. Nothing made sense inside my own head.

And then his mouth landed on me again. The pull it had as he sucked on my clit, a soft but steady suck as it went deeper and deeper into his mouth, toed the line between pleasure and pain.

That line he played with oh-so-well.

The moan bellowed from within me as the orgasm gained momentum.

The feel of his body against my inner thighs, his mouth on my clit, his fingers plunging into me; I was so acutely aware of every inch of him touching me, desperate to feel what I couldn't see or touch.

"Gage!"

He knew I was coming.

And what I loved best was his ability to read my body. He didn't increase his pace, his intensity.

Steady.

He kept it steady, allowing it to build. It was climbing in me, fast and hard. I struggled to keep my legs flat under him as my toes curled.

My muscles stiffened as the peak hit. The tiniest sounds of pleasure came from my open mouth, almost struck speechless. I was erupting from the inside out, my entire body felt as though it was about to burst into flames.

The wave washed over me, the orgasm taking hold of my body. My hands pulled on their restraints, needing to grip something as it tore through me. Settling for the silk of the tie, I pulled it in my one good hand, gripping it tight, as the convulsions began to slow.

I came down from the high, my body relaxing under his grip.

His fingers slowed but didn't retreat right away. Eventually, he slipped them from me, rubbing my wetness along my pussy.

His mouth resorted to peppering me with kisses, the nerve endings on fire everywhere his lips touched me.

"That was amazing," he said. "Amazing to watch you come apart in my hands."

The shifting of the mattress under me was my clue he was

moving around. The casted arm was released first, and he placed warm kisses on the exposed fingers. "Does your wrist feel alright?"

"Hmm," I cooed, still unable to form words.

His hands went to my other wrist, falling from the bedframe like a stone. As he removed the tie from my eyes, his were there, staring back at me. The soft lines around the outsides indicated a smile I couldn't quite see on his face.

"I'm not done with you yet," he whispered along my cheek. "But fair warning, this second half won't last. It's been too long."

And he laughed.

And I realized I'd missed that sound. All of this, I'd missed all of this, so much.

"I don't care," I told him. "I just want to feel you inside me."

With his one good hand, he pulled me over and on top of him.

"Fuck, Harper, saying things like that is making it worse. I won't last ten seconds."

Straddling him, his hard cock coming up between my legs, I reached down and gently rubbed the head with my thumb. He rolled his head back into the pillow as he groaned out loud. The droplet of precum glistened in the waning sunlight, and I skimmed it from the tip of his dick. His eyes jerked toward my movement, growing wide, as my finger made its way to my lips.

Slowly licking my finger, I swirled it around in my mouth, sucking on it once the taste was long gone. My first indication of how much he enjoyed the show was watching the slow swallow along his muscular neck. The way he grabbed me by my hips and rubbed his dick against my pussy was the second.

"First warning, Harper. Get me inside you, now." He reached down, trying to move me while gripping his cock in his hand.

But I wouldn't let him. I was stronger than I looked, especially with the advantage of being on top and him only having one arm.

Using my good hand, I pinned his to the bed.

On bent arms, I lowered my face to his, our lips about to touch. But I hovered above him, and an amused smile slid across his face.

"You're enjoying this, aren't you?" he asked.

My equally smug smile matched his.

But then he surprised me by flipping us over, my back crashing onto the bed.

"Your shoulder, Gage!" I yelled.

He laughed. "Well," he said while spreading my legs and pulling me to the end of the bed. "If you'd have listened to me, I wouldn't have to do this."

Gripping his dick, he rubbed it along my pussy, teasing me now.

"Get ready, baby. This is going to be hard and quick."

Plunging forward, his cock filled me. Completely.

Once fully seated, he froze, his head back, eyes closed. Thankful I could now see, I took full advantage and watched each muscle in his torso tense and contract. His biceps bulged as his thrusts began.

"I missed this," he breathed out. "Fuck, I missed this, baby."

His rhythm continued to increase, faster and faster, as he plunged himself fully inside me. The intensity of each movement, each thrust, caused me to call out every time. He was reaching parts of me he never had.

A sudden burst came from him, frantic movements as he held me in place by my hips. His fingers dug into my skin as I gripped his wrist with my one hand, steadying myself.

"Fuucckkk!" he growled. "Harper, I'm coming, baby."

He was breathtaking to look at. All hard, ripped muscles now covered in a light sheen of sweat. The veins in his forearms protruded from the exertion he put his body through. It gave him a godlike appearance as he peered down from above.

Eventually, his shoulder gave out, and he needed to collapse onto me, which I didn't mind one bit. Rolling to his side, I could feel his eyes on me. As I started getting up, to make the dreaded walk to the bathroom, he stopped me.

"Stay put."

Coming back with a warm washcloth, he wiped me clean, then tossed it on the floor. Plopping back on the bed next to me, his hand went into my hair, playing with the strands.

"I like you as a blonde."

Nodding, I rolled his way as a huge yawn escaped.

"Take a nap, beautiful," he said. "But I'm waking you up in a bit."

My eyes found him, curiosity filling them.

"You didn't think we were done, did you?"

CHAPTER 34

Gage

Waking up the next morning, my body was sore. But it was a welcome sore. We spent a good part of the night reacquainting ourselves with each other's bodies. I forced one eye open as I lay on my stomach to find Harper still sound asleep next to me. Filtered light streamed through the curtains as the sunrise announced a new day over the Atlantic. It bounced off her now golden blonde hair that splayed across her pillow as if she were a goddess.

And she was. She was my goddess.

Handed to me by God, or some higher power.

To save me.

Dealing with my feelings over losing my best friend blindsided me. I'd lost my mom as a kid, and that didn't even touch how this affected me. Her sticking by me not only showed her love, but it also gave me clarity.

Clarity on how I wanted the rest of my life to look.

"The wheels turning in your head are really loud," she said, then chuckled. Rolling toward me, I was met with her bright smile and even brighter eyes against her tanned skin. "You good?"

Reaching out, I took her cheek in my good hand. "I'm better than I've been in a while, beautiful, all because of you."

Her wrist with the cast was the one closest.

"How's that feeling?"

It didn't help that we had physical reminders of the accident still on our body. But only a couple more weeks and we would both be rid of what bound us to that day, at least tangibly.

"Itchy, hot, annoying, but it doesn't hurt anymore."

She reached out with her good hand to my shoulder, caressing it. I'd stopped sleeping with the sling this past week, and it had been feeling okay.

"All types of healing going on," she said.

"Thanks to you," I told her. "This trip was exactly what we needed, what I needed."

Her lips were soft and warm when they landed on mine. The kiss held so much in it, but most of all, it held promise.

Promise that she would be there for me.

And never leave.

"I know we have another night here, but what would you say to us heading home tonight?" Looking for her reaction to my words, she only continued to listen. "I have a meeting with my father this week that I've been dreading." Rolling over onto my back, we both sat up in the bed. "But I've got some renewed energy about it now, and some new ideas I'd like to outline and present to him."

Her gaze was one of pure joy. "Of course," she said with excitement. "Should we go home now?"

Shaking my head, I pulled her to me, content for the first time in so long, and she knew it.

"Nope, tomorrow gives me plenty of time. Besides, there's still more to do here."

She hopped out of bed, ran to the bathroom, and turned the

shower on. Popping her head out the door, she gestured to me as I still lay in the bed.

"Get up!" she ordered. "Let's go. Carpe diem."

Rising from the bed, I marched straight to the shower to join her. Before seizing the day, I would seize her one more time.

THE BRIDGE LEAVING LBI was dotted with lights across the top that, from a distance, gave it the appearance of a string of pearls. As we drove over it, Harper's mood turned melancholy. Thinking back to my childhood vacations and their final days, there was always that yearning for them to never end. I understood as she turned and watched the island disappear in the rear window.

We'd spent the day walking through the streets of the small beach town, searching for every house she stayed in as a child. Once we found all but one, we went for lunch at a café she swore was there twenty years ago. It didn't look it, but I didn't argue. The food was good.

The day rounded out with a shopping trip to the renowned surf shop, Ron Jon's. Stepping inside was like stepping back in time with nostalgic surfboards hanging from the rafters and beachware stacked on every surface. Of course, we each walked out with a new hoodie that had the traditional logo on it. The smile it put on her when we both had them on was priceless.

She nestled into my shoulder once we hit the highway. Knowing she would sleep, I pulled my laptop out before we left, hoping to get a jump on some meeting notes.

"Tommy, how long will the drive be?"

We also had Tommy's cousin somewhere behind us, driving my new car home for us. Once he got it to Manhattan, I gave Tommy a day off to get his cousin back home.

"Says just under two hours, sir."

Plenty of time to draft my outline.

"A RE you sure he's going to agree to this? What makes you think he'll change his mind now, all of a sudden, just because you have this new plan?" Chase asked. He was pacing in my office, quite nervous about the meeting with our father.

I called Chase in early this morning to go over the business model I finalized yesterday. It was full of ideas I'd been thinking about for months, but not until Harper and I went away did it all seem to fall into place in my mind.

The main proposed change was going to be the work week. We were one of the few companies that were in person five days a week, all due to my father.

I wanted to change our model to hybrid, like most of the world. Our father had been resistant when I first suggested it, wanted to hold true to his old higher standards.

And all current research proved that employees were happier with a hybrid schedule. I was able to put together statistics that proved our employee retention rate was lower due to our model. And to overcome that, we'd lost money.

And *that* bottom line was the winning hand I would play against my father.

The other main component to my plan involved Chase and a major change in his role, trying to capitalize on his strengths rather than highlight his weaknesses. Allowing him to take over the sales department gave him more freedom to travel and be out of the office. Entertaining the client is what he did best, so he should be doing it.

Sitting at my desk, my nerves were quite calm considering what was at stake. My father could put his foot down on all I had to say and continue with his plan to sell the company, cash out on his fortune, and ride off into the sunset.

The buzzer on my desk phone chirped.

"Yes," I called into it.

"Gage," Maryellen said. And thank God she remembered, today, of all days, not to call me sir. "Your father is here."

"Send him in."

Chase and I sat together on the couch in the sitting area. A fortified front together. Even though he wasn't completely on board with all my ideas, he agreed his main job was to back me up on everything.

"Ready?" I asked him.

"We have to be, right?" he answered.

As the door opened, in walked the man who dealt with his wife deserting him, and our family, the only way he knew how. By diving into his career, and this company, and not picking his head up. Not once.

Chase got his coloring from him. Our father's hair was light brown, his eyes light too. They even had the same walk. Yet, I looked more like my mother, my dark coloring from her Mediterranean roots. And we both got our height from him, though it seemed age had already started chipping away at his six-foot, two-inch frame.

But as he strolled into my office, we were seeing a completely different man right before our eyes.

For starters, he wore…jeans.

This was a man who wore a business suit almost every day of his life, even in the comfort of his own home.

And with his jeans, he had on a polo shirt. A pink polo shirt.

That showcased a tan he had.

"Boys!"

Even his tone was different. He put his arms out, I guess expecting a hug. Chase and I shared a confused look as we approached him with apprehension. An awkward three-person huddle was all I could call it before we separated and sat down.

The look that shrouded his face was not one I expected. He looked…sentimental. And I didn't know if that was a good sign for us or not.

"I missed you both," he said.

Terms of endearment were not prevalent in the Parker household, so Chase and I were at a loss.

"Yeah, Dad, us too," I said. "You've been traveling a lot. How's that been for you?"

Leaning back and crossing an ankle over his knee, he looked as though the travel had done him some good. More good than anticipated.

"Retirement is what I've needed, boys." Looking around the office, his eyes settled on the bar. "Is it too early?"

"Um, no, I don't think so. We can celebrate your arrival, why not?"

I stood to prepare the drinks when Chase chimed in. "It's never too early in my book," he said, then laughed.

The three highball glasses balanced in my hands as I made my way back to them.

"Pappy," my father said, approval dripping from his words.

We brought our drinks together over the table separating us, and each took a long sip of bourbon. The hope that they could calm the nerves flapping around in my gut was high.

"Gage, I wanted to say how sorry I am about Jared," he started.

As much as I knew the topic of him would likely come up, it didn't make it any easier. Especially since my father didn't come back for Jared's memorial. I wouldn't say I was shocked by that, but it hurt, nonetheless.

"I know how important he was to you, and he was to many of us. His loss will be felt."

As much as my father seemed to have changed, he was still him, thinking about the company.

"I took a tour of the floors before making it to you. Things are running smoothly, boys. I'm impressed." He took a long swallow of his drink before placing the tumbler on the table. "We all know why we're having this meeting. But there are a few things we should discuss first that might play a role in any decisions made today." Leaning forward on his knees, his hands came together as he stared ahead at the floor.

"I, um, met someone."

The room went silent.

Chase and I chanced a look at one another, his eyebrows rising at the news. The way our father delivered the news, it was if he felt we would be disappointed in him. Finally, looking up, he glanced at each of us, one at a time.

"Are you boys okay with that?"

"Dad," I blurted out. "What do you even mean by that? You're a grown man. Your wife left you decades ago. Why wouldn't we be okay with this?"

The concerned look on my father's face morphed slightly at my words. Looking at Chase to see his reaction, I couldn't read him, his face a blank slate.

"Dad," I said again, this time more in control of my emotions. "I can only speak for myself, but I think it's great that you've met someone."

Leaning forward, his hands rubbing together in a nervous ball, he shifted his attention to Chase. We both did.

"Hey," Chase started. "Don't look at me. I'd never stand in the way of you getting some, Dad. Shit, I thought you were anyway, just not saying anything, to be honest."

That got a laugh out of all of us and lightened the mood.

"She, uh, we met in Italy. But she's from the States, from California actually. She's a widow and her name is Sara."

His face lit up as he spoke of her. And for the first time, possibly in my life, I saw my father as a human. Not just the person who cracked the whip on me and Chase our whole lives to do well in school in order to take over this place. Not just the person who stomped around here nervous about the bottom line. Not just the person who thought only about the company and not his sons.

But a human who needed the comfort of another human.

And he was transformed now that he had it.

"Boys," he said. "I'm sorry. For so many years of, well, just being me." Sitting back, he spread his arms out as he looked around the office. "You both are doing well here. I do want to hear your plans for the future, but I already know that they'll be exactly what Parker Financial needs."

Of course, I was pleased that the company was staying with us, with the Parker family, and with my brother and me.

But we gained something much more valuable today than a billion-dollar company staying in our power.

We got our dad back.

When I walked into the brownstone, it was obvious Harper wasn't home yet. There was a feeling of life in this place when she was here, and it was absent at the moment. She didn't know it yet, but I wasn't letting her go back to her apartment. I didn't care if we were moving fast. Almost dying forced you to realize that every day you must…live. And I didn't want to live another day without her waking up in my bed.

She had her appointment today to get her cast removed.

One physical reminder gone: check.

Once I was done with physical therapy, maybe my brain would be able to shut off some thoughts of the accident for a while. But for now, every daily activity was still affected by the injury I sustained that fateful day, prolonging my grief in the process.

But Harper was right in her explanation. The little place in my brain where I tried to put the pain grew each day, allowing me to tuck more and more of the sadness away.

"Gage?"

"I'm out back," I yelled to her.

These simple moments of her coming "home" and calling out to me. I didn't take them for granted. I savored every one of them. Standing up to meet her as she came through the sliding door, I was greeted with the most beautiful creature wearing a huge smile.

"Hi," I said. "Let me grab you a beer. I didn't know when you'd get home."

"Wait," she said, stopping me with her hand on my arm. "Tell me how today went." She sat on the couch, the anxiety clear in her voice.

The call I left her while she was at the shop went to voicemail and then she had to run to the doctor, so we missed each other all afternoon.

"Believe it or not, it went better than I could've expected." My smile rivaled hers.

"Oh, Gage, thank God, I'm so happy for you." She reached out and grabbed my hands with both of hers.

Looking down, I realized the cast was indeed off. Her left wrist and lower arm were significantly lighter in color than her right. Reaching out, I rubbed the dimpled skin.

"How's it feeling? What'd the doctor say?"

"All good. He doesn't even think I'll need PT." She leaned against the back of the couch looking so relaxed. "I have more good news. When I was leaving the shop, I went by my apartment to grab some stuff, and I saw Rex, the bodega owner." She sat up to finish her story, her smile widening. "Maria got accepted into the program I suggested at New York Presbyterian. She's seeing a doctor."

Pulling her legs onto my lap, she instinctively cuddled into my side.

"Of course she did, and of course she is. That doesn't surprise me one bit, because you're an amazing person, Harper Wilson."

We sat back in silence, enjoying the chirp of some nearby crickets.

"Want me to get you that beer?" I asked her, starting to sit up.

I felt her shake her head against my chest. Content with not having to move, I settled back with her in my arms, happy to have our night ahead of us.

Our lives ahead of us.

"I have something else to tell you," she said. But her tone changed. It was more serious.

Sitting up, I needed to see her face and read what was going on. My anxiety shot up immediately. But as soon as I saw the tiny smile form on her lips, the calm settled in again.

"I think it's news you'll like," she said. "Well, I know you'll like it." She sat and pulled away, sitting across from me on the couch. "I think you know I'm a pretty independent person."

There was no truer a statement. But I was confused where this could be going, so all I did was nod.

"Now that the cast is off, I knew I'd be able to go back to the club soon," she said. "I stopped there after the appointment. It had been a while since I'd seen some of my friends there. I actually ran into Pete, which was great."

Her smile made me realize that the club had been a part of her life long before I came into it. She had connections there that meant something to her.

"I like Pete," I told her.

"He's great," she agreed. "And I'm going to miss him."

I wasn't sure I heard her correctly, and she knew that.

"So, this decision was made by me, but for us. I don't want to be out at night anymore, away from you. If I have to work a few years longer at Fiona's to save up for my own shop, I will."

I was torn about how to react. She knew this was going to make me happy. But it stemmed from a very turbulent moment in our past. If I acted too happy, it would bring all of that rushing back.

"Harper," I said. In that one word, my feelings of her wanting to be sure she made the right decision, yet happy at the same time she quit, all came through.

"I know, Gage. And again, I made this decision, all me." She reached out and put her arms around my neck. "I mean, your sexy body, those caramel eyes, and how good you use your hands may have had a little to do with it, but it was *my* decision."

We shared a laugh before we joined for a kiss.

"Well, I appreciate you making that major change in your life for us. That couldn't have been easy to do," I said, stroking her cheek. "We should have Vic and Pete over soon."

She nodded, then fell back against the couch. Kicking her shoes off, she curled into my hold even more.

"What did you need to get at your apartment?" I asked as I relished the feel of her in my arms.

The evening was cool for the end of July, perfect for us to spend our entire night on the patio. Maybe get some takeout and watch a movie.

"Just some basics, some more underwear, and stuff like that."

And I knew I had to just do it. Especially after what she just announced.

"Harper," I said. "I think we should head back there and get the rest of your things."

Her body went completely still underneath my arm.

We talked about this.

She knew I wanted it.

And I knew she was afraid.

And maybe it was too much change for one day. But there was no reason for her to leave. None at all.

Eventually, she sat up and looked at me. Really looked at me. With a face I couldn't read and it made my heart still for a beat as I held my breath. But then the smile slid across her lips.

"Yeah," she said. "I think we should."

I let out the breath I was holding. "Yeah?" I couldn't contain the excitement in my voice.

Laying back against me, she was about to settle into my arms, but she sat up again.

"But all my plants are coming, too," she said, a tone of warning in her voice.

"All of them? Even the boot?" My whiny voice earned me a scoff at first.

Then she giggled and poked me in my ribs. "Yes, even the boot. That's my favorite one. I found that boot under a bench, just left behind. Who leaves behind one boot?"

Fucking adorable. Everything about her was adorable.

And sexy. Her talking about a boot filled with dirt was making me want to take her upstairs and do dirty things to her.

"Maybe someone who knew the boot was gross and it should go in the garbage?" I responded.

She giggled even more as I poked her in the side, our tickle fight escalating. My hand was all over her waist, and she was afraid to fight back, I knew, for fear of hurting me.

"Stop, Gage!" she squealed. "Please, stop!"

I did stop. And I noticed happy tears sprang from her eyes now that our battle ended. Wiping them away, she looked around the patio, taking in our surroundings. The sun had set in the time our talk took place, casting an amber glow into the yard. The lights I'd hung at the beginning of the season lit the space above us.

"I love it out here," she said. "It's probably my favorite spot in your entire house."

Looking at her as she scanned the patio, I didn't say the Hallmark words that came to my mind. Love turned me soft, really soft. Instead, I reached up and pulled her to me.

I knew I was walking the path I was meant to, with her.

"I think I see me putting an old bike in that corner, and filling a basket on it with flowers," she started. "And maybe have a planter made out of the seat." She looked at me, excitement filling her face.

I let her ramble on and on about what she wanted to do once she moved in.

Turning my house into our home.

Epilogue

SIX MONTHS LATER...

Harper

Coming home from the shop, my arms were full of groceries as I kicked the door of the brownstone closed.

Since it was Friday, Gage worked from home, but he still had Tommy bring me to and from the shop even if he didn't go to the office. I protested at first. But he persuaded me by explaining that it was Tommy's job, his livelihood, and he still needed to work each day.

I had more groceries than normal since we were heading to LBI for the weekend. Most people didn't appreciate how beautiful the beach was in this region even in the middle of January. A deserted beach town is the best type of beach town. And we were having a warm spell, in the fifties this weekend, so I was excited.

"Gage?" I called up the stairs.

The footsteps above told me he heard me and hopefully that meant he was done working and packed to go. My bag got packed last night, knowing we wanted to leave as soon as I got home.

The freight train known as Gage Parker came barreling down the stairs, with a bag over his shoulder.

"Finally," he said with a huge grin across his face. "You got the food?"

"Yep."

He decided we'd rent a house this time. Since the shop was closed on Mondays, and he worked remotely that day now as well, we could stay until then. A refrigerator full of food was in order since the island kind of shut down over the winter, with very few restaurants open.

"Victoria said she wants to come next time," I said as I grabbed the cooler bag to put the food in. "Her and Sam seem to be doing pretty good. They've been talking for a couple months now."

Gage came to my rescue and grabbed the now too-heavy bag for me.

"Maybe the first weekend we head down once the weather is warm, we'll ask them to come," I said.

"Okay," Gage said, looking thoughtful. He started for the garage door. "Your bag is at the bottom of the stairs. Let's get going."

Grabbing my things, turning off the lights and locking up behind me, I met Gage by the trunk of the truck. He put all our things in the back, but I took hold of his arm before he could walk around to the front of the car.

"Want me to drive?" I asked him.

"No, I'm good," he responded.

Nodding slowly as I made my way around to the passenger seat, I was hopeful he was.

My offer to drive got denied because I think it was the next demon he wanted to face. And he faced it. The drive down the Garden State Parkway was uneventful, mainly because of the time of year. If it were the warmer months, the traffic would have been horrific. But he did well, and he smiled wide as we drove over the LBI bridge.

"The house we're going to looks like it's on the bay," I said, looking at the map on the phone. That got me a little giddy inside.

"It is," he replied. "Only a few more blocks."

As he turned left onto Fifteenth Street, I couldn't believe the driveway we were pulling into.

"You rented this house?" I squealed. "Gage, oh my God, I can't believe you remembered."

The house we were sitting in front of looked nothing like the house from almost twenty years ago. But on this lot was the house my family and cousins' family rented together one year. It was filled with so many joyous memories for me. Gage and I walked by it last summer on our last day here.

"You remembered?" I asked, looking across the front seat at him. "Oh my God, you remembered." My eyes wandered across the multiple floors of the now mini mansion that stood in front of me. The trend on the island has been to knock down the older, run-down small summer shacks and build homes that could be lived in year-round.

The house stood three stories tall with a huge wraparound porch in front. The cedar shakes were still new enough that they held their brownish color, but over time, they would be a weathered gray. I already knew without seeing that the entire back of the house would be a wall of windows to take in the view of the water.

I couldn't wait to get inside and take a look.

He squeezed my hand as I sat staring at the house, but let it go and jumped from the truck. His excitement rivaled mine as he jumped out of the car.

"C'mon," he said, grabbing my hand. "I'll get our things later. Let's go take a look."

We hurried to the front door, and Gage took a key from his pocket, which struck me as odd, but I thought maybe they made prior arrangements. I knew I'd never get used to his world and the number of people he had that did things for him.

Holding the door open, he allowed me to walk in first.

It was stunning. The white, tan, and light blue color scheme was exactly how I would have decorated a beach house if I owned one. The colors of the sea, sand, and sky.

"Oh, Gage, it's beautiful," I said, turning toward him. "Thank you so much for renting it for our weekend." Running to him, I wrapped my arms around him, my face against his chest.

"C'mon," he said, "Let's look around a little more."

He took my hand, and we walked through the wide entranceway that led straight into the living space. You could see straight through to the back of the house from the front, and as predicted, a wall of windows showcased the water. Although, at this time of night, it appeared like a black hole. But in the morning, it would be a breathtaking sight.

"This couch looks so much like yours," I said. "Well, ours." I corrected myself. He got upset when I didn't refer to the contents of the brownstone as ours. It was still something I was getting used to.

I noticed that Gage was standing off to the side of the room, watching me as I looked around.

"What?" I asked in his direction.

"Nothing," he said. "Just enjoying watching you being so excited."

But then I noticed something on a side table. It was a framed picture.

Of Gage and me.

And I started taking a closer look around. Walking to the mantle over the fireplace, I found another framed picture.

Of me with my parents when I was a child.

"Gage?"

I gasped as I turned to him.

His hands fidgeted between going in his pockets and out as he worked hard to maintain eye contact with me. Eventually, his eyes scanned the room, but then came back to mine. He slowly started taking measured steps until he got within inches of me. Reaching out, he took both my hands in his.

"Gage," I whispered. "What's going on?"

GAGE

"WELCOME HOME," I said. She was confused as I took her hands in mine. And they were trembling. I only hoped I'd done a good thing here. This was a huge step I took without even consulting her. But we both knew this island was special to her, and now special to us both.

Her eyes instantly filled with tears as she took in her surroundings once again, picking up on additional personal details. She saw the bouquet of pink flowers on the kitchen island, and then the New York City skyline painting on the wall she knew I'd been admiring from a local gallery back home. But eventually her hands left mine and covered her mouth in awe as the moment took over.

"This is ours?" she asked, her voice still a whisper. She started wandering around the room, admiring the furnishings and décor. The designer I chose was recommended highly in this area and I was pleased with the outcome. It appeared Harper was as well.

"It is," I finally said, nervous how she would respond to the news. "And listen, if you don't like how the designer decorated, it can all be changed. Just say the word."

She was standing in front of the fireplace as I spoke. Picking up the photo of her with her parents, she wiped at her face quickly.

When I messaged her mother asking for some old photos, she said she had the perfect one. It was of the three of them standing on a small dock along the bay. I knew immediately it was the dock on this property.

And Harper knew that, too.

The boat she told me about was in the background of the picture, tied to the wooden post of the dock with a simple yellow rope. And the smiles on the three of them were of pure joy.

Using two hands, as if the frame would break, Harper put the photo carefully back in its now-sacred spot on the mantle. She turned in my direction, her head tilted downward and facing the floor. As her eyes drifted up, her feet started in my direction, her pace shifting from a walk to a run.

Jumping into my arms, I caught her and held her tight against me. Only then did I feel the shudder of her quiet sobs against my chest. My hands gripped the back of her head, threading through her hair, holding her face to my shoulder.

"It's perfect," she said through her tears. "Absolutely perfect."

"Baby," I said, kissing the top of her head. "I hope these are happy tears. This was all to make you happy."

All she could do was nod repeatedly. She couldn't speak, even when she tried. I put her down, looking into her face. Wiping her cheeks dry, her smile surfaced, and a laugh escaped her mouth.

"I can't believe you did this," she finally got out. "How the hell did you do this?"

When we were here last July, I put the wheels in motion. Turns out, the house was on the market. It was a simple transaction, nothing needed to be done out of the ordinary. Redecorating took some time, and Maryellen spent some days down here handling much of that for me.

"Anything for you, baby."

Her excitement returned, and she wanted to see more of what

she now knew to be her beach house. Spinning out of my arms, and with renewed vigor, she ran through the place. Up the stairs, out on the deck, into the backyard.

"We have a pool?" she yelled.

"Oh my God, have you seen the outdoor shower? It's gorgeous, I can't wait until it's warm enough to take my first outdoor shower."

"It looks like fifteen people can sit around that firepit!"

"How many bedrooms does this place have?"

"What is that space downstairs going to be for? And why are there so many refrigerators?"

Her questions were hitting me so fast I couldn't keep up.

Then she finally made it to the kitchen. It was a gorgeous, top-of-the-line chef's kitchen. But that wasn't why I was happy she'd made it to that room.

She walked around the space, admiring the fine woodwork and the stainless appliances. But then her gaze settled on the large island. Hoping she'd finally seen it, I waited.

Her eyes went to the large bouquet of pink peonies. It was a monstrous bundle of flowers, probably the largest I'd ever seen.

"They're beautiful," she said quietly.

And then a small gasp escaped her.

And I knew she'd found it.

With a shaky hand, she reached out for the tiny offering sitting atop a pink silk bow.

As she picked it up, she turned toward me. And I made sure to be by her side when she did.

"Harper," I said. "You've made me the happiest version of me these past nine months."

The ring shook in her fingers, so I took it, gripping her left hand.

"I don't want to spend another day not knowing that we'll spend our life walking side by side, together."

Perching the pink diamond ring at the tip of her finger, I continued.

"Harper Wilson, will you marry me?"

There were no tears in her crystal blue eyes as she looked up at me.

There was only clarity.

Total and complete clarity as she answered me.

"Yes," she said. "A thousand times yes, in a thousand lives, yes. I want nothing more than to be your wife, Mr. Parker."

I slid the ring on her finger and admired the pink stone on her hand. She held her hand up and did the same.

"It's beautiful, Gage," she said as she extended her hand in front of us. The gem sparkled in the dim light, looking even bigger on her petite hand.

"But we do have one problem."

My head snapped down to hers.

"Harper Parker, that's a mouthful," she said, and broke out in laughter.

Picking her up by the waist, as her legs wrapped around mine, I answered her against her ear.

"Harper Parker sounds amazing. To me, it sounds very professional."

She barked a laugh as I carried her toward the couch.

"Oh yeah, what profession?" Her laughter was like a song as it filled the walls of what would be another home of ours.

"Well, you do have this dream job you've always been talking about," I said. "I'm sure you can be creative with that name for your shop someday."

Setting her on the couch, I sat next to her and took her hand in mine to admire the ring I'd just put on her finger. She made it look even better.

"I was thinking you should start considering that business

model I suggested. You know, about doing your wedding accounts from an off-site rather than having a shop to pay rent on."

The return on investment of walk-in floral orders did not warrant paying rent on a shop, especially in New York City. And Harper was intrigued by my suggestions and the model I presented.

"All it really requires is some industrial-sized refrigerators."

Her head snapped in my direction. It was starting to make sense to her now.

"And maybe a big mahogany table to work on, and do other things, too," I offered.

She stood up from the couch, her confusion and excitement still rolling from her body. I knew I was throwing a lot at her for one day, but that's how we rolled.

Life was fast in our lane.

"Gage," she said, more a question than a statement. "What have you done?" She walked to the other side of the room, looking for something. "Where is the door to the lower level?"

She pulled open a door that led to a closet, then a half bath. "Gage, what have you done?"

Walking to where she was now freaking out, I grabbed her by both her hands and tried to calm her.

"I haven't done anything other than buy a few refrigerators, just in case you were ready to start out on your own," I told her. "But if you are, there's space here, and back in New York, for you to do it."

She shook her head in disbelief as she made her way to me.

"Gage," she whispered as she threw herself into my arms. "My God, you've done all of this for me?"

Wrapping her legs around my waist, my hands, as if on auto-pilot, went to her ass as I started the walk with her, this time up the stairs.

"If I could give you the world, I would, Harper."

Her head snuggled against my chest as I made our way to our bedroom.

"What was that you said about a mahogany table?" she asked.

I laughed, deep and long, before answering her.

"I have two on order, one for each house. And they're being put to use whether you're using them for floral arrangements or not."

Dropping her on our bed, she giggled as I fell next to her.

"What will we do until they arrive?" she asked, a seductive tone to her voice.

Pulling her close, aligning our bodies, my hand made its way to the button of her jeans. Wood surfaces would come, but the christening of this house would be in our bed.

"Well, if you didn't notice, we have a pretty big dining table downstairs, any guess what wood it's made of?"

Her laughter filled the room. It was a gorgeous sound.

But more importantly, another day completed with a smile on her face.

The End

Buy My Books Here

My Website

Amazon

Acknowledgments

It was fun to write a book taking place in a location in my own backyard, New York City. Living only 17 miles from Manhattan would make one think I make it in often, but we don't. But creating this story has reignited my desire to spend more time in one of the best cities in the world.

Of course, I couldn't have put this together without the help of some awesome people around me. Dani Galliaro, my editor, helped form this story into more than it could be, thank you!

Emily Michel, my longtime proofreader, always has my back to find mistakes I've left on the table. Thanks Emily!

Niki, my cover designer, really made some magic this time. I can't thank her enough for the beauties she's created and the time she gives me. I look forward to what we will continue creating together. You're the best Niki, thank you!

Thank you to my readers, old and new. Without you and your positive feedback, I might sit staring at my computer. Yes, just staring.

My street team…there are no words. You go above and beyond with the time you devote to me and my work. Thank you, thank you, thank you!

And, as always, the love and support from my family is what keeps me going with my writing. The unwavering support I receive from them, especially during deadline times, will always be appreciated.

Onto the next book…

Newsletter Signup

Would you like to receive monthly updates? Would you like sneak peeks on the next books in the series? For that and more, sign up for my monthly newsletter at:

https://www.kristaswansonauthor.com/

Author Bio

Krista Swanson lives in New Jersey with her husband of 29 years. They have three children but are now empty nesters. Traveling across the US and Europe is in their plans. She loves the beach, mainly the Jersey beaches, which she feels don't get the love they deserve.

When she's not writing, she is most definitely reading. Her lifelong love of reading romances gave her all of the ideas busting to get out of her brain. While doing either, though, the mug in hand will not have coffee in it. The blasphemy—it will be tea!

She's newish at the social media thing, but working hard at it. You can find her on TikTok and Instagram at *kristareadsandwrites*. Also hop on over and join her Facebook reader's group, *Krista Swanson's Booklover's Besties.* Make sure to sign up for her monthly newsletter on any of those platforms for the most recent news, freebies and giveaways.

9 798989 876 06 278